THE REINVENTION OF ALBERT PAUGH

The
Reinvention
of
Albert Paugh

A Novel

Jean Davies Okimoto

ENDICOTT and HUGH BOOKS

THE REINVENTION OF ALBERT PAUGH
Copyright © 2015 by Jean Davies Okimoto

All rights reserved, including the right to reproduce this book, or portions thereof, in any form. Published by Endicott and Hugh Books, Burton, Washington. www.endicottandhughbooks.com

Okimoto, Jean Davies.
  The reinvention of Albert Paugh : a novel / by Jean Davies Okimoto.

  pages ; cm

  ISBN: 978-0-9894291-3-9 (paperback)
  ISBN: 978-0-9894291-4-6 (hardcover)

  1. Retirees--Fiction. 2. Divorced men--Fiction. 3. Man-woman relationships--Fiction. 4. Vashon Island (Wash.)--Fiction. 5. Love stories, American. I. Title.

PS3565.K46 R45 2015
813/.54
2015903063

Book design by Masha Shubin
Man with Dog Silhouttes © 2015 Michael Hostovecky

LCCN 2015903063

3 4 5 6 7 8 9

For Joe

We must let go of the life we planned, so as to accept the one that is waiting for us.

-Joseph Campbell

ACKNOWLEDGEMENT and AUTHOR'S NOTE

I AM GRATEFUL TO DR. DON WOLCZKO, NOT ONLY FOR HIS PROFESsional expertise in advising me about veterinary medicine, but also for his careful reading and suggestions for the novel.

Librarians are among an author's most trusted friends, and I am deeply appreciative of Rayna Holtz, formerly of the King County Library System, who invested so much time and provided detailed line editing and oversight.

I also benefitted from the professional expertise of Jim Devine, Linda Milovsoroff, Deputy Sheriff Isaac Patino, and Dr. Hugh Straley and I am grateful to each of them.

Once again, my talented editor Ali Bothwell Mancini offered objective insights; as did Juli Morser, herself a fine writer, who gave valuable input. Susan Riemer is an excellent proof reader and Masha Shubin, the designer for Endicott and Hugh Books, is a delight to work with and I'm grateful for the creativity she brings to every book.

Dr. Al Paugh and all the characters are imaginary; however, a few of the names mentioned are of actual people and are used with their permission. Vashon Island is a real place and the various landmarks, businesses and institutions in the novel are a combination of both actual and imaginary places.

JDO

Chapter I

AL DIDN'T QUITE KNOW HOW HE GOT SIDETRACKED. HE'D NEVER thought of himself as an impulsive person, it was rare that he did anything without thinking it through and he certainly had every intension of taking Bert, his chocolate Lab, to Point Robinson. It was a beautiful fall day and Bert was eager to get to the beach where he loved to swim and retrieve his rubber frog. Of course, Al was supposed to get exercise, too. But instead of going to the beach like he'd told Eleanor he'd be doing—the past eight months he'd been very dutiful about always letting his wife know his whereabouts—somehow, he inexplicably ended up going in the opposite direction. He drove to town and turned off on a side street, Ober Lane, and that's where he stopped and parked his truck. Changing his destination had not been the result of a deliberate, rational process. It felt more to Al as though he'd been transported magically like Dorothy when she was whooshed away from Kansas, except that he was Albert J. Paugh, D.V.M. and he'd landed around the corner from the Island Animal Clinic, his former place of employment, which was not Oz.

Al didn't want to be seen by anyone he knew so he parked near some bushes and scrunched down in the seat and pulled the brim of his Husky baseball cap so it covered the top half of his face. This probably wasn't going to be that effective in obscuring his identity, because his truck stuck up over the bushes. Also, his distinctive hair, a big bunch of salt and pepper frizz, stuck out from the back of his head like the tail of an elderly French poodle in need of grooming.

Someone recognizing his vehicle wasn't a concern because he didn't drive something unusual that would attract attention, like his friend Martha Jane Morrison's ancient red Mercedes. Al had an old gray Toyota truck, and Vashon Island was home to numerous old trucks, most of them, like his, unwashed and well past their prime. He didn't have a recognizable license plate, either. Eleanor had wanted him to get one with the letters PAWS, which would relate to his name and occupation, but he never got around to sending in the form, and then it seemed to disappear. When Eleanor nagged him about it and accused him of being passive-aggressive, she was probably right. It was hard for him to tell her he thought it was silly. Just because he was a vet should he have a license plate that says "paws?" Would a surgeon have one that says "knife?" Or a dentist have one that says "teeth?" Al didn't think so. It wasn't professional. But it wasn't worth trying to explain that to Eleanor. Avoiding conflict wasn't anything new for him; throughout their marriage there were very few things he thought were worth arguing about. But ever since everything started falling apart, Al had tried even harder not to upset her.

Bert was lying on the floor on the passenger side, which was a good thing because many people knew Bert, and he would have been easily recognizable sitting up on the seat. Al was pleased that Bert seemed stoically resigned to the fact that they hadn't gone to the beach, as only dogs can be when life hasn't met their expectations. He had his frog in his mouth. It was his favorite object to retrieve, a very sturdy little water toy about the size and color of a tennis ball with a short rope attached. Bert preferred it to swimming after sticks that Al found on the beach.

Al peeked out from under the brim of his cap so he could see the entrance to the clinic. A dark-haired woman wearing a bright red blouse was going up the walk, and at first he couldn't tell who it was. But as she got closer, from her brisk walk and the way things seemed to jiggle, Al saw that it was Marilyn Henderson.

Eleanor couldn't stand her. Actually, Eleanor found fault with a lot of people, but she was especially negative about Marilyn ever since they went on the Audubon Christmas Bird Count three years ago and Marilyn spent the whole time talking to Al. Marilyn was probably in her late fifties, although she looked pretty young. Well, both pretty and young, Al had to admit. Also divorced. He thought she looked a lot like Hope Solo, the Olympic goalie, only not so lean—more flesh, he thought—which probably accounted for the jiggle. With her long, dark auburn hair and her bouncy gait, Marilyn reminded him of an Irish setter, although not a puppy. Middle aged, a little on the heavy side. On the Bird Count, Marilyn had talked about her worries about her corgi, Eloise, and the little tumors Eloise had, lipomas, which were benign. (Al had done a fine needle aspirate and there was nothing to worry about), but the lipomas still made Marilyn quite anxious, and he couldn't just brush her off, could he? Eleanor said the way he was so attentive to Marilyn was inappropriate and he missed seeing a snowy owl, which served him right. He certainly would have wanted to see that snowy owl, but in truth, Al didn't know how to get rid of Marilyn. It wasn't like the office where you have a fixed amount of time and the next appointment is waiting and everyone understands that they have to leave when their appointment is over. Well, almost everyone. Al could think of a couple of people, like the Dog Whisperer wannabes, who always wanted to discuss at length articles they'd found on the internet about various dog behavior problems and he'd have to try to nicely get them to leave. It was difficult for him to cut people off, and he had to admit that running a tight practice in terms of time had never been one of his strengths.

He scrunched down a little lower and watched Marilyn walking up the steps with Eloise on a leash, and then he saw something she was carrying and he sat up and leaned forward to get a closer look. It was just as he thought. Marilyn was holding a small blue baggie. Al fumed. He knew exactly what was in it and it was totally unnecessary. He'd run into Marilyn at Thriftway a few weeks ago and she'd said Eloise was doing great, so this was probably just a yearly check up. It was ridiculous, bringing a specimen when there was absolutely nothing wrong with that dog (except she was too fat). Maybe those chain clinics that owned laboratories insisted on a specimen at every visit, but it was a racket. And Al knew he would be shocked if the lab technicians even glanced at the dog shit. They probably threw it all away, or knowing them, sold it for a hefty price to flower growers, marketing it as a specialty fertilizer or something. Al folded his arms across his chest and glared at the clinic. *How could I have done such a thing?* I never should have sold to Jerry Kincaid. Now he is bringing all the greedy ideas he learned at that big clinic to *my* practice. What a crock!

And what was that on the windows? Al craned his neck, trying to get a better look. Some kind of fancy shades? What happened to the beige curtains with the little black paw prints on them. Many people commented on them, they were perfectly good, why the hell has Kincaid gotten rid of them? New shades! What a waste of money. Well, I suppose he can afford things like that with the fees he's charging for specimens.

Al started the truck. "Let's get to the beach, buddy," he said to Bert. He had seen enough. He'd been avoiding the clinic since last December and now he just wished he'd kept it that way.

Driving to the beach, Al tried to calm down. He was supposed to avoid stress—they'd really emphasized that at the cardiac education classes when he went to rehab—but he couldn't get the picture out of his head of that blue baggie and the windows with those fancy shades. He fumed all the way to Portage, on the isthmus that links Vashon to Maury Island, and was still pissed off as he drove across Maury and down into Point Robinson Park.

There was only one car in the parking lot when he arrived. A blue Subaru sedan with Oregon plates. Not anyone he knew. Good. Probably someone visiting the island. Bert leaped out of the truck, still holding the frog in his mouth. He had some arthritis in his hind legs, the beginning of the hip problems that troubled so many Labs. Al usually had to help lift him up into the truck, but when they arrived at the beach or the park, Bert would jump down like he was still a puppy. He trotted ahead of Al down the hill toward the old Coast Guard house. When he got to the bottom of the hill, Al looked around and didn't see anyone who lived nearby out for a walk. Good. He was still in a foul mood and didn't want to run into someone he might know. Someone who'd ask about Eleanor, and then he'd be stuck talking to the person when he'd prefer to hide his head in the sand. Maybe ostriches were on to something.

He followed Bert as he loped across the lawn toward the beach and the lighthouse. When Al got to the edge of the shore, Bert dropped his frog at Al's feet and jumped around in circles, barking with excitement, waiting for Al to throw it. Al leaned over, picked up the frog by the rope and flung it out over the water. And then Bert was off, galloping, splashing, then swimming—absolutely joyful. Watching Bert always helped Al. He was a role model for him. Bert lived in the moment, a skill Al wanted to acquire but found difficult. Within a few minutes Bert was back, shaking water all over Al, dropping the frog, ready to go at it again. As Al bent down to pick up the frog, he saw someone he knew. Not good. It was Dave Murphy, their plumber, trotting down the hill from the parking lot, carrying his fishing pole and tackle box. Dave waved, and not wanting to be rude, Al waved back, but was very relieved when Dave turned in the opposite direction, obviously not wanting to shoot the breeze. As Al got ready to throw the frog again for Bert, he heard Dave whistling. Still carrying his pole and tackle box, he whistled as he was rounding the bend near the lighthouse. Now there's a guy who loves retirement. No doubt about that. Dave had been talking about his retirement while he put in their new bathroom fixtures. Eleanor's idea. Al thought the old ones had been fine, but she was in charge of the house, and these past months when everything went south, Al was for anything that would make her feel better. Dave did a nice job on the bathroom, but as Al watched him disappear down the beach, he wondered if Dave was the kind of guy that had loved his work. Maybe Dave had his fill of toilets and temperamental septic tanks and with retirement felt free at last. Free to follow his bliss as Joseph Campbell said. Al shook his head. *Why did that name pop into my head?* Funny how that was, when the other day he'd forgotten the name of the dentist he'd been going to for twenty-five years. Al couldn't remember the year, but quite a while ago, Eleanor insisted he attend a lecture series with her based on a Joseph Campbell book and all he could remember now was something about bliss. That was it, following your bliss, or finding your passion—something like that. His friend Ted Krupnik didn't have any trouble with retirement and following his bliss. He and his wife Millie had left a few weeks ago on the Semester at Sea program and wouldn't be back until December. They'd sail to sixteen different countries and study the art, music, religion, government and history of each place. Ted loved stuff like that, but it was hard for Al to relate to being on a ship and stopping at all those different countries. He felt discombobulated whenever he was away from home and besides, he didn't think there were many places in the world as serene and beautiful as right here on Vashon Island. He was happy to learn about the other places from the Travel Channel.

He threw the frog for Bert and watched him leap into the water. Bert swam back with his frog held gingerly in his mouth. With his dark head gliding along, he could almost be a seal. Bert had passion for swimming after his frog. Al envied him. Why wasn't he happy like that? Al breathed in the fragrance of the sea. The early morning showers had left rain-washed sunlight, a lemony light that filled this golden day of autumn. It was so beautiful and the air was crisp, the kind of fall day that always made Al think of the first football game. The kids on the island had all gone back to school the day after Labor Day and now the beach was almost deserted. I should be enjoying this freedom more, he thought. I should be whistling and trotting along at the edge of the water, just a happy chappy like our plumber. Now that Eleanor needed him less—hardly at all—he could fill the hours any way he wanted. Well, they were getting filled now all right—filled with regrets. Actually, it was just one big regret that

Al couldn't ignore anymore. He'd made a mistake. A huge mistake. He'd sold his practice and he never should have done it. That was his bliss and always had been. (Al didn't need any lecture series to figure that out.) *What the hell was I thinking?* But he hadn't been thinking straight. That was the whole thing. Al knew it probably wasn't fair to blame Eleanor, but part of him did.

Al looked at the sunlight dancing on the water. The only sound was the barking of sea lions on the yellow mid-channel buoy to the east. The splendid day made him feel even worse. How could he be so negative when he was standing on the edge of this shining blue expanse, surrounded by such beauty? What a jackass. Maybe it would help his state of mind if he got moving. He was supposed to exercise and he wasn't getting much throwing the frog.

The next time Bert brought it back, Al stuffed the frog in his pocket and headed down the beach at a brisk pace. To get his heart rate up with a little more movement, he swung his arms quite high and marched along lifting his legs in a somewhat sloppy goose step, imagining he was a soldier in the French Foreign Legion. He wondered if there still was such a thing. Maybe he could join up for a tour or two. Although since he didn't care much for travel, it probably wasn't a good idea. Al marched along watching Bert, who didn't seem to miss his frog and was perfectly content to go on up ahead sniffing things in the sand and chasing the seagulls. Like most dogs, he was very adaptable, a quality Al admired very much.

There were huge driftwood logs, whitened by the salt from the sea, along the higher slope of the shore where the tall beach grass began. Bert must have found something there because he stopped sauntering along the edge of the water and walked up behind an enormous mass of driftwood. It looked like it may once have been the roots and lower trunk of a gigantic evergreen. All he could see of Bert was his hind end and his tail wagging. Al hoped he hadn't found a bird or a fish carcass. Nothing smelled worse. Al experienced all animals as sentient beings and often felt Bert was almost human until he saw the delight Bert took in rolling in rotten dead stuff.

Al walked toward the huge log, hoping to pull Bert away before he got into something really putrid. But when he was near the slope where the beach grass started, he saw that what interested Bert wasn't dead. A woman was huddled almost in a fetal position with her head buried in the crook of her arm and her knees drawn up to her chest. Al could see right away she was crying. Her shoulders were shaking slightly and she made little sniffing, sobbing sounds. Bert stood next to her, wagging his tail and nuzzling her face. She leaned against him and slipped her arm around his neck, oblivious to the wet doggie smell and his salt-water soaked fur covered with patches of sand.

In his professional capacity, Al was accustomed to women weeping when their beloved dog or cat had to be euthanized. He felt deeply for them, and comforting anyone in that situation came naturally. He knew what their loss meant, how it felt. But outside of his prescribed role, he often felt awkward with people. He didn't know how to make small talk, and he found it especially uncomfortable to know what to say to most women. Not that he didn't like them—he'd always been attracted to women. When he was in college and first began to date, he would prepare by thinking of topics to talk about, and if he ran out of material, he'd invent something and say he'd heard it on NPR. But out of the blue, like today just coming across a woman who was upset, was another matter. If it had been a dog in distress behind that driftwood, he wouldn't have hesitated for a second. He would have quickly gone right over to it. But it being a person—a woman—he had no idea what he should do, if anything.

Then Bert saw him and came trotting over, and Al wasn't sure if he should turn back or continue walking across the slope. But if he turned back, that would be turning his back on the woman and that didn't seem right. So he went across the slope. He kept walking in her direction trying to decide if he should say something to her. "Do you come here often?" finally came to mind, but that seemed wrong because it sounded like a pick-up line in a bar. Al had stopped the goose stepping when he'd first seen the woman and now he strolled, hoping to appear casual while trying to think of something to say that would be right. When he was a few feet from her, he found himself slowing down as some words actually did occur to him. "Um, are you okay?" he mumbled.

The woman seemed very embarrassed and wiped her eyes and sat up a little. Al was relieved to see that she wasn't anyone he knew. She looked to be about his age, late sixties maybe, although he knew it was hard to tell age. She had a long, thin face with a slim nose and a wide mouth and hair that was kind of fluffy, kind of light reddish brown with some grayish white in it. She nodded but didn't say anything else. Al took that to mean she was okay, so he and Bert continued down the beach.

They walked across the grass to a trail that went up through the woods and hiked along there for a while. The trail ended at the upper lot where he'd parked the truck, and that seemed like a better way to go back than along the beach. He didn't want to pass the driftwood lady again. It was more than just the familiar awkwardness he wanted to avoid. Al recognized that he probably had developed almost an aversion to women who had problems that weren't animal-related.

As he lifted Bert to help him into the truck, his cell phone rang. It had a regular ring, like an old-fashioned phone. He liked the sense of history it evoked. Al was no Luddite, but technology was moving at whirlwind speed and the old-fashioned ring gave him a feeling of continuity. He closed the passenger door, glancing at the phone to see who was calling. No surprise: Eleanor. He decided not to answer. He decided he needed a few more minutes to himself. Besides, Eleanor always left a message.

Al climbed into the truck and thought it would be a nice idea to listen to his music, B.B. King's "Let the Good Times Roll" and his classic, "The Thrill is Gone." Eleanor hated blues. One technological invention that Al thought was pretty good was the set of little earphones you could plug into an iPod and listen without bothering anyone. Being in his truck, sitting there without having to mess with earphones, just hearing his favorite tunes as loud as he wanted, made him feel like a younger man. He leaned back against the headrest and listened to one more song, and it occurred to him that being a retiree, he could stay there, sitting in the truck with Bert listening to music for quite a while, maybe even most of the afternoon. He had no responsibility to anyone for anything except to Eleanor and Bert. It was a hard thing for him to get used to, the fact that no one needed him to care for their animals. Al sighed and scratched Bert behind his ears, thinking how odd it was that so many people had needed him to help them through illness, injuries, and the death of their beloved animals, and now there was this void. And he couldn't be a vet anymore even if he wanted to since he signed a non-compete clause when he sold his practice to that jerk Jerry Kincaid. Taking care of Eleanor had consumed everything for a while, but now even Eleanor didn't need him much.

B.B. was now singing "Rock Me Baby" and Al turned down the volume to listen to Eleanor's message.

"Al, I hope you'll be home soon. I need to talk to you." That was it, not what he was expecting because he'd been sure she was going to ask him to stop at Thriftway or run some other errand. Eleanor was often abrupt, so that was nothing new. But she sounded very serious and her tone worried him because at her last check-up, she'd been given a clean bill of health. Dr. Abrams, her oncologist, said the prognosis was excellent. She had a good chance of living many more years. He told her to think of herself as cured, to visualize seeing herself continuing to be healthy (he was big on visualizing). And Eleanor didn't have to come back for six months, and if everything was okay, she wouldn't have to come back at all unless there was a change in her health. Dr. Abrams said there was no reason for her not to expect to resume a full life. It was an enormous relief, but also hard to digest. It was like living in a house you were told could crumble and crush you at any moment, and then being told it was sound. It left him off-balance with a vague confusion in the space the stress and fear had occupied.

WHEN HE GOT HOME, BEFORE going into the house, Al wiped off Bert's feet in the mudroom. Eleanor insisted they not come in the house unless Al took off his shoes and wiped Bert's feet. It wasn't unreasonable, he knew, and he and Bert were both used to the drill.

"Nice walk?" Eleanor opened the mudroom door from the kitchen. It smelled like she'd been cooking something with a lot of garlic. She was a staunch believer in the healing properties of garlic. Al thought she'd overdone it a bit—almost everything they ate, now that she was cooking again, had at least three or four cloves of garlic in it. But he'd never say anything.

"Fine. How're you feeling?" Al looked up from where he was kneeling, wiping Bert's back paws.

"Fine."

"Good." Al waited, but she didn't say anything else. She just went back to the kitchen. She must have changed her mind about wanting to talk. Al finished wiping off Bert's paws and went to his study and closed the door.

He had a very nice leather desk chair that had been in his office at the clinic that he did not want Jerry Kincaid to have, so he'd brought it home. He'd also hung his diplomas and a beautiful painting of a golden retriever standing on the edge of a lake, surrounded by brilliant fall foliage. Al loved the painting; it had been a gift from one of his clients, Evelyn Murdoch. He had been with her dog Cassidy through the last days of his life. The euthanasia took place at Evelyn's house, which overlooked Tramp Harbor. Afterward, Al helped Evelyn bury Cassidy and spoke a few words about what a wonderful dog he was. The painting and the diplomas and the chair made his home office seem a bit like his office at the clinic. But what was the point? he asked himself every time he looked at them. He didn't have a practice anymore. Al flopped down in the chair and opened his laptop.

After about fifteen or twenty minutes, there was a knock on the door. Eleanor opened it and stood in the doorway of his study, staring at him, which Al thought was odd. Then she finally said. "Al, we do have to talk."

"Can it wait a few minutes? I'm in the middle of something."

He pulled the screen down over the keyboard, covering up the game of Solitaire.

"No." Eleanor still stood in the doorway. "Let's talk in the kitchen." She quickly turned, so Al put the laptop on his desk, tried not to let out a tired sigh, and obediently followed her. Then Bert got up from where he'd been lying under the desk, stretched, yawned, and followed Al.

The afternoon sun was streaming in the kitchen, and as Al sat at the table across from Eleanor, he noticed how spotty the windows were. All of them covered with a hazy film made up of little grayish dots. Another project he'd have to add to the list.

Eleanor's illness had dominated both their lives, and Al was beginning to realize that was why he hadn't faced the loss of his practice. Taking Eleanor to the clinic in Seattle had been a whole day affair. It took fifteen or twenty minutes to get to the ferry, and they always allowed an extra twenty minutes before the boat was scheduled to leave so they would be sure to make it. Then the trip across Puget Sound to the ferry dock in West Seattle took another twenty minutes. Add on at least a half hour to get to the clinic on Capitol Hill, park the car, and check in at the chemo unit at the hospital. They'd spend most of the day there and Al would read to her as she lay in the reclining chair. Eleanor loved Jane Austen. *Pride and Prejudice* was her favorite, and Al tried to be a convincing Mr. Darcy when he read the dialogue, although it seemed to annoy Eleanor. She would shake her head and purse her lips, and Al decided she must be irritated because his Mr. Darcy never matched the voice in her mind: a deep voice, with a proper aristocratic English accent. He suggested he read some Mark Twain and that went over a little better.

When the treatment was over, they'd make the same trip back to the island, which could take even longer if they ended up coming home at rush hour. What a hassle compared to the sparse Vashon traffic where there were only a couple of blinking lights at stop signs—not even a stoplight on the whole island.

The chemo was very hard on Eleanor. The drug she was on, cisplatin, caused nausea, vomiting, some hair loss, fatigue, and severe flu-like symptoms. It also made her taste buds change so that everything tasted like metal. Al took over all the housework, which was new for him. Up until Eleanor got sick, they'd pretty much had a marriage which could have come right out of the fifties. Al mowed the yard and took the garbage to the dump, and Eleanor did the laundry, shopping, cooking, and dishes (although Al did load the dishwasher.) They also had a house cleaner, Tiffany, who came once a week and dusted, cleaned the appliances, changed the sheets, vacuumed and mopped the floors. A shy, hardworking young woman, she was attending Tacoma Community College, and the house sparkled each week after she came. Because of the housework Tiffany did, Al assumed taking over Eleanor's household tasks wouldn't take too much time. It was a bit of a shock when he found out how much time everything did take. The shopping for instance. He couldn't get out of Thriftway in less than forty minutes. Especially when he'd run into people who'd ask about Eleanor. A few weeks ago a lady whose name he couldn't remember came up to him in front of the organic bananas and asked how Eleanor was doing.

"Great," he told her. "Eleanor's in the home stretch."

"Glad to hear it. I remember when my sister had chemo and she was violently ill and it didn't go well at all ...." Then she launched into a detailed account of her sister's experience and Al couldn't figure out how to escape. He didn't want to be rude since the person was telling how someone they love suffered, so he stayed with his cart parked in front of the bananas for twenty minutes and listened, and then the woman finally said to be sure and give Eleanor her best and Al said he would. But of course he couldn't because he didn't know who she was. Often at Thriftway Al found he spent a lot of extra time escaping down a different aisle than the one he needed just to avoid people. And then all those decisions about the food. Thirty-seven different kinds of crackers for example. Besides not knowing what Eleanor would even be able to eat and keep down.

Eleanor was a person who needed to be in control. And to have something destructive happening in her body that she had no control over left her with a sense of helpless rage, the brunt of which sometimes landed on Al. He really felt bad for her, deeply and truly sorry, and his sensitivity to Eleanor's suffering helped him manage the times when he felt on edge, was irritable or impatient. He'd soldiered on, trying to stifle any negative feelings, and eventually developed a technique that he found quite useful when Eleanor was the most difficult, the times when he thought he was on the verge of losing it. For the most part he could handle it when Eleanor lit into him, but it was the hardest on him when she was awful to other people. Those were the times that inspired Al to create the technique, a kind of visual imagery that turned out to be successful in helping him cope. He imagined Eleanor was one of his patients. When Eleanor, fuming, accused Tiffany of stealing a bottle of Shalimar perfume and taking her favorite lavender silk scarf, Al visualized his wife with a furry face and black nose as he tried to calmly reason with her. (Both items turned up, but Eleanor could never bring herself to apologize.) Often when Eleanor was yelling at him, usually about how he'd screwed things up—like not doing the laundry right—he would tap into his best self, by picturing a gift he'd gotten from the family of one of his early patients. They'd made up a little award certificate after Al was able to save their German shepherd, who'd been hit by a car. He was a wonderful dog and had been Al's patient since he was a puppy. He had to tell the family that Fritz had a fractured spleen and the only hope was to do a splenectomy, surgery to remove his spleen. It was a difficult decision for them as the odds were that Fritz might not survive the surgery, but they wanted Al to operate, and Fritz made it. Not only made it, but went on to live another six years in good health. The sign they made for Al had been done in calligraphy. The mom had taken a class in calligraphy at Vashon Allied Arts, and on a beautiful parchment scroll it said, "To our kind, gentle, beloved Dr. Albert J. Paugh, who saved the life of our faithful dog, Fritz. This certifies that you are the World's Greatest Veterinarian. With our deepest gratitude, The Crosby Family, Gary, Dale, Dan and David."

And so Al tried to be that guy for Eleanor, and he thought he had come through for her, which was why that afternoon in the kitchen, he found himself blindsided.

"Would you like a drink?" Eleanor asked.

"This early?" Al glanced at his watch. "It's only two-thirty."

She leaned forward and placed her hands on the table, folding them. The way she was sitting reminded him of the people on panel discussions on TV. He supposed they must be directed to sit like that, so they wouldn't talk with their hands. Al thought it was very distracting watching people on TV move their hands around.

Eleanor glanced at the cabinet where they kept the liquor. "Well, yes. I guess it is early." She looked out the window.

She seemed to be struggling to get started, and Al wanted to get it over with since he suspected it would be a litany of all the things he was doing wrong. So he gave her a little prompt. "You said you needed to talk?"

She nodded, then abruptly stood and went to the cabinet with the liquor and took down a bottle of red wine. "It's not too early for me." It was a bottle of Cabernet, the kind that had a screw top. She looked quite determined, and then pleased with herself, as she opened it without asking Al for help. "Sure you don't want one?' She brought a glass down from the shelf next to the sink.

"No thanks." Al began to feel agitated and wondered if he needed to visualize her as a patient.

"Well, Al—" Eleanor sighed as she brought the wine to the table and sat back down. She took a sip, then set the glass down and folded her hands again. "What I have to tell you ... ," she paused and looked out the window again. "This is very hard," she stared at her lap and then back at the window. "These windows are really dirty ...."

"Is that what this is about?"

"No," she said, sharply. "Not the *windows*." She looked at her drink and took a deep breath. "It's that—" she took a big gulp of her wine, swallowed and said, "I have to tell you that I can't go on—"

"*You can't go on? ...* Dr. Abrams just said the prognosis was good!"

"Not with my *life!*"

"Then what?"

"With ... With this marriage," she said quietly.

"With what?"

"I can't go on with this marriage."

"Our marriage?" he mumbled.

"Yes. Our marriage."

"You don't want to go on with our marriage," Al repeated, not able to believe what he was hearing.

"That's right, I want to get a divorce."

"You want to get a divorce," Al repeated, thinking he sounded like a goddam parrot.

"That's right." Eleanor sniffed.

He was stunned. He didn't know how long he stared at her. Finally Al went to the liquor cabinet and took down a bottle of scotch. He got a glass, then opened the refrigerator ice cube compartment, then closed it and just dumped the scotch in the glass. He leaned back against the refrigerator and took a big swig. "What the hell's going on?"

"Come sit down." Eleanor looked up at him.

"I don't want to."

"Fine. Whatever."

"It's not fine. What the hell is this?"

Eleanor's eyes filled with tears. "It'd be easier for me to talk with you if you'd sit down."

Al wanted to tell her that for most of the past year all he'd thought about was what was easier for her and he was sick and tired of it ... but he stopped. He put his drink down on the counter ... *Maybe the chemo had fried her brain. Maybe she had a loose screw. Or several. Oh shit. Now she was going to need help with a mental condition.*

Al willed his mind to visualize her with the furry face and the black nose; it didn't take that long for the transformation, he'd gotten so much practice. He saw Eleanor as a Labradoodle. Then he visualized the glowing letter from the Crosby family about how he had saved Fritz. *You can do this*, he told himself. He'd done hard stuff before, he could do it again. If she was crazy he would handle it, he just would.

Al brought his drink to the table and sat across from her and closed his eyes for a minute, gathering his thoughts. "Why don't you start from the beginning." He reached for Bert and stroked his head as he pondered the Labradoodle, wondering how much of the personality might be Lab and how much poodle.

"Maybe it started with my diagnosis," she said. "At least I think it probably did."

Al nodded and scratched Bert's ears a little.

"You always think more about your mortality as you age. Everybody does. But then if you get really, really sick—"

Al gave another understanding nod.

"All that time to think, while I was at the chemo unit—"

"It must have been so hard," he murmured, seeing a nice wet black nose.

"And I realized that I wanted a different life. I don't know how much time I have left, none of us do, really. But I had a huge wake-up call and I know I don't want to spend it like this."

"Like what?" Al asked pleasantly with an understanding smile.

"Living with you. And that dog."

"What's the matter with Bert?" He sat forward. "I thought you liked Bert?" No matter how hard Al tried to use his visualization technique, the Labradoodle disappeared and became Eleanor. Al couldn't convert her pale blue eyes, the parchment skin pulled tight across her high cheekbones, and her thinning grayish blonde hair (she always resented his curly mop because Al had more hair than she did). He was unable to get his mind to transform her to anything canine, to be anything other than his wife. And when his technique completely failed him, he got angry.

"What's wrong with Bert?"

"Oh, isn't that just something. Isn't that just the way it's always been? I say that I don't want to live with you and the dog, and all you can talk about is the *dog*. Our whole married life you always cared more for those dogs than you did for me!"

"That's not true." Al was hurt. Hadn't he stayed by her side, been at her beck and call the whole time these past months? Did he have to point that out?

Eleanor seemed to see that he was hurt. She reached for the wine and poured more into her glass.

Al folded his arms across his chest. Then he drank more scotch. Finally he muttered, "I didn't realize you thought our marriage was so terrible."

"It's not that terrible, but it's a polite, empty marriage—at least I feel empty. We might as well be roommates. Only it's worse than having a roommate because I keep hoping I'll feel loved, and I thought after you sold your practice it would change, but it didn't and you just got more distant and withdrawn and— and I had to get *cancer* to get your attention."

"That's harsh! You got sick right after I had my heart attack and sold my practice!"

"Don't shout."

"I'm not shouting. Or maybe I *should* so you'd think everything wasn't so polite!"

Eleanor's jaws twitched and she put her elbow on the table, rested her chin in her hand and looked out the window. Bert needed a drink and walked over to his water dish by the back door and lapped up the water. Eleanor drummed her fingers on the table. "I hate that he gets water all over the floor," she said. "And besides that, he stinks. When you take him to the beach, he rolls in some horrible dead thing and he smells hideous."

"I wipe him off—"

"Not good enough. You don't wipe him good enough!"

Al's arms flew up. "And that's grounds for divorce?"

"And you never listen to me. You make me repeat everything I say to you—"

"I don't hear as well as I used to, Eleanor. Haven't you ever heard of age-related hearing loss?"

"That dog makes the tiniest little itty bitty whimper and

you're right on it, going to him to see what he wants, so I happen to know there's nothing wrong with your hearing. Like I said, you never listen to me and that's all there is to it."

"So her majesty has spoken. She who must be obeyed." On the TV show they used to watch, *Rumpole of the Bailey*, Rumpole always called his wife "She-who-must-be-obeyed" and it always made Al chuckle. But he wasn't chuckling now. Not only was he very upset—but confused, too. He always felt bad for Eleanor, having been so sick. But he was mad and worried about her and also hurt. Al had a mess of different feelings, like a whirling web of bewilderment in his brain, and it made his head throb. He put his hands on his head and massaged his temples and then he rubbed his eyes.

Eleanor looked out the window again. "Look, I don't expect you to understand, Al. But I've had months to think about this and I've never been so sure of anything. Dr. Abrams asked me to visualize myself in the future and to see myself cured and when I did that I visualized myself in a different life."

"You visualized yourself without me."

Neither of them spoke. The silence that lay between them was cold and tense. Finally Eleanor took a sip of her wine. After a minute she set the glass down. "I want to sell the house, and I intend to buy a place near Ruth Ann and then I'm going to travel. You never really wanted to—to travel—I know that. I can hardly get you to leave the island."

Al didn't know what to say. Eleanor sounded sane, but maybe people could sound sane when they were about to do some really crazy shit. So he said, "Well, before you go off and do something rash, maybe it would be good to talk it over with—"

"I'm talking it over with *you*. That's what I'm trying to do here, Al."

"I was thinking like with a counselor."

"A shrink." she bristled. "You think I need a shrink. Listen, I'm not crazy because I want a divorce. Half of marriages end in divorce and all those people aren't nuts."

"Not at our age. Getting a divorce in your sixties is pretty weird, Eleanor. We're getting close to seventy, for crissake."

"No it isn't. I've been reading about it. It's much more common than you think. Since 1980 divorce numbers have doubled for people over sixty-five—there's even a name for it. It's called Gray Divorce."

"I don't care if they call it the Black Plague—since when did you care about being trendy?"

"I didn't say it was *trendy*. There's a difference between trendy and a trend, for God's sake ... and it isn't just men running off with some younger women. Trophies, bimbos, young little hotties, that sort of thing. A lot of older women are choosing to divorce, they're the ones initiating it."

"So that makes it right?" he snarled.

"It's right for me."

Then they each withdrew and sat in the cold silence that now felt ugly to Al.

Finally he asked her if anyone else knew about this.

"Ruth Ann, of course."

"Of course."

"Why wouldn't I tell my own daughter?" Eleanor assumed he was being sarcastic.

"I didn't mean it that way. It just makes me feel bad, that's all. I really did try with her, you know." Al didn't say it, but his stepdaughter reminded him of a chow. They often only bond with one person and can be indifferent to everyone else, and for Ruth Ann, her mother was that person. Ever since Al and Eleanor got married when Ruth Ann was fifteen, Al had been odd man out. They didn't have any big battles or rows, Ruth Ann was civil to him, but Al felt he might as well have been part of the furniture.

Eleanor poured herself more wine. "I never said you didn't try. But it didn't help when she and Robert separated—"

"I was trying to be supportive—you have to admit he was cheap, and him with all that money. When we went out to dinner with them, he'd take the bill and nickel-dime the whole thing, whipping out his little calculator on his phone to make sure he

didn't pay more than his share. And then bringing his own popcorn to the movies ... stuff like that. Look, all I did when they
separated was tell her I thought he was a jerk and that she was
better off without him. I wanted her to know I was on her side. I
thought I could connect with her."

"Well, she certainly remembered it when they got back
together, " Eleanor said. "A lot of good *that* did."

Al had to admit Eleanor was right about that. Ever since he
made the mistake of being honest, if he answered the phone
when Ruth Ann called, she hardly said a word to him, just asked
to speak with her mother. Not even very civil anymore. "But you
didn't like how selfish and cheap he was, either," he reminded her.

"Maybe, but at least I knew enough not to say anything. I
knew she wanted him back."

"How was I supposed to know that?"

"Just forget it. It's water under the bridge." Eleanor took a sip
of her wine. "It doesn't matter anymore."

"Because I don't matter anymore, I suppose, is what you
mean."

"That's not what I said. Look, I'm trying to get through this,
Al. This isn't easy for me, but I have to tell you that there's a
town house near Ruth Ann that she thinks will be perfect. I'm
going down to Portland this weekend to look at it. I'm not sure
how long I'll be gone, but when I get back I'll be putting the
house on the market."

"Does Dr. Abrams know about this?"

"No. Why should he?" she snapped.

"Moving is very stressful and you've had lung cancer and—"

"I know what kind of cancer, for God's sake."

"Well, a divorce, moving, all that stress, and stress elevates
cortisol levels, the hormone ... it's bad for your immune system
and then what will you do all day? Ruth Ann has her job. I just
don't see how this makes any sense, at the very least I think you
should—"

"Ruby's looking at it with me."

"Ruby?"

Eleanor nodded.

"Ruby who?"

"Ruby Nakatani. How many Rubys do I know?"

"I have no idea how many Rubys you know. I have no idea about any of this, as a matter of fact. I don't know what's been going on here."

"Well, Ruby doesn't want to leave Portland. Her sister's there. She wants to downsize— that house is too big for her now—and we've decided to get a place together," she said, quietly.

Al couldn't look at her. Slowly, he got up from the table, poured more scotch in his glass, turned and left the room. He went to his study and sat down with his laptop and tried to resume the Solitaire game, but he couldn't concentrate. Bert followed him and lay at his feet. Al looked at the certificate on the wall from the Crosby family, the people who respected and appreciated him. He read the words in a sad attempt to lift his spirit and avoid the fact that with Eleanor he hadn't been good enough. It wasn't a new feeling: not being good enough. It had been with him as long as he could remember, always lurking in his psyche like a shark unseen underneath a calm ocean. As an adult in his profession, he managed to ward it off, but it only went deeper and never disappeared.

Al didn't know how long it was before Eleanor came in to the study. He'd lost all sense of time. He heard her open the door and when he looked up from the laptop, he saw that her face was red and blotchy, like she'd been crying.

"You'll be fine, Al. This island is overrun with single women and the ones with dogs—which is most of them—they're all in love with you."

"News to me," he said, hoarsely.

"You just don't get it."

"I wish you wouldn't say that. You know I hate that line about men not getting it."

"Sorry."

"But I *don't* get it about this divorce, Eleanor. And I don't get it about Ruby, either."

CHAPTER 2

A L TRIED A FEW MORE TIMES TO SUGGEST A COUNSELOR, BUT ELEANOR was having none of it and proceeded to get ready to leave for Portland. They avoided the kind of de-coupling that involved tearful talkathons, dissecting the minutia of their marriage, and somehow he never got around to asking about Ruby. Eleanor had characterized their marriage as being like roommates, but that was exactly what Ruby was: Eleanor's roommate at Mills College and for decades they'd remained in close touch. What Al couldn't get his head around—was why she wanted to trade one roommate in for another?

It seemed surreal to him the way they behaved before she left. While Eleanor packed and made phone calls to realtors, Al avoided her by spending time at the beach, where he numbly stumbled across the sand and rocks as if he'd just been thrown in the frigid water of Puget Sound. Later, when he left the beach, Al did what he'd most recently imagined: sat in his truck for hours with Bert listening to music.

He decided to expand his musical journey and get out of his blues rut, so he tried a little country music. He played Lucinda Williams "Car Wheels on a Gravel Road." It seemed to speak to him, especially the part that went *There goes the screen door slamming shut … You better do what you're told … When I get back this room better be picked up … car wheels on a gravel road.* When Al listened to Lucinda sing that song, in his mind he just sang "truck wheels" instead of "car wheels" and then it really resonated.

Finally, when he did go home—usually when it was time to feed Bert—Eleanor spoke politely to him, and he was polite to her. When his stupor began to clear a little, and he was able to think about it, their relationship didn't seem much different to him than it had before she got sick. Except that Eleanor was divorcing him. They had slept in separate bedrooms ever since Eleanor said his snoring kept her awake, so there wasn't any change there. Actually, it was quite a while ago that they began sleeping apart; Al thought it might have been during one of the Bush administrations, but he wasn't sure if it was the old Bush's or W's. When he thought more about it, he was sure they hadn't slept together since the Clinton administration. He remembered going to someone's house for dinner during the Clinton sex scandal, and there was a lively and heated discussion about whether you could be trusted to behave with integrity when it came to the country if you cheated on your wife. And right after that Eleanor said his snoring bothered her and she asked him to sleep in the guest room.

Their robot-like courtesy continued through the week. And although they avoided any talk of their marriage, the night before she left for Portland, Eleanor cooked him a very nice dinner. Old fashioned comfort food: roast chicken, mashed potatoes and gravy, and green beans, then chocolate cake for dessert. He wondered if she felt guilty. He was at the beach with Bert the next morning when she drove off, so they even avoided saying goodbye.

AFTER SHE LEFT, AL DIDN'T know if he missed Eleanor. He thought maybe it hadn't hit him, but after a few days, he began to take some pleasure in wrecking the house. Not getting out a sledge-hammer and smashing things to bits, he wasn't going off the rails or anything like that. He just began to omit taking off his shoes and wiping off Bert's paws when they came home, and he let the dishes pile up and he left food out and his clothes were all over the bedroom floor, and he didn't hang up towels in the bathroom.

Things like that. Al found living that way very satisfying. Leaving the toilet seat up, too. He liked that.

Eleanor had been very fastidious about food. They mostly ate fruit and vegetables, chicken and fish and no red meat. She was very big on kale. They ate bushels of kale. On his first trip to Thriftway after she left, Al got potato chips, Fritos, two kinds of cheese (cheddar and gouda) and Triscuits (the original—not whole grain), salami, hot dogs, some donuts (both glazed and chocolate covered) and in the wine section he saw they were having a special on Rioja Vega from Spain for $7.88. Al thought he should get some. It certainly was a good deal and then maybe he could go back and get some Mexican food to go with it. Like some tacos and corn chips and salsa, and refried beans, or just nachos with tons of cheese on top. Of course, that wouldn't exactly be Spanish, like paella or something traditional, but Al was sure nachos would be very good with the wine. As he was reaching for a bottle, a woman whose cart was next to his reached for a bottle, too. She had a long face and dark eyes, with fluffy red-brown hair with grayish white in it. She looked kind of familiar, but the island was full of familiar faces and it was hard to know just where and how you might have met someone.

She smiled at him. "I'm feeling better now."

He mumbled, "That's good," as he set the bottle in his cart and quickly wheeled out of the wine section because he couldn't figure out who she was.

He headed over to the deli section to get some potato salad and eight pieces of fried chicken and while he was waiting for them to weigh and wrap it, he heard someone calling his name. He hoped it wasn't a friend of Eleanor's.

"Al!"

He turned to see Marilyn Henderson pushing her cart past the bakery section, smiling and waving at him. He suddenly wanted to hide, but he was stuck since he was waiting for the fried chicken.

"Hi, Marilyn." Al hoped he sounded pleasant and casual. She stood next to him and looked up at him. Her head came to about his elbow. Al didn't think she was a short person, but he was six feet five inches tall and everyone seemed short to him. Eleanor was almost six feet and Al always thought his height was one of the reasons she married him. He didn't weigh a lot for his height and Eleanor told him that the first time she saw him, she thought of an upside down broom stick with a giant Brillo pad on top of it. She was referring to his mop of curly hair and said it affectionately, at least he thought it was meant that way. In college he had a roommate who called him "Fat Albert," which the guy thought was hilarious since Al was so skinny. Al never told him he didn't like it; his roommate was the kind who would have just kept it up more. He hadn't stayed in touch with the guy, not like Eleanor and Ruby. Al wondered if Marilyn knew anything.

"How are you, Al? We sure miss you." Marilyn patted his arm.

He wasn't sure if it was supposed to be a comforting pat. "Can't complain," he tried to smile. "So, how's Eloise these days?" He didn't think she'd seen him when he parked behind the bushes outside the clinic. He hoped not.

"She just had her annual shots and check-up. Dr. Kincaid—he says everyone should call him 'doctor'—he wants Eloise to have some lab work done, but he says it's just routine."

"I'm sure it is." A routine way for him to jack up the bill.

"Would you like to say hello? You seemed to be in hurry when I saw you here a few weeks ago."

"I thought that's what we were doing now—"

Marilyn laughed and put her hand on his arm again. "I mean to Eloise. She's in the car and I've just got a few things to pick up. How 'bout if I meet you? We're parked right in front of Ace Hardware."

"Okay." He got his chicken and potato salad and went to the checkout. Al always liked Eloise, he was happy to say hello to her. She was a Pembroke Welsh corgi—they were very smart, loyal little dogs. Very popular. Of course, those dogs were best known as the preferred breed of British royalty, and Al supposed that was part of their appeal. As much as Americans prized democracy, he knew there was a fascination with royalty. Al remembered

Marilyn telling him about a folktale that said Queen Victoria was riding along in her carriage and there was the limb of a tree blocking the road, and an elf came out of the bushes and made two corgis appear, one was the Cardigan Welsh corgi and the other was the kind Marilyn had, the Pembroke Welsh corgi, and they moved the tree out of the way so the Queen's carriage could pass. Al thought it would be nice if an elf would come out of the bushes and move Jerry Kincaid out of the way so he could have his practice back.

He waited in front of Ace Hardware and in a few minutes Marilyn came out. "I'm the blue Dodge van over there. Eloise usually curls up on the front seat." Al followed her and waited for her to put her groceries in the back of the van. Then she opened the door on the passenger side and picked up the dog.

"How ya doin', Eloise?" Al put his hand out for her to sniff. She licked it so he scratched behind her ears. "Looks like she's doin' great."

"What about her lumps? You know her best, do they seem the same to you?"

"I can check her if you want."

Marilyn slid open the back door of the van and got in and sat holding Eloise by her collar next to her on the seat, while Al leaned in and carefully felt her abdomen. Eloise was very calm, and didn't seem bothered by his long fingers probing her belly. "They're benign." He smiled down at Marilyn and Eloise. "Just like they've always been. Nothing to worry about."

"Dr. Kincaid said I could have them removed if I wanted." She put Eloise on her lap, and lay her cheek against Eloise's head for a minute. "But I just don't know. What do you think, Al?"

"It's only a cosmetic thing. I don't think they bother Eloise at all and I'd hate to put any animal through unnecessary surgery. It's hard on them—the anesthetic, the stitches, wearing a cone on their head so they won't bite the stitches while it heals. But of course, it's your call." Al knew he'd better leave before he told her just what he thought of Jerry Kincaid. Insisting on *Doctor*

Kincaid—what a pretentious prick. "I've got to get back, nice to
see you Marilyn."

She hopped out of the back seat with Eloise, put the dog on
the passenger's seat and closed the door. Then she grabbed Al and
gave him a very big hug. He could feel her breasts squishing into
him right above his belly button. "Thanks, Al. You're the best."

Al trotted across the parking lot to his truck, trying not to
look like he was running away. He held the cloth grocery bag
close against his chest, hoping he wouldn't squish the chicken
and potato salad. Marilyn certainly had seemed grateful, but he
didn't know if her big hug had been a little over the top. Al didn't
like to admit it, but Eleanor was right about him, the part about
not getting it about women. He'd never known how to read the
signals. People hug each other all the time, who's to know what
means "we're pals" and what means "I'd be very interested in
jumping in the sack with you?" Now with dogs, it isn't compli-
cated at all. It's very clear when they like you, or when they were
afraid, or suspicious or provoked to anger. And when they loved
you, you could count on their devotion like the sun coming up
each day. The only thing wrong with them is that they die before
you do and it breaks your heart.

Was Eleanor right? *Did* he care more about the dogs he'd had
over the years more than he'd cared for her? The whole subject
was confusing to him.

As Al got in his truck, Marilyn waved from her van as she
left the parking lot. Al didn't get it about women, he admitted
to himself. Eleanor was right about that. But he wasn't sure she
was right when she said he cared more about his dogs than her.
He didn't think that was exactly true. It was just that you could
count on dogs.

Bert smelled the chicken and potato salad, so Al put the bag
behind the seat so it wouldn't tempt him too much, although
he knew Bert wouldn't go after it. Bert only had problems with
food and impulse control when Al's back was turned, which Al
thought was perfectly natural. In his practice, the clients who
annoyed him were the ones who acted like a Marine drill sergeant,

treating the dog as if it were a new recruit perpetually in boot camp. Those people didn't understand dogs, expecting rigid obedience like that. Like expecting perfection, which in Al's opinion wasn't natural in people or animals. He always wished Eleanor understood that.

As Al backed out of the parking space, he stopped to let a woman pushing a cart cross in front of him. It was the woman from the wine section. It was odd that she told him she felt better, reporting on her emotional state right there in front of the special on Rioja Vega, as if they knew each other. Very strange. But her red-brown hair with the grayish white and her long face did seem to belong to someone he'd seen recently. Then it came to him— the driftwood lady. She was the lady crying that Bert had found. Well, he thought, glad she's better.

WHEN HE GOT HOME FROM Thriftway, since all the plates were dirty, he ate the chicken and the potato salad out of the carton. Eleanor would be appalled. How had he missed how rigid she was when they first met? Rigidity was often mistaken for strength, but he'd come to recognize the fragility that lay beneath the taut exterior. A need for rules and limits without which the organism feared it would whirl out of control and disintegrate. At least he understood that now. But when they first met—a hundred years ago—actually it was twenty-four, he realized he hadn't seen much beyond how physically attractive she was and what appeared to be a predictable, not excessively emotional temperament. And they did have a few things in common, such as cross-country skiing, liking Thai food and birdwatching. Although their taste in music wasn't the same, and Al loved to dance, but not Eleanor. She said she felt everyone looked at her because she was so tall. Occasionally she'd agree to slow dance, but that was it. She also didn't share Al's passion for animals. Not that she especially disliked them, only that she hadn't grown up with animals and was mostly indifferent.

But no doubt about it—Eleanor was a very lovely woman. A

tall, Nordic-looking blonde with high cheekbones and large, dark blue eyes. She said Al was the only man who made her feel petite and he'd certainly enjoyed their physical relationship back then. He thought she pretty much did too. Had she been pretending? How was he to know what it took to have a good marriage? His parents' marriage had been a minefield that ended with a terrible explosion. Although he supposed that was another thing that bonded him and Eleanor. When they were in high school, they had both experienced the divorce of their parents. Divorce wasn't that common for people of their parents' generation and he and Eleanor found they could relate to each other around what it had been like. The circumstances of the divorces were very different, but what they both had seen was the bitterness, almost hatred, that their mothers had for their fathers. Al was sure that was why he had avoided marriage for so many years. He'd had several long relationships that ended when the women wanted to have kids, an idea that made him very skittish, and they'd left him for someone more suitable.

And what about their age? That obviously didn't mean anything. He and Eleanor were both older when they got married. Al was forty-two and Eleanor had just turned forty. She was divorced, but it wasn't a rebound thing when she met Al; she'd been divorced for eight years. He thought being older was in their favor, that they probably knew what they were doing. If Eleanor had misgivings about marrying him, she didn't show it, although maybe she'd hidden it because she seemed very confident at the time. The fact that he had a secure job and a solid income was appealing to her. Not that she was a golddigger. Just the opposite. She had her own family money—when Eleanor was in college her mother had died and Eleanor had inherited a substantial amount. She was leery of any man she thought might be interested in her for her money since her ex-husband had been a deadbeat who couldn't hold a job. Also her father was an alcoholic, and Al always thought she was suspicious of men in general.

Al's memories of their marriage seemed to surface most when he was eating. He was on his fourth piece of chicken and thinking about how Eleanor said the way he chewed food so loud annoyed her, when the phone rang. The landline. Eleanor had wanted to keep a landline because they lost power a lot on the island when there were high winds, but the phone lines always seemed to stay up through everything. They had a generator, so they could use it to get power to charge cell phones, but Eleanor didn't have faith that it would always work. Generators were among many things she didn't trust. Al didn't want to interrupt his lunch, so he ignored the phone and continued eating one of the chicken wings. When he was at Thriftway, he thought eight pieces might have been good for both lunch and dinner, but he seemed to be eating most of it. He was chomping on a drumstick next when his cell phone rang. Al wiped his hands on his pants, then got the phone out of his shirt pocket. It was Eleanor. He supposed he should answer. He hadn't talked to her since she'd left.

"Hello."

"Al?"

"Hello, Eleanor." He chewed on the drumstick.

"It didn't sound like you—"

"I had my mouth full."

"Oh."

"I'm eating fried chicken." He mentioned this with no small degree of satisfaction as fried chicken, or fried food of any type, was forbidden in their house. This made him think of French fries. Maybe for dinner, he'd go to the Red Bike and get a hamburger and a double order of fries.

"Look, Al. Marcie thinks there might be people who want to see our house and—"

"Who's Marcie?"

"Sorenson. Marcie Sorenson, the realtor."

"Oh."

"I had called her before I left about listing it and I was going to wait until I got back from Portland, but she wants to get going as soon as possible. Marcie says the market is improving and it's a good time to list it."

"Real estate people will say anything to get a listing."

"Well not Marcie—her husband's a very successful lawyer in Tacoma and they're extremely well off. She has her own agency and she can afford to be very selective about her listings. Marcie's *not* desperate for money—"

"Have you seen their bank account?"

"Of course not. That's ridiculous."

"I'm just saying you never know about people. Maybe they made a lot of bad investments and are in debt or she plays online poker and loses all the time, you just don't know."

"I didn't call to talk about the Sorenson's finances."

"All I'm saying is you might think somebody is rich, but you don't know everything about people, that's all." He finished the drumstick and picked up a thigh. Like you and Ruby, he thought, but didn't say it.

Eleanor was quiet for minute. Then she continued, all business. "The house has to be clean for the listing and then the other thing Marcie does is stage the house."

"What's that?"

"Make it look as attractive as possible, making changes here and there."

"What kind of changes?"

"She won't know until she sees it. But I do know we need to take down all our personal things so the prospective buyers can imagine themselves in the house—"

"Like what things?"

"Family photos, art work, things like that."

"My diplomas and the painting of the golden retriever?"

"Right."

"Well, I don't want to do this."

There was a very deep sigh and a long silence while Al chewed on the chicken thigh.

"I wish you wouldn't chew so loud."

"Too bad," he said, smacking his lips.

"Oh for heaven's sake—I certainly don't want to grab up all your stuff and heave it out on the road. We can be civilized about this. I'll be back tomorrow to get the house ready for Marcie to stage and of course, while it's being shown and you're living there, it has to be kept spotless. I think the dog should be kept out of the house as much as possible."

"I can't deal with this right now, Eleanor. I have to go." And he hung up.

Al thought of visualizing her as a patient and a dachshund came to mind, but he decided not to bother. What would be the point of trying to avoid getting angry? Why wouldn't he be mad that she was just bulldozing their life and there wasn't anything he could do about it? Legally, Eleanor could actually do whatever she wanted with the house—it was in her name. And community property wouldn't be a factor in their situation. Eleanor had insisted on a prenuptial agreement when they got married, and she'd maintained her own separate property and they hadn't co-mingled any finances. Everything was separate. For over twenty years Al had used money from his salary to buy the clinic building on installment from Jim McDoogal, the vet he worked with, so he owned it free and clear when Jim and Betty retired to Hawaii fifteen years ago. When Al sold it this past year to Jerry Kincaid, whom Al now always thought of as Greedy Jerry, the proceeds weren't co-mingled either—they just went right into Al's account. Eleanor owned the house and they split the taxes, insurance and utilities. She tallied up the grocery bills and he paid half every week. But Al bought Bert's dog food separately and took care of all his expenses. Eleanor insisted on that. There'd be nothing to untangle or fight about. The real estate lady's rich lawyer husband and those of his ilk wouldn't be buying any new sports cars from what they made off of the Paugh divorce, Al thought. At least that was some consolation. Everything separate, nothing co-mingled ... Come to think of it, he began to wonder if there was anything he and Eleanor ever did co-mingle in their lives. Was that why she said it was a polite empty marriage? When you have joint finances, you have to make most decisions together. He wasn't sure, but he imagined in a good marriage like his friend Ted and Millie's there was give and take, and you negotiate, and fight and makeup and have fun shopping for the new refrigerator together, stuff like that. But Eleanor bought everything for the house, that was her domain. And Bert was Al's responsibility because she wasn't interested in him, and when Ruth Ann lived with them, Al was left out of any parenting they could have done together. Eleanor went on trips with Ruby because he didn't like to travel. Al loved to dance, but Eleanor wouldn't dance, so they never did that together. When his favorite blues band, Bill Brown and the Kingbees, played on the island, Eleanor told him to go ahead without her. He did once, but people wanted to know where Eleanor was and that was awkward for him so he never danced with anyone and never went again. Maybe Eleanor was right. Maybe as marriages went, theirs was just melba toast.

He was pretty stuffed from finishing the chicken, although he did leave a little of the potato salad for later. He'd gotten sleepy so Al went to the bedroom for a nap. Bert followed and started to lie down on the floor, but it occurred to Al that it would be nice to invite him on the bed. Bert was a little reluctant at first because he usually wasn't allowed on the furniture. Even though Al's bedroom was separate from Eleanor's, she had insisted the rules pertain to the whole house. Eleanor became very irate about dog hair. She wasn't allergic. She just hated it on principle. Al lay on his back and Bert's head was on his chest. After a little while, Bert rolled over on his back and lay with his legs in the air. Al wondered what it felt like to lie like that so he decided to copy Bert and he put his legs in the air too, with his legs bent at the knees and his arms bent at the elbows while his wrists dangled. It seemed to take some pressure off the spine, maybe that was the point of it. While Bert and Al were lying on their backs, Al thought about Eleanor's money. She hadn't squandered the pile she inherited like her brother Howard had. Talk about deadbeats, Howard was a real loser—blew all the money on the stock market. (Eleanor hadn't spoken to him in over twenty-five years.) But Eleanor wasn't cheap, in fact she could be generous. She and Ruby moved to Seattle after they graduated from college, and moved in with Ruby's mother. Mrs. Nakatani was a widow and was having trouble making ends meet, and to help her, Eleanor paid off the mortgage on Mrs. Nakatani's house. So she could do really wonderful things for people. But Al still didn't think having so much money had done her any favors, especially coming into that money at such a young age. The money made it hard for her to stick with anything. In college Eleanor had majored in elementary education, and she got a teaching job when she and Ruby were living with Mrs. Nakatani. But she didn't last the year. Eleanor didn't like how the school was being run and she got annoyed, not only with the administration, but also with a lot of the other teachers on the staff. After that she became a professional volunteer, going from one organization to another, but nothing lasted too long. Being a perfectionist, Eleanor was always critical of how things were managed. If she needed to earn money like most people did, she would have had to stick with something and learn how to get along with people better.

He began to get uncomfortable lying with his legs in the air like Bert's, so he turned on his side to get a little shut-eye. Bert began snoring and Al found it a comforting sound, like a nice inboard motor boat putt-putting along the shore. As he closed his eyes, he imagined one of those beautiful old Century mahogany boats from the fifties.

Al had no idea he was so tired, he thought it was just going to be a little nap, but when he woke up, it was after eight. He hurried to the Red Bike so he could get there before nine when they stopped serving. He had a hamburger and double order of fries and enjoyed them very much. Whenever he went to the Bike with Eleanor, she'd always have seaweed salad and sushi and although Al liked sushi, too, the regular pub grub they had always made his mouth water. It wasn't just their house Eleanor took charge of—she was in charge of their stomachs, too. Al was sure she'd been well intentioned, caring about his health as well as her own. But there was no denying she'd become judgmental about it, and eating with Eleanor wasn't any fun.

When he got home, Al thought he should probably pick up the house a little before Eleanor got back. He still worried about her. He couldn't just turn that off after being with her through all her cancer treatment, and Al cared about her. If she saw what the house looked liked she'd be furious and all that anger wouldn't be good for her. It wouldn't be good for him either. But he decided to turn in early and do it in the morning. He smiled at Bert. "Why bother doing something today if you can put it off to tomorrow, right, Buddy?"

THE NEXT MORNING, AL WAS in the bathroom picking up towels from the floor when the phone rang. He went to the kitchen to answer it, hoping it wasn't Eleanor. He didn't feel like talking and he was sure she'd be pissed that he'd hung up on her the day before. But he was pleasantly surprised. It was one of his favorite people on the island, or anywhere for that matter. Martha Jane Morrison. Al only hoped he could be as sharp as she was if he made it to ninety. Actually, she must be about ninety-two now, he thought. He remembered going to her ninetieth birthday party and that had been a couple of years ago.

"Albert, it's Martha Jane." Martha Jane is the only person who called him Albert and from her it sounded fine.

"How are you?" He leaned back against the counter. "I knew it was you from reading your name on my phone. It's great to hear from you."

"I wonder if I'll ever get used to the way people know it's me before I even say anything. It always seems like magic to me and then I imagine they might be clairvoyant." She chuckled. "You know I try to keep up with things, but the gadgets are moving so fast it makes me dizzy. No one seems to write letters anymore, for example."

"I think that's right, I guess it's kind of a lost art."

"Indeed. Well, dear, for a minute I almost forgot what I called for, but I do know because I'm calling about Maria Montessori. I'm worried about her. She's just the most wonderful cat—"

"She is. She's a real gem."

"Albert, I know you're retired. And I hate to bother you, but there's something wrong with Maria ... with her paw ... she's limping and licking it all the time. But when I try to look, I don't see anything. I don't see any blood, like a cut—but I'm afraid that might be because my eyesight isn't so great and I'd feel so much better if you, since you know her and everything, if you might stop by and have a little look. I truly don't intend to do this all the time, dear. I completely understand that you're retired, so maybe just this once?"

"I'm flunking retirement, Martha Jane."

"You're doing what, Albert?"

"I'm flunking retirement. My retirement is a failure, it's not going well at all."

"Oh my. That doesn't sound good."

"No it isn't. In fact things are actually falling apart."

"Oh I'm so sorry. Is there anything I can do? Can I help with anything?"

"I don't think so. But I'd be happy to take a look at Maria."

"Oh, thank you, Albert. When do you think you might be able to drop by, dear?"

"How 'bout now? I can be at Baker's Beach in fifteen minutes."

"Splendid. I'll have tea for us."

As Al drove to Baker's Beach, he realized the truth of his situation having finally said it out loud to Martha Jane. He *was* flunking retirement. And now it looked liked he'd flunked marriage, too.

Chapter 3

Martha Jane's house was nestled in a little cove on the west side of the island between Baker's Beach and Hormann Road, a hilly lane that ran parallel to the water. The back of her house faced the cove and although her front entrance gave the house an address on Hormann Road, she always told everyone she lived on Baker's Beach. Al could see why because Martha Jane didn't have much in common with the Hormann Road people. A lot of them had torn down old beach cabins to build fancy houses; there were even a couple of mini-mansions and they didn't fit at all with the four timeworn, weather-beaten houses at Baker's Beach.

Al had last been to Martha Jane's early in the spring for the wedding of her next-door neighbors Howie Frankel and Mark Bromley. Howie and Mark had been together for almost thirty years and like a lot of gay couples on the island, they got married after Washington state made it legal in 2012. It was a small wedding in early spring. There were only about a dozen guests and Al was very pleased to have been invited. They'd invited Eleanor, too, but Al assumed it was a courtesy since they hardly knew her and he doubted they minded when she didn't come. Eleanor had gone with Ruby on one of those college alumni tours—they often went on those. The Mills Alumni Association organized at least nine different tour packages throughout the year, and Eleanor and Ruby were on one called Treasures of Ecuador, which went to the city of Cuenca and the Amazon rainforest. Al thought what they had right here on Vashon—Island Center Forest—was plenty enough forest for him. It was a 363-acre nature preserve, and to experience it, he didn't have to go through security and worry about packing the right size toothpaste and take change out of his pockets and wonder if his socks had holes in them. Besides, it didn't cost anything.

When he got to Baker's Beach, Al parked in Martha Jane's drive behind her old red Mercedes. She was one of a number of people in their nineties on the island who still drove. Mostly they didn't drive at night, or off island, and usually just ran a few errands around town. Although in the fall, Martha Jane went on expeditions on the back roads to harass deer hunters. She could barely see over the top of the steering wheel, and Martha Jane relished the fact that it seemed to terrify the hunters to see someone her age behind the wheel.

As Al got out of the truck, Mark and Howie's dog Tanner came off their porch to greet him. He was a handsome dog, a young German shepherd who had been the best man at their wedding, wearing a boutonniere on his collar, a yellow tulip like the ones that Mark and Howie wore. Martha Jane had been the maid of honor, and the ceremony was held on the beach. It was a wonderful wedding. And very special, Al thought, to have a ninety-two year-old maid of honor and a best man who was a dog. He was just as glad that Eleanor had been in Ecuador. Not that she was against gay marriage or anything like that, but she had staunch opinions about what was proper and the right way to do things. For example, she never wore white before Memorial Day or after Labor Day, and objected if Al wore a baseball cap indoors (God forbid in a restaurant), and was highly critical of teeth picking or women applying makeup in public. So Al knew a dog participating in a wedding ceremony would have been a stretch for her.

He didn't know in what condition he'd find the cat, but his vet bag was still well stocked with most anything he'd need. He kept it that way in case Bert ever required treatment. It had his stethoscope, thermometer, packs of suture material, a surgical pack with thumb forceps, hemostats, operating scissors, lidocaine for local anesthetic and the pentabarbitol that was used for euthanasia. As he came up the steps, Martha Jane waved through the window and then met him at the door. "Albert dear—I'm so glad you're here. I can't thank you enough." She had to crane her neck to look up at him. Her voice was weak and raspy with age. "Please come in. I've been terribly worried about Maria."

The house had a damp seawater smell along with a hint of cedar and mildew. It was a summer place smell that many cottages, cabins, and camps seemed to have. Hers also had the odor of oil paint in the mix. Eleanor would have been uneasy there, it was so cluttered. In the middle of the living room that doubled as Martha Jane's studio was a large table covered with tubes of paints, palettes, little jars, and brushes. Canvases were propped against every wall and at least a half dozen leaned on the furniture. Some of the paintings seemed finished and a few looked like works in progress. And there were books. Piles and piles of books. On the floor, the windowsills, every table—except the one that held the art supplies. Even the seats of the furniture were covered with books, although the sofa had one book that lay open, face down next to a big furry orange heap that was the cat. Martha Jane had adopted her from Vashon Island Pet Protectors, one of the local animal shelters, and not long after she got the cat, she made a slipcover in fuzzy orange fabric. Rather than worry too much about cat hair, she thought it would work well if the sofa matched Maria Montessori.

Al motioned to the couch. "If you sit on one side of her, I'll be on the other."

Martha Jane took the book off the couch and sat next to Maria, and then Al eased himself down on the other side. "Let's just sit here quietly for a few minutes to get her used to me." He set his bag on the floor next to his feet. "Looks like it's her right paw."

"I'm surprised she's not licking it right now, you must have a calming effect." Martha Jane slowly stroked the cat.

"I hope so. I'll start patting her too in a few minutes."

Al found it quite relaxing sitting next to Martha Jane, looking out at the water while they both stroked the cat. This isn't practicing veterinary medicine, he told himself, he was just helping out a friend. After a few more minutes, Maria began to purr, and Al gently lifted her paw. He bent down for a closer look and saw that one of her claws had overgrown and had grown back into the toe pad, which was infected. He explained to Martha Jane what had happened. "It's very common and easily treated."

"It's my fault. I should have been paying attention and not let her claw get like that. I feel bad about it. But to tell you the truth, Albert, I never seemed to get around to going to that new vet. I mean to ... but then the days go by ... and I don't seem to accomplish things like that." She bent down and put her face next to Maria's. "I'm so sorry old girl, you dear, sweet kitty."

"I'm going to slide her on my lap and then if you'll help hold her, I'll clip the claw and remove the piece from her toe pad."

Al got his hemostat and with a swift motion was able to clip the claw and pull it out. Maria's claws dug into his lap, but she was remarkably calm. "What a good girl," Al said, stroking her head. "You've got quite the cat, there. Wonderful temperament— it's obvious she's been well loved."

"You always know the right thing to say." Martha Jane patted his arm.

"I guess I feel on firm ground when it comes to animals, but not much else in my life, I'm afraid." Al put the hemostat back in his bag to clean with alcohol when he got home. "Do you have some topical antibiotic?"

"I'm not sure ...."

"Something like Neosporin?"

"Oh yes, I have some, at least I think I do."

"If not, I can pick some up for you. But Maria should have that put on her paw twice a day for about a week."

"I'll go check."

It took a while and Al could hear Martha Jane shuffling around, but then she was back with a tube of Neosporin. She sat next to Maria on the couch and put a little of the ointment on her paw. "I'll have to write it down, you know. I don't remember whether or not I've done things sometimes, so I'll make a little chart for Maria and check off the two times each day for her medicine." She looked up at him, "That's how I try to keep from getting discombobulated ... but of course, it doesn't always work."

"It sounds like a good way to keep track." Al smiled and picked up his bag. "Be sure and call me if she's still limping after a day or two."

"Oh, you don't have to run off, do you dear? Can you stay for some tea?"

"Well, sure ... thank you." Al patted the cat and then followed Martha Jane into the kitchen. "Can I help you?"

Martha Jane chuckled. "I seem to still be able to make tea," she said, as she filled the kettle and took it to the stove. She walked very slowly with short steps. "But I have to say there are times when it does get discouraging not to be able to do some things that I used to do. Like today, I really didn't want to try to stuff poor Maria into that little crate to take her to that new doctor what's-his-name."

"Kincaid. Jerry Kincaid."

"Oh, yes. Well, no one can take your place, Albert." She brought two mugs to the table, then went to the cupboard and brought back several boxes of tea. "Most of these are herbal. I hope that's okay."

"Sure, I'll try this one. We always have it at home. Eleanor only gets herbal tea." He put a tea bag in the mug and waited for the kettle to whistle. "You just sit down and I'll get the kettle when it's ready."

"Thank you, Albert." Martha Jane held on to the edge of the table and slowly, and it seemed to him painfully, lowered herself into the chair. Al wondered if her arthritis was bothering her more these days. She finally sat, and sighed with the effort it had taken. "Most of my friends hate Betty White, you know."

"I don't believe I know her. Is she here on the island?"

"The movie star. She turned ninety recently and my friends think she gives the rest of us a bad name. I guess 'hate' is too strong a word. They don't really hate her. But my friends think that she has set this standard for those of us who are still above ground, and of course, none of us can measure up to it, and then my friends end up not feeling good about themselves. There's no question about it, aging is the slow deterioration of your physical self—mental self, too, for that matter—and we have to accept it. My friends just think there are people like Betty White that make it more difficult." Martha Jane picked up one of the boxes. "I like this Celestial Seasonings tea, especially this Bengal Spice. Heavenly. I suppose that's why they named it Celestial. It does make it seem heavenly with a name like that, don't you think?"

"I do."

"It's strange about words. Sometimes I find myself stymied because I can't remember the most ordinary word. When I was younger, in my seventies, and even my early eighties, it used to bother me until I could come up with the word or the name, whatever it was. But now I think that's a waste of time. It doesn't matter, really. Now what were we talking about, Albert?"

"Betty White and the tea, I think."

"Betty White, well, I've had enough of her. And tea? You said you get this same kind at home—tell me, how is Eleanor?"

"Fine, I guess." He tried to sound normal. The kettle whistled and Al jumped up. Saved by the whistle, he thought, as he brought the kettle to the table, filled their mugs and then returned it to the stove.

"You had quite a scare, but things look better for her now, I take it."

Al sat down again and stirred the tea. "They say she's out of the woods. She always took good care of herself, she never smoked—that's one of the reasons she thought it was so unfair she got lung cancer. Eleanor always ate healthy food, exercised, stayed in shape—"

"I'm in shape." Martha Jane chuckled. "Round is a shape."

Al laughed with her. What a great quality, being able to laugh at yourself. He wanted to be able to laugh at himself like that, but right now he didn't think his situation was so funny. They sat quietly and drank their tea. He could hear Martha Jane's kitchen clock ticking, and somewhere down the beach, a dog was barking.

"Well, look who's here." Martha smiled as Maria came in the kitchen and rubbed up against Al's legs. He reached down to pet her and she jumped up in his lap.

"You're one of the few people she'll approach that way." Martha Jane took a sip of her tea. Then she put the mug down. "Albert, what's wrong? I can tell you're not yourself. Is it Eleanor?"

He nodded.

"Oh I'm so sorry. I thought you'd said she was doing so well."

"She is. Her last CT scan and chest X-ray were clear. Her usual vigor and strength are back, and her oncologist said she had a good chance of living many more years." He looked down at Maria and stroked her back.

"Well, that's certainly a relief."

"It is. But she wants a divorce." Al hadn't intended to tell her, but it seemed like he wasn't in charge of anything these days, even what came out of his mouth.

"A divorce?" Martha Jane leaned forward. "Eleanor wants to divorce you?"

Al nodded.

"I can't believe it." Martha Jane stared at him. "I have to say, I can't believe I heard you correctly. I sometimes get things mixed up. You did just say Eleanor wants a divorce."

"You heard it right. She's going to move to Portland and live with her old college roommate. They're very close—they've traveled together and see each other a lot. I knew they were good friends but ...."

"Oh, I see." She put her mug down.

"Eleanor's daughter Ruth Ann lives in Portland and Eleanor and Ruby ... they've been good friends for a long time. They travel together."

"Yes, you just mentioned that."

"Did I?"

"You said they travel together."

"They were in Ecuador when I came to Mark and Howie's wedding."

"I suppose you're wondering if they're gay ...." Martha Jane took another sip of tea. She certainly wasn't one to beat around the bush, Al had always known that about Martha Jane. He stroked the cat and looked out at the beach. A driftwood log was floating by, carried by the current and two seagulls were sitting on it, having a ride.

"Maybe ... well, probably ... I mean, I guess it's been in the back of my mind ever since she told me, but I didn't ask her. We avoided really talking about it, but I know anything's possible. There are homosexual and bisexual animals, you know—it's all kind of a continuum, I think. And not just among mammals like us. There are many species where homosexual behavior has been observed, in social birds and mammals—especially the sea mammals and of course, the primates, like us. And dragonflies are really interesting. Male homosexuality has been inferred because they've seen characteristic cloacal pincher mating damage in a large number of the males and that pincher damage indicates sexual coupling. And then of course, there's Roy and Silo—"

"Who? I don't believe I know them? Here on the island?"

"Not here. Roy and Silo are two male chinstrap penguins in the Central Park Zoo who became internationally known when they successfully hatched and cared for an egg."

Martha Jane was quiet for a while. Then she said, gently, "Albert dear ... putting aside the penguins, what about you and Eleanor?"

"It's easier to talk about dragonflies and penguins." He tried to laugh, but it came out like a snort.

Martha Jane chuckled a little, although she looked sad.

"It not so much about whether the relationship is sexual with her and Ruby that I'm wondering about, honestly. It's crossed my mind of course, but it's not the main thing I've wondered about—"

"An affair doesn't have to be literally sexual. There are affairs of the heart, of course."

"And that's what I'm wondering about, when it comes to me and Eleanor. I'm wondering more about if we loved each other. Did we ever really love each other?"

"Do you think you did?"

"I suppose that's a continuum too, like sexuality, maybe a range, or something that's quantitative." Al got the kettle and refilled his mug. "If I'm honest, I think I loved her because she loved me. Or seemed to in the beginning. And over the years I interpreted her presence and reliability as love. And Eleanor is a stable person. That was probably it. Reliability seemed like a good and solid kind of caring. It was something I hadn't seen a lot of—my mother was an actress—"

"I didn't know that. It sounds very glamorous."

"Not from my perspective, probably not my parents' either. They both were in theater—my Dad was a director. They started out in New York where my brother and I were born. It was an erratic, uncertain life, and neither one of them achieved the level they wanted. I've always thought my mother was like a trained seal that had to do all kinds of tricks and flips and dives to get a little fish, the fish being the sweet sound of applause."

"Fish can sustain a person, but I don't think applause does."

"No, it's more like a sugar high with no nutrients, like empty calories. People crave more and more, but it doesn't ever really feed them. My mother craved it all the time. She was very beautiful and emotional, charismatic and mercurial—"

"Quite different from Eleanor then—personality I mean. Eleanor is very good looking."

"That she is." Al nodded and looked at his watch. "Well, I better get home. I didn't mean to go on about all this. Eleanor wants me to get the house ready for a real estate person who's coming." He took his mug to the sink.

"She wants to sell your house? So soon?"

"Eleanor said having cancer made her think about how she doesn't want to waste any time in moving ahead with her life."

He laughed, but was afraid it sounded bitter. "I guess living with Ruby has been high on her bucket list."

"Have you thought about where you'll live, Albert?"

"No, this just happened and I don't know what the hell I'm doing, actually." He went to the living room and picked up his bag.

Martha Jane was grinning when he came back in the kitchen. "I may have a solution. Now I don't know for sure, but if you'd like, I can check on it. JoAnne McKee is looking for someone to rent her house. In fact, I know she was going to talk to Emma Amiad about it, Emma is a real estate agent and she knows everything about houses on the island. JoAnne's house is right here on Baker's Beach—the one next to Howie and Mark's. JoAnne's a psychiatrist, you know. Or is it psychologist? Maybe psychoanalyst? I get them all mixed up. Well, whatever she is, she's going on a book tour with the book she says is her life's work, *The Hoax of Penis Envy*. And then she has a teaching position as a visiting professor somewhere. I forget the name of it. Some place in London. But Albert, it might be a perfect solution for you ... renting her place until you figure out your next step. Shall I go ahead and ask her about it? I think she'll be coming over to the island in a few days. She's lives in Seattle, you know. The house here at the beach has been her weekend place.

"It's too bad this didn't happen sooner—" Martha Jane scowled. "Oh, Albert ... I didn't mean it that way. Things come out wrong. I don't think it's too bad that Eleanor didn't come to this decision sooner—that's not what I meant at all. You know I'm so sorry about you and Eleanor—what I meant was Maggie Lewis's house across the road was available—she was looking for someone. But her cousin is there now, Bonnie Douglas, a lovely woman about Maggie's age who has had some kind of trouble, something very sad, but I don't remember what, just that Maggie thought it would be good for her to stay on the island for a while.

"That's what happens, you know. Things about people, some of the details, just don't seem to stick. But I do have her name right, I'm quite sure. It's Bonnie ... I know that's correct. Perhaps you've heard that Maggie Lewis and Walter Hathaway have

rented an RV and they're putting on theater workshops in rural
areas and Indian reservations that never get a real author to come.
They'll be gone for three months, until sometime in December, I
think. Did you happen to see Walter's play *A Goose Called Hope*?
We had it at Fred Weiss's meadow and I had my acting debut. I
actually had two parts. In some scenes I was a goose and in others
I was in a crowd scene as one of the townspeople."

"I saw the play, and I loved it." Al gathered up the boxes of tea
and took them to the cupboard.

"What was I talking about? You know I try to say as much as
I can as fast as I can so I don't forget what I intended to say, but
I'm afraid I forgot."

"Maggie's house and renting the other house here?"

"JoAnne's. Right. Shall I call her?"

"Won't hurt to ask, I guess. But she'd have to okay a dog.
Anywhere I go I'll have Bert."

"You and Bert would be a wonderful addition to Baker's Beach.
I'll give you a call after I've talked with JoAnne."

Al thanked Martha Jane and bent down and kissed her cheek.
He adored her. Martha Jane had groupies on the island and Al
was one of them. There were a number of people, mostly in their
sixties and seventies, who hung on her every word, even when she
nattered on and they couldn't always follow her. It was her spirit
everyone loved. At ninety-two, Martha Jane had a curiosity and
optimism about life that you usually found in the very young and
after being with her, he always wondered what it took to have an
attitude like that. Maybe people like Martha Jane were just born
that way, the way some dogs have a wonderful temperament. You
can see it in puppies, some are born anxious and fearful, while
others come into this world brave and calm.

WHEN AL GOT BACK TO the Burton Loop and pulled into his drive,
he saw Bert standing at the back door whimpering, and there
parked in front of the garage was Eleanor's black, shiny Volvo. Al
contemplated leaving his truck running, flinging the door open,

jumping out to get Bert, leaping back in and then roaring back down the drive. He'd go to Agren Park where they'd walk on the trails for a few miles and after that maybe stop for lunch. Pizza might be good. The classic kind with lots of cheese and pepperoni ... Al sat in his truck considering what he'd have for lunch while he gazed through the trees at Quartermaster Harbor, where the sparkling water danced and the breeze rocked their neighbor's sailboat on its buoy ... A sailboat would be nice ... Maybe he and Bert could just sail away somewhere ... around Manzanita and then over to Gig Harbor. He could have lunch at the Tides Tavern and order a burger for Bert, too, before they sailed away along Colvos Passage. Al stared at Eleanor's car. He shook his head and berated himself. They were cowardly fantasies, the escapist thoughts of a weakling, and as much as he wanted to leave, he knew he had to face Eleanor. She who would not be happy.

"IT LOOKS LIKE A CHIMPANZEE was living here!" Eleanor shrieked the minute Al came in. "I can't believe what you did to this house!"

"I'm sorry. I was going to straighten things up, but then Martha Jane called—she was worried about her cat and I thought I should help her so I said I'd stop by."

"Straighten up? *Is that a joke?* This looks like a job for the health department and how could you forget? I distinctly *told* you I was coming this morning—"

"I didn't see how I could say no."

"You never do, Al." She said with a big exasperated sigh. "You say yes to every animal on this island—you've always put animals before me and all I wanted was for the house to look good for Marcie so she could see its potential. But you've left this place like a pigpen, like a bunch of drunken fraternity boys live here!"

"It won't take me long. I'll clean it up."

"What the hell were you thinking, making a mess like this? Were you just trying to spite me?"

"I was going to clean it up this morning, like I told you."

"I had to call Marcie and reschedule."

"Fine."

"Well, it's not fine. I want to move ahead with this and I don't appreciate this delay. Look at this place!"

Al saw how unnerved she was, red-faced, practically shaking, standing on the floor covered with muddy paw prints, in front of the sink piled with a week's worth of his dirty dishes and chicken bones and newspapers all over the place and he felt terrible that he'd upset her so much. "Eleanor, just sit down and take it easy. I'll clean everything up."

"Oh, Al." Eleanor slumped in the chair at the kitchen table.

He went to her and put his hand on her shoulder. "It'll be okay. I'll fix it."

Then she started to cry, deep painful sobs that tore at his heart and he knelt next to her with his knees up against the legs of her chair. His eyes filled with tears and he held her with his long arms enfolding her as they both wept.

CHAPTER 4

EVERYTHING AL OWNED FIT IN HIS TRUCK AND A WEEK AFTER ELEANOR went back to Portland, he moved to Baker's Beach. He was grateful to Martha Jane for suggesting JoAnne McKee's place because there weren't that many rentals on the island. There used to be a hostel where people stayed in teepees but Al heard it closed. He didn't like to think about what he and Bert would have done. He supposed they might have patched together a lot of temporary vacation type rentals in different parts of the island, but he knew changing their home every few days would have been hard on Bert. Not that it would have been a piece of cake for him, either. Al liked to be in one place. Of course he knew he could have stayed in their house on the Burton Loop until it sold, but he couldn't stomach the idea of being told to vamoose every time some prospective buyer wanted to look at it. To say nothing of having to keep it looking like a magazine with all the fancy staging things Eleanor and the realtor were doing. There'd be hell to pay if he didn't promptly make the bed, do the dishes and keep the whole place a dog hair free zone. The sooner Al left, the better.

As far as Eleanor went, he was still in shock that she was leaving him to live with Ruby. And he still didn't quite know if she was leaving him *for* Ruby, or just leaving and then would be living with Ruby. It was more than semantics it seemed to him, but in the final analysis Al thought it probably didn't matter much. The result was the same. Eleanor left, and he and Bert were moving to Baker's Beach.

Al's clothes were all stuffed in garbage bags and he'd gotten big cartons from Thriftway for all his other stuff: his computer, books, a big pile of veterinary medical journals, his CDs and DVDs, diplomas, various framed family photographs, the letter from the Crosby family and the beautiful painting of the golden retriever. His only furniture was the chair he'd taken from the clinic and Bert's bed, a huge red plaid pillow stuffed with cedar shavings he'd gotten from Pandora's Pet Products on the island. He also boxed up Bert's bowls, toys, leashes, bags of dog food and treats, and the medical supplies he'd kept from the clinic.

It only took him about a half hour to load his truck. He carried his chair and Bert's bed first, then the boxes, and on top of those he lay the garbage bags filled with his clothes then fastened it all down with bungee cords. The truck bed was crammed, but as he loaded the last of it, it didn't seem to be that much stuff to have accumulated in his sixty-seven years. It wasn't as though he'd deliberately tried to lead a life of simplicity. It was just that he'd never been much of a consumer and the thing he really cared about was the clinic, and it was now the property of Jerry Kincaid.

The For Sale sign was already in front of the house; Eleanor hadn't wasted any time. As he drove away, he recognized that he wasn't feeling anything. Not mad, sad, glad, afraid or even relieved. Nothing. Maybe he was just numb. Before he turned on Vashon Highway, he stopped at the Burton store to get a big bag of potato chips, Lay's Classic—his favorite, and a six pack of beer. As he parked, he thought his stuff piled on the truck made him look like Jed Clampett, only he and Bert were the only two in the hillbilly family. But he didn't run into anyone he knew at the store and he was glad of that.

Al was looking forward to living at Baker's Beach. Beyond the cove, the beach had long stretches where there weren't any houses at all. He and Bert would probably be able to walk a long way without seeing anyone, which would suit him just fine.

It only took him about fifteen minutes to arrive at JoAnne's house, but as he drove down Baker's Beach road, it seemed like a whole world away. Al parked in front of the house, and as he and Bert were getting out of the truck, he saw a woman walking back from the mailbox. This time Al recognized her right away. It was the driftwood lady.

"Pretty day," she said.

"Sure is." He shut the truck door.

Bert went to her wagging his tail and she put her hand out for him to sniff.

"This is Bert."

"Yes, we've met." She leaned down to pat him. "Hi Bert, aren't you a handsome guy." She glanced up at Al while she continued to pat Bert. "Looks like you've got a pretty big load for the dump there," she said, smiling. "So you're helping clear out JoAnne's place?"

"Um, no actually, I'm moving in. This is my stuff I'm about to unload."

She laughed nervously and looked embarrassed. "I saw the garbage bags and ...."

"My clothes."

She looked puzzled.

"In the garbage bags."

"Oh I'm sorry, I didn't mean to suggest anything like—well, you know what I mean—"

"Well, actually they are kind of ratty." Then Al didn't know how to keep it from going downhill even more. She kept saying she didn't mean his stuff looked like garbage, and he kept saying it was okay because it was all pretty terrible and probably belonged in the dump anyway, and then she just smiled kind of a crooked smile like she couldn't wait to get away, and then she scurried off to her house saying she'd better go in and look at her mail. She went into Maggie Lewis's house across the road and Al figured she must be the person Martha Jane had mentioned, Maggie's cousin, who was staying there. Al didn't get her name, but then he realized he'd only introduced Bert. People seem to introduce dogs more easily than themselves, he'd noticed.

The house Al was renting was the smallest one at Baker's Beach. It had two bedrooms, a combination kitchen and dining area, and a living room with a fireplace and built-in bookshelves. The bathroom had a shower tub combination and was pretty small but had some nice blue and white tile. JoAnne McKee often had weekend renters, so there weren't any of her personal things around. In fact, it was kind of like those well-equipped hotel suites they advertise for business people, with a kitchen and a little dining and living area. It had dishes and pots and pans and cooking utensils, even a nice coffee pot. Al saw that he wouldn't have to buy anything. Eleanor had let him have some sheets and towels from their house. She chose the ones for him to take. The sheets seemed okay, they had faded green and yellow stripes. The set of towels were light green and kind of stained and frayed, but Al didn't care. He didn't see any point making a big deal about bath towels. She also gave him some blankets, but one had some moth holes. But again, he didn't want to fight about moth-eaten blankets. Al did wonder if Eleanor hadn't had cancer whether he would have gotten irritated with her about the crappy stuff she gave him. He supposed that was possible.

It took him less than a half hour to move his stuff into the house. Al dumped all the garbage bags on the bed and then carried in the boxes. The first thing he did was put Bert's water bowl and food dish in the kitchen. Then he chose a cupboard for his food and treats. In the larger of the two bedrooms, Al put the old green and yellow striped sheets on the queen bed and covered it with the blanket with the moth holes. He placed Bert's bed in the corner, but then it occurred to him that Bert could sleep on the queen bed with him every night. What a happy thought. Al whistled as he went to the living room to unpack the boxes.

The bookcases in the living room were the kind with adjustable shelves, so Al changed them around and put his diplomas and the framed letter from the Crosby family on the top shelf. Eleanor had kept their TV but she let him have the CD player, so he set that up on one of the shelves and then unpacked his books and music. He didn't think he should nail anything in the walls, so Al propped his painting of the golden retriever on the top of the bookcase. JoAnne had internet service which he'd pay for with the other utilities and when Al set up his computer and put in the password listed on her instructions for the house, "AnnaFreud," he got on the internet right away.

Baker's Beach Road sloped down toward the cove and JoAnne's house was toward the top. Off the kitchen-dining area there was a deck where you could look out over the tops of the neighbors' roofs and see the beach and the expanse of the cove. It had several teak chairs and a small round table with an umbrella, and as soon as Al had everything put away, he got the beer and potato chips and headed straight for it. One of the chairs had an attached ottoman, and that's where he sat. With his feet up, the bag of potato chips on his lap, a beer in his hand and Bert at his feet, Al looked out at Baker's Beach and the cove and thought this was going to be very good. He didn't miss his old house. Al also didn't miss Eleanor, which kind of bothered him.

When he'd finished his beer and half the chips, he went in to get another beer and his iPod and headphones to listen to some blues. From the kitchen window, Al saw Bert go down the deck steps that led to the yard, probably do his business and maybe mark the territory a bit. He never worried about Bert wandering off or getting lost. Bert wasn't a runner. While Al was trying to remember where he'd put his iPod, his cell phone rang. He recognized one of the Vashon phone number prefixes, 463, so Al answered it.

"Hi Al, this is Marilyn."

"Hi, Marilyn." He hoped it wasn't more concern about Eloise. There was nothing wrong with that dog.

"I know this is really last minute, but I wondered if you'd like to come over for dinner tonight?"

"Oh, well, I was going to go to Thriftway pretty soon, but—" Al didn't know what to say. She had taken him by surprise and it had never been easy for him to say no to people. But then he thought maybe she was a good cook, so he said, "Well, sure, I guess so. I mean, thank you, Marilyn."

"Come about seven, that's not too late, is it?"

"No, that's fine. Um, where do you live?"

She laughed. "Sorry about that. I live on Madrone Drive. It's a lane off of Cove Road and actually my house is a walk-in. It used to be a weekend cabin that I've winterized and remodeled. You park on Madrone, and then I'm about a quarter of a mile in from the end of the lane. You'll see my van there at the beginning of the trail."

"Okay, thanks. I'll see you at seven."

Al would never get used to how fast news traveled on the island. He was almost certain Marilyn had heard that Eleanor had left him and was taking pity on him. And what about Bert? It seemed too soon to be leaving Bert alone in a strange house, but Al didn't think he should have asked her if he could bring him. And then he remembered he should have asked Marilyn if he could bring some food or something. That's what Eleanor always asked when anyone invited them to dinner. Al was wondering if he should call Marilyn back to ask about that when he noticed that Bert hadn't returned. Rushing outside, Al didn't see any sign of him on the deck or in the yard. This wasn't like Bert, but Al berated himself for not keeping an eye on him.

"Bert! Here boy!" Al ran down the steps. "Bert! Here Bert! Come!" He waited in the yard for a few minutes, continuing to call him and when Bert didn't show up, Al decided to walk around each neighbor's house. Bert never ignored Al unless he'd found food, and after going around Howie and Mark's house and Martha Jane's, Al went across to the only other house at Baker's Beach—Maggie Lewis's, which was where he found Bert. In the garbage. The can next to the shed was tipped over and Bert was having a feast.

Just as Al got to her yard, Maggie's cousin came out of the house. "Oh my, well, Bert has certainly found some fun." She laughed good naturedly.

"I'm sorry about this." Al started picking up the garbage.

"No big deal. Here, I'll give you a hand." She picked up a milk carton and started gathering a bunch of orange peels.

"There's no need for you to do this." Al was embarrassed that

Bert had made this mess and here she was picking it up. "I'll take care of it, really. Please don't."

"Then how 'bout if I hold open the bag for you."

"Well, okay." Al didn't want to get into another awkward conversation where he insisted she not help, and she insisted she would help. Although, she actually seemed to be kind of a mellow person. If a dog had gotten into their garbage, Eleanor would have been really pissed. Things like that always set her off.

Bert kept trying to eat the garbage that remained on the ground. "There might be some chicken bones—I just hope he hasn't gotten to them," she said. "Would it be okay if I got something for him from the house to distract him. Like a piece of cheese?"

"Great idea."

Maggie's cousin went in the house and came back with a handful of little cheese pieces and went to Bert, who was licking a yogurt carton, and offered him the cheese. He preferred it to the yogurt and she easily coaxed him to follow her inside her house and then she shut the door.

As Al got the last of the garbage in the bag, through the window he could see her petting Bert and feeding him cheese morsels. She didn't seem to be sad the way she'd been behind the driftwood, but you never know about people—about what might set them off. But she obviously liked dogs and if he kept things at a cordial distance, Al thought she would probably be a nice neighbor. Eleanor had gotten mad at most of their neighbors over the years (they made too much noise on their deck, or when they had company the guests parked on the edge of their lawn, or they trimmed a branch of a tree on Eleanor's property, and on and on) and then she thought Al was disloyal to her if he was friendly to them after she'd just called them to complain. It would be refreshing to get along with your neighbors.

Maggie's cousin opened the door and Bert came out wagging his tail, but he didn't charge out, he sort of ambled. Al knew he liked it there. Bert loved cheese.

"I've got it all picked up," he said. "Thanks for keeping Bert out of the way."

"He's welcome any time."

"I'm sorry about the mess. Look, I've got a bungee cord—why don't I bring it over to fasten on the lid of the can?"

"That's really nice of you, thanks."

"It's nothing, really. It'll just take me a second to find it."

"Oh, by the way, I'm Bonnie Douglas. I'm Maggie Lewis's cousin." She held out her hand.

"My hand's sticky." Al felt awkward touching someone after he'd been picking up garbage.

"I have Bert's drool on mine."

Al laughed as he shook her hand. "I think mine is worse. I'm used to dog slobber. I'm Al Paugh—Bert and I will be living across the road for the next couple of months."

"Well, let me know if you need anything. Cup of sugar, or whatever." She smiled.

Al thanked her and he left to get the bungee cord. When he came back, she was inside so Al didn't see her again. It only took him a minute to get the lid secured, and after that he went back to his place to shower.

Al began to whistle as he got ready to shower, but as he climbed in, he banged his head on the shower curtain bar, and the whole thing fell down in a big heap. "Damn," he muttered, as he picked the thing up and got it back in the brackets. Being so tall, hitting his head was not an infrequent occurrence, but he'd need to remember how low that rod was. He'd probably discover a lot of things to get used to in the house, but basically he didn't think it would be hard to adjust to living at Baker's Beach. Not at all.

He never quite got around to calling Marilyn, so he decided to take Bert with him when he went to dinner. It didn't feel right leaving him alone the first night, and Bert was very comfortable staying in the truck. Al gave him a big rawhide bone for him to chew on in case he got bored.

Al wasn't familiar with Madrone Drive SW and was glad Marilyn's directions were detailed. Vashon was like that, with all kinds of little side roads that had places back in the woods that you'd never know were there. He parked next to her van and left the windows open a crack for Bert.

Walking through the woods on the trail, Al thought how pretty it was, but he wondered what it would be like on a dark, rainy day. The house on the Burton Loop where he and Eleanor lived, or used to live, had a lot of light and Baker's Beach had a lot of light, too. He wasn't so sure he'd want to live back here in the woods like Marilyn, but each to his own, or her own.

As Al got close to the house, Eloise barked like crazy. Al felt bad showing up empty handed. He had thought about stopping at Thriftway to get a bottle of wine, but then he had to clean up Bert's garbage mess and didn't have time. All he had at home was beer, and Al thought showing up with a couple cans of beer might be tacky.

Marilyn held Eloise and opened the door. "Glad you found it, no trouble, I hope."

"Nope. Your directions were good." He bent down and let Eloise sniff his hand. "Hi, Eloise. You're a good watch dog."

"I told her you were coming and she was very excited. She just loves you, Al."

"Oh, well, that's very nice." Al followed Marilyn inside and at first it was hard to tell that they had left the woods because she had large ferns in pots in every corner of the small room that seemed to be a kitchen, living room, dining area and bedroom all in one. There was a wood stove in the corner and hanging over it was a wood carved sign that said, "Goddess Grotto," and there were chunks of crystal quartz on the window sills. A large display case had about a dozen crystals of various sizes and took up most of the wall behind a brass bed that was covered with a printed thing that looked like it came from India. The place smelled like marijuana, or maybe it was incense. Or both. Marilyn wore a long, light purple flowy dress. Al couldn't help noticing that it was very low cut and dangling above her breasts was a piece of rose-colored quartz.

Eloise had a bed in the corner, and Al thought the dog bed

might be the only thing in the place he could relate to. He bent down to pat Eloise.

"How's she doing?"

"Oh, Al. I'm not worried about her at all. Ever since you put your hands on her at Thriftway I knew she would be fine. Did you know that you're a natural healer? You could be a shaman."

"I'm a Cougar, actually."

Marilyn put her hand over her heart. "Oh, is that your spirit guide?"

"Washington State Cougars, that's where I went to veterinary school." He didn't know what to say after that, and then he looked around at her house and did something he hadn't done in years, since before he was married. When he didn't know what to say to a girl, he'd make up something and say he heard it on NPR. So he said, "You know, I heard on NPR that a recent study determined that ferns cleanse the air and eliminate over thirty-five percent of the toxins."

"I'm not surprised." Marilyn smiled. "Scientists often prove just what is ancient wisdom, which is really the divinity of nature." She went to the kitchen area and got a salad from the refrigerator and began tossing it. "It's what we believe. I'm a Pagan, and ferns are an essentially feminine plant. They embody the female divine principal and the sacred feminine, the Goddess." Marilyn took a dish out of the oven and motioned him to the table. "Have a seat, Al. Everything's ready."

She brought the salad and then the casserole dish that was filled with brownish goo; Al thought it might have been beans and rice mixed together, but it didn't look like either one.

"Shall we bless the food?" She sat down and reached for his hands. Then she bowed her head. She was silent for a minute then she said, "Bless this gift from our mother Earth."

As he sat holding Marilyn Henderson's hands, Al wondered what he was doing there. After she said the blessing she kept holding his hands, and he didn't know what to do. She leaned forward and looked deeply into his eyes. "I'm so grateful you're here, Al. It means so much to me."

Then after what seemed to him like an hour, she let go of his hands and shoved the pot of brown stuff toward him. "Help yourself, don't be shy."

"Thank you." Al took a small helping and then a lot of salad.

"Oh, I forgot!" Marilyn jumped up and got a bottle of wine and a couple of glasses that were sitting on the counter. "This is blackberry wine that I got at the Goddess Festival at Paradise Ridge last year." She poured some in their glasses and then lifted her glass. Then she leaned forward and looked deeply into his eyes again and whispered softly, "To our friendship."

They clinked glasses, and Al took a sip and thought it tasted a lot like cough syrup. But the salad was fine and to his surprise, the mystery stuff was actually very good. Marilyn was a talkative person, which was lucky for him because he didn't have to worry about what to say. All through dinner, she talked about how she'd discovered what she called clear quartz and how it was known as the "master healer" and the power it had to release and regulate energy. "It's all about the planes, you know. The physical, emotional, mental and, of course, the spiritual plane. It balances them. And revitalizes them, too, of course. And balances the chakras. It's essentially a deep soul cleanser."

She went on like that for the rest of the dinner, and after they'd finished she brought out some tea. After that Al wanted to leave, but he needed to use the bathroom, and she pointed to a door to the right of the woodstove. Al excused himself and went to the bathroom door, opened it and walked smack into the low doorjamb—*bonk!* He stumbled back and was rubbing his head when Marilyn jumped up and leaped across the room.

"Oh, Al. That must hurt," she cooed, and reached up and lay her hand across his forehead. Then she leaned the rest of herself against him and pulled his head down and kissed him on the mouth. Al had been very eager to escape just a few minutes ago, but it felt good to be holding a very warm person and Marilyn was very attractive and he forgot about the crystals and the goddess things that he couldn't relate to, but found he was relating

on a physical plane. But then she put her hand on the zipper of
his jeans and began to lead him toward her bed.

"Marilyn, I was on my way to use the bathroom."

"Oh, that's right." She smiled and went and sat on the bed.
"I'll be right here."

Al backed away from her and went into the bathroom, this
time remembering to duck his head. After he'd finished and was
washing his hands, Al looked in the bathroom mirror, which was
surrounded by little pieces of quartz and wondered what the
hell he was doing. He needed to think this through. If he didn't
change course, he was about to have sex with Marilyn Henderson
and it seemed to him this would not be a very good idea, so he
ducked his head and rushed out of the bathroom and thanked
Marilyn for the dinner and said he really couldn't leave Bert any
longer and had to go. Then he fled down the trail to his truck. It
was lucky that there was a full moon that night or Al wouldn't
have been able to see a thing and was sure he would have fallen
flat on his face.

CHAPTER 5

THE NEXT MORNING AL LET BERT OUT AROUND SIX-THIRTY, AND AS soon as he came in, they both went back to bed. Eleanor didn't believe in sleeping late, so even if Al wanted to on weekends, she made it clear that she didn't approve. He found it hard to sleep when someone was walking around making little disapproving clucking noises. Baker's Beach was much quieter than his old neighborhood, and Al wondered how late he might have slept if his cell phone hadn't rung. Maybe he would have slept until he got hungry, and that could have been very late because that food at Marilyn's had been surprisingly filling.

When Al saw it was Eleanor, he thought about not answering. Then he felt guilty. He had the creepy feeling that she knew all about him almost going to bed with Marilyn Henderson.

"Hi, Eleanor."

"How are you doing, Al?"

"Fine." He reached over and patted Bert's head, thinking it would have been nice to be Skyping so she could see Bert on the bed with him. "How are you?"

"Fine."

Then nobody said anything and Al wondered why she called.

"I wanted to tell you about the papers I sent you. Also, Marcie said there has been a lot of interest in the house."

He yawned and got out of bed and went in the kitchen to

get the coffee going. There was another silence while he ran the water to fill the pot.

"What?" Eleanor said, "I can't hear you."

"I didn't say anything."

"I thought I heard something."

"It was the water. I'm making coffee."

"You're just getting up?" It was only a question, but there was that familiar little edgy judgmental tone that meant, "just getting up *now*, you lazy schlub?"

"I was out late." He said with some satisfaction, but then hoped she didn't ask where he'd been because he thought it would be mean to tell her he'd been with Marilyn even though Eleanor was the one who didn't want to be married anymore.

"Well, I won't keep you, but I wanted to tell you that King County has what's called a Simple Divorce Packet—you get it online. It's for people like us."

"What are people like us?"

"For uncontested cases of divorce. I've downloaded the forms and filled them out—all they need is your signature. I sent them this morning, so as soon as you get them, just sign them and send them back to me. Then I'll be assigned a case number and it should take about ninety days. It's really quite simple."

"What do these simple papers say?"

"Just that one spouse believes the marriage is irretrievably broken and the other agrees. That would be you. There's also fee. It's $299 and I'll pay that."

"That's very generous of you, Eleanor."

She went right on talking, as if she hadn't heard him. "And Marcie suggested that the house would look better if the lawn was mowed. She said she could hire someone, but I thought I'd check with you. Since you have a lot of time, I thought you could swing by and do it."

"I don't think I can do that, Eleanor."

"Oh."

"I have plans today."

"I see. Well, how 'bout tomorrow."

"Tomorrow, too. I think you should just tell Marcie to hire someone because I'm not really sure when I'll be free."

"Oh? Really?"

"Yes. I'm very busy."

"Okay, well, just thought I'd ask. No harm in trying, right?"

"Right." He was about to say good-bye but then didn't. "Eleanor?"

"Yes?"

"Well, I just wondered how you're feeling?"

"I'm fine."

"I mean, health wise and everything."

"Never felt better. But thanks ... thanks for asking, Al. And be sure to send the papers back right away. I included a stamped envelope addressed to me."

"Okay." He almost said providing the stamp was very generous of her, but instead he just hung up.

While Al waited for the coffee to finish brewing, he wondered why did she think he'd go over to the house and mow the lawn? It seemed to him that if you dumped your husband you wouldn't expect him to mow the lawn. But maybe it was just force of habit since for almost twenty-five years he'd usually done what she'd asked. She probably thought, I'll just ask good old Al. Was it because she thought I was a nice guy? he wondered. Or just a chump? He supposed he'd never know. Anyway, the result was the same: nice guy or chump ... she didn't want to be married to him anymore. She was sending papers she'd signed that said their marriage was irretrievably broken. He might as well sign that he agreed. What was there for him to contest? The only thing he'd like to contest in his life right now was the sale of his practice to that jerk Jerry Kincaid.

As he got in the shower, he remembered to duck his head so he wouldn't hit it on the shower rod, and for a few minutes as Al stood under the warm spray, he started to feel guilty about not mowing the lawn for Eleanor. But when he finished showering and dried off on the crummy towels she'd given him, the guilt evaporated.

After he fed Bert, they went out to get in the truck, but Bert spotted Bonnie Douglas going to her car and took off galloping across the road. Bert danced all around her with his tongue hanging out and his tail wagging joyfully. She bent down and he sat in front of her obediently, and she put her cheek next to his head for a minute and then hugged him.

"It's a good thing you like him." Al said, as he crossed the road and went over to them. "I'm afraid he can be a pest."

"I think he sees me and thinks cheese." She laughed. "But I really do like him. He reminds me of my parents' dog, they had a chocolate Lab." Bonnie opened her car door.

"They're great dogs." Al held Bert's collar. "Well, don't let me keep you. I just thought I'd better stop Bert from slobbering all over you."

"Bert's welcome to visit me anytime. I really miss having a dog," She said, opening her car door. "See you later."

As Bonnie backed out of her drive, Al let go of Bert's collar and they went across the road to his truck. Watching her drive away, he thought how nice it was to have a neighbor who liked Bert, but he did wonder why she didn't have a dog. She seemed to love them.

ON THE WAY TO THRIFTWAY, Al listened to B.B. King and thought what a pleasure it was to be going to the store without a list. Eleanor always gave him a list and would be annoyed if he couldn't find what was on the list and substituted something. "Al, I told you to get red grapes and I didn't mean green grapes, and if they're out of red grapes, it would have been better not to get any grapes at all. Now I'm stuck with green grapes that I don't even want." That sort of thing was typical—the littlest thing with Eleanor had been a big friggin' deal. And she was like that even before she got sick, he reminded himself.

Al enjoyed thinking about getting whatever he wanted at the grocery store. Maybe he'd stock up on some frozen pizzas—maybe those California Pizza Kitchen ones. He also hoped he wouldn't run into Marilyn. The whole thing the night before seemed extremely awkward. She'd said stuff about their friendship. Al didn't know they had a friendship. Their relationship, if it could be called that, was that she talked to him about her dog. A lot of guys would have jumped into bed with her. Maybe he'd been a fool.

Introspection was not something that came naturally to Al. But having his life turned upside down seemed to lend itself to it, and he began to wonder exactly why it was that he hadn't gone to bed with Marilyn Henderson. After all, it wasn't that he had a lack of interest—he found her very attractive and he started to imagine what it would be like to have sex with Marilyn. It would probably be very exciting, and in his mind decades slipped away and he didn't have any worries about performance either. He was virile and confident like the men dancing around the kitchen with their wives in the Viagra ads—did couples really dance around the kitchen like that?—he and Eleanor certainly hadn't ... well, when he had this exciting sex with Marilyn, he didn't need anything like those pills, and they didn't dance around the kitchen either; they just got right to it. But the more detailed the fantasies became (Marilyn was very passionate and uninhibited), he began to feel bad and kind of sad, too, and Al realized that he hadn't switched gears from being the husband of someone, and of someone with cancer—and deep down he didn't think a guy in that situation should be having sex with other women. As he pulled into the Thriftway parking lot and got out of the truck, he thought that was why he hadn't gone to bed with Marilyn Henderson. It was probably as simple as that, even if Eleanor had signed a paper that said their marriage was irretrievably broken.

IN THE FROZEN SECTION, AL was carefully studying the various kinds of pizza when he saw Evelyn Murdoch rushing toward him. She was an anxious bird-like little woman who always seemed to be out of breath and perpetually in motion. A few weeks ago he saw her at the post office and helped her carry in a bunch of packages, and she told him how her new dog was doing. It was another golden retriever like her dog Cassidy, the one that he'd euthanized and helped bury last year.

"Oh Al, I'm so glad to run into you." She came at him so fast, her cart almost literally did run into him.

"Hi Evelyn, how are you?" Al put his hand on her cart to keep it from banging against his hip. He thought of mentioning that the painting she'd given him looked nice in the house he was renting, but if she hadn't heard about him and Eleanor, he didn't want to bring it up.

"Well, I'm fine, but it's Olivia I'm worried about—there's something strange about her mouth—she keeps kind of yawning and licking her mouth and pawing at it, and I can't figure out what the matter is."

"It could be a stick. It's pretty common with Labs or any dogs that chew sticks to get a little piece of a wood wedged in their palate between the cheek and teeth."

"Oh, Al," Evelyn grabbed his arm. "Really? Do you think that's it?"

"It's one possibility, but you ought to have her looked at."

She moved closer, still clutching his arm. "I wonder, I mean I know it's out of your way, but do you think you could swing by my place and have a look? Just this once, I mean, I know you're retired and everything." She sounded a little desperate as she ran a hand through her white, curly hair. Al thought she looked a little like a miniature poodle, although her personality seemed more Jack Russell-like. Evelyn had huge blue eyes and a small face that made him think of a curly white-haired china doll. He realized he'd never noticed her eyes before. They were pretty.

"I'd need to get my groceries home first. Some of the stuff I'm getting is frozen and some ice cream—it's frozen, too, of course. But I guess I could come after that."

"Thank you so-o-o much. And I'd be happy to pay you, of course."

"Oh no, this just a friend thing, not a real house call or anything."

"Okay, well, that's great. I'm still at the same place at Tramp Harbor." Then Evelyn jumped forward and threw her arms around him and squished her body into him, and it was embarrassing because Al was sure everyone in Thriftway saw Evelyn Murdoch clutching him in a hot embrace in front of the frozen food.

"Um, I better get going Evelyn."

She smiled up at him, with her arms still around him. "Right. The sooner I let you go, the sooner you can come to me." She laughed. "And see Olivia."

Evelyn went rushing away and Al got several pizzas and then went to the ice cream section and got stuck there. So many choices! Then he kind of went nuts in a rush of freedom and started wildly throwing a bunch of containers in his cart, but when he had over a dozen, he remembered he didn't know how big the refrigerator's freezing compartment was at JoAnne McKee's house. Al put them all back and decided to be more selective. He'd get three. It took him a long time, but finally he chose three Ben and Jerry's: Chunky Monkey, Chocolate Peppermint Crunch, and Chocolate Therapy. Al liked the sound of that one. Especially since his life was unraveling.

On the way home, he thought rating ice cream could be a good project. He could eat his way through all of Ben and Jerry's and write a little review of each flavor. Maybe Thriftway could post his reviews, although maybe that wasn't such a good idea since he had always tried to encourage his clients to keep their dogs from gaining too much weight and here he'd be making quite a show of eating ice cream, even though the reviews weren't about dogs eating ice cream. But then, since he wasn't a practicing vet anymore, maybe this wouldn't be a problem. Al thought about this all the way to Baker's Beach. But weighing the pros and cons of writing ice cream reviews began to make him feel silly, and he was glad to get home where he could drop off his groceries, get his medical bag, and be on his way to Evelyn's to see her dog. At least when it came to dogs, he didn't feel silly.

Evelyn's house, a small dove gray Craftsman with dark green shutters, was nestled in a stand of fir trees on a bluff overlooking Tramp Harbor. But the secluded, pristine setting was in sharp contrast to the interior of the house. Al had been inside one other time, when he'd euthanized her dog, but he'd forgotten how cluttered it was. Evelyn's level of craftiness seemed to hover close to hoarding, and he felt slightly claustrophobic the minute he stepped inside. Every inch of the living room and kitchen was covered with some project or another. That day she was making jam and canning vegetables and there were glass jars covering every surface of the kitchen. She was also working on a quilt, which Al guessed explained why most of the furniture was also buried in pieces of colored cloth. Paper towel tubes that were in the process of being painted and stuck with sequins and bunches of dried flowers and grasses and ribbon were scattered in piles covering most of the floor.

As soon as Al got there, he wondered if Olivia had eaten some of the craft supplies. Some dogs had unusual appetites, like the great dane that ate forty-three socks, but he didn't want to worry Evelyn unnecessarily and besides, she hadn't said Olivia exhibited digestion problems.

Al spent about ten minutes feeding treats to the dog and talking to her, and then asked Evelyn to hold Olivia while he went to his bag for exam gloves and hemostat. Kneeling on the floor next to the dog, Al gently opened her mouth. As he had suspected, there was a small stick about an inch long wedged in her palate between the teeth and her cheek. Luckily, the stick came out easily and didn't break off. He was able to remove it with one quick motion. Then he felt her palate where the stick had been.

"There's a little swelling, but that's to be expected and nothing to worry about. A young dog like this will heal quickly." Al took off his exam gloves. "Do you have a trash can where I can throw these?"

"It's under the sink. Thank you so much, Al," her voice quavered and she seemed to be tearful as she hugged the dog.

Al took the exam gloves to the kitchen and Evelyn followed him, whipping piles of fabric off the kitchen table and chairs, insisting he sit down and have some blueberry pie. "I picked the blueberries this summer at Kaplan Farms here on the island and froze them. They freeze very well, you know."

"I didn't know that."

"They certainly do, you'll have to stay and have the pie, so you'll see what I'm talking about. You'd never know that they'd been frozen. You really wouldn't."

"Thanks, I'll take your word for it, but I should get going." He didn't want to be rude, but he wanted to leave. Everything in her house was so chaotic, he felt a headache coming on.

"Al, I insist." Evelyn grabbed his hands and pulled him toward the chair. "You do like pie, don't you?"

He nodded.

"Well, then. You can't leave without a piece of Evelyn's famous blueberry pie."

"Okay, well, thanks." Al didn't want to hurt her feelings so he sat down.

He patted Olivia while Evelyn went to get the pie. Olivia was a good dog, a beautiful golden retriever, although she was a little smaller than Evelyn's last dog, Cassidy. Al thought it was wise that someone as frenetically energetic as Evelyn had chosen a breed known for its mellow temperament.

"I saw in *The Beachside* that your clinic is now going to be called Kincaid Animal Clinic. I thought that was too bad, to take 'Island' out of the name," Evelyn said, as she cut the pie. "Why don't you open a little clinic, Al—with just a few of your special clients—like me!" She laughed. "A lot of people our age keep working and just cut back a little. You could have a nice little part-time practice."

"Can't be done." Al tried to sound matter-of-fact, but hearing that Jerry Kincaid re-named the clinic after himself pissed him off. *Kincaid* Animal Clinic, what an egomaniac, that jerk.

"Would you like a little French vanilla ice cream with your pie?"

"That'd be nice."

"Why can't it be done?" Evelyn asked. "One scoop or two?"

"Two, thanks. Because I have a non-compete clause for five years. It was part of the contract when I sold the clinic to Kincaid." To that greedy s.o.b. "I can't open a practice on the island. But I could somewhere other than Vashon if I was willing to move."

Al looked out the window and saw a tugboat pulling a barge across the harbor, and he wondered if he could anchor a barge off the island, maybe off Point Robinson and then people could bring their dogs and cats to him in little boats. To ferry the clients he could have a couple of twelve-foot Lunds with little motors and they would just putt-putt right out to the barge. Al was imagining his barge clinic as Evelyn came up behind him. Leaning close to him over his shoulder, she put the pie in front of him on the table. As she did, she brushed her cheek against his and Al jumped. Evelyn laughed and then got pie for herself and sat across from him.

"Dig in." She grinned.

"Thanks." Al felt edgy, but took a bite of the pie and it was good. Very good. "This is delicious."

"Thank you. I love to make pie. I actually like pie better than cake."

"I do, too. Come to think of it."

"Well, I'll make an extra pie for you, the next time I make one," she said.

"Oh, no need for that." Al mumbled with his mouth full.

"I'd love to. I've always had a special place in my heart for you, Al. Ever since you helped me through the last days of Cassidy's life and gave that beautiful eulogy." Then Evelyn put her fork down, and leaned forward. "You are a dear, kind, gentle man and I'd like to see more of you, Al. No use beating around the bush at our age."

Al looked down at the plate and quickly ate the last few bites of pie, pointing to his mouth like he couldn't talk because his mouth was full.

"You understand what I'm getting at, don't you?" Evelyn looked very directly at him.

Al wiped his mouth with the napkin. "I suppose you've heard about me and Eleanor."

"Yes, and I don't mind saying that I think she's a fool."

"Well, thanks, Evelyn." And he did appreciate her saying that, and he smiled, and before he knew it she had slid onto his lap and they were kissing. She tasted like blueberry pie. Al didn't mind Evelyn Murdoch kissing him. And he couldn't help kissing her back but then she put her hands on his shoulders and leaned back and looked up at him, "We don't have a lot of time to play games at our age, do we?"

And then he wondered, what was he doing in this little house at Tramp Harbor surrounded by colored pipe cleaners, painted paper towel tubes covered in sequins, ribbons, piles of fabric and canning jars, with Evelyn Murdoch on his lap? Al shook his head. His life was turning into a mess and things were just happening to him. "I think I'd better go now," he blurted and moved Evelyn off his lap as firmly but as gently as though she were a little terrier he was lifting off the exam table.

"Thanks for the pie. It was very good," he muttered, as he galloped to the door, stumbling over paper towel tubes. Even though he was stuffed from the blueberry pie, all he could think about was getting home to Bert and having some Chocolate Therapy.

CHAPTER 6

AFTER ABOUT A MONTH, EVEN THOUGH AL STILL APPRECIATED THE freedom of living alone, the intense pleasure of it began to wear off bit by bit, as if a little blanket of fog was rolling in each day. By mid-October—as B.B. sang—the thrill was gone. Now accompanying the dampening of his excitement was an increasing level of agitation as he obsessively questioned what the hell he was doing with this life. The only thing conclusive was his divorce. Eleanor had filed the papers he'd signed with the court and paid the fee, which she emphasized, and it was on track to be final in December.

He had avoided going to Thriftway at the hours when he thought he'd run into former clients, especially Marilyn Henderson and Evelyn Murdoch. It opened at 8:00 a.m. and closed at 9:00 p.m. so Al would usually go as soon as it opened or about twenty minutes before it closed. He put a new message on his voice mail that said, "Hi, you've reached Al Paugh. I'll be away for a while but will return your call when I get back." He wanted people who called, mainly Marilyn and Evelyn, to think he was out of town. They were leaving a lot of messages, usually invitations to dinner; both of them wanted to feed him, and he found it bewildering. Evelyn left a message about making a pie for him, and he did want that pie. But not enough to call her back.

Al's days got shorter. Not only because there was less daylight in autumn as the year began to draw toward a close, but because he was sleeping later and later, and going to bed earlier and earlier. He also took naps. In between the naps, during the remaining few hours when he was awake, he'd be hard pressed to say what he did. The days just fizzled and dwindled away. He organized his CDs, re-shuffled the music on his iPod, took Bert for longer and longer walks, worked crossword puzzles (supposedly good for the brain) and fooled around on the internet. He'd gone off island to buy a little TV and he watched that quite a bit. The news was depressing, so Al watched Animal Planet and the Food Network even though his cooking mostly involved putting frozen food in the microwave. None of these activities was satisfying, but after he'd been living at Baker's Beach for about a month, he got an email that gave him a lift. It was from Patricia Waterton, Director of the Vashon Animal Shelter.

Dear Al,

Our fund-raiser for the shelter this year will be a beautiful calendar featuring twelve fabulous Vashon Island dogs, one for each month. VAS will receive proceeds from each entry fee and of course, the profit from the sale of the calendars. Our committee decided we'd try to get them out and ready for sale by Thanksgiving, to get the jump on the Christmas rush. I'm writing to officially ask you to be our judge and select twelve dogs from all the entries. You were the unanimous choice of our committee, I might add.

Please give me a call if you're interested so we can discuss the details. We sure hope this can work for you, Al, we can't think of a better judge! I look forward to hearing from you!

Warmly,

Patricia Waterton
Director, Vashon Animal Shelter

Al was so moved by this invitation he got a lump in his throat, but the emotion immediately made him feel ridiculous. How pathetic that it meant so much to be asked to do this little job, one that didn't take any skill. Even a three-year-old kid could sort through a bunch of photos and choose twelve nice looking dogs. His reaction was over the top, that was for sure, and it was also a barometer of the extent to which his life was crumpling. But he didn't want to dwell on that. Why ruin such a nice thing? He was the unanimous choice of their committee—that was very good to hear—and getting the email that morning was the most gratifying thing that had happened in months. Al wanted to enjoy it.

He replied to the email right away accepting the job, and then he got Bert's rubber frog and they headed for the beach. It was a sunny morning with a bright blue sky and Al could see the snowcapped peaks of the Olympic Mountains. It amazed him how much brighter everything looked.

As Al threw the frog for Bert and watched him swim, he thought about the role of judge and what criteria he would use to choose the dogs for the calendar. It would be important to have an equal number of males and females. So the first thing he would do would be to divide the photos according to gender. He'd need to tell Patricia that the entry form should indicate that the photos should have the age and gender of the dogs written on the back. And it would be very good if some mixed breed dogs were chosen, and maybe some older dogs, gray around the muzzle, to celebrate their longevity and give them a measure of dignity. It wouldn't be just a cutsie-poo calendar, but something that reflected the journey, the seasons, the life cycle of dogs. So there could be puppies, middle aged, and elder dogs, and an equal number of mixed and pure breeds. Something for everyone.

Bert swam to the shore, but instead of dropping the frog at Al's feet, he kept it, ran down the beach and was soon out of sight beyond the curve of Baker's cove. Al went after him—it was unusual for Bert to take off like that, and as soon as Al rounded the curve of the cove, he saw the reason. Bert had dropped his precious frog at the feet of their neighbor, who was sitting on the sand behind some driftwood. What was her name again? She'd told him the other day when Bert ate her garbage, but Al couldn't remember it. Very frustrating these memory glitches and happening more and more frequently, which sometimes worried him, but mostly he just found it annoying.

"Hi," she said, cheerily. But there was a sadness about her, and as Al got closer he could see she'd been crying. He wanted to leave, but thought he should say something first.

"That's quite a compliment that he's brought you his frog."

"And I'm honored." She stroked the top of Bert's head. "I don't know how he knew I was here."

"Dogs have an extraordinary sense of smell. It ranges from 100,000 to 1,000,000 times more sensitive than a human's, and in bloodhounds it's 100 million times greater. To locate a smell, dogs use their wet noses to determine the direction of the air current that contains the smell they are following."

"I knew it was better than ours, but not to such an extent—that's amazing."

"Elephants can smell water up to three miles away."

"Really?"

Al looked at his watch. "Well, gotta get going. Come on, Bert."

Al headed back toward Baker's Beach, and the little buzz he'd had at the prospect of being the calendar judge faded like yesterday's news. How wimpy. Bert and I find our neighbor again alone and crying, hunkered down behind driftwood, and I mention elephants. And what a phony, looking at my watch like that. Pretending I have to be somewhere. Who am I kidding? Even if I will enjoy working on the calendar, it's just a temporary diversion and I'll be right back where I've been: not able to work because of that crappy non-compete clause and not figuring out what else to do. The only thing Al knew was that he didn't want to be hanging around his neighbor, what's-her-name. He felt lost enough without knowing about anyone else's problems.

Leaving the beach, Al saw Martha Jane by her car, struggling to carry two cloth grocery bags. He ran over to her. "Let me get these for you."

"Thank you, Albert. I thought if I had one in each hand it would balance them and I could manage. They're not very heavy, you know, but I'm wobblier than I think I am. I'm unbalanced. My legs are wobblies—they're on strike." She laughed. "Have I told you that little joke before?"

"Maybe, but keep telling it. It's good. Listen, Martha Jane, you should let one of us know when you have things to carry."

"You're all very kind, I couldn't have better neighbors than you folks. But I always imagine I'll be able to do things. No one really likes to ask for help you know, Albert. It's not part of our culture."

He offered Martha Jane his arm and they walked up to her house. "Don't you love these crisp days?" She smiled and sniffed the air. "I love watching the leaves turn on the bigleaf maples. Every morning there's a little more gold." He helped her up the steps and stood on the porch while she opened the door. "You must come in for coffee now, Albert." She smiled and looked up at him. "Unless of course, you're busy. I don't want to keep you from anything."

"I'd love coffee. Do you think Maria would mind if Bert waited on the porch for me? How's her paw doing?"

"She'd hardly notice Bert—Maria sleeps most of the time. Quite like I do. What else was it you asked?"

"About her paw?"

"Right. Well, thanks to you, Albert, it's healed just beautifully."

He carried the grocery bags into the kitchen and put them on the counter. "Can I help you put anything away?"

"Oh no, thank you. I can do it later. I'll just put the milk and cheese in the fridge. The coffee is from this morning—I should have mentioned that. But I thought we could warm it up in the microwave."

"That's just fine. I do that with mine a lot."

"How are you getting along at JoAnne's house?"

"The house is fine."

Martha Jane got two mugs from the cupboard and poured the coffee. "Cream and sugar?"

"Black is fine."

"I usually warm it for about a half a minute," she said, putting a mug in the microwave and setting the timer. After it beeped she brought it to him. "Besides the house, Albert. How are things?"

"I'm not fine."

"Oh?"

"I'm kind of a mess, I think."

"You don't look like a mess." Martha Jane brought her mug to the table and slowly lowered herself in the chair across from him.

"At least that's something." He laughed, hoping it didn't sound bitter.

"You're quite a handsome man, you know."

Al didn't know what to say. It made him feel weird.

"Do you think you're depressed, dear?"

Al sighed and thought about it. "Maybe that's it, I sleep a lot and I feel apathetic, it's hard for me to feel enthusiastic about anything or at least have any energy that lasts. The truth is most of the time I feel like a failure."

"Oh that really is too bad ... you're such a wonderful man." Martha Jane patted his hand. "And you still have so many good years."

"Thanks, but that's just it. It makes me feel like a jerk—guilty, I guess. Even after my heart attack, I'm relatively healthy and I have enough money, not a lot—but enough, and I live on this beautiful island and I should be doing something with my life, but I'm not. I'm not doing anything. I see guys like our plumber, Dave Murphy, and he goes fishing and seems perfectly happy, and my friend Ted Krupnik and his wife Millie are gone for six months on the Semester at Sea. Most of my retired clients—well, my former clients—they travel, some play golf, visit their grand-children, go to committee meetings, volunteer, garden, take up a musical instrument. They all seem to enjoy being retired. When I face it—I think I'm just a very one-dimensional person. My work was everything to me. I loved it and when I try to picture what I could do without my work, I get stuck. I can only picture Jerry Kincaid at my clinic with my patients. And I get mad that I let it happen." Al sipped his coffee. Shit, he sounded so whiney. He hated that. He didn't know what it was about Martha Jane that got him talking to her.

"You might try making a list."

"What kind of list?"

"Oh, you know, of all the things you might like to do. Things to learn, groups to join, volunteer jobs, things like that. It would be a start. You wouldn't have to pursue any of it if you didn't want to, but just begin to think about it."

"Maybe I'll try that."

"And Albert, if you're still feeling so unhappy, you could try a counselor."

"I wanted to go to one with Eleanor, but she didn't want to."

"Well, this could be just for you."

Maria Montessori came in and jumped in his lap. "What a nice girl." Al stroked her and she started to purr.

"She doesn't do this with anyone else. You're quite special, you know." Martha Jane drank her coffee then put the cup down. "Oh, Albert, I meant to tell you, I'm having the neighbors in for dinner. Howie and Mark are taking the train across Canada on a fall foliage tour and I'm having a little send-off. It's Sunday night. I hope you can make it, it'll be a potluck."

"I'd love to. Although I'm not much of a cook."

"It doesn't matter. It's about being together. Just pick up something from the deli at Thriftway, Albert, that would be fine."

"They have good potato salad."

"That would be perfect."

On Sunday night, Al couldn't decide if he should just bring the potato salad in the containers from the deli or put it in a bowl. Eleanor would know what was appropriate. Of course, if Eleanor were going to a potluck, she would cook something very good to bring. He hadn't heard from Eleanor in quite a while. Al wasn't sure if he missed her exactly, but maybe he did a little because he didn't seem to be thinking of her in such a negative light. Eleanor was an opinionated, rigid, anxious, uptight person—that was all very true—but she had her good qualities. She was capable, efficient, generous, dutiful, and reliable. Al pulled his cell phone out of his shirt pocket and called her.

"Eleanor?"

"Al … Hi, how are you?"

"Okay, and you?"

"A little frustrated. The second offer on the house fell through. They couldn't get financing."

"Sorry to hear that."

"Marcie says there are people who have an appointment to see it this weekend. She thinks they look like good prospects. I sure hope so—it will be good to get it settled." She paused, "Al, was there something you wanted?"

"I wanted to know how you are."

"I'm fine. I'm enjoying Portland."

"That's nice." He didn't know what to say after that and there was a silence.

"Well, I guess that's it then—"

"Eleanor, if you go to a potluck and you bring something, like potato salad from the deli, do you think you should put it in a bowl? Or just bring it in the containers?"

"Really from the deli? To bring to a potluck?" Just the idea of such a thing seemed to offend her.

"That's what I said."

"Well, if it has to be from the deli, at least put it in a bowl. And you should put some parsley around the edges to dress it up a bit."

"Okay, thanks. And your health is okay?"

"I'm doing really well, thanks for asking. Ruby and I are planning a trip to Belize. We're going to learn how to scuba dive."

"Glub glub."

"What?"

"I was just making a little joke."

"Oh. Well, okay then, I'll say good-bye now."

They hung up and Al got a bowl from the cupboard and took the potato salad out of the refrigerator and dumped it in. He wouldn't have enough time before the potluck to get the parsley Eleanor said should go on it. Al looked over at Bert, who was sitting on the living room couch. "Well, Bert, it won't be up to Eleanor's standards, but it will have to be okay the way it is." He didn't think he'd call her again.

Chapter 7

AL HELPED MARTHA JANE TO THE CHAIR AT THE HEAD OF THE TABLE then went back to the kitchen to get his bowl of potato salad. He thought it looked puny as he set it between Howie and Mark's beautiful platter of roast chicken and grilled vegetables and the gorgeous salad his neighbor across the road brought. (What the heck was her name anyway? He was embarrassed to ask.) There were also quite a few bottles of wine on the table. Both red and white, and not cheapies either, like the kind he always bought. That was another embarrassing thing: he forgot to bring wine. Everyone else had and the bottles were all open on the table and people just helped themselves. He filled his glass with one of the whites, a good bottle of Sauvignon Blanc, and it made him feel like a freeloader.

"Please sit down, everybody." Martha Jane motioned them toward the table. "Since Al and Bonnie are the newest to Baker's Beach, they should have the view, and then Howie, let's have you on the other end, and Mark on the water side next to me."

Al sat next to Bonnie, relieved Martha Jane has said her name. What was her last name? He stared at the salad she brought, trying to remember, then looked out at the trees on the bank of the beach. It has something to do with trees. Forest? Bonnie Forest? That didn't sound right. Then it came to him. Douglas. Bonnie Douglas. Like Douglas fir. Al smiled. A little triumph, remembering her last name. A reassuring victory over the decay of his brain.

As they took their seats, Martha Jane looked at the food. "You know it doesn't seem right to call it a potluck when I didn't contribute a pot of anything."

"You don't need to provide a pot, you provide the luck. We all have the good luck to know you, Martha Jane." Howie raised his glass.

Al raised his glass with the others. "To Martha Jane," they toasted and clinked glasses. Al admired Howie and how clever he was with words. He wished he were more like that, but conversation never came easily to him, except with animals.

"Now I think we should toast Howie and Mark's train ride across Canada." Martha Jane raised her glass. "Bon voyage!" Everyone chimed in, and Al thought of saying "whoo-hoo, choo-choo," but he didn't think it would be appropriate. He was starting to wonder if he knew how to act with people.

"I took that trip years ago," Bonnie said. "It was wonderful. We flew to Vancouver and then took the train east. We had a day in Jasper National Park and it was stunning. And as you get farther east, the colors are spectacular."

The platter was passed around, and Al helped himself to some of the chicken and vegetables, wondering who the "we" was that Bonnie mentioned. But it didn't seem right to ask.

Mark took the platter from Al. "We actually wanted to take the trip all the way to Nova Scotia, but it's a twenty-one day trip and costs an arm and a leg. So we're doing the shorter one that goes to Toronto. We'll be away from Tanner for nine days and we thought that would probably be long enough for him," Mark paused, smiling, "and for us, too. We miss him when we're away—we sure appreciate your taking care of him for us, Bonnie."

"I'm delighted to have him. I love dogs."

"I'm curious, Bonnie, you love them—why don't you have a dog?" Martha Jane asked. Al had wondered that too, but didn't think he could ask without prying. But no one ever minded when Martha Jane was direct; she could ask people anything.

Bonnie sipped her wine. "I don't think it would be fair to the dog when my life is in limbo the way it is. And I suppose I'm not ready."

"Well, we're glad you can take Tanner. I have to say, it's also reassuring to leave knowing there's a vet right here at Baker's Beach," Howie turned to Al. "You'll be available in case there are problems, right?"

"For sure. But Tanner's a young, healthy dog. Nothing's going to go wrong."

"Oh, I know, but we're still glad you're here, Al. How are you settling in?"

Everyone looked at him, and Al had just taken a big bite of chicken, so he pointed to his mouth as he chewed while he thought of what to say. He swallowed, then finally said, "Bert really loves the beach. It's great to be able to go right out the front door and be walking on the beach in just a couple of minutes."

"Sounds like retirement is agreeing with you." Mark took some potato salad, and then passed the bowl to Howie.

"I've been asked to judge the calendar contest for the Vashon Animal Shelter, so I imagine that will keep me pretty busy." Al wiped his face with his napkin.

Martha Jane looked out at the beach. "Say, does anyone know why that tent is going up at the Wiggins place down the beach?"

"Bert and I saw it on our walk this morning, and I wondered, too," Al added, very pleased the subject had changed from his retirement.

"I saw it too." Bonnie took some more potato salad. "I love this, did you make it, Al?"

"Actually no, Thriftway did."

"Good for you, the sign of a great cook is knowing what's good at the deli." She laughed and Al laughed with her. A big laugh, louder than what was called for he thought, but he couldn't help it. Bonnie put the bowl of potato salad back on the table. "It's a huge tent—I wondered if there's going to be a wedding there. Does anyone know?"

"Now I do remember. I did hear Carl Wiggins is having an

enormous sixtieth birthday bash," Martha Jane said. "There are a lot of people coming from all over. They've booked most of the B & Bs and weekend rentals on the island."

"We picked a good time to leave town." Howie chuckled.

"Right. A good time to escape with Carl Wiggins's friends contaminating the beach." Mark didn't laugh.

Bonnie took another helping of chicken. "I take it he's not your favorite neighbor, " she said as she cut the chicken.

"Let's say there's a history." Mark reached for the wine. "We're not exactly the Hatfields and the McCoys, but—"

"We never came to blows," Howie interrupted. "Not that I didn't think about taking a swing at that sniveling jerk. From the minute they moved in, his wife Sondra was always hassling us about our chickens. I mean if you're going to live in the country, people are going to have chickens, for God's sake. And Sondra was annoying as hell, but mostly we ignored her. But when I saw Carl drive over her rose bushes and Sondra came home that afternoon and went ballistic and accused *us* of doing it, and even insisted we replace them—that did it! We escalated."

Mark grinned. "We bought a rooster."

"I hadn't realized that was the history behind the rooster," Martha Jane said. "Or maybe I did and forgot." She sighed. "That's certainly a possibility. I have to say the Wiggins aren't my favorite folks either, but I do love when Jordan, their grandson, visits. He's a darling boy. I suppose he'll come for the party."

"He is. He's a great kid," Mark agreed. "But I'm very glad we won't be here and it's wonderful knowing Tanner will be in such good hands." He lifted his glass to Bonnie.

CARL WIGGINS'S BIRTHDAY PARTY WAS held the following Saturday. It began with a bang. Literally. Al had just turned on *King5 News at Ten* to hear the sports and the weather report, when there was a huge boom. Then another and another. Bert leaped off the bed and crawled under it. Al went out on the deck and saw bursts of color exploding and shooting stars rocketing high in the dark sky, then floating down in a great arc of sparkling star-like confetti. Al didn't like fireworks. The Fourth of July was his least favorite holiday, and although he could appreciate celebrating the signing of the Declaration of Independence, he wished a tradition had developed that wasn't so distressing to animals. Couldn't people just sing "Yankee Doodle Dandy" and have a hot dog? And he especially thought it was unnecessary for a guy to shoot off all that stuff to celebrate his birthday. What was wrong with some candles on a cake? Al went inside to check on Bert.

He wished he had known that afternoon that those absurd fireworks were going to be shot off tonight—he could have given Bert some acepromazine. It was always a good idea to give animals the sedative at least forty-five minutes before the event so it would be in their system, helping to calm them so they'd be fairly relaxed when the damn fireworks started exploding. Luckily, Bert was only mildly upset with fireworks. He usually hid under the bed and with the acepromazine he often went to sleep. He handled it a lot better than some dogs; Al remembered having to stitch up a standard poodle that threw himself through a glass door on the Fourth of July.

He got down on all fours and reached under the bed for Bert. "It's okay, buddy." Bert scooted closer toward Al, trembling slightly and Al patted his head. "I'm going to get you some medicine and you'll feel a lot better. I'll be right back."

In the kitchen he got a small piece of cheddar cheese from the refrigerator and rolled it between his fingers to soften it. Then he took the pill from his bag and pressed it into the cheese. He filled Bert's water and went back to the bedroom, putting the water dish next to the bed and reaching under the bed to give Bert the pill. He was relieved when Bert ate it. Like many dogs, Bert wouldn't even eat a favorite treat if he was too anxious. Al turned on the television and then sat on the floor reaching under the bed to pat Bert, while he waited for the sedative to take effect. The floor was hard, so he pulled the pillows down and sat on them. That was better. He was fairly comfortable except for hearing the local news while he waited for the sports and the weather. It was true about local news—"if it bleeds, it leads"—and with the fireworks exploding right out there on the beach, Al didn't want to sit through the reports of fires, burglaries, and murders. He reached for the remote. Flipping through the channels he found a show that looked nice, *Rick Steves' Europe*. The episode was called "The Best of Hungary" and they were showing 19th century castles and some Gypsy orchestras. The Gypsy orchestra went on for quite a while, and Al thought it was very invigorating. During an especially lively tune, Al thought he heard some banging, like someone pounding on the door, but then decided it was just the bang of the fireworks and he turned up the volume even louder. The Gypsy orchestra was drowning out a lot of the fireworks. Good, he thought. But then he looked up and had a shock. He couldn't believe it—next to the television, standing over him, was his neighbor, Bonnie Douglas. She was right there. In his bedroom! He was speechless.

"Al!" She was breathing hard. "Tanner's gone! I knocked and knocked—but you didn't hear me—I looked all around the outside of the house for him, and I ran over to Howie and Mark's and there's no sign of him!"

Al scrambled to his feet, turning down the volume on the TV. "I'll get a flashlight and help you look."

"I brought one." Bonnie held it up.

"Good. Another one won't hurt." In the kitchen, he grabbed his jacket and flashlight from the shelf next to the back door.

"Will Bert be okay?"

"I'm leaving the TV on and the lights. But he's pretty out of it. He never panics, just gets a little jittery with fireworks and I gave him some acepromazine. After it gets in his system, he'll go to asleep." He looked out at the fireworks, shaking his head. "I really hate those things. Okay, let's go ... oh, I better bring a couple of short disposable leads—and my bag, too."

"Oh God—in case Tanner's hurt?"

"He's probably fine and just found a place to hide. It's just a precaution."

Al put the porch light on and they hurried down the steps

to the road. "I feel so awful about this," Bonnie shouted, trying to be heard over the noise. "Tanner started panting and pacing when the fireworks started, and I got him a fresh bowl of water. He came in the kitchen and was drinking it, and then I opened the door to the deck to see what was happening on the beach and he bolted through the door, practically knocking me over. I ran after him, but he's so fast, I lost sight of him."

"Which way did he go?"

"Away from the beach toward the woods between the house and Walter Hathaway's, but I don't know how far he got."

"Dogs often will hide somewhere. Let's go back to your house and start moving out from there. You'd be surprised what a small space even a big dog can get into."

"I'd rather not split up, if you don't mind. I feel pretty shaky— can we just stay together while we look?"

"Sure. I'm positive Tanner knows your voice. Dogs are incredibly tuned into people and language, so I'd suggest calling him every few minutes." Al looked at his watch. "It's almost ten-thirty. I would think the fireworks will be over soon."

"I don't know how he can hear me until they quit going off."

"Dogs' hearing ability is twice that of ours. And they hear higher frequency sounds. If he's not too far away, I think he'll be able to hear you in spite of the fireworks."

"*Tanner!*" she called. They walked across the road, while Bonnie kept calling the dog as loud as she could, "*TAN-NER!... TAN-NER!*"

At Bonnie's, Al went to the front porch and shined his flashlight in the space under the steps. There was no sign of the dog, so they walked all around the house looking for any area that might have an opening under the foundation. While he shined his light along the foundation, Bonnie continued calling Tanner, moving her light slowly across the yard.

Al trotted over to her. "I'm sure he wouldn't go toward the beach where the fireworks are. Let's try the carport back of the house—you probably looked there, but let's just try again."

"Maggie and Walter rented an RV for their trip so Maggie's car is still here." She looked up at him. "Let's hope he crawled under it." They got to the carport, and Bonnie crouched down and shined the light under the car, but the dog wasn't there. "My car's parked in the drive," she said, "I checked before, but I suppose we should look there again in case he came back from wherever he was and hid under there."

"Might as well."

"*TAN-NER! ... TAN-NER!*" They headed across the lawn toward the road where Bonnie's car was parked. "*TAN-NER!*" Bonnie's voice cracked, and it was sounding more and more desperate. Al glanced at her and saw that she was shaking. "Here, take my jacket—"

"I'm okay, really."

"It's getting chilly and I don't need it." He took off his jacket and leaned down and put it around her shoulders. His hand brushed her cheek. It was damp with tears, and Al put his arm around her. "We'll find him."

They stood on the lawn near the road with the fireworks lighting up the sky behind them, and Al held her until she stopped trembling. "I'm okay now, thank you." She stepped back. "Thanks for the jacket. But now you'll get cold."

"I'm cold-blooded, like a reptile."

That made her laugh, and she walked toward her car, shining the light. She bent down by the car to look under it. But again there was so sign of Tanner.

"Going home to Mark and Howie's house seems the logical place he'd go, but you said he went toward the woods. Is that right?" he asked.

"That's what I thought. Although it seems like a blur, I was so upset."

"When they're that distressed, they don't always do what we think is logical. Let's check over at Howie and Mark's again, and if we don't find him, we'll walk through the woods and check at Walter's cabin."

As they walked across Baker Beach Road, there were huge explosions of fireworks, one after the other lighting up the sky with gold, pink, white, purple, blue and green sunbursts. "That has to be the finale," Bonnie said.

"Let's hope."

"Great," she muttered. "Now we just have to put up with all the smoke in the air."

"I take it you don't like them either."

"I don't. Although I did like sparklers when I was a kid. We'd wave them around, and I'd pretend mine was a magic wand." Bonnie looked up at him. "I wish I had one now."

"A sparkler?"

"No, a magic wand so I could make Tanner appear."

They circled Howie and Mark's house shining their flashlights, and looked under Howie's truck, while Bonnie continued to call for the dog. "Do you think now that the fireworks have stopped he might come back on his own?" she asked.

"It's hard to predict, but he might." Al swept the light across the yard. " I suppose you checked the chicken coop?"

"I did," she sighed, "but we can look again. I'm not that familiar with chickens, so Howie and Mark have hired a girl who lives down the beach to take care of them. When I looked in there, they didn't seem too upset with all the noise and flashes of light. And of course, Tanner wasn't there."

"Why don't you just sit here on their porch while I go have a look? Take a break."

She smiled at him and nodded.

Al could hear Bonnie calling Tanner as he walked through the garden on the way to the chicken coop. It occurred to him that he didn't think of her as the driftwood lady anymore. Turning in circles every few feet, he shined the light over the yard and the house, and when it passed over Bonnie sitting on the porch, he thought there was something familiar about the color of her hair, that tawny-like brandy color, only with the white in it. She was sure easy to be with, he thought. Probably because a woman upset about a dog had been an everyday occurrence for so much of his life.

Unless Tanner had dug under the fence of the area where the

chickens were kept, Al was pretty sure that he hadn't gone in there, but he'd check just in case. An electric fence surrounded the area to keep out raccoons. Opening the gate, Al went in and found the chickens roosting in the hay on the tall shelves of the coop. He looked thoroughly, but the dog wasn't anywhere to be found either inside or underneath the coop.

Bonnie was still calling for Tanner, but her voice sounded hoarse, and when Al got back to the porch, he asked her if she wanted to go back to her house to get some water.

"No, let's keep going. I guess going into the woods is next."

"Have you been in the woods with Tanner before?" he asked.

"A few times. Maggie asked me if I'd go over and check on Walter's cabin every so often, and there's a path I've taken through the woods. It's close to a ravine that goes between the properties."

"A ravine?"

"Yes, there are steep banks on either side of it."

"Do you know if there's a culvert?" Al walked faster and Bonnie had to scurry to keep up with him.

"I'm not sure."

"That could be where he is, if he went into the woods. There are culverts all over the island for drainage."

From the path that led to Walter Hathaway's cabin, Bonnie shined her flashlight to the east of the path where the ravine began. "It's fairly steep, it goes back toward where Baker Beach Road curves."

Al stopped walking. "Okay, instead of trying to get down into the ravine from here, let's go over to the road and head into it that way. The culverts often are put right under the road to keep the runoff from flooding."

The road was very dark. The only street lights on the island were in town, and the new moon, just a sliver, was partly covered by clouds. The voices from the birthday party carried up from the beach, and a few minutes after Bonnie and Al reached the road, they heard a band start playing.

"Oh great. Just what we need. Now he'll never come out from wherever he's hiding." Bonnie frowned, glancing up at him.

"Maybe he'll like the song."

"'Thank God I'm a Country Boy'"—you think Tanner likes that? No way."

"What kind of music do you think he likes?" Al was glad she was lightening up. He worried about how fragile she seemed.

"Oh, he likes blues. I'm quite sure. And some James Taylor."

"Sweet Baby James, right. I can see that a dog like Tanner would appreciate him." Al smiled down at her. He couldn't see her very well in the dark; they were both holding the flashlights in front of them, but it felt like she was smiling back. They walked all along in silence for a while, and Al hoped that she wouldn't fall apart again if his theory was wrong. He'd never say it, but his greatest fear was that the frantic dog would have run across Vashon Highway and gotten hit by a car.

"Maybe they're trying to play some kind of seventies medley—doesn't that sound like "'I Write the Songs?'" Bonnie asked.

"I know for a fact that all dogs hate Barry Manilow."

"You say that with authority." She laughed.

"Of course, I'm a vet. I know these things."

"And cats?"

"They *really* can't stand Barry Manilow."

"Thanks for your coat, by the way. I'm not as cold now." She started to take it off.

"That's okay, just keep it for now." Al lifted his coat back over her shoulders.

At the curve in the road, they stopped and shined the lights down the bank into the ravine. The woods were dense, covered with huckleberry and salal, and there were large sword ferns, dead logs, brambles, salmonberry thickets, and broken branches everywhere. "Look, there's no point in both of us going down there. I'll be carrying my bag and will need my other hand free to hold onto some of the branches on my way down. Why don't you start calling him again and stay up here and shine the light for me?"

"Okay ... but be careful. All we need is a vet stuck in a ravine with a broken leg." She tried to laugh, but her voice caught in her throat. "At least take your jacket back. The blackberry vines are vicious."

But he had already started down the ravine. Al could hear the band playing "Don't Go Breaking My Heart" as he headed down the bank. The ground was dry, it hadn't rained much the past few weeks, and he was grateful for that. Long ivy vines choked the maples, alders and firs, but the worst were the blackberry bushes. She'd been right about that. He put his arm out to move a thick vine away from his face, and the end of it flew against his hand, and the thorns tore at his flesh. They *were* vicious. He could hear Bonnie calling the dog as the band played on, and when he got to the bottom of the road, they were playing "Breaking Up is Hard to Do." He'd have to ask Bonnie if Tanner liked Neil Sedaka. He didn't think so.

Al stopped and listened. He wished the damn band would shut up ... he thought he heard something. "Bonnie, can you come down a few feet and call him as loud as you can."

The light bobbled as she came down the bank. "*TANNER! ... TANNER!*"

It was a whine, a pitiful little cry, and Al was sure the dog was nearby. He walked through the thick brush toward the sound, and in the hillside next to the road at the bottom of the ravine was a culvert.

"Bonnie, there's a culvert and I think I hear him! Shine the light down at the bottom of the hill that goes down from the road."

"Is this where you think it is?" She swept the light farther to the east.

"Right. Just keep it there."

The light shone on a culvert that was about four feet in diameter. Moving as fast as he could without tripping, Al reached it, got down on his hands and knees and looked in. A few feet from the opening ... panting and shaking, was the frenzied dog.

❀

CHAPTER 8

"HELLO, BOY." AL WAITED QUIETLY ON HIS HANDS AND KNEES AT THE opening of the culvert to see if the dog would come close to him. "Well, Tanner. You got yourself quite a hiding place there," he said softly. "Let's go now. How 'bout it?" The frantic dog continued to pant, and when Al inched closer and reached in, Tanner growled and snapped. From the top of the ravine Bonnie held the light on the culvert, and Al could see saliva dripping from Tanner's mouth as he shook with fear.

Al stood up, backed away from the culvert, and called up to Bonnie. "It looks like I'm going to have to give him injectable acepromazine. Do you think you can make it down here? I'll need you to hold the light as I get the injection ready." He reached in his pocket and took out the disposable leads.

"I'm on my way."

Al could see the light bobbing from side to side as she moved down the steep bank, holding on to the larger branches of the trees as she went. "Take your time," he called. "The last thing we need is a dog sitter with a broken leg."

"Not to worry. I'm part mountain goat."

In a few minutes she was standing next to him. Bonnie bent down and looked in the culvert. "Oh Tanner, you poor thing. Why don't you come out now—come on boy ...." She moved in closer and stuck her hand in the opening with her palm up, hoping he'd remember her, but she was greeted with the same response Al had gotten: a low growl. She moved back next to Al. "How do we do this?"

"Just shine the light in my bag while I get the sedative ready. When I have it ready, shine the light directly in his eyes. It'll blind him while I loop both leads around his neck to control him. Then I can give him the injection."

"Do you give him the shot in his neck?"

"That's right." Al got the injection ready while she stood above him with the light.

"Okay, I think we're all set." He got on his knees at the opening of the culvert.

"Where do you want me to be?"

"Just move to the right a little and stand with the light so it shines over my right shoulder."

"How's this?"

"Get a little closer so my shoulder doesn't make a shadow."

"Better?" Bonnie moved so her knees were almost touching his back and held the flashlight so the light was well inside the culvert.

"That's good. Now shine it right in his eyes. Ready? ... *Now*."

The light blinded Tanner, and Al lunged toward the dog and quickly looped the leads around his neck, pulling his head away from him. "Okay, well, let's hope my long arms are good for something." Al held him as firmly as he could. Tanner was still growling and struggling, but with his right hand, Al was able to give him the injection, swiftly inserting the needle in the dog's neck and keeping it there, slowly counting to five.

Tears sprang to Bonnie's eyes, but she held the light without wavering. She felt terrible for both the dog and for Al. It was hard for her to see how Al could be so calm and steady with a writhing, growling dog inches away from him. It seemed to last for hours, but it wasn't long before Tanner stopped fighting and stumbled against the side of the culvert.

Al stood up and moved away from the entrance, then placed the needle back in his bag and took the leads off Tanner and put them in his pocket.

"Are you okay?" she asked.

Al nodded. Leaning back against the trunk of the fir, he smiled at her. "I'll wait about five minutes and then I can carry him out."

"You're kidding. Up that bank? That dog must weigh eighty or ninety pounds."

"You look cold."

"I'm okay." She zipped his jacket and tried to push up the sleeves that hung almost to her knees. "You can't be serious about carrying him."

"It's the only way—if you can just take my bag and hold the light we'll be all set." Al picked up his bag.

"Great. And what if you fall and get hurt?"

"Then you can call the medics or send for the sheriff." Al laughed.

"I don't think this is funny. I'm serious—shouldn't we get some more people to help?"

"I can do it. I know I look old, but I'm not frail." Al patiently held his bag.

"I didn't say you were frail, and you don't look that old."

"Just sort of old." He laughed again.

Bonnie sighed. "Look, I'm just wanting to be cautious, okay?"

"Point taken. But I'm not planning to go up the bank here. We just came down this way because it was where the culvert probably was, near the road." Al pointed to the west. "I'm going to go along the bottom of the ravine until we get near your place. The ravine is much shallower there. It's not nearly as steep and it'll be much easier to get him up the bank. Okay?" He handed the bag to her.

"All right," she said, reluctantly taking the medical bag from him. "And I didn't mean you were sort of old, either."

"Fine. I suppose I am though. I'm sixty-seven." Al brushed off his pants and stretched his arms.

"Well, I'm sixty-five."

"I can see the headlines in *The Beachside*. Sort-of-old Medicare recipients rescue dog from ravine." He went back to the opening of the culvert. "Okay, let's get this show on the road. You've got the light?"

"Got it." She shined the light inside the culvert as Al crawled in and dragged the dog out. Then he leaned down and positioned his arms under Tanner's belly. "Okay, here we go ... heave-ho." Slowly getting to his feet, Al lifted the dog. Tanner was conscious and whined a little, but he was woozy. Staying close to Al's side, Bonnie held the light and they headed east, moving carefully along the bottom of the ravine.

It took them over a half hour to reach the bank near the house. In the daylight without anything to carry, it would have taken all of ten minutes. But Al had to stop to give his arms a rest, carefully putting Tanner down in a nest of ferns. "Do you ever wonder how Lewis and Clark made it?"

"They would have been toast without Sacajawea."

"Agreed."

"This was a little harder than I thought." Al laughed as he picked up Tanner again.

"You know we can stop anytime and I can get some help."

"No need. We're almost there." Al was breathing hard as he picked his way over broken branches at the bottom of the ravine.

"I don't believe in heroes." The flashlight bobbled as she walked up the bank to avoid a big log. "Or proving anything. Being able to ask for help takes strength."

"There's always been a controversy about Meriwether Lewis and how he died. It's never been proven whether it was murder or suicide. He was supposed to have gotten pretty depressed." Al walked more slowly, trying to catch his breath.

"Who wouldn't, schlepping along in the forest in all that rain."

He stopped and took a step up the bank, holding Tanner securely while he balanced the dog's weight against his thigh. "Can you shine the light up the bank, I think we're pretty close to the back of the house."

As Bonnie shined the light through the woods, about fifty feet from them at the top of the shallow bank, they saw the outline of the carport and the shed that was behind the house. She turned and grinned. "You made it!"

"We did," he wheezed.

"Why not put him down and rest a few minutes before heading up the bank to the house?"

"No, I'll kick at the end like a long distance runner." Al began to slowly struggle up the bank. "Besides, if I stop I'm afraid I'll never get going again."

"Just wait a second and I'll run ahead and get the porch lights and the carport lights on, then you'll be able to see better." Before he could answer, Bonnie scrambled up the bank and in a few minutes the lights came on.

Al's legs felt like rubber as he carried the dog up the porch steps. Bonnie held the door open for him. "His bed is right there." She pointed to the corner next to the woodstove where the large fleece bed took up a big chunk of the small room. Carrying Tanner to the bed, Al stumbled but held tight to the dog as he caught himself and then gently lowered him to his bed.

"You're really strong, you know." Bonnie closed the door.

"My legs feel like Jell-o. I thought I was in better shape than that."

"Well, you made it, Tanner made it, and I could do with a drink. How 'bout you?"

Al gave her a thumbs up and flopped down in the chair next to the woodstove. He was still out of breath. "Actually, a glass of water first would be good."

"Will do." Bonnie went to the kitchen. "Maggie doesn't keep any liquor in the house. Walter's a recovering alcoholic so she doesn't drink either. But I bought wine and I've got a bottle of Cabernet," she called from the kitchen. He heard her open the refrigerator. "And there's some Chardonnay left. But I'm afraid that's it."

"Cabernet's great."

Bonnie returned with a glass of water for him and went back to the kitchen to get their wine.

"Al—you're bleeding." She set the wine down on the table

next to him and took his hand. There was a deep scratch along his knuckles and around into the palm.

"I didn't know I had that. Must have been the blackberry bushes. That happens a lot, actually. I'll see that I have a cut or a bruise and I'll have no memory of how it got there. Do you think it's a sign of senility?'

"Undoubtedly. Happens to me, too. One of the first signs that we're over the hill. Drink your wine and I'll get something for your hand."

"It's not a big deal." Al said, but she had left the room. He drank almost half the wine, practically inhaling it, then looked at his hand. He really didn't remember getting cut. Weird. Probably just concentrating so hard on getting the dog out of there without falling on his ass. Macho macho man. She said I was strong— must've fooled her, he thought, chuckling.

BONNIE CAME BACK WITH A first-aid kit and a damp washcloth. She pulled up the ottoman and sat in front of him. "Hold out your hand."

"Okay, Rachett."

"Who?"

"Nurse Rachett."

She grinned. "Right. I'm an evil bitch." She washed the cut and then put a little Neosporin on it. Al stretched his legs and lay his head back against the back of the chair while she put gauze over the length of the cut and secured it with adhesive tape.

He closed his eyes. "You have a nice touch."

"Thanks."

"Are you a nurse?"

She nodded. "I was a hospice nurse for most of my career."

"Is this a terminal injury?" Al sat up and looked at his hand.

"No. But we're all terminal. We had a lot of gallows humor in my work. One kid—everyone seems like a kid to me now, but I guess he was in his forties—anyway, he was a very funny nurse that was on the shift after mine, and in the staff room he'd flash a T-shirt he wore under his clothes that said: 'SPOILER ALERT:

Everyone Dies.'" Bonnie put the tape and gauze back in the first aid kit.

Al laughed, and shaking his head said, "What can you do but laugh." He was quiet for a minute, then looked down at his hand. "Thanks for tending to my injury."

"Anytime. Thanks for rescuing Tanner." She raised her glass to him.

"Anytime."

She put the first aid kit back and returned with the bottle of Cabernet. "Just in case we need more of this medicine." She set the bottle on the table next to his chair, and then sat across from him.

A hospice nurse. Maybe she'd been so sad those times he found her behind the driftwood because it all caught up with her, seeing people die all the time. He was curious about her, but he didn't want to just come right out and ask. Al couldn't think of what to say, and she seemed to withdraw. So they just drank their wine and both looked at the floor or at Tanner lying in his bed.

"Maggie's house is nice," he said, finally. "She's your cousin, is that right?"

Bonnie nodded. "Our fathers were brothers and we were close when we were kids. But there was a time when we didn't see that much of each other because our fathers had a falling out. Maggie's father was bipolar and he had all these get-rich schemes. My father was always loaning him money, and I suspect he got burned one too many times. But Maggie and I never completely lost touch, and having her house this fall has been a godsend." Bonnie looked sad and poured more wine in her glass. "You know how it's said God never gives you more than you can handle?"

"I've heard people say that."

"I think it's crap."

Al didn't say anything.

"My husband died of cancer this past May. In Corvallis, where we lived. My folks lived in Seattle and my father is in the early stages of Alzheimer's. My mother was handling everything, caring for him, and in June my mother was taking their dog Susie to the vet when a drunk driver hit them and killed both my mother and Susie."

Al closed his eyes, shaking his head. Finally he looked at her. "I'm sorry," he said, so quietly, his voice was almost a whisper.

Bonnie nodded. "Thanks." She took a sip of her wine, and didn't say anything for a few minutes, just stared at Tanner, who was snoring now. Then she looked at Al. "Well, anyway, I came to Seattle to help my father. Without my mother, he just spiraled down and down. Maggie suggested Vashon Community Care for Dad, and that's another godsend. You probably know, their facility has both assisted living apartments and skilled nursing ... it's been a wonderful place for him—and this island, well, it's helping me put one foot in front of the other."

"You were very sure-footed in the ravine." Al smiled.

"If anything happened to Tanner, I don't think I could bear it." She looked up and he could see tears in her eyes. "Thank you for helping me."

"Anytime," he said, quietly.

She stared at Tanner and sipped her wine. After a while she looked up again. "So tell me, why did you become a vet?"

"Well, there's the long version and the short version." Al yawned. "I'll just give you the short version."

Bonnie glanced at Tanner who had begun to stir. "Is he okay?"

"I'm sure he'll be fine, but he'll want water when the sedation wears off. It would be good to put his water bowl near him, and I can check on him in the morning."

"You were going to tell me the short version," she reminded him.

"Oh, right. Well, it starts with my family. I think it was Tolstoy or someone like that—I'm not much of a one for remembering quotations—not like Martha Jane who has a remarkable memory for them."

"She does. It's pretty amazing. I hope I'm half as sharp at her age."

"I think everyone who knows her feels that way. I may have even gotten the quote from her that 'all happy families are alike and each unhappy family is unhappy in its own way.' Without any of the boring details, the gist of it is that I had the kind of family where, at least in my perception, the only member of the family that I could count on was the dog—"

"The only one you felt loved you?"

"I suppose you could say that. It's not a great tragedy in the grand scheme of things, that's just the way it was, the way it seemed to me anyway, but I'm sure it's a contributing factor as to why I chose work where I could care for animals. Not only for their own sake and well-being, but I know how important they are to people, the kind of role they can play in a person's life."

"What kind of a dog did your family have?"

"Rex was a collie. Lassie was very popular on TV and my mother was an actress. I think she brought Rex home because she associated having a dog like that with film stardom. Maybe she thought it would rub off on her. He was a gorgeous collie."

Al drank his wine and looked away, embarrassed. But when he glanced at Bonnie he could feel his heart speed up ... and then it was if her image had been brought into focus so it began to register ... her coppery, tawny and white hair, the long face, the beautiful dark eyes. *A collie.* She reminded him of a collie. There was nothing new about people reminding him of dogs; he was sure it was something his mind conjured up to help him relate to people better. But he couldn't remember a single time in his entire life, not once, that anyone had reminded him of a collie.

Al gulped his wine and then suddenly felt ill. His palms began to sweat and his heart lurched. The reaction was bizarre. Only one explanation: it had to be some time lapse thing, a delayed response from carrying Tanner, and with the exertion and then the wine he'd drunk so fast, it was just now hitting him. He'd already had one heart attack. He should go home and rest.

He looked at his watch. "Oh, man. It's really late. I've got to check on Bert." He jumped up and hurried to the door, mumbling thanks for the wine. He had to get out of there.

CHAPTER 9

❧

A L HAD A FITFUL SLEEP. IT WAS UNUSUAL FOR HIM: HE WAS AN EXPERT at compartmentalizing, and with ease would block from his mind most things he found troubling. Most of his life, nothing much ever kept him from a good night's sleep and he always thought this was a strength. He suspected he had learned very early in his childhood to detach from the chaos around him. But Eleanor never saw it that way. She accused him of being shallow, not caring enough about anything to let it interfere with his precious sleep. Al found it interesting that being able to detach was now valued so highly by many people who were attracted to Buddhism, but there was no point in telling that to Eleanor.

Lying awake staring at the ceiling, Al remembered the time Eleanor, who thought of herself as a select steward of the environment, took it upon herself to roam the island checking to see if any construction was being done without the proper permits. She justified her vigilante permit patrol by her conclusion that the King County building department was understaffed and it was up to citizens to help in these efforts. She said her vigilance was similar to people helping thwart terrorism at airports by looking around and reporting any suspicious bags left unattended. Eleanor would go to a construction site and ask to see the permit, and would then report anyone who balked to the King County building department. Septics were also her specialty.

When it came to scrutinizing them, she was really on a roll. She literally went sniffing about and reported any septics she suspected of leaking into Puget Sound to the King County health department. This did not endear her to her neighbors, to put it mildly. When she was met with hostility, as she inevitably was, she expected Al to share her indignation. Al wasn't in favor of sewage going into the Sound, not by any means. He contributed to the Vashon-Maury Island Land Trust and was a strong believer in its mission to protect the natural ecosystems and the rural character of the island. Often volunteering for Land Trust work parties, he certainly saw himself as someone who wanted to protect the environment. But joining Eleanor as a deputy in her septic police didn't sit well with him, and he was extremely uncomfortable with the idea of ratting on the neighbors. Eleanor saw his reluctance as a total lack of commitment to preserving the environment and made no secret of her deep disappointment in him. There was no use in arguing with her, her rigidity rivaled all the concrete in Grand Coulee Dam. (Al had read recently that it had taken 12 million cubic yards of concrete.)

He lay there wondering if Eleanor had always been this way. Was she self-righteous and rigid when they first met, and he just hadn't seen it? Had he learned to detach so much that he was in a fog about people, especially women? Absent-mindedly, he stroked the gauze and the adhesive tape that Bonnie had used to bandage his hand; he felt his heart flutter and worried again that he had overdone it carrying Tanner out of the ravine. His regular check-up with Dr. Chan, his cardiologist, was coming up later this month, but if his heart didn't calm down, he supposed he'd have to get in to see him sooner.

Al got out of bed and went to the kitchen to make some tea. He remembered Chamomile was supposed to have a calming effect, and he found some in a box of assorted herbal tea bags. He made it in the microwave, and as he waited for it to beep, he looked across the road at Bonnie's place. The porch light was on, but the rest of the house was dark. It was weird not being able to sleep. This never happened. He'd always heard that there could be a feeling of dread, of impending doom that sometimes preceded a heart attack. But this didn't seem like dread; it was more like he was jittery, hyped up with an agitated case of nerves. Maybe his heart was misfiring or something. He'd give it a day to calm down and if it didn't, he'd call Dr. Chan.

But in the meantime, there was only one thing to do: throw himself into his work. But he didn't have any work. So he'd have to throw himself into the only job he did have, which was judging the contest for the calendar. They wouldn't have all the entries in for a while, but Al thought there was no reason he couldn't start getting ready by creating a rating chart and listing all the categories on which he would judge each entry. As he drank his tea, he decided that first thing in the morning he would work on the chart on his computer and print out a stack of rating sheets. Having a plan seemed to relax him, and as soon as he got in bed, Al fell right to sleep.

THE SUN ROSE AT SEVEN-THIRTY and by eight Al was hard at work developing the rating charts. Since the purpose of the calendar was to raise money for the shelter and promote animal adoption, he concluded that it wouldn't be helpful to feature dogs that weren't appealing. It would be counter productive to feature dogs that looked aggressive and would scare people—although he'd known many such dogs whose fierce looks belied a kind and gentle nature. But he'd have to look for dogs with great appeal, and since the shelters usually had many more mixed breed dogs than purebreds, he would choose a disproportionate number of mixed breed dogs. Eight mixed breeds and four purebreds would be about the right ratio, he decided, and he'd organize them according to color, size, gender and age. Then he would rate each group according to whether they looked alert, playful, affectionate, loyal, cuddly, and on the appearance of overall good health—with a premium on a good coat and bright eyes.

By late morning, he'd finished making the chart on the computer and was printing it when someone knocked at the door.

Bert went with him to answer it and it was Howie, carrying a plate covered in plastic wrap that Bert found very interesting, trying to keep from jumping as he raised his nose up to sniff.

"Hi, Al. Mark and I have something for you." Howie held the plate higher, while he patted Bert's head. "Got a minute?"

"Sure, good to see you. Come on in—how was your trip?" Al always thought Howie looked like a bloodhound, although with a slightly narrower face and hair like a gray Afghan; whereas Mark seemed to favor a beagle. It was their sturdiness and reliability that put them both in the hound family in Al's mind.

"Canada was fantastic," he said, holding out the plate. "Mark made these for you—cranberry scones. Bonnie brought Tanner back this morning and told us what happened."

Al grinned. "I love scones, thanks!" He took the plate from Mark. "Yeah, it was quite a night. How 'bout coffee?"

"That'd be great."

In the kitchen, Al got mugs from the cupboard. "The Fourth of July is bad enough for animals, but for a guy to shoot off all that crap for his stupid birthday, it's just asinine. I'm not very aggressive, but I wanted to go over there and punch the guy out." He poured the coffee. "Cream?"

"Got any non-fat milk?"

"I do." Al got the milk, and took it to the table with the coffee and sat across from Howie.

"It's probably good we were out of town—we might have joined you." Howie poured some milk in his coffee. "Got a spoon?"

"Sorry." Al grabbed a spoon from the drawer and handed it to him.

"Thanks," Howie stirred his coffee. "It never even occurred to us that Bonnie would have to deal with fireworks. It's October for God's sake. Tanner becomes incredibly anxious, and you probably remember, we always came to you to get tranquilizers for him before the Fourth."

"I remember. And his distress was certainly exacerbated having you gone." Al picked up a scone. "These look great. You said Mark made 'em?"

Howie nodded. "One of his specialties. We wanted to thank you for all your help. Bonnie said you were amazing, the way you figured out Tanner was in that culvert and carried him all the way through the ravine. She started joking that there should be a Super Vet action figure named Al."

"She said that?"

"She did." Howie took one of the scones. "Al, the Super Vet."

Al was pleased, but the moment of pleasure was fleeting. He looked out the window at the clouds rolling in with the tide. "Right, we could set up a stand, and sell them outside the Kincaid Animal Clinic."

Howie sipped his coffee. After a few minutes he said, "You really miss working, don't you, Al."

Al nodded. "I never should have sold my practice. What a fool."

"It was after your heart attack, right?"

He nodded again. "When I had my heart attack, they did a coronary angiogram and my left coronary artery—that's the one they call the widow maker, well, it had a partial obstruction and they put in a stent. They didn't find any other blockage. The weird thing was that it just came out of the blue. I didn't have any risk factors, no heart disease in my family, not a smoker, no high blood pressure or high cholesterol, not overweight—and the heart muscle wasn't damaged, but it was infarcted. I went to cardiac rehab for a couple of months. The Washington State Veterinary Medicine Association has an online newsletter, and I put a notice there for someone to take over my practice for two months while I was in rehab. Jerry Kincaid responded and ran my practice for me. It was just supposed to be temporary, but he really wanted to be on the island. His wife had grown up here, and when the two months were up, he made an offer to buy the practice. I had been told to avoid stress, and had gotten depressed with the whole thing. I found out depression can go along with a heart attack. Anyway, I was pretty low and exhausted, and Eleanor convinced me I should sell. And right after that she got sick."

"You sure had a lot on your plate. I know they say sometimes a crisis can bring people closer, but I guess the opposite happens, too."

"Do you ever wonder who 'they' is?"

"You mean 'they' in the 'they say'?"

"Right. Sometimes I wonder who 'they' are, but I suppose it means the common wisdom." Al grabbed another scone. "These really are good," he said, taking a bite. "I guess Eleanor and I weren't strong enough to weather everything." Al looked at Bert, who sat at his feet, patiently staring up, hoping some crumbs would fall his way like manna from heaven. "Listen, enough of this misery." He shook his head. "I was glad I could help Tanner. He's a great dog. How's he doing this morning?"

"Fine. Seems very happy to be home with us."

"I'll bet." Al smiled. "So, the trip was great you said."

"It was. The leaves were spectacular and we met a lot of nice people on the train. Our favorite was Quebec City. We loved it, probably could have spent a week there. And basically, we both just love Canada. The people are wonderful, and their culture seems much more humane and civilized to us." Howie stood up. "Well, better get back. We've got a pile of mail to go through, and the laundry and all that stuff that piles up when you're gone."

Al went with Howie to the door and Howie gave him a hug. "We can't thank you enough."

"I'm glad I could help, Howie. And tell Mark the scones were delicious. Anytime he makes too many, I'd be glad to take them off his hands."

THE AFTERNOON PATRICIA WATERTON CALLED Al to let him know the calendar entries had been submitted and were ready to be picked up, Al was pleased; the moment to judge the contest had arrived. In fact, he was more than pleased—it bordered on delight, which he knew was a little silly considering the job didn't require any skill. By giving it a great deal of thought and preparing the rating sheets, he admitted he had tried to puff it up, exaggerate what was required when the task could just as easily be accomplished if he threw all the photos up in the air and picked twelve that Bert stepped on. But he should enjoy it while it lasts, he thought, as he drove to the shelter to get the entries. Because as soon as he picked the winners and his tenure as judge was over, he'd be right back facing the emptiness of his life and the nagging question of what to do with himself. In the past few weeks he'd had the sad recognition that the happiest he'd been since he sold his practice was the night Tanner was rescued. He'd felt energized, capable, useful and needed. The way he'd been on a regular basis when he had his practice. Well, he certainly couldn't sit around waiting for some poor dog to get stuck in a culvert. Al sighed as he turned off Wax Orchard Road into the drive of the shelter. But at least his heart had settled down since then. He'd made a point of trying to eat better and exercise and he guessed that was something.

The Vashon Animal Shelter was located at Patricia and Paul Waterton's house. They had three fenced acres, and the dogs waiting for foster care or adoption were kept in the large daylight basement. It was a non-profit agency: the Watertons received a small amount of rent, but no salary, as it was basically a volunteer operation. Patricia did most of the work since Paul was a pilot for Delta Airlines and was frequently gone, although he did help out when he was home. They were a nice couple. Al liked them both. Paul had asked Al to play golf once, but since Al wasn't a golfer, nothing else came of it.

Patricia was on the phone and waved to Al when she saw him walking up the path. He was immediately greeted by a boxer and a shaggy black dog with white paws, lacking any discernible heritage. Patricia covered the phone whispering, "I'll just be a minute, Al."

Al bent down and let the dogs sniff his hand, and they jumped around him wagging their tails. The doors to the crates were all open and he didn't see any other dogs. Patricia usually had good luck finding foster homes and the shelter had an impressive record of adoption. The boxer had a lot of gray around his muzzle, and Al thought he was probably going on ten or more. Older dogs were hard to place, especially if they had health problems. Al identified with the hard to place senior dogs.

Patricia got off the phone and rushed over to hug him. "Oh Al, it's so good to see you. I've missed you!" She was a large, big-boned woman with warm brown eyes and a nice smile. Her straight gray hair was cut short and Al had never seen her wear anything other than a VAS sweatshirt with its logo of a dog and cat in a heart. Patricia turned sixty last May and had a great party, which Al had loved. He usually wasn't much for big groups, but this was his kind of party. A big picnic had been held in the Watertons' yard with all the people who'd adopted dogs from the shelter bringing their dogs. They had prizes and treats for the dogs and a lot of beer and wine for the people. It was loud, very loud, with barking and laughing and much chasing around: dogs chasing dogs, people chasing dogs. Eleanor was in the middle of her treatment and didn't go, which was just as well. She would have hated it.

The hug seemed to last more than a few seconds, and Al began to get uncomfortable. He patted her back and stepped away. "Good to see you, too."

"It's just not the same without you." Patricia ran a hand through her hair. "The new vet won't treat our animals for free anymore."

"That figures."

"I don't mean that we just loved you because you didn't charge us." She smiled up at him. "I guess to be fair, I admit Dr. Kincaid does give us a discount."

"Why be fair?"

Patricia laughed. "Well, anyway. We certainly miss you." She went to her desk and picked up a box. "All the photos are in here——we had a great response," she said, grinning. "We got 113!"

"I can see I have my work cut out for me." Al took the box from her and went to the door. "I'll be sure and get these back as soon as I can."

"Great." Patricia stood next to him and put her hand on his arm. "You know, Al. You are one of my favorite people on this island." She lifted her face up to him.

Al gave her a shaky smile, feeling uneasy.

"I get tired of eating alone when Paul's gone so much. He's got the route to Hong Kong this month. Why don't you come for dinner tonight?"

"Oh, well. Thank you, Patricia. But I can't come tonight."

Patricia moved closer and hugged him again, but he clutched the box of photos to his chest with one hand, and it got squished between them. "I've got to be on my way now," he mumbled. "Bert's waiting for me."

Patricia stepped back and grinned. "Thought it was worth a try, Al." Then she chuckled, watching Al run out the basement door.

AL WAS COMPLETELY BAFFLED. HE always thought Patricia and her husband seemed quite happy. Was the island full of hanky-panky and he'd been totally oblivious? Hanky-panky ... what kind of dumb geezer word was that? ... he sounded to himself like someone's maiden aunt. Maiden aunt? There was another one. There were lots of single women who were somebody's aunts. Who ever said maiden aunt anymore? What century was he living in? These were the kinds of things his grandmother would say. Al cringed as he thought about his grandmother. What a nasty piece of work she was, and what a contrast to his beautiful, crazy mother. With love supposedly coming in those two packages, no wonder he preferred dogs. Eleanor was probably right about him. She always said he didn't get it about women. Touché. He probably didn't get most things having to do with people. Mostly women, unless it related to their animals.

Al stopped by the post office on his way home, and as he was getting out of the truck, Marilyn Henderson came out of the post office and bounded over to him.

"Oh, Al! Just the person I wanted to see! I've left a lot of messages for you, but since I never heard back, I thought you were on a long trip somewhere."

"Oh, well, I've been pretty busy."

"Now that I've caught up with you, I have something I've been wanting to give you. I've been carrying it around in my car, just hoping I'd run into you."

"I really need to get going, maybe some other—"

Marilyn moved close to him and threw her head back. "You

wouldn't want to look a gift horse in the mouth, now would you?" She puckered her mouth like she was about to kiss him.

"That's an interesting expression. The origin is that horses were always scrutinized as to their health and general constitution by examining their mouths, checking their teeth. But it was considered an insult to do that with a horse that was given as a gift."

Marilyn grabbed his hand. "Come on Al, my car's right down here. It'll just take a minute."

Marilyn pulled him across the parking lot to her blue Dodge van. As they approached, Eloise began barking and jumped up against the window on the passenger side.

"It's okay, Eloise. I'll be with you in a minute," Marilyn said, sweetly. "Doesn't she look wonderful. You know I had my neighbor, Janet Greenbaum, take Eloise's photo for the VAS calendar contest. Janet is this amazing photographer and the portrait of Eloise perfectly captured her beautiful little animal spirit energy. I hear you're judging the contest this year—that is just so great." She went to the back of the van and lifted up the rear door. Al stood behind her trying not to look at her butt as she bent over and reached into the back of the van.

"Ah, here it is. Just for Al." Marilyn pulled out a small turquoise glazed ceramic pot which held a little fern. "This is from a cutting of one of my ferns. They say the best gifts are when you give part of yourself and—"

"Do you ever wonder who 'they' are? I've been thinking about that lately—you know, like 'they say'—who are 'they'?"

"I don't know, but this is a little part of something I love that I want you to have." Marilyn handed him the pot, while Eloise continued to bark and throw herself against the window.

"I'm sorry I couldn't quite hear with Eloise barking."

"*I said* ...THIS IS A LITTLE PART OF SOMETHING I LOVE THAT I WANT YOU TO HAVE." Marilyn shouted, then turned to glare at a woman coming out of the post office who was staring at them.

"Thank you." Al said, awkwardly holding the pot in front of him.

"My pleasure." Marilyn glared at the woman again, then

smiled sweetly at Al, and jumped in the van, while Al stood in the post office parking lot holding the plant. She put down the window, gazing at him as though she wanted him to say something. When he didn't, and started to walk to his truck, she called, "I know that little fern will love you and thrive being surrounded by your good aura. Be sure and let me know how it goes, Al. I'll give you a call and let's get together soon! Take care."

WHEN HE LEFT THE POST office, instead of going home to Baker's Beach, Al found himself driving to Burton where he took a left by the Burton Store and drove slowly around the Burton Loop. When he came to his old house, he stopped his truck across the street from it. The For Sale sign was still up and he wondered if there were many people interested in it. The yard looked in pretty good shape—Eleanor must have found someone to mow it for her. Al couldn't figure out why he wanted to look at the house. It wasn't as though it held a store of beautiful memories. But it had been his home, and everything in it and the way they'd lived had been predictable. That is, until his heart attack and Eleanor getting cancer. He wondered how she was doing. It seemed strange to him that he mostly had unpleasant memories of her these days. Maybe it made it easier to accept what had happened. Because there had been good times. Especially in the beginning. Al remembered when he made the final installment on the clinic and Jim and Betty McDoogal had a big going away party at the Burton Lodge at Camp Burton before they moved to Hawaii. The night of McDoogals' party, before he and Eleanor left for the Burton Lodge, Eleanor had given him an expensive bottle of champagne to celebrate his ownership of the clinic. A local band, the Royal Islanders, had been hired for the party. Eleanor never liked to do anything but slow dance. If she ever danced fast, she said she thought people were looking at her and judging how she danced. But slow dancing with a partner was something she occasionally enjoyed. The Royal Islanders played a lot of old favorites of the McDoogals' generation, songs like

"Autumn Leaves," "Stranger in Paradise," and "Love is a Many Splendored Thing." Al loved dancing with Eleanor. She was tall and elegant and her head fit right against the top of his shoulder, in the crook of his neck. And they danced that night until after two in the morning, and he remembered having more champagne after they got home. And making love. Al closed his eyes; he felt a lump in his throat. "Love is a Many Splendored Thing." That was a beautiful song. He put his truck in gear and headed to Baker's Beach.

CHAPTER 10

THE PHOTOS WERE SPREAD ALL OVER THE KITCHEN TABLE. EACH photo had a number that corresponded to a number on a master list at the shelter office, which recorded the owner's name and contact information. The system guaranteed impartiality. With only a number on the photo, Al had no idea who owned the dogs. When it came right down to it, owning dogs, or any animal, wasn't a concept he ever liked. He much preferred the idea of guardianship. To be an animal's guardian conveyed the special responsibility humans had to care, protect, provide for, and watch over the animals entrusted to their care.

Al began to arrange the photos in three main groups: puppy, middle aged, and senior. Then within each age group he would make sub-groups of purebred and mixed. Originally he thought gender would be another category, but when he looked at the photos, he realized that if he knew the gender and the general age of the dog, he might have a clue to its identity. It was good he hadn't been given any information like that. As he sorted through the photos, even though he didn't know with certainty each dog's age, he made a guess and sorted all the photos into the three piles. Then Al stared at the piles, trying to decide how many of each age group the calendar should have. Since they needed twelve photos, the obvious thing would be to choose four from each of the three age groups. But he knew puppies were the most appealing, and he wondered if maybe the calendar should be weighted toward more puppies. But then he thought about how senior dogs were the most difficult to adopt. Maybe having more senior dogs would help promote their adoption. For a second he considered getting advice from Patricia Waterton—but when she had invited him to dinner, it didn't seem like it was only dinner she had in mind, and he concluded asking for her advice might not be a good idea. He'd have to make these decisions himself. After all, when they asked him to be the judge, they said the choices were completely open-ended and totally up to him.

Al felt it was quite a responsibility and decided to think about it over lunch. He'd go into town and have a hamburger at the Bike. Everyone called the restaurant the Bike, although the name was Red Bicycle. It was named for a famous Vashon Island land-mark: an old red bicycle sticking out of the trunk of a tree. It was stuck there about seven feet off the ground so that it looked as if the tree had tried to eat the bike and had then grown around it. In the waiting room at his clinic, Al had kept a children's story about it called *Red Ranger Came Calling* by Berkeley Breathed. He'd taken it with him when he moved his stuff out. He did not want Jerry Kincaid to have his *Red Ranger* book. Kincaid could get his own books.

His mouth watered as he thought about lunch. The Bike's Santa Fe Burger would be nice. It was an Angus patty with jala-peno, jack cheese, avocado, lettuce, tomato, onion, and pickle and all their burgers came with your choice of soup, salad, fries or coleslaw. He would have fries. He'd go back to eating more healthy stuff when he'd finished judging the contest.

The Bike was the kind of place where you just walked in and seated yourself. But when Al got there, he saw Evelyn Murdoch sitting near the door with three other women and she spotted him before he could turn around to leave.

"Hi! Al! Excuse me, ladies." She jumped up and pranced over to him. "I thought there was something wrong with your phone—I've been leaving messages for you."

"Oh, well—I've been very busy." Seeing her jump up like that, he realized why he always thought of her in Jack Russell terms, even though her white curly hair made her appear more poodley.

"Well, never mind. Here you are, and I have something I've made for you. Just a little token of my appreciation for how wonderful you were to help Olivia. I'd love to bring it over. Where are you living now Al?"

"Oh, there's no need." Al thought if she came to his house, he might not know how to get rid of her. But he couldn't think how he could avoid accepting her token of appreciation, whatever it was. That would be too rude. He'd better go to her house and then make a quick getaway. "It's very nice of you to have something for me. I'm just having a quick bite and then I could swing by your place after I'm through lunch. I have Bert in my truck, so I could just pop in for a minute. Would that be okay?"

"Absolutely." Evelyn beamed and gave his arm a squeeze. "I'll be waiting for you."

Al went to the corner of the restaurant near the back door, hoping he wouldn't see anyone else he knew. He ordered a beer with his Santa Fe burger. He didn't usually drink at lunch, but he felt a little unnerved seeing Evelyn. She was a nice woman, and her blue eyes were beautiful. Just too jumpy and skittery of a person, and her house was a mess with all that jumble all over. But he had to admit he did feel some kind of connection to Evelyn, probably because the two of them had gone through Cassidy's euthanization together and then he'd helped her bury him. And of course she'd given him the beautiful painting of a golden retriever, which he prized.

It had started to rain when Al pulled up in front of Evelyn's house and he jumped out of the truck and trotted quickly to the door, pulling the hood of his parka over his head. Evelyn flung open the door as soon as he knocked. She must have been sitting by the window waiting for him.

"You've got to come in out of this rain, Al," she insisted.

"Bert's in the truck—I really need to—"

"Just for a minute." She tugged his sleeve and pulled him inside. Al was surprised; for such a little woman, she was quite strong. Her house looked just as chaotic as it had the last time he was there when he came to extract the stick from Olivia's mouth. Looking at all the stuff she had piled everywhere, he wondered again if Evelyn was some sort of hoarder, maybe a Granny's Attic addict. The furniture was still buried in pieces of colored cloth, and paper towel tubes were scattered all over the place like before. But now on the floor there were piles of dried leaves and rolls of chicken wire and pieces of red and green felt and some sort of sparkly white stuff everywhere. Evelyn darted into the kitchen and came back with a jar and held it up to him.

"This is plum jam. I meant to give it to you when you were here helping Olivia, but I forgot. I had a fantastic amount of plums this year." She picked up what looked like a tiny red felt hat with white sparkly trim. "I almost wrapped it in this but I thought it was a little early."

"Thank you for the jam." Al put the jar in the pocket of his parka. "Well, I better be on my way. Bert's out there in the truck."

"Wait! I have something for Bert, too." Evelyn ran to the kitchen and came back with a little red felt bag, which was closed at the top with a white ribbon. "I made these dog treats myself. No preservatives, all organic. I bake them and the dough is made from chicken broth, whole wheat flour, garlic, parsley, honey, and an egg. Olivia loves them." She moved closer. "I heard you were the judge of the Vashon Animal Shelter calendar contest, Al. You know, there are a lot of goldens on the island, but Olivia has this little adorable ridge on her nose that distinguishes her. It's charming don't you think?" She winked at him.

Evelyn handed him the little bag of treats and then hugged him. Her head came to the middle of his chest, and he remembered how she'd ended up in his lap after he ate the blueberry pie. When they kissed then it had been nice, but also made him very uncomfortable. In fact, the only time hugging Evelyn hadn't felt awkward was when he held her as she wept after Cassidy died. Al patted the top of her head. "I really have to go, Evelyn." Then he patted her back and pulled away from her. "Thank you for the treats. For me and for Bert."

"I know you need time, Al," she said, as she held the door open for him. "But we never know how much we have left, do we? Just think about that, will you?" Then she put her arms around his neck, stood on her tiptoes and kissed him.

As SOON AS AL GOT in the truck, he opened the little bag of dog treats and handed one to Bert, who lunged at it, almost inhaling it, his mouth like a slobbery vacuum. It had been very nice of Evelyn to make special organic dog treats. She was a nice woman. Maybe he was a fool. Was it right what she said about his needing time? Eleanor hadn't been gone very long, but he was facing the fact that their marriage hadn't been much of a marriage for years. He didn't think getting involved on the rebound really applied when you'd been living in an emotional drought. Rebound from what? From an arrangement of convenience? Maybe that was the most he could say about him and Eleanor. There certainly hadn't been any passion for years. Al drove along Tramp Harbor and thought about Marilyn Henderson. She seemed to be a passionate person and he found her very attractive. Any man would, but he always wanted to escape when he was around her for more than a few minutes. She seemed like gooey taffy that he might get stuck in. Evelyn didn't give him that gooey taffy feeling, but her jumpiness and the way she talked a mile a minute made him nervous. If she were a dog, she'd bark all the time, one of those high-pitched annoying little barks. But at least she liked dogs. So did Marilyn.

FOR ALL OF THE NEXT week, Al used the rating sheets he'd made and sorted through the photos. He wanted to give each and every one of the 113 careful consideration. He assigned points for the various attributes on a scale of one to five, with five being the highest rating, and then totaled the score, attaching the rating sheet to each photo. By the end of the week, he had chosen three finalists for each month. He'd ended up deciding to just go with the three obvious age groups: puppies would be chosen for January, April, July, and October, and middle-aged dogs would be in February, May, August, and November. The senior dogs would be in March, June, September, and December. The majority of the dogs in the calendar would be mixed breed, with four purebred dogs in April, June, August, and December.

Getting to the final three for each month had been difficult, there were so many appealing and photogenic dogs. But he did admit to having a bias against dogs wearing clothes. He debated quite a long time about whether it was fair to eliminate those dogs when it was their guardians who had a problem allowing them to just be dogs. As if being a dog wasn't good enough and the animal had to be adorned with something to give it a more human appearance. But he was the judge, he reminded himself, and he judged dogs less attractive if they wore clothes or accessories, even if it wasn't their fault. Once he became clear about that issue, he quickly eliminated the ones that were wearing scarves, little bow ties and hats. One golden retriever even had on a little Santa hat, an obvious ploy to be chosen for December, and it was one of the first photos he put in the reject pile.

It was getting close to the deadline when his choices had to be given to the shelter, and Al decided not to look at the photos for at least a day to see if he could bring a fresh eye to the process. He left the twelve groups of finalists spread out on the kitchen table and headed to the beach with Bert.

IT HAD BEEN WINDY THE night before, bringing more leaves off the trees, and a few branches were scattered across the path. Al zipped up his parka. The wind had died down from the night before, but it was still breezy and there was a chill in the air. Winter would be there soon. No matter how cold the day, Bert always wanted to swim and Al had Bert's frog in his pocket, although he never threw it as far when it was cold like this.

He decided to walk north along the cove, rounding the corner where they'd be out of the wind a bit. The water and clouds were both battleship gray, and the dreary day was only brightened intermittently on the bank where a smattering of yellow leaves stubbornly clung to the branches of the vine maples. There was a high tide and he'd forgotten to look at the tide chart before he left the house. He looked out at the choppy water and the tide seemed to be coming in. Better not go too far and get stuck as the tide swallowed the beach, he thought, stopping at the first bend after the cove. Bert had been trotting ahead and came back and jumped around, barking with excitement as Al pulled the frog from his pocket. He threw it less than six feet into the water and Bert charged after it, giving no indication that he felt short-changed by the short distance. Al envied Bert the most when he watched him at the beach. If only he could find such simple plea-sure. Judging the contest had given him something to look for-ward to, but as soon as he picked the final twelve, the job would be over. Bert swam back, shook water all over Al, and dropped the frog. As Al bent down to pick it up, he looked at the rocks on the beach, actually really taking note of them. There were all shapes, sizes, and colors. Each had a unique and subtle beauty. Maybe he could polish rocks. Al threw the frog again and Bert bounded into the water. But what would he do with all the rocks once he'd polished them? What would be the point exactly? Al was thinking about what to do with polished rocks when he saw Bonnie coming toward him. She waved and as he waved back, he realized he hadn't seen her since the night of Tanner's rescue.

"Kind of a crummy day, but at least it's not raining," Bonnie said, as she got within earshot. "And the wind's not as bad as last night, so that's good."

"Always look on the bright side of life." Al said, and then for some reason he started to whistle the tune.

"Ah, a Monty Python fan—of course." Bonnie grinned.

"Aren't you?"

"Of course." She laughed.

"I can't remember all the words though, just the tune." Al watched Bert swimming back with the frog.

"It's a great tune. Listen, Al—I'm glad I ran into you. There's something I've been meaning to ask you."

"Oh?" Al had trouble looking at her. He bent down and picked up a rock, wondering what it would look like if he polished it. He could get a little machine. They had machines for that, maybe it wouldn't cost too much.

"I wonder if I could borrow Bert?"

"Bert?" He felt a strange sense of relief. He stopped looking at the rocks. "You'd like to borrow him?"

"Okay, I know this is kind of an odd request, but I don't know if you remember what I told you the other night about my father ...."

Al nodded. He remembered everything about that night.

Bonnie looked at her watch. "Actually, I need to get back. If you're going back maybe we could walk together and I can tell you."

"Sure. Bert's never ready to leave, but he's always very accommodating." Bert swam to shore, shook again and dropped his frog, which Al scooped up and put back in his pocket.

The water was getting higher and they walked close to the bank while Bert ran up ahead, chasing a seagull. "My father's memory is pretty well shot. He still knows me and I'm grateful for that. He never talks about my mother or what happened, but as I probably told you, their dog that was killed in the accident with my mother was a chocolate Lab. And I thought since Bert's a chocolate Lab, it might give Dad some comfort to have a visit from him. It's kind of an experiment—I honestly don't know what will happen. There's always the chance it could backfire and not bring comfort at all, just trigger a lot of pain. But I thought it was worth a try. Do you think it sounds crazy?"

"I don't really know what's crazy anymore. To me dogs are the most comforting creatures on the planet, so it would be worth a try." Al watched Bert, who had stopped to sniff something near the edge of the water. He hoped it wasn't a jellyfish. "Bert! Come on boy!" Bert ran over to them, and Al bent down to pat him. "Bert likes most people and he really likes you, so I think it would work out fine."

"We bonded over the cheese that day." Bonnie laughed. "But listen, I really would be uncomfortable taking him by myself."

"Oh, he'd behave himself for you, no problem."

"It's not about Bert. It's about me. Ever since Tanner ran away from me, I'm kind of gun shy. I couldn't handle it if anything happened to Bert while I was responsible for him. I don't mean that I think some old guy at Vashon Community Care is going to set off fireworks and freak out Bert."

"I'd agree that's not a concern."

"Right. But anything can happen to anyone, anytime ...." They could hear the cry of a kingfisher as it sat on a branch near the bank in front of them. Bonnie took a tissue from her jeans pocket and blew her nose.

"I'd be happy to go with you when you take Bert to meet your father."

She looked away, wiping her eyes. "You could stay in the car while I take him in, you wouldn't have to meet my Dad or anything."

"I'd be honored to go in with Bert."

Bonnie watched Bert trotting ahead of them. She stopped and dug in her pocket for another tissue. She pinched the bridge of her nose, then wiped her eyes again. "Thanks, Al."

They left the beach and walked single file along the path to Baker's Beach Road with Bert in the lead, followed by Bonnie, then Al. Bonnie said her father always seemed a little better, a little more alert in the morning, and they decided to go the following Tuesday.

Al said goodbye to Bonnie and went in to work on the calendar. He felt cheerful as he made a fresh pot of coffee and settled in at the kitchen table to choose the twelve winners. He enjoyed Bonnie's company, and the best thing was he could relax with her because all she needed from him was the use of his dog.

Chapter 11

AL CHOSE THE FINALISTS FOR THE MIXED BREED SLOTS FIRST. HE wasn't sure why, but he found it considerably easier than trying to choose the four purebred winners. But by mid-afternoon on Monday, he had finally made his selection. There would be a German shepherd puppy for April, a senior yellow Lab for June, a Yorkshire terrier that he thought might be middle aged for August, and a gray and white shih tzu puppy for December. The dogs were all so appealing, he hadn't realized when he accepted the job how difficult it would be to choose only twelve. He wondered if the people whose dogs weren't chosen might be a little disappointed. But he was sure it wouldn't be much of a problem since it was all in fun and for a worthy cause. He was eager to drop the winners off at the shelter office to keep from re-thinking his choices. Maybe he could ask Bonnie if she'd mind if they stopped there on the way to visit her father on Tuesday. That way he could tell Patricia someone was waiting in the car and he could make a quick getaway.

Al got up early Tuesday morning and boxed up all the entries, separating out the photos of the twelve winners, which he put in a manila envelope. He made a list which he'd keep of the numbers on the winners' photos and their designated months in case anything got misplaced at the shelter office or on the way to the company that was printing the calendars. The calendar had previously been designed, and all Patricia had to do was scan the photos and pop them in the computer file along with the names of the twelve dogs, and then get it off to the printer. It was a printer in California that did bulk rush jobs and Al wanted the back-up list in case anything went wrong.

A few minutes before ten Bonnie called. "Hi, guess this is it. Time for the big experiment. If you're ready, I'll meet you and Bert out by my car."

"Oh, you're driving? I guess that makes sense. Taking my truck would be a little crowded with both you and Bert in the passenger seat."

"I'm happy to drive. After all, you're doing me the favor."

"Actually, I need a favor." Al realized he wasn't used to asking people for things and thought he sounded uptight. "Would it be okay if we swing by the shelter on the way to see your father? I need to drop something off. It would just take a minute," he said apologetically.

"Sure, no problem. I can wait in the car with Bert."

"Great. Thanks." That hadn't been too hard. Now he could tell Patricia he had to get going because Bonnie and Bert were waiting. Maybe he'd misunderstood her dinner invitation the other day, but he didn't think so.

IT WAS RAINING WHEN HE went out to Bonnie's car. He'd put Bert on his leash and brought a towel to wipe him off before they went in to meet Bonnie's father. Bert had a way of walking through every puddle he saw, and Al didn't think it would bode well for the experiment to come to the care center with a wet, muddy dog. He opened the back door for Bert and then got in front next to Bonnie, holding the box of photos and the envelope of the winners' photos.

"I haven't been to the shelter. I'll need you to tell me where to go," Bonnie said, as she backed her car out to Baker's Beach Road.

"It's on Wax Orchard Road in Frog Holler, a little north of Camp Sealth. It's in Patricia and Paul Waterton's house—Patricia is the Vashon Animal Shelter director."

"In their house? They must have a lot of room."

"She only handles dogs. The cats are kept at a different person's house, Rhonda Bragassa's, but it's the same arrangement. They foster a lot of the animals with different people around the island. Patricia and Paul have quite a few acres, and the house has a big daylight basement where they keep the dogs when they're not outside. The shelter is a nonprofit, funded entirely from donations, and she gets some kind of a stipend from having it at her house." Al looked at the box on his lap. "I'll be glad to drop this off. Judging this thing was harder than I thought."

"A lot of cute dogs, I'll bet." Bonnie turned onto Wax Orchard Road.

"Right. They were all appealing—they all looked very likable. Of course, I'm only talking about their looks. I think Will Rogers said he never met a man he didn't like, or something like that. I can't say the same for people, but I've probably never met a dog I didn't like. Even the ones that have been difficult, I can usually understand why from the way they've been treated ... or mistreated, which is more the case."

"Dogs were always a big part of my life, both as a child and an adult." Bonnie glanced at him for a second, then looked ahead at the road. "I'd like another dog, but I can't imagine when I'd be ready. I don't even want to go in the shelter with you when you drop off the photos."

"Because you might be tempted?"

"My husband and I always got our dogs from shelters. The kids would go with us and we always came home with a mutt that turned out to be a wonderful addition to our family. The last dog we had, Chloe, was a shepherd Lab mix. She looked a lot like a shepherd, although she loved to swim like a Lab. She was loyal and protective—a terrific watch dog, but loving and gentle. She and my husband had cancer at the same time, although she had a more merciful death. If I went in the shelter with you, I'd just be faced with how uncertain my life is. Frankly, most of the time I feel like I'm treading water, and it's hard for me to imagine allowing myself to attach to anything. I mostly feel shell shocked—especially first thing in the morning. Not sure why mornings ... maybe just facing another day."

"My wife had cancer." Al pointed to the road ahead. "It's up here—240th and it's about a half mile after that."

"On the right?

Al nodded. "The drive is by the big blue mailbox that has the black metal cut-out of the dog on top. The sign for the shelter is back a few feet from the road."

"Martha Jane told me about your wife's cancer. It's tough ... I know, and I just, well ...." Her voiced trailed off as she turned right on a gravel road. It wound through the woods for about a quarter of a mile to end in a clearing in front of a fifties' style ranch house. "Shall I just park in front here?"

"That's fine. I'll only be a minute." Al turned to Bert in the back seat. "Stay," he said firmly. "I'll be right back."

It was still raining as Al headed up the long path that led to the back of the house. Bonnie's life made his present situation pale by comparison, like tragedy-lite, or not even that. Not any kind of tragedy. Just a pitiful little unraveling. It was hard for him to imagine what it must be like for her, losing her husband, then her mother, and having her father not the person he once was, the way it is with dementia. And her dog at the same time. And her parents' dog. It made him think about people in wars or earthquakes, who lost everyone in their families. Unimaginable grief. How did people go on? And what was the deal with the kids she'd mentioned, where were they?

As he went to the back of the house, he could see Patricia at her desk. Pulling his parka around the box of photos and the envelope, he went down the steps and knocked on the door.

"Hi Al." She opened the door, grinning, as if they were conspirators and shared a little secret.

Al held out the box. "Hi, well—I've got them here. The winners are in the manila envelope on top, and they're all labeled with the month I've chosen for each dog."

"Oh, I can't wait to see. Do you have a minute so we can look at them together?"

"Sorry, I've got to run, Bert is in the car and Bonnie—"

"Bonnie?" Patricia raised her eyebrows.

"Maggie Lewis's cousin. She's staying in Maggie's house while Maggie and Walter are gone. We're bringing Bert to visit Bonnie's father at Vashon Community Care."

"I didn't know Bert was a therapy dog." Patricia seemed surprised.

"Oh, he's not. It's just an experiment."

Patricia took the box over to her desk. "Well, I can't wait to see these. And even though the calendar doesn't come out for a while yet, I'll be calling the winners personally. And after the winners have been notified, I'll send a generic email to our list of everyone who entered the contest, announcing the winners. We've found this cuts down on people calling to find out the results. It's been so great over the years to see how invested people are in this."

"I'll look forward to seeing the calendar when it's done." Al turned to leave. "And thanks for asking me to be the judge. I liked doing it." Al didn't think he'd go into how much it had meant to him. It would sound like he didn't have much of a life, which of course, was true.

"Our judge always gets a complimentary calendar." Patricia went to the door and threw her arms around him. "Thanks, Al!" She pressed into him and tilted her head, raising her chin and gazing at him.

"Say hi to Paul when he gets home." Al mumbled, stiffly leaning away from her.

Patricia threw back her head and let out a big hearty laugh. She kissed him on the cheek, then let go of him. "Will do. Thanks again, Al."

VASHON COMMUNITY CARE WAS LOCATED north of town on Vashon Highway across from the Episcopal Church. It was an attractive three story building that had opened in 2002, although there had been a nursing home on the island since the late 1950s; and before that its roots dated back to 1928 when it was a boarding house and working farm. A senior care provider, it had thirty-nine assisted living apartments and thirty skilled nursing beds. Bonnie glanced at Al as she drove in and parked in the lot on the north side of the building. "The staff knows we're coming with Bert to visit Dad, but we'll need to check in at the desk."

"Have you told your father we're coming?" Al asked.

"I did, but I doubt he'll remember. In the beginning, when he'd forget recent conversations or events, my mother and I thought it was just normal aging. But when we looked back, we could see that it had been the early stages of Alzheimer's."

"I forget stuff—it's a little frightening." Al unbuckled his seat belt.

"We all do, but in the early stages of Alzheimer's people gradually become slower at grasping new ideas. They repeat themselves continually and lose the thread of what's being said. They become confused and show poor judgment, and find it harder to make decisions. They typically lose interest in other people and activities and sometimes they'll blame others for taking their stuff, becoming paranoid. And as it gets worse, they become confused about where they are or they can wander and get lost—all that sort of thing. With my father it spiraled down after my mother died and now, although he's still eating and not incontinent, he rarely communicates with anyone. We don't know how the grief has affected the progress of the disease, but all the symptoms became so much worse after he lost my mother. And Susie."

"But he does know who you are?"

"Oh yes, but when I'm with him, he doesn't say a lot, mostly just stares. His eyes are vacant, like there's nobody home." Bonnie sighed. "I guess I'm hoping Bert might create some kind of little spark." She looked across the parking lot. "Rain seems to have stopped—shall we go in?"

Al nodded and got Bert out of the back seat. He patted him and snapped on his leash. "He doesn't seem too wet. Guess I don't need the towel."

"No need to worry. The staff couldn't be nicer—the island is lucky to have this place."

Al followed Bonnie inside and waited while she checked in at the front desk. "Do you think he'll be okay in the elevator?" she asked. "I know some dogs get anxious."

"I don't think he's ever been in one. We might as well find out. I have treats in my pocket to encourage him." On the way to the elevator, they passed several people in wheelchairs and a lady wanted to say hello to Bert, so Al stopped while she patted him.

"What a big one." The woman and Bert were at eye level. "We don't see big ones here much." She patted his head. "We can have dogs, but the limit is twenty pounds and the dog has to be at least two years old. We can't have puppies, of course. Some of us are messy enough as it is." She laughed. "What's its name?"

"Bert," Al told her.

"Gert, that's a fine name. I had an Aunt Gert—Gertrude, but everyone called her Cannonball because she was from Wabash, you know Wabash, Indiana. She was kind of a cannonball, too. A lot of fun, my Aunt Gert." She turned and wheeled down the hall.

Al caught up with Bonnie, who was waiting by the elevator. "Bert—Gert, it's all the same to him." He smiled as they got in the elevator. "I didn't quite get it about the cannonball though, did you?" Bert walked right in the elevator and although he started to pace a little as the door closed and it started upward, he seemed pretty comfortable. "So far so good."

"It's a song about a train, I think. A folk song ... 'The Wabash Cannonball.'" Bonnie said as they got out on the second floor.

Her father's room was halfway down the hall on the right side. As they passed the rooms, Al was struck by the photos of the residents, often a photo of a person when they were much younger. A reminder that this was a person who had a full, vibrant life. Sometimes there was a short paragraph, a little biography of the person. What a leveler age was, he thought. Bonnie stopped outside the third door from the end of the hall. On the wall, next to the door was a smiling photo of a nice-looking man with brown eyes and auburn hair, white at the temples. He had a long face and Bonnie looked a lot like him. Al thought it must have been taken when her Dad was about sixty or so. Under the photo was just his name, "Ralph Douglas."

"Dad?" Bonnie knocked on the door. There was no answer, so she opened it a little. "I'm here Dad, with some visitors."

Bonnie's father had a one-bedroom apartment. It was just under 600 square feet with a living area and kitchenette, bedroom, and bathroom. The door from the hall entered into the kitchenette and the small living area was adjacent to it with a large window at the end of the room. Al wasn't one to pay much attention to furnishings, but he thought the warm colors of the tan couch and the maroon chair made it seem cozy. On the wall over the couch there was an Impressionist style painting of what looked like beautiful red cranberry fields with a barn and trees in the background. Her father was sitting by the window when they came in. It would have been hard to know he was the same man in the photo; his long face was so thin, it seemed almost emaciated, and his hair lay across his skull in what looked like sparse pieces of white thread. He raised his hand slightly when he saw Bonnie.

She went to him and bent down and kissed his cheek. "I've brought my neighbor Al and his dog here to see you." She motioned to Al to come over.

"Dad, I'd like you to meet Al Paugh and his dog." She looked at Al, "This is my father, Ralph Douglas."

Al held out his hand. "Pleased to meet you, Mr. Douglas." Bonnie's father's hand was cold and skeletal, but he offered it and let Al shake it. Then Al kneeled next to the chair and brought Bert close, and Bonnie's father put his hand out for Bert to sniff.

"I have a treat if you'd like to give it to him." Al reached in his pocket and pulled out Bert's favorite, a little piece of freeze-dried beef liver. The treats were expensive, so Al saved them for special occasions. He held Bert back by his collar as he handed the treat to Bonnie's father. Bonnie smiled when she saw her father take the treat and hold it out for Bert. Al let go of Bert, and in a second he'd slurped up the treat from Ralph's bony hand.

"I hope he didn't eat your hand, Mr. Douglas."

"Ralph. Call me Ralph." His voice was raspy, hardly more than a whisper. "No, my hand's fine." He kept his hand extended toward Bert, and Bert began to lick his hand with his huge wet tongue. Ralph didn't draw his hand back, but looked tenderly at Bert.

"My Susie," he mumbled, looking up at Bonnie, and then he reached out to Bert and put his frail arms around Bert's shoulders and began to weep.

Bonnie knelt next to her father and held him, laying her head against his thin shoulder and wept with him, the two of them clinging together next to Bert, awash in grief.

Chapter 12

"I'M STARVING. DO YOU WANT TO STOP FOR LUNCH?" BONNIE PULLED out of the care center parking lot and turned right toward town.

"Sure. I could use some lunch. Good idea." The morning rain had stopped and the sun was breaking through the clouds. The way it fell on her hair made him think of an apricot or fresh apple cider with foam the color of coconut. He certainly must be hungry.

"Will Bert be okay in the car?"

"He'll be fine. He'll get a good walk on the beach after we get back." Al reached into the back seat and patted Bert's head.

"And it's my treat."

"You don't need to do that," he protested.

"Well, it wasn't the easiest visit, having two people totally disintegrate." Bonnie kept her eyes on the road. "I never know when I'm going to get blindsided."

"I don't know, grief always seems to me like the weather, like when it's sunny and all of a sudden there's a downpour. And not much warning."

"It's been like that for me. Not always in any predictable stages like denial and anger and whatever. Want to go to the Mexican place? Casa Bonita?"

"Great. I'll have a burrito." Al's mouth began to water, and he couldn't help thinking about how Eleanor didn't want them to eat Mexican food because she didn't think it was healthy.

"And I'll have a margarita." Bonnie laughed. "And some food, too. But I feel like I need a drink."

"I'd like a margarita, too." Al lifted his chin, folding his arms across his chest as he leaned back in the seat. Eleanor had been quite rigid about drinking during the day. She thought it was decadent.

CASA BONITA WAS ONE OF Vashon's oldest restaurants, having been under the same ownership since its opening in 1996. Al thought it was a treat to be going there. He held the door open for Bonnie, and they walked to the back where there was an open booth. Sitting across from her, he looked around at the colorful, hand-painted murals of Mexican scenes. He especially liked the one of a huge black and gold sombrero and wondered what he might look like in a sombrero. In the background, Mexican music played. Al thought the place was cheerful and charming. Too bad Eleanor had never wanted to come here.

A pitcher of water and two glasses were brought to the table, and Bonnie assumed the role of hostess, pouring water for each of them as their server came back with chips and salsa. "I always fill up on all the chips, and then I can't finish what I ordered," she said, grabbing a chip and dipping it in the salsa.

Al sipped his water, then took a chip and dipped it in something that looked like a bean dip that had come with the salsa. "It's true about not eating one chip. Any kind of chip. Probably true about chocolate, too. And maybe a lot of other food, although not kale, I don't think."

He looked at the menu and was trying to decide between the Super Burrito or the Combination where you could combine three things. If he got that, he'd choose an enchilada, a taco and a tostada. He went back and forth, trying to make up his mind between the Super Burrito and the Combination. It was a hard choice.

"I feel like getting a Margarita Grande." Bonnie looked at her watch. "But maybe I shouldn't, it's only 12:30."

"Who cares." Al said. "I'll have one with you."

Bonnie laughed. "Great. That was easy."

"I am easy." Oh hell, what did he mean by that? It just popped out and her dark eyes met his for a second and he thought he felt his face flush. He couldn't be blushing, that was too weird. The restaurant was warm and they were in the back near the kitchen.

"What're you going to have?" she asked.

He quickly looked down at the menu. "I've been going back and forth, but I'm going to have the Super Burrito with beef with a side of extra sour cream and guacamole. I want to make sure I get enough of that. I love sour cream and guacamole."

"Maybe I'll have that, too." Bonnie said, "although maybe it's too much, but probably anything would be. I haven't had any appetite for a long time. In fact I only started to want to eat again the night after we got Tanner out of the ravine. Being scared seemed to shake something up, getting my adrenaline going, I guess."

After they ordered and the drinks came, Bonnie sat back and didn't say anything for a few minutes. Al nibbled at the salt on the rim of the big glass. That was another thing they hardly had at their house: salt. He wondered when he'd stop comparing everything with Eleanor. She certainly had her good qualities. So maybe dwelling on the things he'd never really liked made him feel better. Things he just had accepted because that was the way it was, and you could never argue with Eleanor. Although in truth, he wasn't the arguing type. He'd just shut up and go along—anything to avoid conflict. Peace, that's what he liked—there were enough explosions and drama in his life as a kid to last a lifetime.

"Do you think he thought Bert was Susie?" Bonnie asked.

"I don't know. But does it matter?" Like did it matter whether Eleanor was really a lesbian, whether she and Ruby had sex, or just some kind of platonic love? Who cares? The result was the same: She left.

"I don't know if it does or not." Bonnie sipped from the big glass.

"I just mean that if the interaction with the dog is meaningful to him," he tried to explain, "well, then maybe it doesn't matter whether the dog your father is connecting with is the same dog or not."

"I didn't know what would happen, and even though it was

painful to see his sadness, I have to think that it's better than staying so bottled up that inside everything is numb. Like it's been deadened." She sighed. "I want to believe it helped him, but really I don't know. I guess I'll just have to see." She glanced down and sipped her drink again. "These are huge. I better take it slow." She set the drink on the table and looked up at him. "You seemed so calm when my dad and I were both crying. A lot of people are really uncomfortable with strong emotions like that—they think they have to get you to stop—they feel like they need to fix it for you."

"I'm used to seeing people grieve over the loss of their animals ... I think grief is grief, whether it's the loss of an animal or a person. You have to just let it roll through, like the current in a river. I suppose that's kind of true, too. Like what you just said—I mean if you stop a river, it becomes stagnant and everything starts to die."

The server came and took their order. Al worried what he said about the river sounded flowery, or like he was trying to be philosophical and erudite. He licked the salt around the rim of his glass and took a big gulp of the margarita.

"I'd like to see if my dad remembers that we were there today, if he remembers Bert. If I wait too long, there's probably not much chance of it."

"We could go tomorrow."

"Really? You're sure you don't mind?" Bonnie looked concerned.

"I don't have anything else to do right now."

"I really appreciate your help. My kids were with me last spring when their father died, and they came to help me when I moved up here, but they have their own lives. I haven't gotten to know many people here, mostly the neighbors at Baker's Beach and the staff at the care center."

"It's no trouble. It expands Bert's life from just chasing his frog." The server brought their food and it looked and smelled delicious. Al reached for the hot sauce and put a few drops on the inside of his burrito.

"This is enormous. I don't know if I can eat it all." Bonnie looked at the Super Burrito and laughed.

"Well, you can take home what you don't eat for dinner. Or whatever." Al took a big bite of his burrito. "Mmm ... excellent."

"It really is good." Bonnie agreed. "Big, but good."

"So, where are your kids now?" he asked.

Bonnie took another bite, then wiped her mouth. "My son is a late bloomer ... I guess that's a nice way of saying he's had trouble getting much that's permanent in his life. He's almost forty and he's not married. He's had quite a few girlfriends, but they don't last. And he's had a problem with drugs—we thought mostly smoking pot—but we're not sure. Rob was never able to stick with school. He went to the community college but couldn't finish. He's a very good carpenter and often had work, but when the recession was so bad he moved home. And it was hard on me and my husband, having him there, seeing him floundering. After my husband died and I came up here to help my dad, Rob stayed in Corvallis. He's living in our house. The mortgage was paid off years ago and Rob is supposed to pay the utilities and taxes, and so far he's been able to. I'm hoping that the death of his father might have jarred him into adulthood more. Mike, my husband ... well, he kept bailing Rob out and it was a big problem in our marriage. Rob's got a good construction job now and I pray, although I'm not sure who listens to prayers, but I do it anyway ... I pray he'll keep it." Bonnie picked up her drink, took a sip, then asked, "Do you have kids?"

"No, I had a stepdaughter, but we weren't close." Al looked toward the mural of the sombrero and took a big drink of his margarita. "You have other kids, right?"

"We have two. A boy and a girl. Our daughter Emily teaches at Boston College in the Graduate School of Social Work. She followed in her father's footsteps—Mike was a professor at Oregon State in the College of Public Health and Human Services. Emily's ex-husband was, I mean, is—he's not dead—although there were times I wanted to kill him, I have to say. Figuratively, of course—anyway, he's a poet and a professor of English literature.

They have two children, Mike, who's six, he was named for my husband, and Luke, who's four. Emily's ex-husband used to say that the young women in college were predatory, describing the way they came on to him. But he wasn't very successful in fending them off. It broke my heart when they divorced. It seems like a good marriage can weather an affair, but I'm sure no one understands anyone else's marriage."

"I didn't even understand mine," Al mumbled. Then he took another huge bite of his burrito. When Bonnie didn't say anything, after a minute he said, "I suppose you've heard all about it."

"Not really. Martha Jane had told me your wife had cancer and that you're separated."

"Eleanor has a good prognosis. It's really wonderful—she had lung cancer and the chemo was a nightmare, I'm sure you know."

"I do. Sounds like she was one of the lucky ones, if she's a survivor."

"She really is doing well. And when her treatment finished and her doctor said she could resume a normal life, she decided she didn't want the life we had, and she's living in Portland with a woman she's very close to—they were college roommates and have traveled together and stayed best friends." Al finished his drink and set it back down on the table. "The thing is, I don't know if Eleanor was really a lesbian or exactly what the deal is, but it's kind of like your dad and Bert. Whether or not he thinks it's Susie. I don't think it matters what the label or the category is about love, if there's comfort or some understanding. Eleanor gets something she needs from Ruby and that's who she wants to be with." Al looked at his watch. "It probably would have been a little easier if I hadn't sold my practice."

"That sounds like it could be an understatement." The server brought their check, and Bonnie handed him her credit card.

"It is." Al tried to think of a joke—he didn't want to seem pathetic, but nothing came to mind. In a few minutes the server returned and Bonnie signed the receipt.

"You really didn't have to treat me, but thank you."

"My pleasure," Bonnie said. "Are you sure you really want to try this again, tomorrow?"

"Sure. I was thinking that since Susie was a Lab, your dad or mom probably threw a ball for her a lot."

"Susie was one of those dogs who always went on a walk with the green tennis ball in her mouth. It was great exercise for both my parents, and my father continued to walk with Susie even as his memory and cognitive abilities began to fail."

"If you think it would be a good idea, maybe we could take Bert out with your dad sometime and see if your dad would like to throw a ball for him. Bert loves his frog, but if I left the frog at home, he'd go after a ball for sure." Al worried the minute he proposed it. Now she'd know he didn't have much to do. "Anyway, just a thought."

AL WAS FEELING A LITTLE buzzed from the Margarita Grande when he got home, and he figured that was probably why both he and Bonnie had been so talkative. He also felt sleepy, but he knew he'd better get Bert off to the beach for his walk. If he took a nap first, there was no telling how long he might sleep. The days were getting shorter and he didn't want to nap and then have it be too dark.

On the beach they headed down their usual route along the cove. The tide was coming in, although in the middle of the cove where the beach was at its most narrow point, there was enough of it left for him to get around. The tide would continue to get higher as it got into November and December, and at Baker's Beach they might not be able to walk in the daytime until spring. Al noted he would have to start going to KVI beach or Point Robinson, where the beach was so wide there was usually room to walk no matter how high the tide.

He threw the frog for Bert and watched him leap into the water after it. What a great dog. He had been proud of how calm and steady he was when they visited Bonnie's father. But Al himself hadn't been all that calm when they first got there. He was sure Bonnie hadn't picked up on it, but the minute they walked in, he'd been uncomfortable seeing so many elderly people. People older than he was, anyway. And it wasn't hard to figure out. The place evoked the threat of his own inevitable decline. Seeing animals age had been so much a part of his life that he wasn't one to deny that as a fellow mammal he'd also go downhill. In a matter of time, he knew in some degree, he'd be diminished physically and most likely mentally. It was only the extent of the decline that was unknown at this point. But decline he would, as surely as the sun rose in the east.

True, the place itself had made him uneasy at first. But what he couldn't quite believe was how comfortable he was with Bonnie. Her life seemed to be as tentative and uncertain as his, and maybe that in itself made him feel relaxed. But mostly he was sure it was because she asked him to help her with dogs: first with Tanner and now with Bert and her father. It was a familiar role, and it felt like a brief respite from the emptiness of his life without his practice.

WHEN AL AND BERT WERE coming up the path from the beach, Martha Jane called to them from her porch. "Yoo-hoo! Albert!" Leaning on the railing, with a quilt around her shoulders, she'd just come out to her deck when she saw him. "Can you stop in? I have something to show you!"

Al had trouble hearing her breathy age-softened voice. He trotted over to her yard and looked up at the porch. "Hi, Martha Jane. Is there anything I can help you with?"

"I'm fine, but oh, yes, Albert. Please come in for a minute if you can. I have the best news! It's for you, dear."

"Sure. Let me take Bert home and I'll be right there."

In a few minutes Al was back, sitting across from Martha Jane in her kitchen with Maria Montessori on his lap.

"The kettle will be ready in a minute. I still call it the kettle, but actually my grandchildren gave me a gadget for my birthday." She pointed to an electric teapot on her counter.

"I didn't know you had a birthday recently. If I'd known I'd have baked you a cake." Al smiled. Martha Jane always gave him a lift.

"I didn't want anyone to know since there was such a big celebration for my ninetieth. We just had a quiet little party for only my family in Seattle."

"No fireworks then." Al stroked the cat.

"Wasn't that just awful? What a vain man to do that and I heard about what happened to Tanner. Thank goodness you were able to help, Albert." Martha Jane shuffled over to the counter and got two mugs from the cupboard and several tea bags, which she set in front of the electric tea pot. "This gadget is amazing. That's what my grandson says all the time. Everything he likes is amazing. It used to be awesome, but now it's amazing. Well, this little number boils the water in exactly ... oh, I guess I forgot the number of seconds, or is it minutes? Well, whatever, no matter. It's very speedy and I love it. It automatically shuts off when the water boils. I can't figure out how it knows that, but it does." She put the tea bags in the mugs and poured the hot water. "Oh my, I didn't ask you what kind of tea you wanted. This is Celestial Seasonings, the one with the tiger. Bengal Spice. I think they must have named it that because the tea is heavenly. I suppose I've remarked on that before."

"I love that kind. It's perfect." Al put the cat down and got the mugs and carried them to the table. It took Martha Jane a little while to lower herself into the chair. He knew her arthritis made some movement difficult, but it inspired him how cheerful she always seemed. He thought about his reaction when he'd walked into Vashon Community Care. It couldn't just have been about old folks. Martha Jane's aging hadn't ever made him uncomfortable, but then he knew her. Although the Wabash Cannonball lady seemed pretty upbeat, too, and he had enjoyed meeting her.

And then it dawned on him. When he first walked in the facility, a few of the women he'd seen reminded him of his grandmother: a cold, critical, unfeeling woman who didn't like him or his brother (although she preferred Jamie, as everyone did.) But she teemed with resentment at being stuck taking care of them while their parents were touring, which seemed like most of the time. His grandmother wasn't physically abusive. She dutifully took care of him, but it was always with a strong undercurrent of hostility, not hiding what a burden he was to her. Al grew up thinking the only way he could please her would be if he didn't exist.

The Beachside was laid out on the kitchen table, and Martha Jane held it up. "Albert, did you see this?" She turned to a page on the inside of the paper and shoved it toward him. "Look at the article halfway down the page there."

"The one that says 'Ober Needs Volunteers'?"

"Yes. They're looking for people to bring their dogs to the Lunch Buddy program at Ober Elementary School. It's a special program for kids who are having difficulty reading and they read the book to a dog. And the dog just has to be able to sit quietly. I thought of you and Bert immediately!"

Al smiled as he read the article. "Thanks. I hadn't seen the article, but truthfully, I might not have picked up on it if I had. I've never thought I was that good with kids. Maybe because I don't have any of my own, but you know ...." He paused to think, "Maybe with Bert there, well—maybe this could be something useful we could do."

"Do you have this week's paper at home?" Martha Jane asked.

"Eleanor cancelled our subscription when she moved, so I try to pick it up when I'm in town, but I can't remember if I got it this week."

"Here take mine." She handed him the paper. "I've read it all."

Al bent down and kissed her cheek. "Thanks."

"You will look into it, won't you, dear?"

"I will."

"Promise?" Martha Jane put her hand on his arm.

"Absolutely." Had it been so obvious to her that he was over there next door treading water? Al thought he'd been putting up a better front than that. But he was grateful to Martha Jane for pointing out the article. Judging the contest was over, and he couldn't make a career of taking Bert to visit Bonnie's dad. Having a regular volunteer job might help him get his act together. Maybe being a Lunch Buddy would be a start.

When Al got home he re-read the article and copied the phone number of the person to contact at the school. Her name was Dodie Solback, and the article said to call her at school Monday through Friday anytime between 9:00 and 3:30. What was today? Since he'd retired, Al often lost track of the days of the week. He pulled out his phone to look at the calendar, something he rarely did since he didn't have anywhere he had to be, except to his surprise he saw that tomorrow he did have something: his appointment for his yearly check-up with Dr. Chan. He'd forgotten all about it. Was his brain getting fuzzy? Maybe he was unraveling. Of course he was. He knew that myelin, the crucial white fatty coating of the nerve fibers that make the connections in the brain work, begins to break down around age forty, and after that as people age, their neural network declines at an accelerating rate. It is all downhill, like a spool of thread unwinding, rolling down Mount Rainier, picking up speed as it goes. But there is normal aging and then there is Bonnie's father and all the others like him. Fourteen million by year 2030, or was it 2040 or 2050? He forgot the year when he'd read about it in *The New York Times*, or was it *The Seattle Times*? His myelin was unraveling for sure.

He'd better call Bonnie to tell her he couldn't go to see her father tomorrow. Al flipped to the contacts on his phone, but instead of calling, he put the phone down and wandered to the TV. Turning it on, he flipped through the channels. He looked for *Animal Planet*. Sometimes he liked that. Then on a Spanish channel he saw some people arguing—the woman was very beautiful and she was furious at a handsome guy. On the food channel there was some kind of a competition going on, and it looked like the judges were making the contestant chefs feel bad. Al realized he hadn't had dinner yet and went to the kitchen. He opened the refrigerator. Then he closed it. What the hell, he had to call her. Time to quit farting around.

"Bonnie?'

"Hi Al."

"About tomorrow … I have to go to the doctor."

She didn't say anything.

"Bonnie?"

"I'm here."

He had trouble hearing her. "Are you still there?" It seemed like she was whispering. Now maybe his hearing was going. Was there something wrong? She sounded odd, nervous or worried or something. Although maybe she was furious he was cancelling, and she was gritting her teeth trying not to yell at him, or slam down the phone. He looked out the window to see if there was a light on at her house.

"I'm here ... you said 'doctor'?" she repeated. "Are you ... are you alright?"

"Oh sure. It's just my six-month check up with my cardiologist and I completely forgot about it when I said I could bring Bert tomorrow."

Bonnie laughed.

"What's so funny?"

"Nothing. You sounded so serious I just ...."

"I felt bad about cancelling. I hate to do that." Al paced in front of the TV.

"Not to worry. You can bring Bert another time."

"Tomorrow's Tuesday—how 'bout Wednesday?" Was he sounding too eager? Like all he had going in his life was a visit to the doctor.

"Great. Dad's usually more alert in the morning."

"I'm sorry about this," he said, nervously.

She laughed again. "Really, it's not a big deal."

They agreed to meet at ten, and Bonnie insisted on driving again. Al was surprised by the huge relief he felt. Maybe he thought any woman would get pissed off if he made a mistake.

CHAPTER 13

IT SEEMED THAT EVER SINCE ELEANOR LEFT, AL WAS SURPRISED BY THE feelings that crept up on him. Maybe his work had consumed such a great deal of his emotional energy that he hadn't reacted that much to anything else. He did think of himself as a reflective person, although he wasn't sure his conclusions about anything were particularly insightful. Especially about women. But he wondered if losing his marriage had somehow jarred his emotions. Maybe he was like an old can of soda that suddenly got shook up and started to fizz unexpectedly. Whatever it was, when he parked in the garage at the Swedish Medical Center and was walking in the dim light toward the elevator, he started to cry. Not great racking sobs, or anything like that, but his throat got tight and tears filled his eyes and spilled down his cheeks. He had to stop to blow his nose. The memory was powerful. Eleanor standing next to the gurney as it was put in the aid car and the medics standing above him, the priority boarding on the ferry, then there was a blank—and then Eleanor was holding his hand, quietly, calmly telling him that he was going to be alright. And he believed her. Eleanor was not a bullshit kind of person. She had been so strong and reliable. You could set your watch by her. The only other time he'd had surgery was when he was eight years old. He had his tonsils out and his mother and father never came to the hospital. They were in a play somewhere. It didn't seem strange to him at the time; they were always touring. But it had been so nice to wake up from surgery and find Eleanor there. Had he ever told her how much it meant to him?

He only had to wait about fifteen minutes to see Dr. Chan, and his check-up went well. Al told him about some of the fluttering he'd had after carrying Tanner out of the ravine and sometimes these strange feelings of apprehension. Dr. Chan was reassuring. "Al, one of the problems for heart patients is that they often become anxious with every twinge. It's a normal response. But you're in great shape and everything checks out. We'll look at the lab results and I'll call you if there's a concern, but your last blood work was excellent, and I expect the same this time. Just make an appointment for six months, and I won't need to see you until then." Dr. Chan shook his hand. "Give my best to your wife."

Al stood at the window of the appointment desk. Six months would be April. He should make it for April Fools' Day. He felt like a fool, not telling Dr. Chan that Eleanor had left him. He'd even asked him how he was doing, if there were any big changes in the past six months and Al had said everything was fine. It had seemed too personal to talk to him about what happened with Eleanor, which Al thought was kind of funny, since Dr. Chan had an intimate relationship with his heart.

He had some time before the next ferry back to the island, so Al decided to stop at HappyPet in West Seattle. He hadn't been able to find a tennis ball at the house for Bonnie's father to throw for Bert. He used to have one, but it had probably gotten misplaced when he moved to Baker's Beach. Maybe he could also get some new special treats that Mr. Douglas could give Bert so they could really bond.

The minute he entered HappyPet, Al felt a little disloyal to the pet supply store on the island. He tried to shop locally whenever he could, but since he'd sold his practice he'd avoided the island store, knowing he'd undoubtedly run into his former clients and would just get pissed off that he couldn't be their vet anymore. Not only did going in HappyPet make him feel disloyal, but the amount of stuff in the huge store almost made him dizzy.

The myriad of choices of food, equipment and supplies was over-whelming. The store also had a large section where they sold tropical fish, birds, little white mice and rats, bunnies, hamsters, and gerbils. Al never liked to see animals living in cages. It made him sad, and as soon as he found the treat section and the dog toys, he bought what he needed and got out of there.

WHEN AL DROVE ON THE ferry to head back to the island, he was suddenly very hungry. After parking his truck toward the front of the car deck, he jumped out and went up to the passenger deck and headed straight for the food service galley. He got a muffin and coffee, then looked for a seat. There were single chair seats in the middle of the boat, and along the windows on either side were rows of upholstered benches facing each other with tables between the benches, like the dining cars on a train. Across from the stairs to the car deck there was an empty one, and Al sat on the bench next to the window where looking south, he could see Mount Rainier. He set his coffee on the table and took a bite of the muffin. Blueberry. Pretty good. Closing his eyes for a minute, he chewed slowly. The relief of his clean bill of health began to sink in. For the past few months he felt like he'd been moving in quicksand, pretending to be a person, when he felt like some-thing not exactly human. Like a vegetable ... nothing juicy, not a tomato, more of a potato or a turnip. And he hadn't told Dr. Chan about all the crap he'd been eating. He sure hoped the lab tests wouldn't show that he'd messed himself up. He'd had a few stabs at trying to eat better, but maybe he should really try now. Al opened his eyes and took a big bite of the muffin while he mar-veled at the splendor of Mount Rainier. This wasn't the first clear day in the past few months when the mountain had been out, but he realized that he'd hardly noticed, having been stuck in turnip mode. Al finished the muffin and was thinking about going back to the galley for a glazed donut. Just a little more living on the edge until he knew the results of his lab work. A few more days of indulgence couldn't hurt anything, could it? Should he? Or shouldn't he? Al sipped his coffee and looked at the mountain, trying to decide about the donut.

"Al!" Evelyn Murdoch stood by the stairs of the car deck and marched over to him.

"Hi, Evelyn," Al gestured to the bench across from him. "Care to have a seat?"

"No. I don't," she hissed. "How *could* you, Al?"

"How could I what?" He looked up at the little curly white-haired woman, her teeth clenched as if in any minute she'd lunge at him, snapping and growling.

"After all I've done!"

Al stared at her and set his coffee down.

"Didn't it mean anything to you?"

He leaned back, folding his arms across his chest while continuing to stare at her.

"Don't give me that blank look. The painting, the blueberry pie, the plum jam, the organic dog treats—"

Al nodded and breathed slowly to exude calm as one would in the presence of a crazy person.

"I even gave you a hint, for God's sake. Reminding you about the little ridge on Olivia's nose and showing you the little Santa hat I made!" She glared at him and hovered over him, fuming.

Al couldn't think of what to say. An earthquake came to mind, and how seconds seem like days while everything is swaying and rolling around. It had been like that in the Nisqually Earthquake of 2001, and Al remembered grabbing Louie, a big Irish terrier and getting under the clinic doorway with him. (Louie was a great dog—he was healing up nicely from having a little tumor removed from between the pads on his paw.) It had been one of the largest recorded earthquakes in Washington state history. He remembered being shocked when he learned it had lasted only forty-five seconds.

"So you have nothing to say for yourself?" She spat out the accusation.

Finally Al said, "I'm sorry, but I don't really understand—"

"The calendar, you idiot! Olivia was supposed to be MISS DECEMBER!" Then she spun around and stomped off.

Al watched Evelyn Murdoch charge around the corner to the stairs to the car deck. He took a bite of his muffin, wondering if he was supposed to run after her and apologize. Whenever Eleanor was mad at him, an occurrence which happened with great regularity, he always ended up apologizing. Mostly just to keep the peace. Then she'd accuse him of making an insincere apology, which of course, was true. And she berated him for not discussing anything, but there never seemed to be much point to it. Al wondered about his impulse to apologize to Evelyn. Force of habit, he supposed, his knee-jerk response to a woman who was angry with him.

Except he had nothing to apologize for, dammit. How did he know she was trying to buy a win for Olivia with plum jam? Actually, that jam was pretty good. So was the blueberry pie. Bert also liked the organic dog treats. And Al loved the painting of the golden retriever that she had given him after Cassidy had died, but it had nothing to do with the contest—she'd given it to him long before he was appointed judge. Why did she throw that in? He hoped she didn't expect him to give that painting back. Al began to feel quite indignant. He'd done his best to be fair and impartial when he chose the dogs to be on the calendar, and he was not the kind of person who could be bought off. He also began to wonder if she'd ever liked him. Maybe the kisses and flirting had all been to convince him to pick Olivia to be Miss December. Al didn't know what to make of it, and it didn't take him long to decide he would just ignore the whole thing. If he ran into Evelyn at Thriftway or wherever, he'd be polite and pretend this conversation never happened. That was the best plan. He finished his muffin and went back to the galley for the donut.

AFTER HE GOT HOME AL took Bert to Agren Park and threw the new tennis ball for him. It was probably completely unnecessary to practice for Bert's visit with Bonnie's father, but he wanted to check out the park before they arrived in the morning, as he hadn't been there in ages. Agren was the only official off-leash park on the island, and the park department provided a dispenser with complimentary dog poo bags. There was also a Sani-can for the people, which would be good in case Mr. Douglas might need to go. The beautiful wooded park was situated on thirty acres with trails that wound through the dense conifer stands. The south portion of the park was level, with a sports field that was used for softball and soccer, encircled by a crushed rock path. Bonnie's father seemed so frail that Al didn't think taking him to any of the beaches would be wise. Walking on sand and rocks wouldn't be good for a person who wasn't that steady on his feet, and at the park Al also wouldn't have to worry about Bert swimming and shaking water on the old man.

Funny how he thought of Mr. Douglas as an old man. What did he think he was at sixty-seven, a spring chicken? Spring chicken, that was an expression his grandmother used to say, no one said that anymore. Besides wouldn't he be a rooster? Although he didn't think he'd ever heard of a spring rooster. Al threw the ball a few more times for Bert, then headed back to the truck. The chicken thoughts made him hungry, and he wanted to stop at Thriftway and pick up one of those nice roasted chickens they had for his dinner. Usually when he left for the grocery store from Baker's Beach he checked with Martha Jane to see if she needed him to pick up anything for her. He might as well check with her, he thought, taking his cell phone from his pocket.

"Hello, Albert." Martha Jane answered right away. "Isn't it clever how I knew it was you!"

"You bet. Very clever." Al laughed. She always lifted his spirits. Every time he called and Martha Jane read his name on the caller ID, she had the same response, and Al found it charming. He actually didn't know if she'd forgotten that her phone could identify the caller and was surprised to see the name, or if she expected to see the name but still found it a delight. It probably didn't matter. Either way she got a kick out of it.

"I took Bert to Agren and I'm on my way to Thriftway and wondered if I could pick anything up for you?"

"That's so kind of you, dear. I think I'm all set, but let me think for a minute …."

She didn't say anything and Al pressed the phone to his ear and wondered if Martha Jane had dozed off. "Martha Jane? Are you there?"

"Oh, now I remember. I don't need anything at the store, but I've been meaning to call you and now here you are. I'm going to be out of town all Thanksgiving week and I wanted to ask you if you could take care of Maria Montessori?"

"I'd be happy to."

"You'll be staying on the island?"

"Right." Al hadn't given any thought to Thanksgiving. Last year they'd spent it in Portland with Eleanor's daughter and son-in-law. And that sure wasn't going to happen this year. He couldn't see being one of the those divorced couples that still spent holidays together. What was the point? If you liked each other's company so much that you wanted to be together on the holidays, why get divorced? Of course, he and Eleanor weren't officially divorced yet, but he still couldn't imagine being invited to Ruth Ann and Robert's. Ruth Ann had barely tolerated him after he'd told her he thought Robert was a jerk when they'd been separated. Hard to imagine that she'd want to see him now that he and her mother were divorcing.

"There won't be much you need to do for Maria, just make sure she has food and water, and take care of the litter box. She doesn't go out much. And she likes you."

"I like her, too. She's a wonderful cat."

"Thank you, Albert. I feel very secure leaving her with you."

"Thanks." He felt a lump in his throat. What was wrong with him?

"Howie and Mark are going to be with Howie's family. So I guess you and Bonnie will be holding down the fort at Baker's Beach. I'm so relieved you'll be here. I was upset thinking I might have to board Maria somewhere. Thank you, Albert, dear."

"My pleasure."

When he got off the phone, he started the truck, but instead of putting it in reverse, he sat there for a minute and then pulled out his phone. Maybe Bonnie needed something at the store. She was a neighbor, too.

"Bonnie? It's Al."

"Hi Al."

"I'm on my way to Thriftway, and I just wondered if I could pick anything up for you? I just checked with Martha Jane and she doesn't need anything … I'm getting a few things and … well, actually I'm picking up a chicken …."

"Oh thanks, I don't need anything. But it's nice of you to ask."

"Do you like chicken?"

"I do."

"Some people don't eat chicken. Only vegetables. But I remember now from the Mexican place, you eat a lot of stuff. Wanna come for dinner? I'm having chicken." Al turned the motor off and looked down at the floor and began scratching his head. What was he doing? First he practically weeps because Martha Jane trusts him to take care of her cat and now he blurts out a dinner invitation to Bonnie. He was going off the rails.

"I can bring a salad."

"What?"

"When I come to dinner. I'd love to come—I'll bring a salad."

"Oh. Wonderful."

"Al?"

"Right, a salad. That's great. Right."

"What time?"

"Oh well, let's see." He looked at his watch. "Would seven work?"

"Sure, thanks. See you then."

Al put on B.B. King and bounced out of the parking lot along the park road. He turned left on Bank Road and headed toward town. B.B. was singing "Playin' with My Friends." Bonnie liked blues. Maybe he could put on B.B. King while they ate the chicken.

CHAPTER 14

❋

As he drove in the parking lot, Al noticed two teenage girls sitting at a card table outside the Thriftway entrance. It looked like it was a bake sale, probably a fund-raiser for something. There were often people fund-raising for various organizations in front of Thriftway, and it had been one of Eleanor's pet peeves. She always said she'd like to be able to go to the store without being accosted for this, that, or the other and made to feel guilty she didn't support their causes. And when they're selling food, Eleanor said, "you have no idea of how sanitary the conditions are when they prepared it—there are no inspections, no health department overseeing it, no regulations whatsoever. You just don't know what you're getting."

Ever since Eleanor left, Al had made it a point to support all the fund-raisers. Especially the bake sales. He found a parking space in front of Eyeland Optical, and as soon as he parked his truck, he trotted over to the girls' table. They were selling cookies to raise money for their senior class trip; various kinds were set out on paper plates covered with plastic wrap. Al bought a plate of chocolate chip. It would be nice to serve them for dessert tonight. He was sure Bonnie would like them. Everyone liked chocolate chip cookies, he thought, as he got a cart and headed into the store.

In the deli section Al studied the roast chickens. He wasn't sure, but he figured one would probably be enough for the two of them. He picked out a nice plump golden brown chicken and put it in the cart. Bonnie was bringing a salad, but he didn't think chicken, salad, and chocolate chip cookies would be enough. Maybe he should get some vegetables and rice or potatoes, and maybe bread. If he made a baked potato, it would be good to have all the stuff that goes in them like bacon bits, chives and sour cream. But then Al remembered the twice baked potatoes with cheese in the deli case. You could just warm them up. He smiled, very pleased he'd thought of those.

Al was at the deli case looking at the potatoes, when someone came up behind him and tapped his arm. He turned to see Marilyn Henderson looking up at him.

"Hi, Marilyn." Al smiled. "How's Eloise?"

"I have to talk to you, Al." Her voice was low and quiet. "Meet me outside in ten minutes."

Al looked at his watch, "I don't know if I'll be ...." But Marilyn had gone. He caught sight of her just as she went whooshing past the seafood section. Wonder what she wants? He hoped Eloise was okay and that Marilyn wasn't anxious about those benign tumors again. She seemed rather fixated on those tumors. He wondered what it would take to get her to relax about them. Some dogs were given Prozac when they had dementia and were extremely anxious, sundowning—pacing at night, that sort of thing. Perhaps Marilyn was the one who could use it. After getting the potatoes, he went to the produce section to get a vegetable. Something green. He could steam some asparagus, or green beans, maybe spinach. Although not everyone liked spinach. Al decided on green beans. He took a plastic bag from the produce bag stand, and went to the bin where they had the beans. He wasn't sure how many to cook, and he stood in front of the beans for a while thinking about it. He decided two big handfuls would be enough, and as he was filling the bag, Marilyn did a drive-by with her cart and said, "Be there, Al."

There was an ominous note in her voice that worried him. Could it be possible that he'd misdiagnosed Eloise and the tumors had been malignant? Al worried all the way to the check-out, and as soon as he paid for the groceries, he hurried out to find Marilyn. He stood by the door, but didn't see any sign of her. Maybe he should walk through the parking lot in case she was waiting in her car with Eloise. She was a cute little dog, and he was sure those tumors were benign, but then you never know. He had an awful feeling in the pit of his stomach as he remembered a case of Addison's disease he had misdiagnosed when he was first starting out. When the blood work appeared normal, he should have gone a step farther with special tests—but didn't. The dog died and Al still felt terrible. He'd never gotten over it.

"Over here, Al." Marilyn motioned to him from a bench outside the store near the stacked grocery carts. Al went over to her, and she gestured to the bench. He guessed she expected him to sit next to her, so Al sat down.

"Al, I think it's important that we process what happened between us."

What was she taking about? Process? Process what? Eleanor had always accused him of avoiding conflict, of being vague, and not really present and direct. Maybe he should try being direct. Al cleared his throat. "I don't know what you're talking about, Marilyn."

"That's what's so sad, Al. Or I should say, I feel sad about it, Al. I need to take ownership of this."

"Ownership of what?" He held his cloth grocery bag on his lap. The chicken was still warm, and he hoped the grease wouldn't leak out.

"You see, Al. I knew that it was too early for you, with Eleanor just having left. But I recognized we'd always been kindred spirits, Al. I remember, on the Audubon bird walk, how you looked at me Al, and the time you always spent with me when I saw you at the clinic, Al. I knew you gave me extra time and it warmed my heart."

He didn't know how to get rid of her at the clinic. He was never good at that. And why did she keep repeating his name the way salespeople do?

"That night at my home, I could tell you felt the magic of our connection. When you looked into my eyes, I could see your soul."

She sounds like Bush and Putin. Al shifted his weight and held the grocery sack a little tighter on his lap.

"So you see, Al. It was very hurtful to me ... I mean, *I* was very hurt when you disrespected Eloise."

"Um, how did I do that exactly?" What the hell was going on here? He'd always done his best with all his patients.

"Well, the calendar, of course. I didn't assume which month she'd be, although I thought Miss May would have been perfect. But any month would have been fine, but when you completely passed her over, well, it was, I mean ... *I* felt like it was a knife in the heart."

"I did my best to be fair and impartial with that contest."

"You sound like Fox News," she snapped.

"I think they say they're fair and—balanced."

"Yeah, well they're full of shit, just like you," Marilyn almost bit his head off and then she stopped, closed her eyes and lay the backs of her hands on her knees and opened her palms. She inhaled deeply with her mouth closed, then opened her mouth and exhaled slowly.

Al clutched the bag with the chicken, and wondered what he was doing there. Maybe he could tiptoe away while Marilyn was meditating. He looked at his watch while she continued to slowly breath in and then slowly exhale. He leaned forward, inching slowly off the bench.

Marilyn opened her eyes and glared at him. "We're not through here, Dr. Paugh," she hissed.

"I don't know what I can say to make you feel better. I did the best I could with that contest." Al tried to be rational.

"Yeah, well your best isn't good enough. And you're not a good enough vet either, because Dr. Kincaid thinks Eloise needs to have her tumors checked on a regular basis so I'm taking her in every other week. At least he knows when to be concerned!"

Al stood up.

"Where do you think you're going?" she growled.

"Home. I'm going home, Marilyn." Al turned and ran to his truck. He wanted to tell her that he hoped she and that crook Kincaid would be very happy together. What a scam, having her come every few weeks so he could feel Eloise's tumors and tell

Marilyn everything was okay to the tune of a hundred bucks or more. Shit. Al headed toward his truck. His life was turning into looney-tunes with that stupid calendar. And to think how seriously he'd taken it, and how much it had meant to him to be the judge. What a fool. Al saw that the high school girls were still selling cookies so he bought another plate, and then went back to his truck.

Marilyn was still sitting on the bench in front of Thriftway, looking like she was continuing to meditate with her hands, palms up, resting on her knees as Al backed his truck out of his parking space. Driving out of the lot, he had to pass in front of her, and he tried to just look straight ahead. But out of the corner of his eye he saw her open her eyes, glare at him and flip him the bird.

Heading home, Al wondered if Bonnie had any expectations of him that he didn't understand. He hated to think that Eleanor had been right that he didn't get it about women. But there was no denying things had turned into a mess with Marilyn and Evelyn. They were both extremely pissed off at him. Could there be anything he hadn't picked up on with Bonnie? She didn't have a dog entered in the calendar contest so that wasn't a problem, and she seemed grateful that he'd helped her find Tanner and then brought Bert to visit her Dad. Bonnie was his neighbor. They were neighborly. That was very nice. And they were both trying to put their lives back together and each could use a friend. Al really didn't want to mess it up with her. Not that he'd wanted to with Evelyn and Marilyn, it had just come out of nowhere. What bothered him the most was the fact that he never saw it coming. He glanced at his watch. Only an hour and a half before Bonnie came. All he had to do was steam the beans and warm up the potatoes. That wouldn't take too long. But he'd have to check out how the house looked.

Al couldn't exactly remember when he'd actually cleaned the house. It had been so liberating when he was first on his own not to worry about it. To just do as he pleased. He'd been oblivious to dust and dog hair and dirt tracked in. To scummy sinks and toilets. He did sort of keep up with the dishes, washing them when he ran out of clean ones, but that was about it. When he got home and carried in the groceries, he looked around and realized the house looked terrible. Very terrible. He put the chicken, beans, and the potatoes in the refrigerator and stared at the mess. Where to start? It was a little overwhelming.

Finally, he decided to start in the bathroom and then work back to the living room and then do the kitchen last. He ran to the bathroom and picked up all the towels from the floor. Maybe she'd want a clean towel by the sink if she wanted to wash her hands. But he didn't think he had a clean towel. The sink and the mirror over it had shaving cream stuck to it and hardened globs of toothpaste and little hairs everywhere. He went to the kitchen and looked under the sink but didn't find any bathroom cleaner so he grabbed the dish soap. He squirted some in the toilet and all around the sink and then scrubbed it all with one of the towels that had been on the floor. He shook out one of the hand towels he'd grabbed from the floor and hung it neatly next to the sink, then took the others and dumped them in the corner of his bedroom. Bonnie would only be in the kitchen and the living room so he could put everything in the bedroom. Al picked up all the old *Beachsides* and other papers and the dirty dishes he wouldn't have time to wash and dumped everything in the corner next to the bed on top of the towels. Then he got the vacuum from the hall closet and tore around the living room with it. Bert seemed shocked by all the activity and hid under the bed.

Al put the vacuum away and jumped in the shower, but he was in such a hurry that he forgot to duck his head. *Damn!* He rubbed his head for a minute, swearing, and then quickly washed and got out of the shower, but the only towel was the small one he'd put neatly by the sink. Dripping wet, he ran out of the bathroom to get a towel from the pile on the bedroom floor, but his feet flew out from under him just outside the bathroom door, which sent him crashing and he landed in a wet heap. Al lay on the floor and took deep breaths, trying not to panic as he thought of himself stuck there, unable to get up as Bonnie came over and knocked several times and called his name, and finally because the door was unlocked, she'd come in and would find him wet and naked lying outside the bathroom on the floor. He closed his eyes, remembering how she'd helped him when he cut himself when they got Tanner. She was a nurse after all, she'd know what to do. She'd undoubtedly seen many naked people. A hospice nurse so she'd seen many naked old men. She was very gentle, he remembered. A kind, soft gentle touch. Maybe he should just lie there and see what happened. Al rubbed his head. Staying there in a naked wet heap waiting for Bonnie to come to him ... *what was he thinking?* Maybe he had a screw loose from the fall. Al felt the back of his head where he'd hit the floor. He'd probably have a little knot but there wasn't any blood or anything. Slowly, he struggled to his feet. His tailbone hurt, but other than that and the bump on his head, he guessed he was okay.

There was a full length mirror on the back of the bedroom door. As Al got up he looked at himself. He'd gained weight. He pulled his stomach in and wondered what he should wear. He never thought about what he was going to wear. Although he had found clean clothes to wear that morning to go to the doctor, but the pants and shirt he'd worn were crumpled in the corner. Al looked in his closet for some clean pants, but most everything was on the closet floor. He finally just put on his jeans and was able to find a clean short-sleeved summer shirt. It was white with red stripes, Al looked in the mirror. He thought it looked dumb. And it was straining the buttons over his stomach. Why was he worrying about this? What was the matter with him? Maybe those women furious with him had bothered him more than he knew.

In the kitchen, he grabbed the roll of paper towel, ran to the floor outside the bathroom, got down on his hands and knees and frantically wiped up the water. Then he ran back to the kitchen and wiped up the kitchen table. He hadn't realized how much food had gotten stuck to it. Al looked at his watch. It was seven. She'd be there any minute. He quickly rinsed the dishes and put them in the dishwasher, then set the table. He realized he didn't have any napkins, so he pulled off two pieces of paper towel off the roll and put them under the forks by each plate. The house he was renting had nice dishes and he was glad of that. They were a glazed earth-color pottery, kind of sophisticated. He found the salt and pepper shakers. They were also kind of classy, made out of pewter, in the shape of two little birds. He put them in the middle of the table. But then he realized he hadn't thought about drinks. There was a bottle of Cabernet he hadn't yet opened and some sort of generic white table wine in the refrigerator, and lots of beer. She'd had wine that night at her house. She'd probably like that better than beer. He was getting the wine glasses down from cupboard when he heard a knock on the door and ran to let her in.

"Hi, sorry I'm a few minutes late." Bonnie held a salad bowl and a small decanter. "Shall I put this here for now?" She motioned toward the kitchen.

"Sure. Great. Martha Jane told me once she thought it was rude when people came right on time, exactly on the dot. She thought it was wasn't nice since people were never ready."

Bonnie laughed and followed him to the kitchen. "Well, then I'm quite polite by her standards." She put the bowl and decanter on the counter.

"Would you like a drink? I'm afraid I don't have a big selection. There's some Cabernet and white wine and beer in the refrigerator."

"I like red wine, thanks. I remember when people thought you should only have white wine with chicken and fish. But now it doesn't matter. Not that I ever cared about that anyway."

Al opened the wine, and poured them each a glass.

"Thanks." She smiled and held up her glass. "Cheers."

"Cheers." He clinked his glass against hers. "Do you want to go in the living room or should I start dinner now while we have our wine? I just have to steam the beans. Do you like beans?"

"I do."

"They're green."

"I like green beans." Bonnie took a sip of her wine.

"And I bought those twice baked potatoes they have at Thriftway, so I just have to warm them up. I wasn't exactly sure how long, though. And the chicken is all cooked, I could heat it up or we could just eat it cold." He was sure he sounded ridiculous. Like he didn't know what he was doing and he wanted her to decide everything. Al rubbed the back of his head where a little knot was forming.

"I actually prefer cold chicken. Sounds strange, I know. Maybe I'm just a cold person—"

"You're not cold."

"Thank you. Well, I'm happy to just sit here in the kitchen and I'd guess the potatoes should take about fifteen minutes." Bonnie put her wine on the table and turned a chair to face him and then sat down.

"Probably at three-fifty, I'd say. The temperature. For the oven." He wanted to sound more capable. Al went to the refrigerator and took out the potatoes, beans and chicken and set them on the counter. At least he was good at carving the chicken. He took a drink of his wine and then got a colander, put it in the sink and began washing the beans. "This is the first time I've had anyone to dinner since I moved here."

"Well, I'm honored." Bonnie looked out the window. "Actually, I haven't had anyone over to my place. I think you were my first guest the night Tanner ran away and that wasn't exactly planned."

"I thought I planned this dinner, but I don't have any appetizers or nuts or chips or anything to have with the wine." He went to the cupboard and began scrounging around. "I think I have some Fritos."

She laughed. "I'm fine, really." Bonnie looked out the window again. "You have a nice view here."

"All the houses at Baker's Beach have good views, I think. And I actually like it a lot better than the Burton Loop where I used to live."

Bonnie nodded. "It's been good for me to be here. I'm grateful to Maggie for suggesting it. Even in the winter when it's so gray and rainy, I still love it. Are you from this area originally? Most people seem to be from somewhere else."

Al got a big pot from the cupboard, filled it with water and put it on the stove and turned on the burner. He brought his glass and the bottle of Cabernet to the table. "I was born in Connecticut. New Haven."

"Oh, were your parents with Yale? My dad was a professor at the University of Washington. I was born and raised in Seattle— one of the few around, I guess."

He pulled out a chair and sat across from her. "My parents met at the Yale School of Drama and I think my older brother was probably the reason they got married young. Not planned, I'm pretty sure. Both of them were in theater; my dad was a director."

"I think you mentioned your mother was an actress, which I thought was fascinating."

"More wine?"

"Sure, thanks." She held out her glass.

Al filled her glass, then his. "Honestly, it was a hard, uncertain life and neither one of them achieved the level they wanted. My mother was often an understudy or had minor roles, or supporting roles at best, and most of the directing jobs my father got were in small shows in upstate New York or Cape Cod, so he was gone a lot. I don't think they were people who should have had kids. Mostly I remember being sent off to our grandmother's."

"You mentioned a brother, were there other kids?"

"Just me and my older brother." Al felt the knot on the back of his head. He didn't want to talk about Jamie. It was not a happy subject. He hadn't seen him in fifteen years and that was fine with him. He noticed the water for the beans beginning to boil and realized that if he put them in now, they'd be done before he'd warmed up the potatoes, so he got up and turned off the burner and went to the oven and set the temperature.

"Hi, Bert." Bonnie leaned down and patted Bert, who had finally decided to come out from the bedroom. "Compared to your background, mine is kind of boring. I lived in the same house in Seattle from when I was born until I went to college."

"From my perspective that sounds very nice. Although we did have a little more stability when my father got a job in the Midwest. He was the artistic director of a regional theater in Columbus, Ohio. It didn't pay well, of course, but it was steady.

But it didn't last long. He had a lot of conflict with the managing director and he finally branched off and founded the Theatre of Northeastern Ohio, outside of Cleveland. We moved when I was about six. We had a small house in Sandusky, Ohio, and our grandmother took care of us most of the time. Both my parents worked their butts off, fund-raising, writing grants, schmoozing with rich theatre patrons. It was a repertory company and brought in a name actor several times a year. When I was in high school, they produced *Picnic*. It had been a huge Broadway hit in the fifties—in fact, Paul Newman's Broadway debut was in that play."

"I didn't know that. But it was a movie, too, as I remember—because I wanted to see it when I was a kid because it had such a nice name ... *Picnic* ... I thought of hot dogs and softball games and lemonade. But my parents wouldn't let me see it. I suppose because it was too sexual or something."

Al put the potatoes on a baking sheet. "Well, it turned out too sexual for my mother because my father took up with the ingénue." He sat across from Bonnie while he waited for the oven. "On a good day, my mother was someone who could turn a minor setback into a ten-alarm fire. So you can imagine the explosion."

"I can." Bonnie sipped her wine. "But at least you had your grandmother, for some stability."

"I suppose, but talk about cold. She was glacial, although I guess they're melting now so that's not the best description. She never melted, her heart never did. She was there in body—but not spirit. I'd say dutiful but detached would be accurate ... except when she did engage, then it was always negative."

The oven beeped and Al got up and put the potatoes in and set the timer. "But my dog Rex ... now he was never detached. Getting Rex was the best thing my mother ever did for me, although I doubt she ever knew how he affected me. She was mostly oblivious to both me and my brother. Mom spent her life chasing fame, which I resented, but knowing my grandmother the way I did, as I got older I could almost understand my mother's craving for recognition."

"I don't know, but hopefully by our age we've gained some

understanding of our parents. I guess I have ... or hope I have, at least for the most part. And it certainly makes it easier with my dad, to hang in there with him." She looked over at the oven, which just had a few minutes left on the timer. "Maybe I'll toss the salad now. I just brought a vinaigrette. Nothing fancy. That okay?"

"It's great. Perfect." Al looked down at her. Her tawny and white hair looked soft and fluffy. Tonight in the kitchen light he thought it looked like cantaloupe and butterscotch with the white part around her face like French vanilla ice cream. He turned away and quickly opened the drawer with the utensils and rummaged around until he found a carving knife and a big fork. He sure was hungry. Al unwrapped the chicken and put it on a cutting board and began to carve it, hoping she'd see how fast and well he carved. But Bonnie was busy tossing the salad, and he didn't think she noticed. He looked down at the buttons puckering his shirt where it strained over his stomach, then he felt the bump on his head again and began to feel silly. Silly and old.

CHAPTER 15

B ONNIE AND HER FATHER WERE SCHEDULED TO MEET AL AND BERT AT Agren Park at eleven, and Al spent the morning doing his laundry. He didn't think he needed to wear anything nice for the park, but in case he and Bonnie decided to have lunch afterwards, he wanted a better shirt than the ill-fitting summer shirt he'd worn the night before. He also hadn't washed anything other than underwear and socks in a while.

As he was waiting for the washing machine to finish, Al decided to brush Bert. Bert shed a lot, although his dark brown hairs mostly showed up on lighter colored furniture. It wouldn't matter in the park, but he thought it would still be a good idea to make Bert look nice. Bert was very cooperative. He liked being brushed and sat quietly while Al gently stroked the wire brush over his back. It made Al smile, thinking about how he and Bert were getting spruced up to meet Bonnie and her father. It surprised him how much he was looking forward to it. Last night, in spite of being so nervous getting everything ready for Bonnie, the evening had ended on a nice note. A musical note, literally, because after they did the dishes together, they went in the living room where Al made a fire, and they listened to some of his early blues: Lightnin' Hopkins, Muddy Waters, Bessie Smith and Billie Holiday. Bonnie said Robert Johnson's "Sweet Home Chicago" was one of her all-time favorites, and she talked about hearing

Miles Davis in person when she was in New York on spring break from college. She'd started college at Radcliffe, but was so homesick that she left after one year and transferred to the University of Washington. "I felt like a fish out of water in the East. Maybe it would have been broadening and built character or something to stick it out, but I missed my family too much."

"I remember Seattle had some of the greats ... Ray Charles, Quincy Jones. But maybe that was before your time," he said, kidding her. "Had you always liked blues?"

"I was at the U in Seattle between Ray Charles and Jimi Hendrix, but I grew up with a lot of jazz ... my father loved Coleman Hawkins, but it was probably in nurses training that blues really resonated with me."

"How did you happen to go into nursing?" Al went to the bookcase next to the fireplace and leafed through a pile of CDs. "I think Hawkins was on a CD, one I used to have, *Classics in Jazz*—at least I think I had it."

"Don't worry if you can't find it." Bonnie slid down from the couch and sat on the floor next to Bert and began patting him. "About nursing ... well, I think it's pretty accurate that for many girls in my generation the main idea was to find a husband by the time you were twenty-two, and if you hadn't found the prince by that time ... then it was mainly either being a teacher, a secretary or a nurse. My grandfather lived with us when I was a kid, and when he became ill with congestive heart failure, I would hang out with him. My mother said she thought I helped him to feel better. I suppose that influenced me and I seem to have the temperament and personality for hospice work." She leaned back against the couch and Bert put his head in her lap. "You know this is the first time I just sat and listened to music in a long time." She stroked Bert's head and scratched behind his ears.

"Really? I'm the opposite. Since I've been living alone, I seem to need music all the time." Al put the CDs back and went to tend the fire.

"I don't know. Music evokes so many memories, I think it made me feel lonelier. But maybe that's because I tried to listen to music by myself." She lay her cheek against the top of Bert's broad head. "Isn't that right, Bert?" She looked up at Al and smiled. Her eyes were so dark and steady, he had to look away. He poked the fire with his back to her. "Did you know that in 2009 the House of Representatives passed a resolution that made Miles Davis's *Kind of Blue* a National Treasure?"

"I did not know that." Bonnie laughed.

"And it was unanimous. Be nice if they could agree on some other stuff and accomplish something."

They began to talk about politics and Al was so comfortable, he didn't want the evening to end, but about ten-thirty Bonnie looked at her watch and was surprised she'd stayed so long. They went to the kitchen and she got her salad bowl and the decanter with the dressing. It was dark, and although Bonnie had brought a flashlight, Al grabbed one and his coat and insisted on walking her home.

They were quiet as they crossed the road. The night sky was lavish with stars, the air was cold and the last of the gold bigleaf maple leaves were scattered across Bonnie's front yard. When they got to her porch, Bonnie looked up at him and thanked him. "This was really nice, Al. Thanks." She lifted her arms to hug him and Al suddenly bent down to kiss her, but she stiffly drew back.

"Sorry—I just—" he stammered.

"Nothing to be sorry about." She smiled and gave him a quick hug. "Thanks again for dinner."

THE WASHING MACHINE BUZZED, AND Al went to load his clothes in the dryer. At least today when he and Bert went to the park to meet Bonnie and her father, he wouldn't have to worry about making the wrong move with her. What a fool. Trying to kiss her like that. Her husband hadn't been dead a year and her mother died and the dog, too. Besides, he wasn't divorced and he hadn't had any word from Eleanor in a while. He was sure she wasn't having any second thoughts; she'd said their marriage was irretrievably broken, they'd both signed the papers and she'd made a big deal about paying the fee. But weird things happen sometimes ... if her cancer came back, he couldn't not take care of her if she changed her mind and needed him ... he really had no idea what he was doing. He and Bonnie were becoming friends ... it was good to have a friend ... he hoped he hadn't screwed it up ... what had he been thinking trying to kiss her?

As soon as the dryer was finished, Al changed his clothes, got several green tennis balls, gave Bert one more quick brushing and headed out to the park. Driving along Wax Orchard Road, he slowed by the farm that had the Rent-A-Ruminant business where the goats lived. The goats were hired to clear unwanted vegetation and Al thought it was a wonderful enterprise. He kind of wondered what it would be like to have a business like that. Although there had been a competitor from another island who was hired awhile back—but it had turned into a disaster when the guy's goats escaped from the area they were supposed to clear. They ate up someone's fancy garden that was going to be on the Garden Tour. Al thought the garden belonged to the people who'd had the fireworks birthday party, although he wasn't positive. But it had caused a big hullabaloo—quite an uproar—maybe with a lawsuit, as he remembered. The island seemed so quiet and peaceful, and it always surprised him when there was trouble like that. It'd be nice if everyone could just get along as well as most dogs do. They usually worked things out.

When they got to the park and bumped along the rough entrance road, Al glanced at his watch. It was a little before eleven. He might as well get some exercise while he waited. Even though he took Bert to the beach almost every day, he had to admit he didn't walk that briskly, and mostly he strolled since the beach was rocky. He liked strolling and he thought it counted as weight-bearing aerobic exercise, but the image of the paunch he was developing came to mind and he began to walk briskly around the park, swinging his arms as he went. Every few yards Bert ran to him with the ball and Al bent down, trying not to break his stride, and scooped it up and hurled it across the field.

He kept an eye on the parking lot. But there was no sign of

Bonnie. He knew it could take a while to get Mr. Douglas organized, bundled up and then out to the car, but by a quarter after
eleven she still hadn't come. Bert was delighted to keep chasing
the ball and Al continued round and round the track, keeping an
eye on the parking lot. He lost count of how many times he'd
been around; he'd probably covered quite a few miles when his
cell phone beeped at 11:26.

"Al—I'm really sorry ...." Bonnie's voice was tense.

"Is everything okay?"

"Not really. Dad has a cold and I talked to the nurse who
thought it would be a mistake to take him out. So we need to
cancel today."

Al bent down and picked up the ball that Bert had dropped at
his feet. "I'm really sorry that he's not feeling well."

"She said he shouldn't have visitors either, other than me ...
nothing to tire him as pneumonia is always the concern."

"I understand. No problem." Al put the ball in his pocket.
"Give him my best, and thanks for letting me know."

"I will. Sorry I didn't call sooner—I had to wait for the nurse."

"Oh, right. Well, take care. And I sure hope he's better."

"Thanks, Al."

BERT STAYED NEXT TO HIM as Al walked slowly to the parking lot.
"Sorry, buddy. That's it for today." He helped Bert in the truck,
then got in the driver's seat and sat there for a few minutes, not
sure where to go next. The afternoon stretched ahead with hours
to fill, and he couldn't think of what to do with himself. Go to
the post office, he decided. He hadn't gotten the mail yet today.

The road to the park was filled with big potholes and the truck
hit a number of them as Al drove out. He couldn't muster the
energy to avoid them as he usually did. Heading into town on Bank
Road, he slowed down in front of a farm that had some large brown
steers in the yard. They had impressive horns and Bert enjoyed
looking at them. Watching him stick his nose out the window,
focusing intently on the big steers and wagging his tail, Al felt his

familiar envy of Bert and the way he found pleasure in so many simple things. And the way he adapted to situations so gracefully, just going to sleep if there was a disappointment, like on the days the weather was too bad to go to the beach. Maybe after the post office, Al thought, he should go home and take a nap.

He turned off Bank Road on to Vashon Highway and didn't notice until he was across from Kathy's Corner, the garden center and nursery, that he'd passed the street that went to the post office. Al ran his hand through his hair, then felt the bump on the back of his head that was still there from when he fell last night. He was in a fog. Just not paying attention. But what did it matter? He put on B.B. King and kept driving and when he got to Burton, Al turned left on to the Burton Loop and then found himself by his old house. He parked across from it and sat staring at the yard. It looked pretty good. The person Eleanor had taking care of it was doing okay. The For Sale sign was still in front. He'd heard from Howie and Mark, who had a realtor friend, that the word was that Eleanor was asking too much and had turned down some good offers. Maybe she was ambivalent about selling. Maybe she wanted to come back some day. Or maybe she was greedy. Al hadn't thought of her that way, but maybe that was something else he just hadn't seen. He probably didn't get it. About anything. B.B. sang "Never Make a Move Too Soon," and it made him think of Eleanor, maybe she'd made a move too soon. Then he thought of trying to kiss Bonnie, and he felt bad. He didn't think that was why she'd cancelled today. He was sure her father really did have a cold. But she hadn't said anything about re-scheduling when her father was better. He'd been too eager. Came on too strong, inviting her to dinner, and he was sure he'd messed it up again with a woman. What was he doing? All he wanted was a friend.

Along Quartermaster Harbor as Al left Burton, he saw the scoters, the little black and white winter ducks. For some reason he never saw them swimming near Baker's Beach. He loved those ducks. They were probably the only thing he did miss from his old neighborhood.

AT THE POST OFFICE, THERE were about three other people picking up their mail, but luckily no one he knew. He didn't feel very sociable. He opened the box, pulled out the mail and shuffled through it. Seemed to be just the usual: a few bills, grocery store flyers, a notice from the Puget Sound Veterinary Medical Association announcing a continuing education lecture, *Canine Socialization and Risk Assessment for Feline/Canine Aggression,* a reminder card from his dentist, and the *Journal of the American Animal Hospital Association*. But there was one letter with a return address he didn't recognize:

GRISWALD, CARLOTTI, AND WONG
ATTORNEYS AT LAW
5555 HARBOR LIGHT DRIVE SW
SEATTLE, WA 98155

He'd wait and open the letter at home. It was probably one of those estate planning firms offering a free seminar. Wonder where they got his name? They didn't sound familiar, although maybe it was someone Eleanor knew.

The November sky seemed bleak when Al got to Baker's Beach, and as he walked to the house, the quiet was broken only by the sound of dry leaves crunching under his feet. He looked over at Bonnie's, but her car was gone. Probably still with her father, he thought, and wondered again why she hadn't said anything about finding another time for Bert to visit him. Well, he was done. That was for sure. He wasn't going to bother her anymore. He'd wait and see if she'd contact him. Like B.B. sang ... never make a move too soon.

Al made himself a sandwich. Peanut butter and jelly. He thought it was kind of silly, eating kid food. But he especially liked the crunchy peanut butter with that plum jam he had. The jam Evelyn Murdoch had made. What a fiasco that was. "It's better just you and me, Bert," Al said as he took his sandwich to the kitchen table. He sat down and looked again at the mail.

He took a big bite of his sandwich and slowly chewed while he opened the letter from the lawyer.

Dear Dr. Paugh:

I am writing on behalf of my client Dr. Gerald Kincaid about your recent violation of the non-compete clause in your contract with him for the sale of your veterinary practice. It has come to our attention that you have both examined and rendered a professional opinion regarding Eloise, a Pembroke Welsh corgi, owned by Ms. Marilyn Henderson, thereby damaging Dr. Gerald Kincaid. I urge you to cease and desist any further violations of your agreement with Dr. Gerald Kincaid. Any further non-compliance with your agreement with Dr. Gerald Kincaid will result in litigation.

Sincerely,
Raymond Griswald
Raymond Griswald, Senior Partner

Al put his peanut butter and jelly sandwich down and re-read the letter. Motionless, he sat staring at the words. Then he read it again. Then once again. Then, the anger began. First with heat that started in his stomach and slowly rose to his face making it as hot as if he'd spent the afternoon on a Mexican beach in July. Al crushed the letter. *WHAT A SHITHEAD!* He pounded the table with such force that it sent Bert scooting under it. *Ow!* Al shook his hand. He closed his eyes trying to calm down. The last thing he wanted was another heart attack. Wouldn't want to give Kincaid the satisfaction. Damages! What damages? What a *SHIT* that guy was. *A total shit.* And Marilyn. My God ... who'd have thought? She must really have a screw loose ... and all because of? Because of *what?* What was the matter with these people?

CHAPTER 16

AL DIDN'T SLEEP WELL. AT FOUR IN THE MORNING, HE WOKE UP AND couldn't get back to sleep. He probably didn't want to go back to sleep, the dream that had his brother Jamie in it was too disturbing. A nightmare really. Jamie had entered him in a contest of some kind and he stood in a line facing the judges, who were famous actors: James Dean, Cary Grant, and Paul Newman. The other dozen contestants were all little boys about eight or nine years old. They had on tuxedos and were holding a basketball. Each one was supposed to sing a song and then shoot a basket. But he was an adult, the age he is now, and he was naked and he didn't know the song and the basketball kept clumsily dropping from his hands. Jamie and his friends, who were ten and eleven years old, sat in the audience mocking him, and the humiliation was so painful he couldn't run off the stage. He was frozen, unable to move or speak.

Al tried to put the horrible dream out of his mind. He got dressed, quickly throwing on jeans and a sweatshirt and went into the kitchen and made coffee. Then he sat at the kitchen table drinking coffee, thinking, and staring out at the dark, cloudless night. He sat for hours, trying to give himself a pep talk, hoping to ward off the deep wave of worthlessness that ate away at him.

Quit feeling sorry for yourself. Get a life. You're not a victim of famine, war, a terror attack, a plague … or a natural disaster

like an earthquake, a flood, a hurricane, landslide, avalanche, or a
tornado. You're reasonably healthy. You have a nice house to live
in. You have enough to eat. Stop wallowing in self-pity. How could
you let a jerk like Jerry Kincaid tip you over! Get a grip! Chiding
himself every way he could think of, he watched the darkness
slowly become pearl gray, as the light of a new day touched the
tops of the trees along the edge of the beach. He thought about
the sunrise and tried to gain strength from it. From how the sun
had endured for billions of years. How many billions? He got up
from the table and went to his laptop and Googled it.

> "The Sun is about 4.5 billion years old now. It is about
> 300 degrees hotter and about 6% greater in radius
> than when it was first born. It will continue to increase,
> in temperature, luminosity and radius at about the
> same rate for about another 5 billion years."

Another five billion years, that's pretty good. But then he
remembered after that it would burn out and the world would
end. Al shook his head back and forth, literally trying to shake
off the gloom and pessimism.

*This is ridiculous. I've got to move ahead and start thinking about
other people. I know that. I know that's what I need to do.*

Al reminded himself about the Lunch Buddy Program. It
would be a good start. Trying to help a kid and not just dwelling
on his own pathetic life, and Bert would be involved, too, so he
could maybe teach something about dogs. That certainly wouldn't
be a violation of his friggin' contract with that jerk Jerry Kincaid.
Al felt the tiniest glimmer of hope, and went to the living room
to find the issue of *The Beachside,* which had the article with the
details and the name of the contact person.

It wasn't on the desk. He went to the pile in the corner of
the bedroom where he'd dumped stuff when he cleaned up for
Bonnie. Al dug through it, but no luck. Maybe he'd put it in the
recycle. He threw on his coat and went outside around the side
of the house to the bin. It would probably be on top if he'd put

it there. He dug through the papers and magazines, but there was no sign of it. Maybe he'd spilled something on it and it had ended up in the garbage. It bothered him that he had no memory of what he'd done with it. Memory lapses like this seemed to be happening with some regularity and it unnerved him. Like completely forgetting his doctor's appointment the day he was supposed to take Bert to Bonnie's father. He glanced across at Bonnie's house. Her car was there, but there weren't any lights on. In fact, all the houses at Baker's Beach were dark except his.

Back inside Al thought he should get something to eat, although he didn't have much appetite so he grabbed a banana and opened his laptop again. *The Beachside* was online so he could probably find the article there. It took him a few minutes as a lot of articles came up when he searched the site for Ober School, but he finally found it. The name of the person to call was Dodie Solback, and the article said to call her at school Monday through Friday anytime between nine and three-thirty. He looked at his watch. It was only a little after seven.

Al decided to go for a long beach walk with Bert until it was time to call the school. He brought the green tennis ball, still hoping that there might be a time when they could meet Bonnie and her father at the park. He wasn't going to initiate it though. It occurred to him that Bonnie seemed like such a kind person that she might have agreed to the idea just to be nice. He'd know she really wanted to meet again if she was the one who contacted him. That would be best.

HE FELT BETTER AFTER HIS walk. It usually helped his mood, and after another cup of coffee, he decided he would practice reading to Bert to get ready for the Lunch Buddy Program. In the living room, Bert sat at his feet while Al opened his laptop and went to *The New York Times,* which he read every morning, anyway. For the practice he didn't think it mattered that it wasn't a kid's book. But he didn't want to read Bert the depressing bad news it always had on the front page. He went to the *Dining & Wine* section, and read an article called "Inventive Kitchen Mixes Carrots and Chocolate".

"Now pay attention Bert ... 'A new dining experience featuring chocolate and vegetable creations can be found at Chococarr, the Brooklyn restaurant named for the signature dish of Chef Jacob Padillo.'" Al looked down at Bert, who now lay at his feet with his head on his paws. He didn't seem very interested so Al went to the *Travel* section and began reading "A Camel Trek in India." He'd finished the first paragraph about the camel safaris launching out of Jailsamer, a trading center carved out of golden-yellow sandstone, when he got a call on his cell phone.

"Hi Martha Jane."

"Oh Albert, I just love how you knew it was me before I even said a word." She chuckled. "I hope I'm not calling too early, but I saw your light on …."

"No problem. I've been up for hours."

"Good. I hope I didn't interrupt anything?"

"No, I was just reading to Bert."

"Well, could you come over? I'd like to show you where I keep Maria's food and the cat litter and so forth. I got the dates wrong about when I'll be gone. I'm leaving this week, not next week."

"Sure, when would be a good time?"

"How 'bout now? I like to do things when I think of them, if you know what I mean."

"I do. I'll see you in a few minutes."

WHILE HE PUT ON HIS jacket, Al glanced at Bert, who had started to snore. Maybe he'd have been more attentive, if he'd read him a story that had words that Bert knew, like "treat, park, and walk"—or he could just stick those words in every so often in the middle of the article he was reading. Al thought about this as he walked over to Martha Jane's. Probably a better idea would be to give him a little treat every few minutes as he read. That would definitely keep him focused.

"Come in, dear." Martha Jane opened the door when he saw him on the porch. "I'm still in my bathrobe, hope you don't mind."

"You look very comfortable."

"I am. It seems such a bother to get dressed sometimes. Especially when I'm not planning on going anywhere and I like to spend the morning reading." She closed the door behind him. "Tea? Or maybe I should show you where her food is first—yes, let's do that first."

Al followed her to the kitchen where she pointed out the food and water dishes for the cat and the cupboard where she kept the food. "She eats about a half of one of these cans in the morning and then I give her the other half for dinner. She's usually wants to eat between seven and eight, but I'm sure she can wait if that's too early for you to come over."

"It's fine. I'll be up and can come right over."

"I've always been impressed with early risers—they seem to get so much done."

"I don't get anything done." Al was glad that she turned and didn't seem to hear him.

She went to door that went out to her deck and showed him where she kept the litter box and then the shelf in the mudroom where she kept the litter. "I don't think you'll need to change it too often when I'm gone. Maybe just once or twice." She patted his arm. "Let's have our tea now."

They sat at the kitchen table where Martha Jane had her electric teapot plugged in and had set out two mugs and several boxes of tea. "You go ahead and choose the kind you like. I always have the tiger one. You know, the Bengal Spice. I've had my breakfast, but I have some lovely blueberry muffins if you'd like one, dear."

"Just the tea is fine, thanks. For some reason I haven't felt like eating today. Still don't, I guess." Al put a teabag in the mug and poured the hot water over it.

"Is something eating you?"

Al laughed. "I suppose."

"I didn't mean to make light of it. Things don't always come out the way I intend."

Al nodded and sipped his tea. He bent down to pat Maria Montessori, who had wandered in and rubbed against him. Maria jumped in his lap and Al slowly stroked her back. "Things don't come out the way I intend. That's for sure."

"What is it Albert?" She reached across the table and lay her hand his arm.

He felt sad, and awkwardly moved by her touch.

"I don't mean to pry ... I mean if you don't want to talk ...." She leaned back and put both hands around her mug.

"Oh, I got this ridiculous letter from Jerry Kincaid's lawyer threatening me with a lawsuit, and then these women were furious since I didn't pick their dogs for the calendar." Al explained what had happened with Marilyn Henderson. "I think it was a retaliation for not choosing Eloise."

"Maybe not choosing her, I would think." She saw that he looked puzzled. "Not choosing Marilyn."

"I didn't intend to give her the wrong idea. With Olivia, too."

"I don't believe I know Olivia."

"She's Evelyn Murdoch's dog. She was mad I didn't pick Olivia and I was caught totally off guard—I thought we were friends."

Martha Jane poured more hot water in her cup. "There are a lot of women who live alone Albert, who fantasize about having a relationship—they imagine how a relationship is going to be, how it might unfold. I'm pretty sure they comfort themselves with these images and it gives them a sense of future, of something to look forward to." She lifted her teabag from her cup and put it in a saucer. "Just try a muffin, Albert. Don't be shy." She slid the plate of muffins toward him.

"Okay." Al took a muffin. "Thanks."

"Mark made them for me." She looked up at him. "What was I saying?"

"About women."

"Oh, yes. Well, the things they imagine can become very strong and very real to them. Then when real life and real interactions don't match up to all that they've imagined and begun to almost count on, they're crushed and can feel betrayed. And underneath most anger is hurt, I think."

Al shook his head. "It's still hard to understand. I mean, I never wanted to hurt anyone."

"You are a kind man. A kind and handsome man and it's easy to see why women would imagine having a relationship with you. People usually hear what they want to hear and the smallest kindness can be blown up and seen as encouragement."

"I sometimes think I don't pick up on loneliness in other people because it's sort of the baseline for me. Although my brother has made a career out of people's loneliness. Not people—women. Not that women aren't people, but you know what I mean."

"I didn't realize you had a brother. Or maybe I forgot—which is very likely."

"No, you didn't. I probably never mentioned him—we don't have much to do with each other. Really, no contact in years. But last night for some reason I had a dream about him."

Martha Jane sipped her tea. "Dreams are so interesting, I think."

"This was more of a nightmare. Jamie told me once that there was no shortage of lonely women and although he didn't spell it out, he implied that they were his meal tickets."

"Was this in the dream?" Martha Jane asked.

"No, this is who he really is. He got into drugs in the seventies and dropped out of Yale and has lived around various luxury resorts ever since—most of his adult life. He's a parasite, a gigolo. There's no polite way to say it. Jamie looks like Colin Firth, and he had our father's charm and our mother's looks. He took up most of the air in our family. I just don't know why I'd be dreaming of him now."

"I'm not sure about this, but I think sometimes when things in our lives don't seem to be going well, we get memories of other times when we felt bad. Well, at least that's how it's been for me." Martha Jane said quietly. "Maybe that's something my therapist told me. Or maybe my friend. I'm not sure now."

"You had a therapist?" Al was surprised. Martha Jane was the most sane person he knew. "You always seem so cheerful and optimistic."

"I've had my moments, and a bad patch after my husband died. But I try to keep in mind about berry, but I sometimes forget which berry." She glanced at the muffins. "Let me think ...." Martha Jane tapped the table.

"Strawberry or raspberry—maybe it's blueberry?" He tried to be helpful.

"I love blueberries best, I think." Martha Jane looked up and yawned. "Well, I'll think of it."

"I better be on my way," Al took his cup to the sink. "Be sure and let me know if there's anything else you need when you're away and don't worry—I'll take good care of Maria."

"I know you will." She followed him to the door, shuffling slowly. "Thank you so much, Albert dear."

"I'm happy to do it. I don't have a lot going on, although actually, I am going to call the school about the Lunch Buddy Program this morning."

"Good for you. I think that's a step in the right direction." Martha Jane hugged him. The top of her head came to the middle of his chest and he could see her pink scalp through the wispy cloud of white hair.

"I hope so. Wish me luck." He kissed the top of her head.

Martha Jane smiled up at him. "I will—oh, I just thought of it. It's Wendell Berry, not a fruit. He's a person and he said, 'Be joyful though you have considered all the facts.'"

"I'll give it a try." Al hugged her again and as he walked to his house, he looked over to Bonnie's, where now the lights were on in the kitchen. At least she's someone I don't have to worry about fantasizing about me, he thought, and went in to call the school.

CHAPTER 17

WHEN HE CALLED THE SCHOOL, AL LEARNED THAT THE PROGRAM WAS just getting underway and they wouldn't have a boy chosen to be his Lunch Buddy for another week. "Normally, we have to do a background check on the volunteers, but since you're well known in the community we won't need to do one on you!" Dodie Solback had a high, chirpy voice and she announced this news with a degree of enthusiasm that suggested it was comparable to his winning the lottery.

At least they didn't think he was a criminal, Al supposed that was something. During the week that led up to the Lunch Buddy date, Al practiced reading books to Bert. The treats Bert received throughout the reading helped focus his attention, working effectively to make him sit quietly staring at the book. As he read, Al would hold the treat hidden behind the book, and then his hand would pop out every few pages offering the treat. Before she left on her trip, Martha Jane had suggested books that had subtle lessons for the children, but were presented within the context of a non-preachy and very funny story. Al went to the Vashon Bookshop and spent a bit of time saying hello to Consuela, the lovely golden retriever, who was part of the staff, while Nancy and Laurie helped him get the books. *Poodle and Doodle* was about unexpected friendship and adapting to change as a purebred poodle finds itself having to adapt to a scruffy Labradoodle that joins the family. Martha Jane suggested *The Paterson Puppies and the Midnight Monster Party* because she said kids like books about monsters, and the story teaches kids to tame and conquer fear through laughter, humor and joy. Al's personal favorite was *How Do Dinosaurs Love Their Dogs*. Kids are crazy about dinosaurs, Martha Jane explained, especially boys, and Al had been told by Ms. Solback that his Lunch Buddy would be a boy. There were a number of boys who didn't have a father around, and the program had especially wanted to find men for them. She also implied that a man with a little girl Lunch Buddy wasn't desirable for the obvious reasons, but wanted to assure him that it wasn't meant as a reflection on him or his character.

It was a cold, blustery day when Al set out for the school. He put on B.B. King as he left Baker's Beach Road and tapped his fingers on the steering wheel. Just as Al turned into the Ober School parking lot, B.B. belted out one of Al's favorites, "Playin' with my Friends." Perfect timing, he thought, humming along. Getting out of the truck, Al zipped his parka and turned up the collar. "Maybe we'll make a new friend today, Bert." He opened the passenger door and Bert leaped down. Bert looked quite handsome. Al had given him a bath the night before and hadn't taken him to the beach that morning for fear he might roll in something dead and foul smelling. "We wouldn't want to stink up the school, would we Bert? That'd be no way to make a good first impression." After putting Bert on his leash, Al trotted up to the school, carrying a Thriftway cloth bag, which held treats for Bert and the books that Martha Jane had suggested.

Dodie Solback was waiting by the main door. On the phone her high chirpy voice had given him the impression that she was young, but he hadn't been prepared for just how young. She looked like she could be a student at the school, one who was big for her age, but certainly not a teacher. Ms. Solback wore her brown hair in a pony tail and had a little metal stud in her nose. She had on a plaid flannel shirt and olive green cargo pants, and Al thought she looked like she was dressed to go hiking rather than teach school. But then he didn't think he'd been in a school since he was a student himself and no doubt things had changed. He remembered a crush he'd had on his second grade teacher, Miss Leffler, who often wore a powder blue dress that rustled and who wore perfume that smelled like Smith Brothers honey cough drops.

"Oh, no—" Dodie Solback, squealed, as she looked at Bert sitting attentively by the front door. "I'm *so* sorry! I just found out from our Principal that the dogs have to be certified therapy dogs. I just thought that ... well since you didn't need the background check and you're a vet and everything that the dog would be fine, too. But it's not the case. I'm really, really sorry." She was taking quick little breaths as she spoke and seemed very flustered.

"Well, I guess that's it then." Al turned to leave.

"Oh, please stay Dr. Paugh. The Lunch Buddy Program also involves interacting with students in other ways—not just the dog reading activity, which we can do as soon as your dog gets its certification—you can interact and get to know the student today without the dog and then bring the dog, like I said, when it has its certification."

"I don't know, I mean—"

"We have a student who is in the lunch room waiting for you. He'd be so disappointed." Dodie Solback pleaded breathlessly, making it sound like the kid's life depended on being Al's Lunch Buddy.

"Okay, then. I'll have to take Bert to my truck and I'll be right back."

On his way back to the parking lot, Al thought that he'd still take the student the books about the dogs even though Bert wouldn't be there. It could be a good introduction to the whole subject of dogs, sort of a jumping off place for conversation. Al opened the passenger door and lifted Bert's hind end, helping him in the truck. "Sorry, buddy. It's not your fault. I know you would have been great." He took a handful of treats from the bag, giving a few to Bert and putting the rest in the cup holder on the console between the driver and passenger seat, so Bert could enjoy them while he waited. "You stay, and I'll be back in a little while."

Dodie Solback was still standing inside the door to the main entrance and told him again how sorry she was. "It's a new program and we're still ironing out the problems. Not that your dog is a problem, I didn't mean that. I'm sure he's a wonderful dog, but you know what I mean, we're kind of putting the program together as we go."

"Who's the boy who'll be my Lunch Buddy?" Al hoped he didn't sound nervous, but the truth was, being here without Bert made him a little apprehensive.

"I know this sounds strange, but we've decided not to tell our volunteer Lunch Buddies anything about the students, other than their age, of course, and what grade they're in. We want the volunteers to get to know the students themselves without any preconceived ideas. Your Lunch Buddy is a boy in the fourth grade. He's ten years old—his name is Nicholas Figley."

Al nodded and followed her down the hall. The school smelled like a combination of industrial cleaning solution and some kind of fried food, maybe corn dogs, although he didn't think that was it since he'd read in *The Beachside* about a new emphasis at Ober School on fresh, local food in the school lunches. But maybe they hadn't quite gotten up to speed yet on that either.

"As I mentioned when we talked on the phone, the Lunch Buddies meet in the lunch room after all the other students have had lunch so the Lunch Buddy pairs can have the whole lunch room to themselves. We just have one other pair today and you'll both be served the lunch that the students get today."

"I wonder if it's corn dogs?"

"You're right, but it's a chicken corn dog and the entree is always served with a salad, sometimes canned mixed fruit and a fresh treat like an orange wedge or apple slice."

They got to the lunch room and Dodie Solback opened the heavy door and waved to a little boy. He was wearing a Seahawks sweatshirt and sat alone at a big table at the end of the room. In the opposite corner a little girl was sitting with a woman who had the table covered with paper and art supplies. Al followed Dodie as she hurried over to the boy. "Nicholas, I'd like you to meet your Lunch Buddy. This is Dr. Al Paugh."

Al put out his hand and Nicholas grabbed it, "Gimme a paw ... Paw," he said and slapped Al's hand.

"It's Dr. Paugh, Nicholas." Dodie Solback said, firmly.

"Oh, it's okay. He can call me Al."

"Well, I'll leave you buddies now, and they'll be bringing your lunch in about ten minutes. So you gentlemen have a little time to get to know each other."

Nicholas began to run around the table. It was designed like a picnic table only made out of black metal. Al sat on the bench and raised his long legs trying to get them to swing under the table. "Wanna race, Al?" Nicholas punched him in the shoulder as he buzzed around the table.

"Maybe better sit down, Nick."

"DON'T call me Nick! I hate that. I really hate that."

"Sorry. Why don't you sit down? I brought some books—actually, I was going to bring my dog Bert but—"

"I hate dogs."

"You do?"

"Yeah, and I hate to be called Nick because my brother—he's in seventh grade at McMurray—he calls me Nick the Dick." Nicholas continued running around the table. Al thought about grabbing him, but that didn't seem to be in keeping with the spirit of the program.

"So you don't like dogs at all?"

"Hate 'em. They stink, they make dog crap all over the place, they drool and chew up your stuff, and they can bite."

"I guess you had a bad experience with a dog then, is that it?" Al looked across the room at the other Lunch Buddy pair. They were cutting paper and making little hats with cut out flowers on them.

Nicholas zoomed around the table, punching Al on his shoulder each time he went by.

Al pulled the three books out of the bag. "Maybe you don't like them, but let's read about them. I brought some books. One is about dinosaurs and the other—"

"Why read about 'em? I hate dogs."

Al glanced over at the other Lunch Buddy pair. They were

now leafing through magazines, quietly chatting about the pictures and cutting some out.

His knees bumped on the underside of the lunch table. "Okay, so tell me if anything happened to you with a dog, Nicholas."

Nicholas slapped Al on the shoulder as he circled the table, then he slowed down and slumped on the seat. "Nothin' happened. My whole family hates dogs. That's it."

"Here's the one about the dinosaur." Al shoved it toward Nicholas. "How 'bout reading it to me?"

"That's stupid. You brought the book, so you know what it's about." Nicholas drummed his fingers on the table. "You got a cell phone?'

"I do."

"Got any games on it?"

"Games?"

"You know, like apps—*Candy Crush, Angry Birds*—*Zombies vs. Vampires.*"

"No. I don't have anything like that."

"That sucks." Nicholas got up and started to run around the table.

"I think you should sit down again. And we can talk until they bring the lunch." Al looked again at the end of the lunch room where the other pair were quietly chatting away.

Nicholas flopped back down on the seat. "So you like sports?"

"Not really."

"Not even the Seahawks?" he scoffed.

"'Fraid not." Al looked at his watch, wishing they'd bring the lunch. Then at least maybe they could talk about the food or something.

"So what do you like?" Nicholas picked his nose. "What kind of stuff do you do anyway?"

"I like to walk my dog, I like being outdoors, I like to listen to music, on the way here I was playing B.B. King—"

"Never heard of 'em—BB gun! Ha-ha!" He pointed his finger at Al. "Pow! Pow!" He ran around the table and then flopped back down on the seat again. "So what else you like?"

Al scowled, and didn't say anything.

"What else?"

He folded his arms across his chest. "Okay. Well, I used to cross country ski and I read, other than professional things—I mostly read biographies, although I like some poetry—"

"Poetry! I gotta poem for you. Roses are red, violets are blue, you look like a monkey and you smell like one, too. Ha-ha." Nicholas doubled up laughing. Then he repeated it and started in a third time when Dodie Solback came in carrying two trays. She waved as she took the trays to the woman and the girl, "Ladies first," she chirped, smiling. "I'll be right back for you guys."

"That sucks." Nicholas gave an exasperated sigh. "Why should they be first?"

Al couldn't think of an answer and sat there glumly, looking at his watch and wishing this disaster could be over. Nicholas seemed to wind down a bit, and at least was sitting when Ms. Solback brought their trays.

Nicholas stared at the tray. "Oh man, not that fake hot dog again. I hate that thing. They try to fool you to think it's a real hot dog, but it's this crappy chicken stuff and it wouldn't fool a dog."

"I'm going to have to leave right after we finish lunch, Nicholas. I have to let my dog out of my truck."

"Okay." Nicholas drank the milk, making a huge slurping noise with the straw as he finished it. Then he ate the carrot sticks and the orange slices. When he was done, he pulled the hot dog out of the bun and wiggled it back and forth. "What d'ya think this looks like, ha-ha."

Al ate in silence. Nicholas then tore the hot dog bun apart into little pieces, which he rolled up into balls then flicked all over the table. Al thought of suggesting they make a little container out of Nicholas's empty milk carton and try to flick the bun balls into it, sort of a little game. But he didn't think he should suggest it—encouraging his Lunch Buddy to throw food didn't seem appropriate.

Dodie Solback finally came in and Al slowly stood up. His back ached from having his legs hugging his chest as he'd crumpled himself to sit at the lunch table. "I'd better get going now. Bert's in the truck."

"Well, hope you guys got off to a good start." Ms. Solback smiled at Nicholas, who smiled back and sat quietly at the table. "I'll take you back to your classroom now, Nicholas. And you should thank Dr. Paugh for coming."

Nicholas smiled triumphantly. "Thanks!" he shouted and slapped Al on the wrist as he galloped to the door.

Al put the dog books back in the grocery bag and left the lunchroom. The school required that visitors sign in and out in the office, so he stopped there on his way to the parking lot. He was surprised when he looked at the clock to put down his sign-out time. He'd only been with the kid for thirty-five minutes. It seemed longer. An eternity. Al was putting on his coat when Dodie Solback came into the office.

"So, how'd things go?" she asked.

"Not too well. I didn't have games on my phone and I couldn't talk about sports and he hates dogs." Al didn't mention that the only game he could think of to engage Nicholas was throwing food.

"Oh? Nicholas seemed very enthusiastic."

"Really?"

"You seem surprised."

"Well, I guess I am. If it's genuine, then I suggest he's enthusiastic about getting out of his class. Look, I'll check out what it might require for Bert to get certified and then see if it makes sense to continue, but I do think it would be important to pick a kid that likes dogs."

Al couldn't get out of there fast enough. He didn't want to tell Ms. Solback that he thought the kid was a jerk. That was the whole point, wasn't it? That the kids needed Lunch Buddies because they needed some extra attention from adults. If they were perfect little angels, they wouldn't need anything extra, he reminded himself.

Al climbed in the truck and gave Bert a hug. "Let's go home, buddy. It's good they wouldn't let you in there. The kid was a jerk."

CHAPTER 18

🐾

AL DIDN'T FEEL LIKE MUSIC AS HE DROVE HOME. HE WAS FRUSTRATED because he didn't want to let Nicholas Figley get under his skin. A ten-year-old kid, for God's sake. But the kid *had* gotten under his skin. The experience with Nicholas evoked a familiar feeling of alienation for Al, one of not fitting in, being different, not liking fishing, hunting or golf. Not watching football. Not being a regular guy. Never being one of the boys. He'd begun sprouting up in the sixth grade, and because of his height people expected a lot of him. Especially that he play basketball. All through junior high and high school, in fact almost as long as he could remember, he'd been asked if he played basketball, and the reactions were always the same. When people, mostly guys, learned he wasn't an athlete—especially not a basketball player— they thought less of him. And it always ended any conversation. His being that tall and not playing the game was, in its most benign form, a puzzlement to people. In some instances, he was branded with a stamp of weirdness that resulted in avoidance and not infrequently, ridicule. The result was his acute loneliness. His rejection by the other boys was exacerbated by the celebrity status of his brother. A star running back in high school, Jamie made the Ohio All-Star football team when they lived in San- dusky and was an outstanding basketball player to boot. At just six feet, he was shorter than Al, but he played point guard and led his team to the state championship his senior year. When Al got to Sandusky High after Jamie had graduated, there seemed to be a palpable wave of disgust when the football and basketball coaches and their respective teams learned that Al Paugh was no Jamie and wouldn't be even be going out for either sport. There was a narrow path to acceptance and success for both boys and girls. The girls had to be pretty, and the boys had to be athletes. Al knew he shouldn't judge a whole generation on the basis of one kid, but after his encounter with Nicholas Figley, he wondered how much had changed.

On the way back from Ober School, Al thought he'd stop at the pet supply store, as he was getting low on dog food. Maybe he'd get Bert a big rawhide bone, too, since he'd had to sit in the truck instead of getting a story read to him by a Lunch Buddy the way they'd practiced. Al knew Bert didn't mind, and really understood none of it, but he wanted to get him a special treat anyway. At least with Bert, Al felt like a regular guy.

At the main intersection in town, the corner of Vashon Highway and Bank Road, he turned into the US Bank parking lot to get some cash from the cash machine. A lot of the local merchants preferred cash, and Al tried to accommodate them. The parking lot was empty except for a blue Prius and Al parked next to it. As he got out of his truck and walked up to the cash machine, a big scruffy, brown dog leaped out of the back of a truck that was stopped at the intersection. The dog ran toward the bank, and the truck peeled around the corner into the parking lot, screeched to a stop and a guy—fortyish, beefy, and balding, resembling a younger Rush Limbaugh—left the truck running, jumped out and charged after the dog. "God damn you, you stupid mutt!" He lunged at the dog, grabbing it a few feet from Al and kicked the dog, who yelped in pain.

"*Hey, stop that!*" Al spun around and shoved the guy, pushing him back off the dog.

"It's my goddamn dog, asshole!" The guy stumbled, then scrambled to his feet, grabbing the cowering dog as it tried to escape under Al's truck and kicked it again and again with his heavy boot.

Al grabbed the guy's shoulders with both hands and threw him, slamming him against his truck, which set off Bert who began barking and whining. The guy bounced forward and swung at Al, hitting him in his chest, causing Al to fall back, slip and then hit his head on the edge of the front bumper of the Prius, and his head began to bleed. Everyone in the bank had come to the window and watched the guy dragging the dog across the parking lot, swearing and kicking it. Al struggled to get up and was lurching after the guy again when the sheriff 's car sped into the lot. Deputy Sheriff Jake Molina, who had been stopped at the intersection, had seen the whole thing.

"STOP!" Jake Molina jumped out of the car and held out his taser. Al froze next to his truck. He could feel blood starting to drip down his face, but with the taser pointed at him, he was afraid to put his hand up to wipe it. The bald, beefy guy stood still and let go of the dog, who went yelping and crying down the parking lot past Cafe Luna as Deputy Sheriff Molina got between the two men and told them not to move. "Put your hands on top of your head," he ordered Al, who quickly obeyed; then the sheriff held Al's hands with one hand, and with his other hand, he patted him down for weapons. "Okay, now I want you to have a seat in the back of my car while we sort this out." Al walked slowly, he felt tipsy like he'd had too much to drink. He got in the backseat of the sheriff's car and wiped the blood off his face with the sleeve of his parka. Bert continued to bark and whine, jumping against the back window of Al's truck, and Al's heart pounded at the sight of Bert that frantic. The dizziness overwhelmed him and he thought he might be about to pass out, when a part of himself floated up and out of the sheriff's car where he looked down at the parking lot of US Bank and saw the sheriff talking to the beefy, bald guy, saw the people in the bank staring out the window, and saw himself with his head bleeding as he sat in the back of the sheriff's car while Bert barked and whined in his truck. It was as though he were watching a movie from somewhere out in space only he was in the movie sitting in sitting the back of the sheriff's car.

"Did you see what that asshole did? Going after me! I was just getting my dog and he starts attacking me, Sheriff!" The beefy, bald guy shook his fist and pointed toward Al in the sheriff's car. "You better arrest him for assaulting me!"

Floating above the US Bank parking lot, Al watched as another King County Sheriff's car arrived. Now there were two sheriffs' cars in the lot and a bigger crowd with everyone in the bank up against the windows, their noses practically pressed to the glass. Across the street, people were watching from the Hardware Store restaurant, and a small crowd had gathered on the corner in front of the restaurant and on the opposite corner in front of the flower shop.

Jake Molina trotted over to his partner, Deputy Sheriff Louis Hays, and leaned into his car. "I actually saw it, Lou. I was at the four-way and the guy was kicking his dog, and the tall guy in the back of my car intervened and started pushing the guy around. I'll take the tall guy to the sub-station to get his side of the story and his statement, if you can get the other guy's statement and see if he wants to pusue this. Might not be bad to read him the Animal Cruelty statute—I don't know the number offhand, but you can check it on the app. I think it might be a gross misdemeanor, might encourage him to drop this, but we'll have to see."

Al pressed his palm against his forehead and the sense of floating above the parking lot began to subside as Jake Molina came over and got in the car. "I'm going to have to take you over to the sub-station to get your side of the story. I see you've got your dog in your truck there—think he'll be okay?"

Al wiped the blood on his hand on his pants, and held his head again. "Um ... will ... will this take long?"

"Not too long."

Al looked at his truck and saw that Bert was no longer at the back window, now he was just sitting quietly in the passenger seat. "Okay, then ... he'll be okay."

As the sheriff drove Al away, the guy yelled, "I'm telling them to press charges! And you can have the goddam dog for all I care. You and that sack of shit deserve each other!"

When they got to the King County Services Building—the sheriff called it the sub-station—Al stumbled getting out of the sheriff's car.

"You alright?" Jake Molina held Al's arm.

"Just dizzy, I guess."

"We'll get something for that cut." The sheriff took Al inside to the conference room and told him to have a seat. Then he left for a minute and came back with a large Band-Aid. "Head wounds usually bleed a lot, but they're often not that bad. But you should have that looked at when we're through here."

Al nodded and felt his hands trembling as he put the Band-Aid on his forehead.

The sheriff wrote down Al's name and address and verified it after looking at his driver's license. "Look, I saw everything and I understand how it happened. I've got dogs myself. So, I do understand. But unless we hear differently, you'll be charged with fourth degree assault. We should assume that could happen—it's up to the prosecutor—so we need to move ahead with your statement. So now I'll read you your constitutional rights."

Al nodded. He wondered what it was like to be in shock. Nothing seemed real, although he knew where he was and that he was sitting here at this table across from Deputy Sheriff Jake Molina who was very nice to him—calm and friendly as if they were having a normal conversation, only he was about to be read his rights because he was in custody for assaulting someone.

Jake pulled out a sheet of paper and wrote down the date, time, and place at the top and where it said, "Statement of," he wrote in Al's name. "I'll read these to you, and after each number, you'll initial to indicate it's been read and you understand it."

"Okay."

"So it says, 'Before questioning and making of any statement I, Albert J. Paugh, have been advised by King County Deputy Sheriff Jake Molina of the following rights:

1. I have the right to remain silent.

2. I have the right at this time to an attorney of my own choosing.

3. Anything I say or sign can be used against me in a court of law.

4. I have the right to talk to an attorney before answering questions.

5. I have the right to an attorney present during questioning.

6. If I cannot afford an attorney, I can have one appointed for me without cost, if I so desire.

7. I further understand that I can exercise these rights at any time.'"

Jake Molina showed Al the paper and explained that if he wanted to waive the rights in order to make his statement now, he'd sign under a second line where it said, "Waiver of Constitutional Rights. I have read the above explanation of my constitutional rights and I understand them. I have decided not to exercise these rights at this time. The following statement is made by me freely and voluntarily and without threats or promises of any kind."

Al stared at the paper. He wondered if he was a fool to just write a statement of what happened, waiving his rights and not ask for an attorney. But then he thought about Bert waiting in the car and he just wanted to get it over with, so he initialed each line and then signed the waiver.

"Okay, so now we'll need your statement. Think you can write that? Just your side of the story. Just tell what happened."

Al didn't say anything. He didn't know where to begin. "I'm not sure what I should say. See, I'm a veterinarian and that guy was abusing his dog."

"I thought you looked familiar."

"Well, I'm retired now." Al thought about Jerry Kincaid threatening to sue him. Al closed his eyes. His life was going down the toilet.

"Look, you just tell me. I'll just write a summary. That okay?" Jake seemed very sympathetic.

"Sure. I feel kind of dizzy, actually." Al swallowed and then began and told where he was, what he was doing and what he saw. He said he tried to stop the guy from hurting the dog and shoved him away, but the guy kept kicking the dog. Al knew he could seriously injure the animal, so he grabbed the guy and shoved him against his truck. "The guy slugged me, and I was about to go after him again when you came."

"Well, that's how I saw it." Jake Molina wrote it up as Al had described the incident and then had Al sign it.

"Can I go now?" Al started to get up.

"I can't let you drive, Dr. Paugh. I know you've felt dizzy, and you might have a mild concussion. You should be checked out."

"Oh, I'm sure I'm okay."

"I have to insist, sir."

Al slumped in the chair. "But my dog ...."

"Is there someone you can call to get you and the dog? If not, I can get my partner to take you to the clinic and then if we have the okay, we'll get you back to your car."

Al thought of Martha Jane, but she was out of town, visiting her family. So were Mark and Howie. Ted Krupnik was off sailing around in the ocean at the Semester at Sea, and Eleanor— well, she'd be so disgusted with him she'd probably never come. Besides, she was in Portland, so that didn't make any sense anyway. Al sighed and pulled out his cell phone. The only one he could think of was Bonnie. He'd have to call her.

His hands trembled as he looked in the contacts on his phone and found her number. What if she didn't answer, or didn't want to come and get mixed up in this. Who could blame her?

"Hi Al," she said cheerily.

"Bonnie ... um, if you're not busy, I um, wonder if you could pick me up."

"Oh? Do you have car trouble?"

"No." Al looked at Deputy Jake Molina, who had gone into his office next to the conference room. He felt dizzy again and he couldn't think of what to say.

"Al?"

"Uh-huh."

"Are you still there?"

"I'm here."

"Where are you, Al?"

"I'm at the police station."

"Oh."

"Bonnie?"

"I'm here. Sorry, you said the police station?" She couldn't hide her surprise.

"Right. Can you come?"

"Okay ... but I'm not exactly sure where—"

It took Al a minute to think where he was, where the King County Sheriff's Office actually was. Then he remembered they'd just driven from the bank parking lot and were still on Bank Road and it was across from the Land Trust Building.

"Where is it, Al?" she asked again. "Where's the police station?" This time her voice was calm as if she'd switched into crisis mode and was taking charge.

The quiet authority in her tone helped him feel less fuzzy, less out of it. "It's in what they call the Vashon Rural Services Center—it's across from the Land Trust Building."

"I'll be right there."

"Bonnie?"

"Yes?"

"Could you get Bert, too? He's in my truck in front of the bank."

"Sure. It's not locked, is it?"

"It's open ... I'll explain about this when you come."

"Okay. I'll—"

"Bonnie?"

"Yes?"

"Thank you." He slumped in the chair and put his cell phone back in his pocket. He felt both foolish and grateful. He cleared his throat trying to ward off the lump that rose, trying to stay in control.

CHAPTER 19

DEPUTY SHERIFF MOLINA CAME BACK IN THE CONFERENCE ROOM. "Find someone to drive you to the clinic?" He sat down at the computer and began to type.

"My neighbor's coming. She should be here in about ten minutes. I was wondering Sheriff—what happens now? What's next?"

"Depends if the guy decides to press charges." He glanced up from the computer. "My partner read the Animal Cruelty Statute to him. Might discourage him." He looked back at the computer and began typing. "You never know."

Al didn't want to annoy him, the sheriff was obviously busy, but what happened if the guy did press charges? He'd have to get a lawyer ...there were a lot on the island, but the only one he knew that well was Stephanie Griffin and Harold, her eleven-year-old English Bulldog. Harold really needed to lose weight—Stephanie had gotten quite defensive about it. Al thought her specialty was environmental law or something like that, so she probably wouldn't defend someone charged with assault even if she hadn't been peeved at him for telling her that Harold was too fat.

"Sheriff?"

"Yeah?" He continued typing and didn't look up.

"What if they press charges, then what?" Al's head ached.

Jake Molina kept looking at the computer, then shuffled some papers on his desk. "You get notification in the mail saying when to come to court—usually comes in thirty to ninety days. So there's first an arraignment—then a court date. Worse case would be conviction, but sometimes at the arraignment there's deferred prosecution. Might require an anger management program—something like that."

Al knew it usually took the county a long time to do things. Probably the courts were just as slow as all the other departments. Could take a while before he even had a court date, so he might as well wait to get a lawyer. Besides, they're not cheap. Made sense to wait. He looked around the office, at Deputy Sheriff Jake Molina, his uniform and his gun. Al was thinking about how it would be good if animals themselves could press charges against people who assaulted them when he saw Bonnie come in. She stood by the door and he quickly got up and went over to her. His head stopped hurting the minute he saw her.

"Hi, Al." She gave him a quick hug.

"Thanks for coming," he stared at her for a minute, then looked away, feeling sheepish and turned to the sheriff. "Okay for us to leave?"

"As long as you don't drive," he said, briefly looking up from the computer. "Might have a concussion and you should be checked out first."

Bonnie had parked in the small lot in front of the station and Al followed her to the car. When he saw Bert sitting in the back seat, he wanted to rush to him and hug him like those guys in the Army who get reunited with their service dogs. But Bert seemed pretty calm. He just stood up on the back seat and wagged his tail when he saw Al. Al thought he should act calm, too.

"Hi, buddy, sorry you had to wait so long for me." He leaned over the front seat and patted Bert before he got in next to Bonnie. He started to put on his seatbelt, but stopped and turned to her. He covered her hand with his for a minute. "I can't tell you how much I appreciate this. I just want you to know that."

She was quiet, waiting for him to explain. When he didn't say anything, she finally said, "Okay. What happened, Al?"

Should he start with the Lunch Buddy disaster? It had nothing to do with the fight, except that kid had put him in a bad mood. It really wasn't relevant, so he just told what had happened the way he had given his statement to Deputy Sheriff Molina.

"Al, there's blood on your sleeve."

"It's just from where I wiped the cut on my head. It's no big deal."

"We'll go to the clinic. To make sure."

"The dog's the one who should be looked at to see if it's okay. The guy took off without it ... just left it. I hate people who abandon animals, but under the circumstances—with a dirtbag like that—I'm glad he did. Look, I'm serious, that dog might be injured and I need to find it."

"I'm supposed to take you to the clinic."

"Honestly, the cut isn't that bad and they just have a nurse at the clinic and—"

"And I'm a nurse." She nodded. "Okay. But let me tell you about concussions first, and if we're not going to the clinic, you have to listen to what I say."

Al nodded. If this woman told him to go jump in Fisher Pond he'd do it.

"The signs of a concussion can be subtle and you don't always experience them right away ..."

He studied her hair. It was the color of butterscotch. And the white part that framed her face was the color of sugar cookies.

"... the common symptoms are headache, or a feeling of pressure in the head, confusion or feeling as if in a fog, and dizziness ..."

Maybe the color was more between butterscotch and candied yams.

"... there can also be ringing in the ears, nausea, vomiting slurred speech, feeling dazed and fatigued ... Al, are you listening?"

"Right ... dazed and fatigued."

"There's more. There can be irritability, sensitivity to light and noise, disorders of taste and smell. Like I said, these things can be subtle and not immediately apparent. They can last for days or weeks or longer. So you have to avoid physical exertion, and not do any things that require mental concentration."

The white part was more like eggnog than sugar cookies, he decided, wondering why she made him think about food.

"Al?"

"I was listening. You said not to do any concentrating and that won't be a problem because I don't do anything that requires concentration. Lately, being in a fog is just my default position, so it's nothing new." Her eyes were so dark and beautiful it made him feel dizzy.

"Do you remember what happened before you saw the guy with the dog?" she asked.

Al nodded. "Bert and I flunked Lunch Buddy. It's a long story ... I just want to try to find that dog now."

"Oh, all right. I'll help you look."

"Let's just walk a little around here. Often an injured animal will hide."

Bonnie laughed.

"What's so funny?"

"Just *déjà vu* all over again." She got out of the car and went around to the passenger side. She wanted to watch him as he got out and stood up to see if he was steady on his feet.

"You're talking about when you and I were Baker's Beach Dog Search and Rescue, looking for Tanner." Al wanted to hold her.

"Looks like your memory's okay."

He also wanted to kiss her. But he remembered how that hadn't worked out so well when he'd tried before. Besides, they were walking in front of the credit union, and he'd already attracted enough attention for one day. He turned down the street between the Senior Center and the credit union where there were a few parking spaces. At the side of the building Bonnie thought she heard something. Bert heard it too, and ran to the end of the row by a green van and stood by it, barking. Bonnie got there a few steps ahead of Al and looked under it.

"Al ... it's here!"

"Great! I'll go back to my truck and get Bert's leash and then stop in Cafe Luna to get some food to coax the dog to come out. It'll just take me a minute."

"No." Bonnie stood up and glared at him.

"No?"

"I told that sheriff that I'd take you to the clinic and now you want to go running all over the place." She held out her hand. "Give me your keys—I'll get Bert's leash and some food. You stay here and sit quietly. I told you the symptoms of a concussion aren't always immediately apparent."

It was silly, but there was no use arguing with her. He didn't have the energy for it anyway. Al reached under the van and lay his arm down on the pavement so the dog could sniff him. "You're a good dog. We'll have some treats for you, because you're such a good dog, you can rest with us and we'll take care of you, good dog, and everything will be okay. We'll find a home for you and someone to love you, good dog, and we want to give you treats because you're a good dog ...." He kept it up, repeating "good dog" and after a few minutes, Al felt warm breath on his palm and a slight touch from a wet nose.

Bonnie came around the corner with the leash and a muffin wrapped in a napkin. She also carried two cups of coffee. Al kept his hand under the van and motioned to Bonnie. "He's sniffed me," he whispered. "I just hope whoever owns this van doesn't come back right away. I'm afraid this dog would bolt again."

"If that happens, I can see if I can get the driver to wait a few minutes." She handed Al his coffee and the muffin.

"I'll bet you could. You're hard to refuse ... thanks for the coffee." He took a sip and set it down, then tore a little piece of the muffin and gave it to Bert. Slowly, he reached under the van with a piece of muffin on his outstretched palm. "Good dog," he said quietly, and began talking again.

"You could seduce anyone with that voice," Bonnie whispered.

"I wish."

She sat next to him, patting Bert. After a few minutes, Al felt the dog's mouth as it ate the muffin. He gave Bonnie a thumbs up and tore off another piece of muffin, moving his hand closer to the edge of the van. In another few minutes, the dog had moved so its nose was sticking out from under the van. Al took the leash in one hand, and a piece of muffin in the other and as the dog ate, he snapped on the leash.

"Come on, doggie," he called encouragingly, tugging slightly on the leash. The dog crawled out from under the van and Al stroked its head, continuing to talk. Then he bent down and took a closer look under its hindquarters. "Looks like we've got a girl here."

"I don't suppose there's a name on her collar."

Al looked closely at the collar. "No, there's nothing. We can check for a microchip later, but I think it's highly unlikely we'd find one."

"I'm going to call her Princess, since she should be revered and treated with love and respect. Like royalty."

"Let's try to get her to your car now. I don't want to force her, but if you walk ahead with Bert, I'll follow with her and see if she'll come with us." The dog was trembling and panting, but she did walk with him. When they got to the car, without too much encouragement, she got into the backseat with Bert. "Hope you don't mind chauffeuring, but I'll sit in back with the dogs."

"My pleasure." Bonnie looked back at him as she started the car. "Okay, now that we have Princess—you really have to take it easy. I did what you said. We got the dog and now I need to look at that cut and then you have to rest. Nothing physical, nothing that requires concentration."

"Okay. But I'll want to observe Princess for a while. It doesn't take much concentration. I want to see if she can eat and keep food down. See how lethargic she is. Sometimes it's hard to sort out what's a physical trauma resulting from an injury, and the trauma from what she's just been put through. It may take quite a while before we know, and I wouldn't want to try to place her for adoption until she's well and we find out the kind of a home she'll need. Whether she's good with kids and cats, other dogs … all that sort of thing." Al put an arm around each of the dogs.

Princess was still trembling, but she'd stopped panting. He lay his head back against the seat. He was proud of Bert, being so mellow and accepting of Princess. In the rear view mirror, his eyes met Bonnie's. Hers were so dark, and they seemed luminous. Like rich dark coffee, or the darkest chocolate. He sighed. He'd have to think of some way to thank her, but he was too tired.

CHAPTER 20

IT HAD STARTED TO RAIN BY THE TIME THEY GOT TO BAKER'S BEACH. The sky was a grainy pewter, the drizzle making the bare branches silver in the twilight. The wind had picked up and it was cold. Bert jumped down from the car and Al climbed out, coaxing Princess, patting her and pulling gently on the leash. Finally she jumped down and stood next to him, now only trembling a little. "Bonnie, I can't thank you enough for your help with this fiasco. I'll just take the dogs and head home now." He went to hug her, just a friendly thank-you kind of hug, but she stopped him.

"No. Absolutely not. I need to look at that cut and you agreed."

Al nodded. He was hoping she'd forget about it. Finding that dirtbag's dog had helped clear his head, restored some sense of control, and even the possibility that some good might come out of the whole fiasco—if they could find a good home for the dog. "I should take Bert and Princess home," he protested. He'd thought of keeping her himself except that his lease only permitted one dog, although he was sure having it there a short time wouldn't be a problem.

"Both dogs can come in with you."

"But I have to feed Martha Jane's cat."

"I'll feed her for you after I see that cut. Come on now. Quit stalling." Her voice was affectionate but firm.

Feeling ridiculously childlike, Al bent down and patted Princess, then he and the dogs slowly followed Bonnie into her house.

As soon as she got inside, Princess began to pant. Al took her off the leash and she went straight for the wing chair next to the woodstove, hunkered down and scooted under it.

Al leaned back against the door. "I think we should just leave her until she feels safe enough to come out."

"Okay, I'll get some water for the dogs after I check your cut," Bonnie said, turning on the lights. She wrapped her arms around herself and shuddered. "Brrr—then I'll make a fire."

Al wanted to go home. He also wanted to wrap his arms around her. "At least, let me get the fire going."

"No ... Sit." she commanded and pointed to the couch.

"Do I get a treat if I obey?" Al went to the couch and sat down.

"Down," she said with authority.

"You want me to lie down? Really, I—"

"Down," she repeated, interrupting him and Al reluctantly lay on the couch, then Bonnie held her hand up, her palm facing him. "Stay."

"I suppose I would be in the doghouse if I didn't do what you say," Al muttered wondering how far he could carry stupid dog jokes.

"Scoot over a little." Bonnie sat next to him on the couch. "I'm going to take off the bandage and check the cut. I don't think it needs stitches, but I have to take a look." Al looked down as Bonnie removed the bandage. "I'm just going to clean this a little." She got up and in a minute came back with a first aid kit, a little bowl of warm water and some gauze. Gently, she wiped the cut, then put Neosporin on it and a clean bandage.

"Haven't we done this, before?" Al asked. "I get cut and you fix it?"

"Like a broken record. Maybe we're just stuck."

"You were good at all the commands. Sit. Down. Stay."

"We always took our dogs to obedience training."

"What about 'Off'?" Al closed his eyes.

"Off?" Bonnie shut the first aid kit.

"When a dog jumps on you and you don't want it to, you say 'Off.'"

Bonnie smiled and kissed his forehead and went to the kitchen and came back with a mixing bowl filled with water for the dogs. Bert went straight to the water and drank, then sat quietly beside Al, who closed his eyes again and lay his hand across his forehead, dropping his other arm to scratch Bert's ears.

Bonnie started the fire, and it wasn't long before the small room lost its damp chill and Al felt sleepy.

"How's your head?" she asked.

"Hurts a bit, but I'm sure it'll go away."

"Aspirin and ibuprofen can increase the risk of bleeding, so I'll get you some acetaminophen." She came back with a glass of water and some Tylenol and handed them to Al. "No alcohol either," she said, with a sigh, "but I think I'm going to have a glass of wine, if you don't mind. But first I'm going to run over to Martha Jane's and feed her cat." She bent down and kissed his forehead again.

"Really, I can do it," he protested, sitting up.

"Shhh." She put her finger to her lips while she slipped on her jacket. "I'll be right back."

"I feel ridiculous," he muttered, but she was gone. He touched his forehead where she'd kissed him. Twice. What did that mean? Maybe she was taking pity on him. He closed his eyes and realized he must have dozed off because when he opened them, he was surprised to see that Bonnie had already come back and was hanging up her jacket.

"I knew there was a key in the planter box next to the door, so it just took a second to get in—Maria Montessori's such a nice cat—I gave her the rest of the can I found in the fridge."

"Thanks for doing that. But listen, I'll leave as soon as I can get Princess. I'd rather not drag her out from under the chair. If you've got a little food, I'll coax her," he said, sitting up.

"I'll do it," she said, going to the kitchen. "You rest."

"Bert will want it. I remember how you got him away from the garbage with cheese." Al lay back down on the couch. He didn't need to stay here. It was silly and he'd imposed enough. There was nothing wrong with him. He was fine. But he liked being near her. He didn't really want to leave.

"The garbage?" she called from the kitchen.

"When I first moved to Baker's Beach and Bert got in your garbage."

"I do remember," Bonnie said, as she came in with a glass of wine, some chicken and cheese and sat on the floor next to the chair. Immediately Bert was sitting in front of her, staring intently. "I'll give you a piece, too. Don't worry." She patted Bert and tore off a piece of cheese for him.

From the couch, Al watched Bonnie with the dogs. She held the cheese under the chair, and after a few minutes, Princess ate it. Next she offered her a little piece of chicken and the dog inched forward.

"You're very patient." Al smiled as he watched her.

"So are you."

"I suppose so. But today was unreal ... I've never been in a fight before."

"Really?" She looked up, still holding her hand under the chair.

"I remember in preschool or kindergarten—I'm not sure which, but it was when I first started school—and whenever there was some kind of scuffle, the teacher would say 'You're bigger, Albert. You could hurt someone.' I heard it so many times, I suppose it became hard-wired into my brain. Not that I ever wanted to beat anyone up ... I've always thought I was a Ferdinand kind of guy."

"Ferdinand?" Bonnie sipped her wine and patted Princess, whose head was now next to Bonnie's leg. "The only Ferdinand I remember from history was that Archduke Ferdinand guy, the one whose assassination triggered World War I."

"Ferdinand the Bull. He never wanted to fight, just smell the flowers."

She looked over at him and smiled. "Oh sure, the children's story—I loved that story. Everyone should be a flower-smeller, we'd be a hell of a lot better off."

"Did I ever tell you that you remind me of my dog?"

"Of Bert?" Bonnie laughed. "Can't say I see the resemblance." She fed both dogs, moving slowly back as Princess inched out until all that remained under the chair was her tail. "It's working." Al pointed to Princess and gave Bonnie a thumbs up. "Not Bert—"

"You don't want me to feed Bert?" She looked up at him.

"It's fine to feed Bert, I mean it's not Bert you remind me of. It's another dog. My collie. The dog I had when I was a kid, Rex."

"My cold wet nose and hairy body."

"Your hair is the same color. His was kind of tawny ... you know, golden, reddish brown with white, like yours and his eyes were almost black and shaped like yours. And he was tall. Also long legs." He was talking too much. What was he doing?

"Oh, then I guess it's supposed to be compliment?" Bonnie smiled.

Al looked at the ceiling. "I loved that dog."

Bonnie stood up. "They've finished the cheese and chicken. I'm going to get some more, but when I come back, I'll sit in the other chair and see if she'll come to me." She set her wine glass on the table next to the chair.

"Bert will, that's for sure." Al focused at the ceiling. How stupid. Telling her she reminded him of Rex. He pictured that beautiful collie and all of a sudden he started to chuckle, remembering a cartoon he'd seen years ago. It had two frames: in the first one there was a kid with a collie and the kid is shouting, "Lassie! Get help!" and the second frame showed a psychiatrist's office and Lassie was lying on a couch. Al laughed so hard remembering it, he got tears in his eyes. Shit. He closed his eyes and rubbed his head. What a mess I've made of everything. I *should* see a shrink. I really should. Then he drifted off to sleep.

THE HOUSE WAS DARK EXCEPT for a few small coals glowing in the woodstove. Opening his eyes, Al looked around and saw Bert on the floor next to him. It was a few seconds before it registered that he was in Bonnie's house and then everything that happened came back in a flood of embarrassment. He felt his head. It was a little tender around the cut, but other than that, he seemed fine. His memory was obviously fine, too, because he could recall every single event in all its humiliating detail. He looked at his watch. Two in the morning. No reason to stay here. He'd get both dogs and go home.

He didn't see Princess anywhere in the room, unless she had gone back under the chair. Al crouched and looked under it, but the dog wasn't there. Walking quietly, he looked in the kitchen and through the house, but there was no sign of her; then, at the end of the hallway, he saw that Bonnie had left her bedroom door open. He looked in and saw her nestled against the pillow with her lovely face just above the big, dark head of the dog, who was curled next to her. He felt a wave of tenderness which soon became a yearning ache; he knew it was a longing for her and it embarrassed him deeply to be standing in the doorway of her bedroom gawking at her.

Quickly, Al turned and went to the living room to search for paper and something to write with. It would be wrong to just disappear. Women hated that—he at least knew that much. They hated waking up and seeing that the guy they had been with had taken off in the middle of the night. Of course, he hadn't really *been* with her. But still, he should leave an explanation, a proper note thanking her. On the desk in the corner he found a notepad and a pen.

Dear Bonnie,

Thank you again for your help. I feel fine now and I'll call you tomorrow. I saw that you and Princess were asleep and I didn't want to disturb you, so I'll pick her up in the morning. Thank you again for your help today.
I want to take you to dinner to show my appreciation.

Gratefully yours,
Al

He started to write, "P.S. I'm sorry if I offended you when I said you reminded me of my dog," but thought better of it and crossed it out. The way he signed it didn't seem like enough. Maybe he should have said something like "thank you from the bottom of my heart," but he was afraid she might think it was a little over the top in a kind of adolescent sort of way. And he'd already made a big fool of himself.

AT HOME THE NEXT MORNING, Al woke early. It was before the sun rose, and after he let Bert out he made a fire and sat in front of it drinking coffee. The image of the cartoon he'd remembered of Lassie lying on a psychiatrist's couch getting help kept coming back. And it didn't seem so funny in the dark hours before dawn. He didn't think he was crazy. But he knew his life was a mess and he should get counseling because nothing else seemed to be working. Besides, wasn't he the one that suggested going to a counselor when Eleanor announced she was leaving him? So, why not go to one now? Only without Eleanor. Maybe if the court sent him to anger management, which Deputy Sheriff Molina implied might be likely, he could do the anger management with the counselor. Then it could fulfill a court obligation, if that's what came out of all this mess.

Periodically, he went to the kitchen window to look across and see if the lights were on at Bonnie's. He'd take the dog off her hands as soon as she was awake. And that was another thing. Bonnie. He wanted her. And his feelings were getting out of control, and he needed to get a handle on it. Maybe a shrink could help him get his head screwed on better when it came to women. He didn't seem to understand how friendship worked with them. He thought he was friends with Marilyn and Evelyn, and obviously he was blind to their feelings. And with Bonnie, he was the one who wanted more than friendship—that was for sure— and her husband hadn't even been dead a year. What was he thinking? The last thing he wanted was to push her away. He'd settle for friendship if that was what it would be. He'd settle for anything as long as he could still have her in his life.

AFTER AL FED THE CAT at Martha Jane's, changed the litter box, and spent some time cuddling with her, he went to Bonnie's to pick up Princess. At first glance, he was surprised at how well the dog seemed to be doing, but he needed to check her out. In Bonnie's kitchen, he knelt next to her and gently pressed his fingers along her ribs and under her belly. She didn't jump or snap at him, which was encouraging. Whatever bruising would have occurred might not be excessive. He looked in her ears, then held her muzzle and gently looked in her mouth. "Have you noticed her limping? Or licking herself excessively, or panting?" he asked.

"No, and when I invited her on the bed last night, she jumped right up. No problem."

So would I. Al looked at Princess, trying to focus on the dog. "If her kidneys were damaged when she was kicked, there might be blood in her urine. That's something I'll check for," Al said, as he stood up.

"Would you like some coffee?"

"Sure, thanks."

Bonnie poured them each a cup and sat across from him at the kitchen table. "I'm glad she seems to be doing so well," she said, stirring her coffee.

"She's a pretty resilient dog, seems to have a good temperament."

"Al, I've been thinking about her, and it occurred to me that I could foster her. Give her a foster home while we see how she's doing. I can observe her carefully and see how she progresses. And after she's registered with the shelter, I could foster her until she's adopted. I think it can work—she seems happy with me."

Who wouldn't be? Al sipped his coffee.

"It just hit me this morning when I woke up and saw her next to me. What do you think?"

"It's a great idea. I think it's wonderful." I think you're wonderful. Al looked at his feet under the table. Can't he even be around her without feeling that ache? It almost seemed like a craving. Get a grip, he told himself. He looked up. "How's your father?" he asked, trying to focus on something else.

Bonnie cupped her hands around the coffee mug. "I'm supposed to see him today, but honestly, I feel like it's just too soon to leave Princess."

"I could stay with her. Or if you'd rather, Bert and I can visit him. Is he over his cold?"

"Physically he's fine. They always worry that a cold or flu will turn into pneumonia when people are his age, but he's a tough old bird. Been physically strong his whole life. He looks frail, but he usually bounces back." Bonnie stared out the window. "At least he used to." She didn't say anything for a while, but then turned to look at him. "The thing is, he's worse mentally, Al. I guess I just have to face it. The last few times I was there he didn't seem to know me. One time I thought he knew me, but then the next day he acted like he thought I was part of the staff. It's not a consistent incremental loss of memory, it seems to have these spurts. Times when he seems sort of aware, and then others when he's blank and just not there. And it's hard because the times when I think he's somewhat aware, it gives me hope that I can still connect with him. But the next time he doesn't seem to know me, whatever hope I had just gets doused, and then I'm even more sad.

"I shouldn't be surprised. I knew this day would come, but nothing can prepare you. It's like a kick in the stomach. You're staring at this person who you've known and loved and looked up to your whole life. A person you leaned on and needed, and there's a body sitting there, the same eyes are looking at you, but the person has left and you feel abandoned in a terrible way. But I keep chatting and pretending that he knows me, hoping that somewhere in there I'm connecting with some spark that is still him." Bonnie put her hands on the table and stood up. "More coffee?"

He nodded and she brought the pot and filled both cups. "I do think it would be good if you took Bert to see him. I doubt he'd remember you at all, but I'd like to know if he'll respond to Bert. I can call the office and just make sure it's okay." She reached over and touched his arm. "Are you sure you really feel up to this?"

"I do. I'm fine. I think a lot of my problem was being in shock that I got myself into this mess. It made me look at a lot that's been happening, or not happening—which is more the case. Martha Jane suggested I see a counselor awhile back, and I'm going to ask her to recommend someone. The sheriff told me it's possible that the prosecutor could recommend anger management or something like that. I won't know anything for a while. The court will send me a date for the arraignment—there's nothing I can do but wait, and I figure as long as I'm waiting, I'll see if I can get my head screwed on better."

"I don't think there's anything wrong with your head, Al."

"You don't?"

Bonnie looked away, embarrassed. "I'll call Vashon Community Care and let them know you're coming. Late afternoon is a good time, a little before dinner, if that works for you."

"Sure. No problem." Al went over to Princess and patted her. "You're in very good hands, dog. Lucky you."

CHAPTER 21

❖

A L'S HANDS TREMBLED AS HE READ THE "SHERIFF'S REPORT." IT WAS one of the most faithfully read sections of *The Beachside*. There were those who found it of more interest than some of the paper's news stories about things like quilting exhibits, coyote sightings, and problems with the park district pool. Sometimes the "Sheriff's Report" listed 911 calls for medical emergencies, but the majority were of thefts or suspicious behavior. Although the items never identified anyone by name, they did report the location. In the paper that day was an item that made Al feel ill. Sandwiched between "November 12, A ladder was stolen from Island Security and Self Storage and a cheaper ladder was left in its place," and "November 20, Dirt was stolen from Vashon Cemetery," was "November 19, A man was arrested in front of US Bank, 9910 SW Bank Rd. for assault in an altercation involving a dog."

The item in the "Sheriff's Report" was bad enough, but when Al turned the page and saw the headline "Island Veterinarian Arrested for Assault," he couldn't bear to read it. His hands tingled and his heart pounded with such a hammering that he imagined the headline in the next issue, "Island Veterinarian Dies of Heart Attack Reading Story of His Arrest." He put the paper down and held his head in his hands and sat immobilized, unable to think for several minutes. Finally, he sighed and told himself it was cowardly not to read it. He needed to know exactly what was being said so he could defend himself ... but as he picked up the paper and tried to read, the words blurred. Shame engulfed him. Not shame for what he'd done to help the dog. The man didn't deserve to have a dog, and the fact that Al ended up pushing that dirtbag off the poor animal was exactly what he deserved. No, it wasn't that. It was seeing his name in the paper with the head-line "Arrested for Assault." The words *arrested* and *assault* being associated with his name troubled him deeply. It felt unjust and humiliating, and again it triggered a similar cache of emotion that had been buried since childhood.

Bert was lying on the couch next to Al, and Al tossed the paper aside and put his arms around Bert's neck. Bert licked his face as Al closed his eyes and hugged him. Taking deep breaths, holding Bert close to him, he inhaled his wet, saltwater doggie smell. After a while, Al dropped his hands to his lap, but lay his face against the top of Bert's broad chocolate head for a few min-utes more—then buoyed by the devotion and loyalty of his dog, he picked up the paper.

ISLAND VETERINARIAN
ARRESTED FOR ASSAULT

Recently retired Island veterinarian, Dr. Albert Paugh, 67, was arrested in the US Bank Parking lot November 19 for assault in an incident in which, according to Dr. Paugh's statement to Deputy Jake Molina, Dr. Paugh intervened on behalf of a dog. The King County Prosecutor's Office will determine if charges are to be filed against Dr. Paugh.

Al put his head back against the top of the couch. He won-dered how much liquor he had in the house. He could use a stiff drink. Almost everyone read *The Beachside*. Especially the stuff about crime. People were very interested in crime. Look at all the TV shows about crime and the mystery books that were so pop-ular. Although this wasn't a mystery. The perpetrator had been arrested. No mystery there, and everyone knew that he was the one who had been arrested. Al reached for Bert again. He didn't much care for the idea of going out in public. He really wasn't up to showing his face anywhere. Especially Thriftway.

In the kitchen he looked in the refrigerator and through all the cupboards. Good. There was a lot of canned soup and Ramen, and after he finished the leftover chicken, he had enough food for about a week. And he could go to the post office at night when no one was there. The mailbox section was open twenty-four hours, every day. No one would be there getting mail around midnight or later. He opened the cupboard where he kept the liquor. He had scotch and a bottle of vodka. The idea of just anesthetizing himself was very appealing. But he'd told Bonnie he'd take Bert to see her father this afternoon. Probably wouldn't be a good idea to show up drunk. Would everyone on the staff have read the paper? He was considering how he might sneak in to see Bonnie's father when the phone rang. Al's cell phone was on the counter next to the sink. He didn't want to talk to anyone, but he glanced at the caller ID. It was his neighbor Howie, so he answered.

"Hi, Howie." Al tried to sound natural. Not like someone who was had just considered getting totally wasted.

"Al, we just wanted you to know that you have our full support and if there's anything Mark and I can do, just give us a call."

Al felt his throat close up. He couldn't say anything.

"Al? You there?"

Al cleared his throat and ran a hand through his hair. "Thank you."

"Anything you need ... really, don't hesitate to call us."

"How did you know? Aren't you with Mark's family?"

"We are. We'll be back after Thanksgiving, but Mark reads *The Beachside* online and he read the article. Then we got an email from Fred Weiss, who had been eating at the Hardware Store and had seen the whole thing and he told us what happened. He said he was cheering you on."

"Really?"

"That's what he said. And we just want you to know that if we'd been there we would've done the same thing."

"I appreciate that." Al voice caught in his throat again. "I suppose I'll need to get a lawyer, but I haven't gotten that far. It's been hard to think what to do."

"No one could convict you Al, you're the most gentle guy we know. Mark said if it'd been him, he might be charged with murder."

Al laughed. "Actually, there is something ...."

"Anything—you name it."

"Martha Jane suggested a while back that I see a therapist, a counselor—and I haven't done anything about it—but I haven't been able to make anything work out since I retired and after this arrest and all, well, I think I should probably talk to somebody."

"Trust me, I know what it's like. After I retired I got really depressed. My whole life had been theater and without teaching and directing shows, I was kind of a zombie for a while. I couldn't get interested in anything. But I saw a guy for about six months— Barney Klein—and he was great, helped a lot. Then when I directed Walter's play, things began to turn around for me. Hang on and I'll get his number for you."

"Okay, thanks." While he waited, Al shut the door to the cupboard with the liquor and looked out the window. It was cold and breezy, but walking on the beach might be good, and he probably wouldn't run into anyone.

"Okay, got a pen?" Mark asked.

"Oh, just a second." Al went to the desk in the living room. "Okay, all set."

"Barney Klein, 206-303-3313. His office is in West Seattle, so it's easy to get there from the island. The bus goes on the ferry and you can get off at California, and it's just a few blocks to his office. He's in a group with another psychiatrist and a psychologist—there's no receptionist or anything, they each make their own appointments. The number I gave you is his cell."

"Thanks, Howie."

"Wants some advice?"

"Sure."

"Don't wait to call Barney. Just make an appointment and if it doesn't work out or you don't feel comfortable, we can come up with more names for you."

"Okay. I'll call him right now."

"Great, and let's get together when we get back, we'll be home Monday after Thanksgiving."

"Sounds good. Give my best to Mark ... Howie, I ..." Al's voice cracked again. " ... thanks."

"Anytime, bro. See you soon."

Al hung up and looked out at the beach. He was sure taking Bert for a walk would help him feel better, but he worried that if he did, he might lose his nerve about calling the shrink. He had told Howie he would. And he'd probably ask about it when he and Mark got back. He didn't really want to call a shrink when it came right down to it. Although it had been in his mind ever since Martha Jane first suggested it. He supposed the reluctance was having to admit that he couldn't figure things out himself. He'd only relied on himself his whole life, and the idea that his own abilities weren't enough to solve his problems made him feel profoundly inadequate. But he'd told Howie he'd call and he would. Just later. He'd do it—but later. Bert needed his walk.

Al put on his parka and a wool hat and was about to leave for the beach when the phone rang. It was Bonnie. Just seeing her name lifted his heart.

"Hi, Bonnie."

"Just wanted to see how you're feeling today and if I could keep Bert's leash for a while."

"You haven't seen the paper?"

"No."

"There's a story about me getting charged with assault."

"Oh Al, I'm sorry."

"So am I. But you know, there's nothing secret on the island anyway. It would get around even if it wasn't in the paper. I admit I was blown away when I saw it, but Howie called and I feel better. Anyway, sure, you can keep the leash. I have another one."

"I want to take Princess for a walk, but I'm a little worried she'd spook at something and run off. I don't think she would, but I don't want to take the chance."

"That's probably wise. I'm about to leave with Bert for the beach, if you want to join us."

"Great."

"We'll see you in a minute." Al felt like yo-yo. One minute he's devastated about the humiliating article in the paper, and the next minute, at the thought of being with Bonnie, he's Mr. Bliss. Was he bipolar, his mood swinging like that?

THE TIDE WAS GOING OUT, exposing more of the rocks on the gravelly beach. On the shore, the bigleaf maples and alder on the bank had lost the last of their leaves, and the bare branches swayed as the wind swept across the beach. The November sky was steely gray, and the air was cold and damp as it rustled through the fir trees on the high bank, but to Al—he could have been strolling on a tropical beach. Bonnie walked next to him with Princess while Bert trotted along the edge of the water. The leash he'd loaned her for Princess was expandable, but the dog stayed close to her, never venturing out more than a few feet. He got that. He wanted to stay close to her, too.

"Is your head really okay this morning ... no headache or foggy feeling?"

"I'm fine. It just feels strange, though."

"Your head?"

"No. Having someone worrying about me."

"I'm good at worrying. Anytime you need worries—just call my name." She looked up and smiled at him.

He laughed nervously. Al couldn't think of what to say. He wanted to tell her he thought that he probably loved her. What else to call it? She unlocked a playful part of himself he'd forgotten existed. He wanted to be with her all the time. He appreciated her lovely temperament, her openness and kind heart, and he admired her competence and intelligence. It was peaceful to be with her. There was joy. And something he thought had been locked in some mausoleum: Passion. It was hard to comprehend he'd only known her a few months because he felt like he'd always known her—but he hadn't—and that's what worried him, scared him into not trusting his feelings. Was he just wanting to cling to her like she was a St. Bernard sent to rescue him? He looked at Bert, who was sniffing some kelp. "I hope Bert doesn't roll in a dead fish or something. I'd have to wash him so he doesn't stink when I take him to visit your father." Was that all he could think to say? That he hoped his dog didn't roll in something dead?

"My dad probably wouldn't even notice."

"The staff might, though." Al picked up a stick and threw it across the beach for Bert. He glanced at Bonnie. Her cheeks were red from the wind. "Are you warm enough?"

"I love it on the beach, even when it's like this." She pointed to a blue heron standing in the shallow water a few yards away at Peter Point. "There's a perfect log down there, it's almost like a bench. Let's sit a minute and see if he catches anything."

He held out his hand, palm up. "It's starting to rain a little."

"Just a drizzle. Nothing to us in the Pacific Northwest, right?"

"You bet."

When they got to the log, Princess sat at Bonnie's feet and rested her head on Bonnie's knees while Bonnie scratched her ears. "I'm getting attached to her, you know. I thought I'd take her for a ride in the car later this afternoon to see how she does. I'll probably stop at Thriftway to get some dog food."

"I can give you some of Bert's," he offered, as he sat next to her.

"I'll just get a small amount. A few cans."

"After all you've done, at least let me supply the dog food." He leaned closer to her. "And when can I take you to dinner, by the way?"

"Actually, I wanted to know if you had plans for Thanksgiving. I'll be eating at the care center with my father, and I wondered if you'd like to join us?"

"I'd like that very much."

"And I do have a favor to ask you, Al."

"Anything."

"I'm going to be in Boston between Thanksgiving and Christmas visiting my daughter and grandchildren. And I wondered if you'd look after Princess for me?" Bonnie looked at the dog and smiled. "I'm just not ready to have her go to the shelter yet—I want to keep being a foster home for her and I'm trying to figure out what to do, what makes sense. Maggie's coming back in January and I have to make some decisions. I'm hoping being away will give me a new perspective, help things to be more clear."

"I'd be happy to look in on your father, too, if you'd like."

She looked up at him and touched his cheek. "Thank you." She lifted her face to him then slipped her arm over his shoulder to rest her hand on the back of his neck and drew him toward her. They held each other in the light rain while down the beach the heron patiently stared at the shallow water as the tide rolled out to sea. She tasted of salt and he felt tears against his cheek, not sure if they were hers or his.

CHAPTER 22

❧

T HE TEMPERATURE HADN'T DROPPED ENOUGH TO WARRANT SHUTTING off the water to the outside faucets, and Al used the hose on the deck to wash the sand off Bert. Luckily, Bert didn't smell bad. He hadn't found decaying fish or fowl to roll in, so it was just a matter of getting the sand off before he took him to visit Bonnie's father. He smiled, thinking about Bonnie. He didn't want to wonder what it had meant to kiss her. To analyze or dissect it. It happened. It was wonderful. She was wonderful. He felt a little goofy. Like a teenager. But what was wrong with that? Better than feeling like an old fart who was over the hill. They had walked back from the beach hand in hand and he had wanted to kiss her again before she went in her house, but they both seemed to be feeling a little shy and just left each other with a long hug.

Driving to the care center with Bert next to him in the truck, Al put on "Sweet Little Angel" and sang along with B.B. King. "I've got a sweet little angel … I love the way she spread her wings … Yes, when she spreads her wings around me … I get joy and everything … Oh, if my baby should quit me … I believe I would die … Lord I do believe I would die …Yes if you don't love me little angel … Please tell me the reason why!" He thumped his hand against the steering wheel, belting it out with B.B. and although he felt happier than he had in years—maybe ever—he still cut over to Cove Road to avoid the center of town.

He parked in the lot next to Vashon Community Care and stared at the building. How many people would he run into? Would they avoid him? Not want to talk to or be seen near a man who'd been arrested for assault? Al lifted the console between the seats where he'd put the green ball. "Okay, buddy," he said to Bert as he put the ball in his pocket. "Let's stick together. We can do this. 'Love Will Keep us Together,' right, Bert ... like Captain and what's-her-name." Tina? Tahlula? Lucile? No, that's not it. It bothered him to not be able to think of that name, especially as he walked into the care center, a place where people with memory problems weren't in short supply. Al went around to the passenger side, opened the door and snapped on Bert's leash. "Here we go, buddy. Show time."

The lobby was decorated for Thanksgiving with a large bouquet of autumn colored flowers: dahlias, chrysanthemums, and gerbera daisies in shades of gold, bronze, burgundy and orange. In the dining room across from the main lobby, Al saw a table with a centerpiece of gourds and Indian corn. The whole place was lovely and welcoming, and he supposed if folks couldn't be home for Thanksgiving this was as good a place as any. Better than most. He checked in at the desk, and the receptionist said that he and Bert could go right on up to see Mr. Douglas.

As he waited for the elevator, a man who looked to be well into his nineties shuffled by hanging on to an aluminum walker. He stopped and smiled at Bert. "Some pony you got there."

"His name is Bert." Al smiled.

"I had a pony back in Illinois. A little town called Sandwich, near Aurora. A nice brown pony. Name was Scout."

The elevator door opened and Al held it. "Going up?"

"Nope. Just takin' a walk. Goin' to see my girlfriend." He chuckled and shuffled past the elevator.

Al wondered if the guy really thought Bert was a pony, or if he was making a joke or just got his words mixed up, saying "dog" instead of "pony," and then the memory of his pony surfaced. It was hard to tell how a person's mind worked when things got jumbled up. And what was the name of that singer, the one who sang "Love will Keep Us Together?" It was starting to bug him. Martha Jane said it didn't matter if you couldn't remember details and it was a waste of time to fret about it. He supposed she was right. At least he was remembering to feed her cat.

Ralph Douglas didn't answer when Al knocked on the door. He waited a few minutes then knocked again. Maybe he didn't hear well or was in the bathroom or asleep. Al wasn't sure what to do but figured even if Mr. Douglas had been told about having a visitor, he may not have remembered. Slowly he cracked the door open and stuck his head in.

"Mr. Douglas? Ralph?"

He sat in the same chair in front of the large window and looked up and gave a slight nod when he saw Al, but broke into a grin at the sight of Bert. "Susie!" He leaned down and held out his arms.

"Nice to see you again, Mr. Douglas." Al handed him the little bag of freeze dried beef liver. "Here are the treats."

Bonnie's father looked at the little bag, as if he wasn't sure what it was.

"It's for the dog."

"Call me Ralph. Nice to see you, too, and my Susie." He pulled out a treat and gave it to Bert.

"Mind if I sit down, Ralph?"

"Be my guest." Bonnie father looked at Bert lovingly, patting his head with his pale skeletal hand.

Al sat on the couch and pulled the ball out of his pocket. "We probably can't throw the ball very high here—only roll it, but someday we can take ...."

He began to say "Bert." But why not call him "Susie" and refer to him as a "her?" What did it matter? Ralph Douglas probably wasn't going to look closely at Bert's anatomy and if he did, Al doubted he'd connect the dots. If Bonnie's father wanted Bert to be Susie, Bert would be Susie.

... "her to the park," he continued.

"Can I have the ball?" Ralph asked.

"Sure." Al handed it to him, and Ralph leaned down and rolled it the length of the living room and into the kitchenette. It was only a distance of about twenty-five feet, but Bert gleefully galloped after it, sliding across the floor of the kitchenette where he retrieved it.

"That-a-girl, Susie! Bring it here!" Ralph held out his hand. As soon as Bert came back with the ball, he dropped it in Ralph's lap and Ralph immediately threw it again. "She's a good one, my Susie," he said with pride.

"She's a great dog, that's for sure." Al sat back, feeling like Mr. Bliss again as he watched Bonnie's father getting so much joy from Bert. He didn't think Bert would ever tire of the game, but he didn't know about Ralph.

"We've had Susie ever since she was puppy, you know." He scratched Bert's ears, before he threw the ball again. "Smartest dog I ever had."

"I'm glad we could visit. Bonnie was sorry she couldn't come today."

Ralph didn't respond, then threw the ball again, delighted as Bert went after it.

"I think I love her."

"Oh, I love my Susie." Ralph nodded.

"I mean Bonnie. But I don't know," Al sighed. "I don't think I've been very good at it, you know. I mean, I thought I was a good husband to Eleanor. I didn't drink or gamble or chase women ...."

"Susie always chases the ball. A born retriever, you know."

"But I guess there wasn't much passion and that's what I feel when I'm with Bonnie. When I'm with her I feel like I did about Rex, only much, much more so, naturally. She's open-minded and kind, and strong and caring and loves dogs and fun and I love her dark eyes and long face and long legs and her playful elegance. I want to hold her ... well, more than that ... actually. I want to make love to her, but it's been so long I don't really know how that would work out. But we would laugh, I think. Maybe. She's not the kind of person who would laugh at me."

"Susie makes me laugh, the way she slides!" Ralph watched Bert skidding across the kitchenette.

"And it's too soon for both of us. She's not sure what she's doing and where she'll live and I'm trying to reinvent myself since I can't be a vet for five years, except the things I've tried haven't worked out very well. I'd really like to reinvent myself as a good husband, if truth be told. I just want to be with Bonnie. But then I have to worry about what the prosecutor's going to decide about my case and that's just a big mess."

"Susie never messed up. She was housebroken very easily. She's so smart, aren't you, Susie girl?" Ralph took the ball from Bert and put his arms around him.

Watching the two of them, Al felt sad. Bert was doing so much for Bonnie's father. What a shame that the residents couldn't have dogs over twenty pounds. He understood the need for that, of course. Big dogs can knock people over, and there was a good reason to have the limit on size. But it still made him sad.

There was a knock on the door, and Al got up to answer it. Ralph didn't seem to notice; he was in his own world with Bert a.k.a. Susie. The repetition of the game seemed to be soothing to him, and he and the dog had developed a steady rhythm of it.

Al opened the door to an attractive woman with short gray hair and red glasses. "Hi, I'm a volunteer and they asked me to check with you about Thanksgiving."

"I'm Al Paugh—I'm just a friend."

"We have it down that you'll be having Thanksgiving dinner here—"

"Right."

"The staff wanted to know if we could have one of our residents join you. Betty Bagley, she doesn't have any family. She's a lovely person—uses a wheelchair, and I think you'd enjoy her."

"Sure. I'm sure that would be fine. I know Bonnie would like that, but I can have her call you." Al looked at his watch, it was close to five. Ralph would need to be going down for dinner. "I have to leave, but we'll be in touch."

"Okay, great." She looked at Ralph, who stared at Bert with a sweet smile while he petted him. "Hi, Ralph."

Ralph waved. "Hello, dear."

Did he think she was Bonnie? Maybe it didn't matter so much, Ralph seemed very content. Wasn't that the best you could hope for, that a person at the end of his or her life could find some pleasure and not be in pain or feel afraid? The volunteer left and Al went to Ralph and squatted down on his heels next to Bert. "It's time for dinner, Ralph. And dogs aren't allowed so I'll take Susie now."

"Okay." He hugged Bert. "See you soon Susie."

It struck Al how confident he'd been that Bonnie would be happy to have the lady without a family join them for Thanksgiving dinner. How different that was, to feel sure of someone's heart. He didn't want to think of Eleanor and make comparisons, but it was hard not to—the way they operated in the world was so different. It wouldn't even matter if the lady was an irritating person, he knew Bonnie would be kind to her. How many people were there like Betty Bagley? People who ended up in a nursing home with no family. Would he be one of those? The social worker finding some people to have a holiday dinner with him because he didn't have anyone. "Would your family include Al Paugh, he's a nice fellow, and has no family." Oh, man. Is that what it would be like? He'd always have a dog, of course. But what if he got to the point that he couldn't take care of a dog. What then? Al thought about Bonnie, and what he'd said to her father. It had all just babbled out of him, but maybe he was putting too much stock in thinking of a future with her, too much hope. Was it a bad thing to hope? Could he stand it, if she backed off or got to know him better and decided she didn't want him? He told Howie he'd call the shrink, and he knew he should. It was one thing to spill his guts to Mr. Douglas whose brain had turned to mush, but maybe talking to someone who hopefully had all their marbles could help somehow. It had to be worth a try.

When he got home, after he fed Maria Montessori at Martha Jane's, he wanted to call Bonnie to tell her how things had gone with her father and Bert. And to ask her about Betty Bagley

joining them at Thanksgiving. It was an easy name to remember—
Betty Bagley, it made him think of Betty Boop, but the lights
were off at Bonnie's house, and her car was gone. His house was
chilly, and he went in the living room and decided to build a fire.
Bert would like that, he always wanted to lie in front of it. Then
he'd have a drink and make Ramen for dinner. He knew canned
soup and Ramen would get old, but he was sure he'd soon feel up
to going to Thriftway. It had gone so well at the care center, no
one seemed awkward around him. The receptionist, the volunteer, and the guy who mentioned the pony—they'd all been fine.

After he got the fire going, Al went to the kitchen and fed
Bert. He had a few eggs left and broke one over his kibble for
something a little special. What a great dog. He'd been so willing
to retrieve the ball over and over again just from Ralph's small
living room to the kitchenette and back. Al fixed himself a drink.
He had about half a bottle of Johnny Walker, and he took it out
of the cupboard, got a glass, put in ice and poured himself a bit.

Standing by the window, he sipped his drink and looked out.
Still no sign of Bonnie, she'd probably gone to Thriftway to get
food for Princess. She was sure becoming attached to Princess. Al
closed his eyes and took a big gulp of his drink. He hoped she was
becoming attached to him. Then B.B King's song "There Has to
be a Better World" popped into his mind and the part that went
"Everybody I love ... Seems to love somebody else ... And every
woman ... Got a license to break my heart ... And every love, oh
it's over ... Over before it gets a chance to start."

Okay, that's it. Enough. *Just call the shrink like you told Howie
you would.* Al went to the desk where he'd written the number.
After he put in the call, while it rang, he wasn't sure what he
expected. He pictured some cartoony guy with a monocle and
a little pointy beard, with messy hair sticking out all over, an
Austrian accent and a bow tie. But when the message came on, it
was straightforward and the voice was warm. "You have reached
Dr. Barney Klein, please leave your name and number, and I'll
return your call at my earliest convenience." Al cleared his throat,
then left his name and number and said he'd like to make an

appointment and that was it. Not a big deal. And like Howie had said, if he didn't like the guy he could always try somebody else. Or no one, if he could somehow turn things around himself.

CHAPTER 23

"WOULD YOU LIKE SOME MORE MASHED POTATOES, MRS. BAGLEY?" Al asked. Betty Bagley sat next to him with her wheelchair pulled up to the table. She was a tiny woman whose pale lined face was topped with sparse wisps of grayish hair like a dandelion gone to seed. But her blue eyes were bright, and even though she was physically impaired, which had to take its toll, she seemed younger than Bonnie's father. Ralph, although he was frail, was not in particularly bad shape considering his age; but it was the way he was detached that made him seem older. He focused on his food and looked up occasionally, but his eyes had a vacant look, as if he was mostly in his own world and only peripherally there with them.

Bonnie and Al had dressed up for the occasion. Al couldn't remember when he'd last worn a tie. It might have been at the memorial service for one of his clients, about six or seven years ago. And he'd never seen Bonnie in anything but jeans. Tonight she was wearing a dark green dress with a gold necklace, and she looked elegant and beautiful in the soft light of the dining room. The room itself was festive with the aura of a lovely restaurant. On all the tables there were candles and little centerpieces, each with a small ceramic turkey surrounded by fall flowers. You'd hardly know it was a nursing home and assisted living facility.

Mrs. Bagley put her hand on Al's arm. "My appetite is a lot

smaller than it once was. But I do love a turkey dinner and they do such a nice job here—I think I will have a little more, just a small amount, thank you." She smiled. "Oh, and quite a bit of gravy. That's just the best part, I always thought. That and the stuffing. And please call me Betty. "

"I agree." Al put a small amount of potatoes on her plate. "Is that about right, Betty?"

"A little more gravy would be good." She laughed. "It's lovely to be with you. It's so nice of you to include me at your table."

"We're delighted you wanted to join us." Bonnie cut her turkey and took a bite. "It's nice to have Thanksgiving dinner with a group of people."

"I remember some swell Thanksgivings we used to have on the Oregon coast. A bunch of us rented a house at Manzanita for years. None of us had children or any family nearby and we made our own family, if you know what I mean."

"I do know." Bonnie nodded and looked at her father's plate. "Doing okay, Dad?"

"Fine." Ralph continued to eat slowly, mostly staring at his plate.

"The thing about the Oregon coast that was so wonderful was the beach. We all had dogs and they would just run and run. It was a joy to see them. It reminds me of a Mary Oliver poem about dogs not on leashes, although I can't remember it exactly."

"I love her poetry." Al reached for the sweet potatoes.

"Do you now?" She laughed. "I suppose I shouldn't be surprised. Certainly many men like poetry and are fine poets."

"A lot of her poems are about dogs, and I can certainly relate to that."

Betty put down her fork. "I miss my dog so much." She glanced down and knotted her napkin in her lap.

"What was your dog's name?" Al asked.

"Ali. He was a boxer—just the most beautiful boy—we named him for the famous boxer. It was my husband who named him."

Bonnie put her hand over Betty's. "That's a perfect name for a boxer. How long did he live?"

"Oh, he's not dead. Ali's very much alive, but you see when I needed to come here after I broke my hip and couldn't manage on my own anymore, I couldn't have Ali here. There are dogs here, but just little ones. You're not allowed to have a dog over twenty pounds. I couldn't find anyone to take Ali. Donald and I never had children and I've outlived my closest friends, so Ali is at the Vashon Animal Shelter, waiting for a home. Every day I pray someone will adopt him. Some nice family. But so far, no one has."

AFTER DINNER ON THE WAY back to Baker's Beach, they talked about the contrast between Bonnie's father and Betty Bagley. It had been obvious that Ralph hadn't seemed aware of who Bonnie was and had no memory of Al's visit the day before. "They're close in age, but she's really alert and engaged with everything. I felt so sad for her. I can see she's someone who makes friends easily and can enjoy people's company, but I can imagine it's just hard to be without her dog. I wanted to adopt Betty Bagley *and* the dog," Bonnie said with a deep sigh.

"So did I."

"The problem is I'm just not in any position to do much of anything. I don't even know what I'll do about Princess. What if she's like Betty Bagley's dog and just lives at the shelter with no one to adopt her?"

Al turned into Baker's Beach road. "People used to bring stray dogs to the clinic. It was always sad. We'd keep them as long as we could. Sometimes we knew a family whose dog had died in the last year and we'd do a little matchmaking. It was one of my happiest times when we could do that." Al parked his truck in front of his house. He could see Bert's face at the front window. He always appeared there whenever he heard the truck. They had left both dogs at Al's house when they went to dinner. "Would you like to come in for a drink?"

"Thanks, but I'm taking the red-eye tonight and I've got to pack. I'd like to see Princess before I leave, but I think to bring her to my house and then just turn around and bring her back an hour later might confuse her. Probably better just to leave her there." Bonnie unfastened her seat belt. "I'm grateful to you for taking care of her."

"It's not a problem. I always thought I should've had her anyway." Al got out of the truck and went around and opened the door for Bonnie.

"Ah, a gentleman." She laughed and slowly got down from the truck. "I don't seem to even climb in and out of my car without creaking. These old bones ain't what they used to be."

"You don't seem old. You seem, I don't know what it is ... I just feel young when I'm with you. You do that for me. And you looked beautiful tonight."

"Candlelight helps, and the relativity of being with folks in their nineties, but thank you." She reached for him and he kissed her. Al leaned back against the truck and pulled her against him. They were each wearing winter coats and gloves and Al pulled off his gloves and unbuttoned her coat. He slid his arms around her and caressed her back, he kissed her throat and ran a hand through her hair. He wanted to make love. He wanted to tell her he loved her, but just then Bert started barking and the disturbance was enough of a distraction that the words remained in his heart. Al held Bonnie's head against his chest. "Bert seems to be having a problem with the fact that I haven't come in." She tilted her head back and they kissed again, but Bert continued barking and Bonnie started to laugh. "This is so high school!" She looked at Bert barking with his head bobbing up and down in the window. "Only it's not the parents yelling at the kids to come in—it's your dog!"

"Bert is very parental. We look out for each other, Bert and I." Al kissed the top of her head. "Are you sure you don't want to come in?"

"I really can't." Bonnie looked at her watch. "The Vashon Shuttle is coming for me at 10:00." She gave him a quick kiss, "I'll see you in a couple of weeks."

Al buttoned her coat and started to walk her to her door. "Al, just go to Bert, he's getting upset. And if we started in again at my door, I'm not sure I'd make the plane."

"That would be fine with me." He looked at her tenderly.

She touched his cheek. "I really do have to go."

"Well, okay then. Have a safe trip, Bonnie."

He didn't want to leave her. He walked up to his house wishing he'd been brave enough to tell her he loved her.

CHAPTER 24

IT WAS A BAD NIGHT. THE NIGHTMARE WAS LIKE THE ONE HE'D HAD after Jerry Kincaid had threatened to sue him. The details were fuzzy, but something happened that was humiliating, leaving him feeling worthless in a way that was familiar. It also hadn't helped that both Princess and Bert had spent the night on the bed with him, and they were big dogs. Bert always slept with him, but it didn't seem right to let Bert on the bed and make Princess stay on the floor. Life wasn't fair. Al knew that, but at least he could try to be fair to the dogs. And there was something else: his appointment with the shrink at ten that morning—that made him very nervous. And it wasn't with the guy that Howie had recommended. When Dr. Barney Klein called him back, he had told Al his practice was full and he didn't foresee any openings until after the first of the year. But he had recommended a psychologist in the group he formerly practiced with, a Dr. John Dudnik, whose office was near the Pike Place Market. At first Al thought that having Dr. Klein unavailable would give him a way to get out of it. He could tell Howie that he tried, but Dr. Klein couldn't see him. But when he was honest about it, he realized that although he had more clarity about Bonnie now that he admitted he was falling in love with her, everything else was still pretty much a mess. He still had no idea what to do with himself—how to figure out a life without his work. He couldn't just hang around Bonnie and do nothing, just depend on being with her to make him feel happy. Follow her around like a puppy. She'd get sick of that pretty quick and besides, he didn't even know how she really felt about him. Clearly, she had affection for him, but maybe that was it. Maybe he was a kind of diversion, a respite from the grief she struggled with, and he'd never be more than that and she'd move on. And he still had to face the possible arraignment, and then he'd have to find a lawyer and Deputy Sheriff Molina had said it could be months. It was a good bet it wouldn't happen until after the first of the year, which was when his lease was up, and he had no idea where he and Bert were going to live. There certainly wasn't a shortage of things he needed to get a handle on. After thinking it over, Al decided to keep the appointment. But in his mind, it amused him to think of Dr. John Dudnik as Dr. Dud. It made having to tell a complete stranger how screwed up his life was less threatening.

THE PASSENGER BOAT FOR DOWNTOWN Seattle left from the north-end ferry dock several times a day, with the times tailored for commuters. Dr. Dudnik's office was near Pike Place Market, and Al thought it would be easier not to bring his truck and try to park. The boat, which some islanders called the foot ferry, was officially the King County Water Taxi. It had three morning sailings, and Al took the last boat, The MV Sally Fox (named for a beloved island activist), at 8:15, which was due to arrive in downtown Seattle at the waterfront at 8:40. It was about a six block walk to the guy's office, and Al would look for a coffee shop where he could hang out until his appointment.

It was a dreary day, typical for late November. Al found a seat next to a window toward the back of the boat. He had brought a book about retirement that he'd found online, *How to Retire Happy, Wild, and Free: Retirement Wisdom that You Won't Get from your Financial Advisor*. If Dr. Dudnik really was a dud, maybe the book would help. He'd also brought *The Beachside*, which had come that morning. Al started to look at the retirement book;

he'd never been the type for self-help books, although he supposed he'd never been in a position to think he needed one until
now. But the tone of the book was so cheery and upbeat—so
removed from how he felt—he couldn't connect with it. Instead,
he picked up *The Beachside*. He read about a new purchase by the
land trust and a program at the Senior Center where the Vashon
Ukulele Society had performed a medley of Beatles songs—just
the usual, until he turned the page to the Opinion section, where
under *Letters to the Editor* in a large headline he saw his name.

In Support of Dr. Al Paugh

> We are writing in support of Dr. Al Paugh in response to
> the story in the paper last week, which reported his arrest.
> We were witnesses to the altercation that took place in the
> US Bank parking lot, and to us, Al Paugh is a hero. He
> bravely acted to intercede on behalf of a dog that was the
> victim of cruel abuse. The island is lucky to have someone
> as kind and caring as Al Paugh, and we intend to petition
> the King County Prosecutor's Office on Dr. Paugh's behalf
> to request that the charges be dropped. Dr. Paugh has pro-
> vided outstanding care to so many of our animals and there
> are already over four hundred people who have signed our
> petition. The world needs more people who are willing to
> take a risk and get involved when someone perpetuates such
> cruelty to an animal, and Dr. Al Paugh is someone we all
> need to get behind.

> Bruce Fillinger, Barry Foster, Margy Heldring, Dana Illo,
> Catherine Johnson, Dan Klein, David Pfeiffer, Faith Reeves,
> Ann Leda Shapiro, Janie Starr and Kirk Starr

Al read it over five times. Each time the words blurred a little
more as tears filled his eyes. Al looked out at the Seattle skyline;
they were nearing the waterfront, and all he wanted to do was race
back to the island and thank every one of those people. They said

he was a hero! He wished he was with Bert so he could read it to him. He stared out the window and chuckled. He was so happy he could hardly keep still. Maybe he didn't need to see Dr. Dud. Maybe he could cancel. But then what would he do? The next boat back to the island wasn't until 4:30. Al saw the Great Ferris Wheel perched on the edge of the waterfront. Maybe he could ride around on that for a while, then call it a day. That's how he'd retire happy, wild and free ... going round and round on the Great Ferris Wheel. Or he could even go to the Seattle Art Museum or the aquarium. That would really make the trip worthwhile. He especially loved the otters; that could be a lot of fun.

But he remembered how it put a glitch in things when he was in practice and people canceled at the last minute. It wasn't considerate, although sometimes it couldn't be helped if the person had an emergency. Riding the Great Ferris Wheel wouldn't cut it. Al sighed and decided he'd better go. But he could bring the article to show the shrink so Dr. Dud would see that he was a good guy. Make a good first impression.

Al got off the ferry with the other passengers and walked along Western Avenue where he found a coffee shop and got coffee and a blueberry scone. It wasn't as good as Mark's, but it was okay. He'd been so nervous about the appointment, he hadn't had breakfast. Before he left, he'd gone over to feed Maria Montessori at Martha Jane's, and then fed Bert and Princess, but he hadn't had any appetite himself.

While he ate and sipped his coffee, Al read the letter in the paper again, "In Support of Dr. Al Paugh." He could read it now without crying. Now he smiled and read it over so many times he was beginning to memorize it. When he got back to the island, he would write a note of thanks to each person who signed the letter. He could even go to the post office in broad daylight. And Thriftway. He wouldn't just have to eat Ramen anymore. Maybe he'd get salmon and a nice bottle of wine. Al bought another scone and left the coffee shop and ate it on the way to Dr. Dud's. Maybe after the appointment he could have a nice lunch before he went back to the island. He could go to one of the restaurants in the Pike Place Market or Anthony's Pier 66—it was right on the waterfront. He could have their salmon and wine, and it had a gorgeous view of Elliott Bay. Maybe even some oysters. Was November a month when they were good? He couldn't remember. No matter. They'd have a lot of seafood he'd like.

He didn't have any trouble finding the office. It was an old brick building like so many along the waterfront. Al took the stairs to the second floor and saw the office at the end of the hall. He went in the waiting room and took a seat. It was kind of weird. There was no receptionist and two people were sitting in the otherwise empty room. A young pretty woman wearing boots and a fluffy sweater was reading a magazine, and a guy wearing a sport coat was scrolling through his phone. They both looked normal to him, and Al wondered what they had to talk about. Maybe they were a couple and their marriage was having problems. He wondered what would have happened if he and Eleanor had ever gotten marriage counseling. Probably nothing. Which was fine with him, since he was glad they were getting a divorce. He hadn't heard anything about it from Eleanor, and he assumed it was all on track.

A door opened to the waiting room and a guy looked in. He was wearing gray slacks and a blue button-down dress shirt. He looked exactly like the comedian John Oliver. It made Al want to laugh, but he controlled himself. Dr. Dudnik spotted Al and smiled. "Dr. Paugh?" Al nodded and the guy said, "Please come in."

Al was almost surprised the guy didn't have an English accent, he looked so much like John Oliver. Al followed him down a narrow hall to an office, which had the door open. As he closed the door he held out his hand, "I'm Dr. Dudnik—John."

"Nice to meet you."

"Please have a seat." Dr. Dudnik motioned to a chair in the corner of the room. Al went and sat down. He wanted to tell the guy he looked just like the comedian John Oliver, but he thought maybe that wouldn't be appropriate. Then he wondered what was appropriate in the company of a shrink. Al glanced around the office. It looked like a nice little living room. There were several chairs and a nice blue and beige striped rug and two end tables by the chairs and the only thing that seemed a little odd was that they had boxes of tissues on them. There weren't any family pictures around, only some diplomas on the wall behind the desk. And the paintings: a pastoral landscape and a seascape that were pretty nondescript and didn't tell you much.

Dr. Dudnik sat across from Al in a black leather chair. It looked like Al's chair, the one he'd brought home from his office so Jerry Kincaid couldn't have it.

"Did you have any trouble finding the office?" Dr. Dudnik asked.

"No, your directions were fine, and I have a map on my phone. I don't come into Seattle all that much though. I live on Vashon."

Dr. Dudnik smiled." I'll just get your name and address and then maybe you can tell me what brought you here."

"The ferry." Al laughed nervously, then gave him his address. "My address is temporary, I'm just renting because well, it's a long story." Al looked at Dr. Dudnik. "I suppose I should tell you."

"Whatever you think is important, Dr. Paugh."

"Oh, call me Al. What should I call you?"

"I get all kinds of things," he laughed. "Dr. Dudnik, Dr. D., John, Dr. John—"

"So, you're goin' back to New Orleans?" Al laughed nervously again. Dr. Dudnik didn't say anything, Al thought he looked a little puzzled, so Al said, "You know—Dr. John—the blues singer, he does pop and jazz too, also zydeco, but I like his blues best."

Dr. Dudnik smiled. "Oh, right. He's the guy that plays the piano."

"That's one of Dr John's hits—'Goin' Back to New Orleans'— maybe I'll just call you John." Al decided not to mention the he was a dead ringer for John Oliver.

"That'd be fine."

"I like blues. It's really my favorite kind of music." Dr. Dudnik didn't say anything and the silence made him nervous so Al just kept talking. "My wife, I mean she's almost my ex-wife, hated blues. She didn't like dogs that much either, which I probably should have paid attention to in the beginning since I'm a veterinarian."

"I wondered what kind of a doctor you were. Do you have a practice on the island?"

"No. I'm retired, and I think that's the main problem—I've flunked retirement."

"It can be a really hard adjustment for people." Dr. Dudnik nodded sympathetically and then Al just went ahead and told him the whole story. His heart attack, Eleanor insisting he retire, selling his practice to Jerry Kincaid, Eleanor leaving him to live with Ruby, his move to Baker's Beach and meeting Bonnie, the women getting mad at him for not choosing their dogs for the calendar, Jerry Kincaid threatening to sue him, his failure as a school volunteer, and then his arrest.

Dr. Dudnik listened intently and didn't say anything. It wasn't a cold kind of silence, though. Al felt it was encouraging somehow. "I started having some awful dreams that started when Jerry Kincaid threatened to sue me." Al felt upset mentioning it, but he tried to smile. "Isn't that what you do when you talk to a shrink? Tell them dreams?"

"Only if you want to, if you think it means something."

"The main thing I guess is that it brought back a feeling of being humiliated and worthless and I keep remembering something that happened when I was about seven." Al looked at Dr. Dudnik. "I don't know if it matters—I've never told anyone."

"I think if doors need to be opened, they will be—but most likely only when their right to remain closed is respected."

Al looked at the floor. Then he glanced at John Dudnik, then he blinked and looked at the seascape on the wall. Then he just started in, talking about his family being in theater, how they were often gone and how their grandmother had taken care of them and seemed to resent every minute of it. Al paused and cleared his throat. It felt like he was about to plunge off a diving board into cold water, but he made himself do it. "What happened was that when I was about seven, my older brother Jamie, who must have been about eleven at the time—he and his friends—they stripped me and tied me to the tree in our front yard. There were lot of kids playing in the street. My brother peed on me and his friends thought it was funny—kids ran around laughing and pointing at me—it seemed like hours before my grandmother finally heard me wailing and came and untied me. Her reaction was to say 'boys will be boys' and throw me in the bathtub, yelling at me to clean up. She seemed angry at me for the whole thing. I never knew who to turn to. My parents were either gone—or if they happened to be there, they were oblivious to what was going on in our family. The only one I could ever trust was Rex."

"Was Rex your older or younger brother?"

"He was the dog."

"And you became a veterinarian." John didn't say anything for a few minutes. "What you describe is a traumatic experience," he stated, quietly. "And children typically think when something awful happens it's because they're not worthy. It doesn't occur to them that the people who are treating them with neglect or abuse are the ones with the serious problems. And for sure that wasn't just a 'boys will be boys' episode. Your brother's hostility was beyond what is normal sibling rivalry."

"Why do you think he was like that?"

"I don't know him, of course. So I can only speculate in general terms, but when there's a considerable amount of emotional deprivation, siblings can turn on one another to express the rage they feel against their parents. They displace it because it's safer to turn it on a sibling—what your brother did indicates a pretty disturbed boy."

Al knew Jamie was screwed up. It wasn't news, considering the way Jamie had made such a mess of his life. But it surprised Al to feel a kind of relief in the way John described it.

"What kind of a dog was Rex?" he asked.

"A collie. A gorgeous collie. The stability for me growing up was Rex. He was the one on my side."

"It's good you had Rex. Children need to feel there's someone on their side."

"Bonnie, the woman I mentioned, she reminded me of Rex."

"Sounds like a good association to me." John smiled.

"The things is, though, I've got to figure out what to do with myself. Even though I had that heart attack, I'm in good health, but I can't practice for five years because of that non-compete clause I signed when I sold my practice."

John leaned forward. "Al, what have you done since you retired that you've enjoyed?"

"Besides being with Bonnie?"

John nodded, and Al had to think about it for a minute. Then he said, "Bonnie's father has Alzheimer's and lives at Vashon Community Care, an assisted living facility and nursing home. It's a really nice one. He used to have a chocolate Lab like my dog Bert. And I've brought Bert to see him. He thinks the dog is his dog, Susie, and the guy just lights up. I love that. I love watching him interact with the dog. Making that happen for him."

John looked at his watch. "We need to stop in a minute. Would you like to make an appointment to come back?"

"I guess so. Is this all there is? We just talk? You don't have any advice for me?"

"Mostly, I see my job as just helping you figure out what you want to change and what you want to do differently so that things are working better for you."

"So you don't tell me what to do?"

"No. I don't intervene unless I think you're going to hurt yourself or someone else."

"You're talking suicide or murder?"

John nodded.

"Okay, well. No danger of that. Although I imagined strangling Jerry Kincaid. But I suppose that doesn't count."

"I'm not worried about it," John laughed. "If our fantasies were dangerous, we'd all be in trouble."

"I almost forgot. I meant to show you this," he handed him *The Beachside*. "It made me feel great." But soon as he gave Dr. John the paper, Al felt a little silly—like a kid eagerly showing his dad a good report card.

After reading it for few minutes, John looked up and smiled. "You have a lot of fans it seems. I can see why that made you feel great," he said, as he handed the paper back. "Thanks for showing me this."

They made an appointment for the next week at the same time. John took down Al's address and went over his fees, and asked whether Al's insurance had mental health coverage. Al wanted to just pay out of pocket. A psychologist wasn't cheap, but it wasn't as much as a lawyer and seemed not that far off from what Al had charged for an office visit when he was in practice. He shook John's hand and thanked him. He decided he didn't look as much like John Oliver as he'd first thought.

CHAPTER 25

When Al got home, he wrote a thank you email to the people who had written the letter to *The Beachside*. He had all their contact information; they had all been former clients and he wrote the note in a group email:

> Re: Beachside Letter
>
> Dear friends,
>
> I saw your letter in the paper. It meant a lot to me and I'm grateful for your support.
>
> Thank you!
>
> Best wishes,
> Al Paugh

It didn't adequately reflect what the letter had done for him, but he didn't want to overdo it and let them know how low he'd really been. It was true, what he'd told Dr. John. Since he retired, taking Bert a.k.a. Susie to see Ralph Douglas at Vashon Community Care was something he loved. The feeling was probably similar to when he was able to help clients when there was a good outcome from the illness or injury of their dog. It was puzzling though, because Ralph Douglas seemed completely surprised when Al showed up with Bert, as if he hadn't remembered they'd been there just the day before. But their routine must have gotten wired in somehow, because he'd immediately take the bag of treats and offer one to Susie. Then Al would hand him the ball and he'd throw it across the living room into the kitchenette. It seemed as though his concept of time was impaired, but his memory of the activity associated to the motor skills remained intact. Al couldn't help worrying about how his own brain would do as he aged—wondering if he'd be like Ralph. But then there was Betty Bagley just down the hall. If his brain ended up like hers, he'd take it.

On one of his visits he ran into her in front of the elevator. She rolled up in her wheelchair and held out her arms to hug him. Al bent down, and she put her arms around his shoulders. "Great to see you Al!"

"How's it going, Betty?"

"Can't complain as long as I'm on this side of the ground." She laughed and reached out and petted Bert. "What a beautiful dog. What's his name?"

"Bert, but he's 'Susie' to Ralph. He had a chocolate Lab just like Bert. We're here for a visit."

"Oh that's wonderful that you take this big dog to see him. We have a lot of little dogs around here, and they're very cute. But not like my Ali." She looked away for a minute, then met Al's eyes again. "I've been calling the shelter every day to see if anyone has adopted him, but I suppose I've gotten to be a pest. The last time I called, about a week ago, the lady—I forgot her name now—but anyway she was a bit firm with me and said that they'd call *me* when there was any news."

"I guess you just have to be patient, but I know that's not easy." Al said.

"No, it's not easy. When you're old, time is not on your side and patience doesn't seem to be much of a virtue when you want things to happen before it's too late." Betty glanced up at a poster next to the elevator. "But there's a lot going on this time of year to take my mind off Ali. The Vashon Ukulele Society is doing a holiday concert tomorrow, and it's great fun. People sing along and it's amazing how people remember the words, even the poor folks who can't remember their own name, if you know what I mean. And they have kazoos!"

"Kazoos?"

"You know that little horn thing that sounds funny that anyone can play. I asked one of the volunteers if she could find me one, so I could play it with them. Well, I better get going, I'm getting my hair done. There's a beauty shop right here, you know. Nice to talk with you, honey. I'm looking forward to Christmas dinner with you."

"I am too," Al bent down and hugged her.

BERT WAS VERY GOOD ABOUT retrieving the ball in Ralph's apartment. He didn't seem to get bored, just cheerfully ran after it back and forth in the small space. But after one of their visits, Al headed home to pick up Princess and then decided to take them to Point Robinson where Bert could really run and swim after his frog. The tide was coming in and there wasn't much room for them to run at Baker's Beach, but even at high tide there was a wide stretch at Point Robinson. It was a rare clear winter day, and against the bright blue sky the peaks of the Cascades were glazed with snow and Mount Rainer was breathtaking. There wasn't much wind and the water of the Sound was relatively smooth, except for the waves from a large freighter slowly making its way south, bound for the Port of Tacoma. Al threw the frog for Bert, only not too far out. Bert would swim in any temperature, but during the winter months, Al wanted to limit the time he spent in the cold water. Princess was not a swimmer. She was content to stay close to Al and sniff around the beach. Al looked beyond the lighthouse to the driftwood logs that had been battered and pushed by the waves to pile along the far edge of the beach. He remembered the first time he'd seen Bonnie there. She'd been in such terrible sorrow and grief.

He walked over to the driftwood and sat on one of the logs that might have been the place where he'd first seen her. In these weeks between Thanksgiving and Christmas, he'd found himself often looking over at Bonnie's dark house. Her car was still parked in front. She'd taken the Vashon Shuttle to the airport and seeing her car sitting across the road made it seem even emptier without her.

Bert and Princess had been sniffing the seaweed and kelp that lay at the edge of the beach, but came to sit next to him when they saw him on the driftwood. Al watched the freighter for a while and found himself reflecting on his visit with the shrink: something he'd done frequently since his appointment. Especially what he'd said about Jamie. Jamie had belittled him his entire childhood, but the tree incident was iconic and it helped to hear what Dr. John had said—that it wasn't just normal sibling rivalry. Al could understand it if he framed it in the way puppies played: chasing, nipping and tumbling with each other. But if one viciously attacked, there was something wrong with the dog. Jamie had been such a star, it was hard to see him as emotionally deprived, but the veneer of his charm must have been thin, barely covering a really angry kid. Al guessed it did explain the life his brother had ended up with. Living off women sure had a big dose of hostility in it.

But it wasn't just his thoughts about Jamie that had resurfaced so frequently. Dr. John's question, "What have you done since you retired that made you happy?" stayed with him. And—other than being with Bonnie—he always came up with the same answer: the times when he took Bert to visit Ralph Douglas at Vashon Community Care. Al watched Bert, who had run down the beach chasing a seagull. Bert gave Ralph so much pleasure, he wished Betty Bagley could experience the same thing, but her beloved dog was in a shelter. Here was a dog who, through no fault of its own, was flunking retirement home. And there were probably others like it—flunking retirement home because they were too big.

Al stared at Bert, and then it hit him. It was so obvious, he

laughed out loud. *Why couldn't he adopt them all?* He could start a
home for dogs over twenty pounds who belonged to people who
moved to a retirement place where they couldn't keep them. Then
he could take the dogs to visit the people. *Of course it was possible.*
Al laughed again. He felt like Henry Higgins—*By Jove, he's got it!*
He could provide veterinary care for all the dogs because they
would legally be his dogs since he'd adopted them.

Screw you, Kincaid! That jerk couldn't do a damn thing about it!

Al jumped up and began walking back and forth in front of
the log, his mind racing. And since they were his dogs and they'd
be visiting the people who had them before, they wouldn't need
to go through any kind of training to be certified therapy dogs. *It
was perfect!* All he needed to do was to find a place with acreage
to rent or buy. He'd start with just Ali, and he'd bring him to
visit Betty Bagley every day the way he brought Bert to Ralph
Douglas. And then he could adopt more dogs as the need arose.
The care center could tell new residents who had to give up their
dogs that the program was available. He was sure they'd go for it.
It *was* perfect! "Come on, Bert, Princess. We've got work to do!"

Al jogged across the beach to the parking lot. He got the
dogs in the truck, helping lift Bert while Princess jumped in
and sat on the floor. Al started the truck, and before he put it
in reverse, he switched on B.B. King and blasted the song that
always made him want to dance: "Playin' With My Friends." He
bounced along Point Robinson road, singing along with B.B. Al
could hardly wait to get home and look in the paper for a place
to live. With Bert, Princess and his future too-big dogs.

The Beachside had pictures of a lot of places that had at least
five acres; Al was surprised at how many there were. Some had
houses, or what looked like a cabin, and there were other ads for
just land. He supposed he could put a yurt on some land like the
one Fred Weiss had, but then you'd run into putting in a well
and septic, and you could get stuck in the county health department purgatory forever. Probably better to find a house on some

land. He got out his computer and looked online, where there were good photos and more information. But then he remembered what Betty Bagley had said about patience not being such a virtue at her age, and he realized that adopting Ali should be first on his list. After he adopted Ali, he'd ask Patricia if the shelter would keep Ali until he found a place to live. He could pay the adoption fee, fill out whatever forms there were, and pay for boarding until he was ready to get him. He would be surprised if Patricia wouldn't go for that.

It was a relief when he arrived at the shelter and saw that Paul Waterton, Patricia's husband, was in the yard. There wouldn't be any awkward dinner invitations or those squishy embraces masquerading as a friendly hug. Paul waved as Al parked and got out of the truck.

"Nice to see you, Al."

"How's it going? You home for a while?"

Paul nodded. "Seniority is good for some things, I guess. I get my pick of the schedule, so I'm home for the holidays. The thing is though, Patricia has a honey-do list for me as long as my arm." He laughed. "But that goes with the territory. I'm wrapping all our outdoor faucets—it's supposed to get down below freezing tonight."

"Yeah, I heard. Hope it doesn't last too long."

"Say, I heard about what happened. Patricia showed me the stuff in *The Beachside* and I just want you to know that she and I and everyone we know—we're behind you one hundred percent."

"Thanks, Paul. I appreciate that. Is Patricia in the office?"

"It's pretty slow this time of year, but she should be back there."

"Thanks." Al felt his back pocket to make sure he'd remembered his checkbook as he headed around the side of the house. He saw Patricia through the window and then went to the basement door and knocked.

"Al!" Patricia grinned as she opened the door. "What a nice surprise—what brings you here?" She gave him a quick hug.

"I'm here to adopt Ali, Betty Bagley's dog."

"Oh, Al. That's wonderful. She'll be more than thrilled. He's in the other room, I'll go get him."

In a minute Patricia was back, followed by Ali. Al thought he'd seen him when he visited the shelter before. Ali trotted right over, sniffed and then licked Al's hand, while his tail wagged and he danced a little. He was a handsome boxer, a little gray around the muzzle, with a white chest and underbelly and white paws. He was large, Al guessed probably close to seventy pounds. His eyes were alert, and he seemed healthy. Al was glad to see that neither his tail nor his ears had been cropped. For years it had been the fashion, but Al was right in line with the American Veterinary Medical Association in frowning on it. Ali was so friendly and trusting, Al knew he'd been well socialized, which was no surprise knowing Betty Bagley. He pulled out his phone. "I'd like to take his picture to show Betty."

"Shall I hold him?"

"Just for a minute while I get him focused, thanks." He backed up a few feet. "Okay, smile Ali!" Al took the photo. "One more. Okay, great." He put his phone back in his pocket. "He's a handsome dog. And he seems to have a great temperament." Al patted the dog. "I won't be ready to take him until the first of the year. But I'd like to pay the adoption fee now and do the paperwork and pay a boarding fee until I can pick him up."

"That would be great—I can't wait to tell Betty."

"If it's okay with you, I want to keep it a secret. I'm having Christmas dinner with her and I thought I'd tell her then—it'll be her Christmas present."

"You got it. Not a word." Patricia went to the file cabinet and took out some forms. "So you'll be a two dog household now, is that right?"

"Right. But it's a little more than that. I'm starting a new business, a service really. But I've got to work out some details before I can talk too much about it."

"Well, I'm sure anything you do will be a big success, Al." She handed him the adoption forms and Al looked them over, then signed them and pulled out his checkbook. Do you have a boarding fee, so I can add on to the adoption fee?"

"Not exactly, but why don't we just say $20 a day? He doesn't eat that much, but the shelter can also use money. I want to take you for all I can, Al." Patricia winked and reached for a calculator. "I use this thing so much I think I forgot how to add without it."

Al watched as she added up the fees. "Looks like with the boarding fee until January it will be $475. Sure that's okay?"

"Let's round it off to $500."

"What a guy!" Patricia gave him a thumbs up.

Al wrote the check and folded up his copy of Ali's adoption papers. At the door he thanked Patricia and mentioned again that it was a secret.

"I won't forget. Trust me. And Al, I just wanted to say that Paul and I—we're really behind you with what happened with the sheriff and everything. That petition is gathering signatures by the minute."

"Thanks, Patricia." Al smiled. "Means a lot. Believe me."

THE COLD SPELL HAD SET in and although snow wasn't expected, the temperature at night had dropped into the high twenties. Al had a fire going all the time, and the house was toasty. He spent every evening looking at the island real estate listings on the internet, and every day driving by the properties. He was narrowing down the ones he wanted to look at, and then he'd get in touch with the realtor. Marcie Sorenson, the agent who represented Eleanor, was listed as the agent for a couple of the houses that sounded interesting, but he didn't want to call her. Who knew what Eleanor might have told her about him—he'd have to figure out a way to see them without her. Al also spent every day driving around the island with Bert and Princess looking for any "For Sale by Owner" signs, although so far he hadn't seen any.

What a difference to have a sense of purpose. The nights were long and dark as the year drew to a close, but Al couldn't remember feeling so much hope. He was going to dinner to mark winter solstice at Martha Jane's, who had returned from her month-long visit with her family. She'd also invited Howie and Mark, and Al was looking forward to seeing them. Their call when they'd read about his arrest had meant so much to him.

Solstice was a quiet, peaceful time on the island, and Al always wanted to be sure to see the luminarias that a group of islanders set up along several island roads. Other than the few blocks in town, most of the roads on the island had no street-lights, and on winter solstice, the luminarias were the only lights in the dark night, a winding magical path that went for miles. It was a beautiful event, the antithesis, Al thought, of all the commercial stuff around the holidays. The ritual of the island luminarias was never advertised. There was no hype of any kind. Just some folks who quietly and without fanfare created a beautiful path to light the longest night, marking the end of the dark, and the renewal and rebirth of the sun and warmth and light.

Martha Jane had lit candles all over her house, and they ate in a beautiful glow that they all decided made everyone look younger. Howie had made a big pot of chili and cornbread, and Martha Jane made a salad and apple pie for dessert. She gave Al a bottle of Cabernet to take home. "It was wonderful to know that Maria was so well taken care of. I couldn't have a better pet sitter than our own veterinarian."

After dinner they went to the living room and sat in front of the fire. Maria was curled up on Martha Jane's lap. "You know I loved seeing my family, but it's awfully good to be home." She looked at Al. "I was so sorry to hear about all the trouble while I was away."

"Thanks. I have to say, everyone has been wonderful to me. Bonnie picked me up at the sheriff's office after I'd been arrested. I don't know what I would have done without her."

"Oh, you would have figured it out, I'm sure," Mark said. ""How is Bonnie? She's back East right?"

"Visiting her daughter. She'll be back the day after Christmas."

"Howie and I brought a wonderful bottle of brandy. At least

it's supposed to be good. We haven't tried it yet—shall we have a little warmth for solstice?" Mark asked.

"I'm in." Al smiled.

"I can show you where the glasses are," Martha Jane started to get up.

"I know your kitchen as well as my own. Just stay where you are." Howie patted her shoulder. In a minute he came back with the bottle and put it on the coffee table, then went back for glasses.

"I think I'll pass, Howie," Martha Jane said. "The wine we had at dinner is already making me sleepy, and the brandy would probably finish me off."

"Okay, but it's supposed to be really good stuff. If you change your mind, one of us can carry you to bed." He filled the glasses and handed them to Mark and Al.

Al got up and put another log on the fire. "I've been going through the wood at my place so fast, I'll probably need to get another cord to replace it for JoAnne when she comes back in January."

"I hate to think of you not living at Baker's Beach." Martha Jane said.

"Believe me, I'll be back to see all of you." Al raised his glass. "This is the best place I've ever lived. The beach is great—Bert loves it—but it's really because you're the best people."

Howie took a swig of the brandy and licked his lips. "This *is* smooth—excellent."

"Nothing but the best." Mark turned to Al. "Do you know where you'll be?"

"I'm actually going to start a new venture, so I'm looking to rent a place, maybe lease with an option to buy, or just buy—I'm not sure which, but I want at least a couple of acres. Preferably fenced, although I could put in a fence myself." Al grinned. He felt warm from the brandy and mellow from all the wine, so he told them what he was planning to do. "The dogs are too big, it's not their fault they've flunked retirement home. I've already adopted the first dog, a seven year old boxer, Ali—"

"Great name for a boxer." Howie laughed.

"He belonged to Betty Bagley. I'll be having Christmas dinner with her, and it's a surprise—I'll tell her then. I've already adopted him, and the Vashon Animal Shelter will keep him for me until I move."

"This is absolutely a wonderful idea, Albert. I knew you'd figure out what you wanted to do."

"I admit I was pretty stuck there for a while without my practice. But I'm really excited about this."

Howie sipped his brandy. "When I retired, part of what I struggled with was not only that I didn't have my work in theater, but I also had to face that it was the end of my career as I knew it, and I wasn't going to have a career like, say, Daniel Sullivan—the director at the Seattle Rep, who went on to direct in New York. He's won a Tony and had many nominations, and I had to face that wasn't going to happen for me. I can imagine I never had his luck, but I probably didn't have his talent either. But when I directed Walter Hathaway's play here on the island—"

"I was in it, you know," Martha Jane said proudly.

"Yes, and it was a delight to witness your acting debut." Howie blew her a kiss. "Anyway, when I did Walter's play I realized the process is the same. The scale is different of course, from when I directed the big shows at the university. But the creativity, the collaboration, that whole process—which is all that matters anyway—was the same."

Martha Jane nodded and stroked Maria Montessori. "You know you sometimes hear about these people who retire and they take up something completely different from what their career had been. Like a surgeon who opens a pastry shop—that sort of thing. And that's fine for those people. But some people who really love their work can often find something that's related after they retire, the way you're doing, Albert."

"Right," Howie agreed. "That's what I did and Walter, too. Now he's writing plays, and I got an email from him about his wanting to do another one when they get back."

Martha Jane clasped her hands together. "I hope there's a part for me."

Howie smiled. "I'm sure there will be. You're an actress I'd love to direct again, Martha Jane." He set his glass down and was quiet for a minute. "I guess the point I'm trying to make is that you might not work the same way you did, but you may not have to completely reinvent yourself."

"Maybe you have to reinvent yourself as the same person, only different." Mark added. "I think getting older in itself requires a certain amount of reinvention." He reached for the brandy on the coffee table and put a little more in his glass.

"Right." Martha Jane smiled. "I agree. And at my age—I'm over ninety you know—I think being older does require reinvention. You have to reinvent yourself as an older person, adapt to what it means to be diminished physically and have our memories not working so well, just not being as sharp all the way around. You adjust your thinking about your place in the world, how you operate, and it does take some inventing, at least that's what I think." She looked at Al. "Well, enough of that—so Albert, with this new venture, are you looking at any certain part of the island?"

"Not really. It would be great to be near Baker's Beach. But like I said, I'll be seeing you guys wherever I live. The only problem is some of the places I'd like to see are listed by the agent Eleanor is using and I'd like to have someone different, I guess."

"Just call Emma," Mark said.

"Right, Emma Amiad—she only represents buyers and she's great." Howie added.

"Of course, why didn't I think of that?" Al sipped the brandy. "Guess I've been a little preoccupied getting arrested and all." *And with Bonnie. Oh, by the way, I love Bonnie Douglas.* But Al didn't say it. As he'd found before, it was easier to tell Bonnie's father, who wasn't firing on all cylinders. And besides, he should find a way to tell her first.

CHAPTER 26

IT SURPRISES ME THAT I WAS JUST HERE A WEEK AGO." AL LOOKED AT the seascape hanging above the chair, as he took a seat across from Dr. Dudnik. "So much has happened."

"An eventful week, then?"

"It was. I mean, it is. In fact, I thought about cancelling this appointment, but I wanted to come back to tell you what's happened." Al smiled. "I figured out what I'm going to do. In fact, it was so obvious I don't know what took me so long." Al continued, describing in detail how he adopted Betty Bagley's dog and then his plan to adopt other dogs in the same situation. "I can provide the veterinary care since the dogs will be mine. My lease is up at the end of the month—and I've been looking for places to rent and there are some good possibilities."

"It sounds like a great venture for you."

Al nodded, smiling. "I don't really think I need to make another appointment. But you've been a big help."

"I didn't find the solution—you did. Probably deciding to see me just helped you focus," he said. "And I've always agreed with Karen Horney. She was a German psychoanalyst who practiced in the United States—she said that 'life itself still remains a very effective therapist' and I think it's true for people who have the creativity to learn and grow from whatever setbacks life dishes out."

"Horney. That's quite a name for a psychiatrist." Al chuckled, then felt ridiculous. What a dumb thing to say. Sophomoric, that's what it was. Was he horny? Probably, at least for Bonnie. She made him feel like a teenager. He began to get uncomfortable because Dr. John wasn't saying anything. Al looked at his watch. There was still time left, but he couldn't just get up and leave now, could he? He wasn't sure what to do, but then he thought about what John had just said about life being an effective therapist so he said, "Well, I don't know that I've learned much from life when it comes to women. I think I mentioned Bonnie when I was here last week …."

"Yes, you described associating her with the dog you had as a child that you loved."

"Right, and I guess I'll just come right out and say it—I'm in love with her, but I don't know how she feels about me. She's warm and affectionate, and I've felt encouraged. But her husband died a little over a year ago and she talks about not feeling settled. Everything in her life is temporary and I worry that I'm part of that. Like a temporary distraction. Maybe pleasant, but mostly to take her mind off everything she's been through. I'm not sure what to do."

"What do you think your choices are?"

"Honestly, I don't always think of myself making choices when it comes to women. I just seem to go along." Al looked at the paintings on the wall. "Choices? Well, I suppose I could do nothing and wait and see what she does. That's a familiar choice. Or I could act."

John didn't say anything. He just looked at Al as though he were waiting for him to explain more. To say what he'd do, if he didn't decide to do nothing.

Al felt weird just sitting there so he finally said, "Well, I guess I'd tell her I love her and that I want to spend my life with her."

"And that's how you really feel?"

"Absolutely. I just don't know if I'm ready to do it. To tell her." Al tapped his fingers on the arm of his chair.

"Well, let me ask this—what do you think stops you?" John looked at Al thoughtfully. "What gets in the way?"

"That's easy. She'll tell me she doesn't feel the same way."

"Then the next question is always 'could you survive that'?"

"I could." Al sighed. "I'd feel terrible, but I suppose I'd be able to settle on just being friends so I could still have her in my life. It wouldn't be my first choice, but now that I've figured out what I'm doing, there's a lot to look forward to—adopting and caring for the dogs. Taking them to see the folks in the care center. It would help having that going for me if Bonnie doesn't feel the way I do."

Once he'd started talking about Bonnie, Al was surprised that it wasn't as hard as he thought it would be. In fact, it had taken up the rest of the time. It had helped to talk about his fears, and as Dr. John had suggested, it helped him focus. Al hoped Dr. John wouldn't advise him to make more appointments, but he didn't need to worry. As they said good-bye, Dr. John told him his door was always open if Al ever wanted to come back, then he shook his hand and wished him well.

Al couldn't wait to get back to the island and look at more houses with acreage. He was eager to get on with his life and he didn't think he'd ever need to see Dr. John again. At least he hoped not, but he liked knowing the door was left open.

THERE WAS A PROPERTY NEAR Paradise Cove that looked really promising, one where the owners were anxious to sell and had dropped the price. The house, a four-bedroom, two-bath farmhouse, was described as having potential—which Al knew could be real estate speak for a dump. But when he saw it, he thought it was perfect. True, the kitchen and bathrooms were very old-fashioned with linoleum floors and rusty faucets, but three years ago it had been given a new roof, and there was a stone fireplace in the living room that Al loved. The floors throughout, except for the kitchen and bathrooms, were hardwood and sagged a little in several of the rooms, but none of that bothered him. The place needed paint, both inside and out, but the structure seemed solid. It had good bones, as they said. The windows were single pane and the appliances were old, but everything seemed to work. The best thing about it was that it was situated on three and half acres, and one acre was completely fenced!

Since he needed to be in by January 2, he decided to sign a lease with an option to buy. He could move in right away and then if he wanted to buy, he could have an inspection and take his time to think through the finances. Al wanted to have his project be an official non-profit. Financially, he could support a lot of dogs himself, but in terms of what might develop in the future, it would be good to have the non-profit status. It would give it a level of legitimacy, an organization, not just his hobby. Non-profits usually had to have a board of directors. Maybe he'd see if Bonnie wanted to be one. And Martha Jane and Mark and Howie, and if he needed more than that, he could ask Maggie and Walter. On December 23, Al signed the lease.

CHRISTMAS MORNING WAS FOGGY, AND when Al checked the temperature on the weather app on his phone, it was twenty-nine degrees. He hoped he wouldn't have any problem getting his truck started—sometimes it was a little temperamental in the cold. He put on coffee, made a fire and got his breakfast ready while the coffee perked. He cooked bacon and scrambled eggs and gave some of the eggs to Bert and Princess for a Christmas treat, then ate his breakfast in the living room in the front of the fire. The night before, Howie and Mark had given him a plate of scones for Christmas and he ate them with his breakfast. The other gift he'd gotten was from Martha Jane. It was one of her paintings of Baker's Beach, which he'd hang in a place of honor over the stone fireplace in his new house. At the Vashon Bookshop, he'd picked up a gift for Bonnie, Mary Oliver's poems about dogs, *Dog Songs*, which he planned to give her as soon as she got back. After he finished eating, he gave Bert and Princess their presents—they each got a huge rawhide bone.

People didn't send too many cards in the mail anymore, but he had gotten lots of email cards, and many of them had messages of support referring to his arrest. He hadn't heard anything yet from the King County Prosecutor's office, and just hoped it wouldn't drag on and on. He also hoped Deputy Sheriff Molina had been right when he told him that one of the outcomes could be a deferred prosecution on the condition that he attend an anger management class. Anger had never really been much of a problem for him. Al thought maybe Eleanor could have benefitted from something like that. He hadn't thought about her in quite a while, but he did wonder how she was doing and decided to call her and wish her a Merry Christmas. It seemed like the right season for a little good will, and he probably felt more generous toward her now that he had a plan for what he wanted to do with his life. He got his phone from the table next to his bed and went back to living room. He placed another log on the fire, then put in the call.

"Al?"

"Hi Eleanor, I just thought I'd wish you a Merry Christmas."

"Oh, that's very nice. What a surprise to hear from you. How are you, Al?"

"I'm great actually. Things are going really well."

"Really?"

"You seem surprised." He patted Bert and Princess, who had jumped up on the couch next to him.

"It's just that I heard about, you know—well, it was in the paper and everything."

"That I got arrested"

"I left a voice mail when I heard. Maybe you don't remember."

"Oh, right."

"And the divorce should be final soon, in case you're wondering. The ninety days are up, but with the holidays and all, we'll probably get the final dissolution papers in a week or so."

"They send it to us?"

"Right." She was quiet a minute, then asked, "So are you really okay? Being arrested and everything?"

"I really am, Eleanor. I've had fantastic support from people on the island and the thing should be resolved before too long. The deputy sheriff thought the most I'd get might be an anger management class."

"A what?"

"Anger management, you know, a class to teach you how to control your temper, that sort of thing."

"Ha! That's rich. I always wished I could have gotten some passion from you, Al. You're as mellow as they come."

"Let's not go into that, Eleanor." Al sighed. "How's Ruby?"

"Fine. Things are going well and we have an offer on my house. It's supposed to close in about six weeks. Then Ruby and I will be going on a trip to Bali."

"Bali Ha'i will whisper ...."

"What?"

"I'm singing ... 'Here am I, your special island,'" Al sang, "'Come to me, come to me!'"

"What was that supposed to be?"

"I was singing Eleanor, the song ... 'Bali Ha'i' ... from *South Pacific*."

"Oh. Well, whatever." Eleanor paused again. "Are you sure you're okay, Al?"

"Never better. In fact, I've met someone." Al hadn't planned to mention this, but it just came out.

"Really?" Eleanor didn't try to hide her surprise.

"Yes, and she likes dogs."

"I see. Well, thanks for calling," Eleanor hesitated, then added, "and Merry Christmas, Al."

AL GOT OFF THE PHONE and went to the kitchen and was about to pour himself another cup of coffee, but then thought maybe it would be good to have a Bloody Mary. Then he could take a nap if he felt like it before it was time to go to Vashon Community Care for Christmas dinner. He didn't have any Bloody Mary mix, but he did have tomato juice and vodka. He sprinkled some lemon pepper in it and stuck in a stalk of celery. It was very festive.

He sat in front of the fire sipping his Bloody Mary and eating another of Mark and Howie's scones while Bert chewed on his rawhide bone. Thinking about his call to Eleanor, he realized she hadn't been on his mind at all lately. And he also realized he didn't make comparisons like he used to when she first left. But after talking with her this morning, it was hard not to. Eleanor didn't laugh when he sang "Bali Ha'i"—Bonnie would have laughed and sung along with him. He couldn't quite believe he'd told Eleanor about her, but it was true. He *had* met someone he cared for. A lot. More than that—he was in love with Bonnie. He didn't know to what extent it would be reciprocated, or requited—requited?—what a strange way to say someone loved you back. Well, he hadn't wanted to tell Eleanor all that, but he'd reported the basic fact with accuracy. *I've met someone.* Al went to the desk where he'd left his phone, went back to the couch, took another sip of his drink and put in a call to Bonnie.

She answered right away. "Oh Al, I'm so glad to hear from you. How are you?"

"Bert, Princess and I wanted to wish you a Merry Christmas."

"Thank you! Merry Christmas to the three of you. I called Dad to wish him a Merry Christmas, and he seemed pleased—although, I'm not sure he knew who I was."

"I'll be seeing him for Christmas dinner. Wish you were here."

"Me, too. How is Princess? How are you? And Bert, too, of course—can't leave him out. Are you all getting along okay?"

"The dogs are doing great. It's pretty cold here and we all sleep together. Princess seems right at home. She's calm, and she and Bert get along fine," Al paused. "I miss you, Bonnie."

"And I want to be with you—I miss you, too. I can't wait to come home."

"This feels like home?"

"It really does. But it's been good for me to get away—I've realized a lot being here. Seeing my daughter Emily and my grandkids has been wonderful, and I guess the change of scenery has helped me get things in focus better. I've come to some decisions, Al. There's a lot to tell you."

"So have I. I have a lot to tell you, too. I can't wait to see you."

"Me, too. Al . . . I . . . well, me, too."

BEFORE HE LEFT FOR CHRISTMAS dinner at the care center, Al took the dogs to Baker's Beach for a long walk. The fog still hadn't lifted and it blanketed the Kitsap Peninsula and Point Defiance to the south so that it looked like the beach was on an ocean with no land in sight. He could hear the fog horn from the Tacoma Narrows Bridge. It was usually a lonely sound, and Al and the dogs were alone on the beach. It was damp and cold, but to him it was a beautiful day. *Bonnie missed him ... she wanted to come home ... she couldn't wait to see him.* She had really said those things.

After their walk, he showered and dressed for dinner, left the dogs with their rawhide bones and headed for Vashon Community Care. The building looked very festive and matched his mood. Swags of evergreens with bright red ribbons decorated the dining room, and a tall tree with colored lights stood in the hall of the reception area. Christmas carols were playing somewhere, and Al found the seat that was reserved for him with Betty Bagley and Bonnie's father at a table near the window. Betty was wearing a red silk dress and she had on a little Santa hat. Ralph had on a navy blue sport coat and looked very presentable. The meal had been a choice of turkey or ham, and everyone at their table had decided on ham.

"We're a very compatible group," Betty said. "Are you enjoying the dinner, Ralph?"

"Very good." Ralph smiled. He hadn't asked about Bonnie, and Al wasn't sure who he thought he and Betty were, but the food and the holiday music seemed to please him.

After they finished the meal and were waiting for dessert—they'd all decided on pumpkin pie with vanilla ice cream—Al took out two small gift wrapped packages from the pocket of his sport coat. "I've got a little something for each of you." Al handed the little packages to Betty and Ralph.

"Oh my, you shouldn't have, Al. I don't have anything for you."

"Well, actually you do. You'll see."

"Should we open them at the same time?" Betty asked.

"Let me help Ralph first." Al took the gift and undid the

ribbon that Ralph had been struggling to get off the package. He handed it back to Ralph, who took off the paper.

"It's Susie!" He took the gold little picture frame with the photo of Bert to his lips and kissed it. "Thank you," he patted Al's arm. "Glad to have a photo of my Susie. We play ball, you know."

"That's great. Glad you like it." Al smiled and looked at Betty. "Okay, your turn."

Betty pulled her wheelchair a little closer to the table and unwrapped the present. "Oh my, Al. What a beautiful photo of Ali." Her eyes filled with tears.

"There's more. Do you see the little card with it?"

"Right, I see it. Taped to the back of the frame. I'll need my glasses." Betty's purse was on her lap, and in a minute, she'd pulled out her glasses. She took the card from the envelope "Shall I read it out loud?"

"Be my guest."

She put on her glasses. "On December 19th Ali was adopted from the Vashon Animal Shelter by Dr. Albert Paugh and will—" She was crying too much to be able to finish and handed the card to Al, who had gotten up to hug her.

"Merry Christmas, Betty." He held her for a minute until she lifted her head and smiled, dabbing her eyes. "The rest of the card just says that Ali will officially be my dog, but I will bring him to visit you here every day, just the way I bring Bert—I mean Susie—to see Ralph."

"I don't know what to say—" Betty wiped her eyes again.

"That's okay. Meeting you and learning about Ali and then seeing what it means to Ralph to have Susie visit every day has helped me figure out how to spend my time. I think I'll be able to bring Ali to visit you by the middle of next week."

Betty put her hand over her heart. "Al, I'm a loss for words …."

"Where's the pie?' Ralph asked.

"Should be coming pretty soon." Al patted his arm.

Betty stared at the photo of Ali. "I've always thought that the quality of life as you age is about how well you deal with loss—your health, your friends, your home, people you love. And I don't think I was doing very well without Ali, not really."

"I like ice cream with the pie." Ralph said.

"I'm sure it'll have that, Ralph." Al glanced at the servers, who were bringing the pies around.

"Isn't Ali handsome." Betty smiled at the photo.

"He's a great dog, Betty. He was calm and very trusting when he met me. You did a wonderful job raising him. I'm looking forward to living with him. But especially to bringing him to you every day."

"What kind of pie is it?"

"Pumpkin, dear." Betty patted Ralph's hand.

"Good. I don't like figgy pudding."

Betty and Al laughed and Ralph joined in. Al wasn't sure if Ralph knew why he was laughing, but it was great to see him having fun. Bonnie would be glad to hear that her dad was in good spirits. Al looked around the dining room and then at the Christmas tree. He'd sometimes made house calls when he had his practice. Coming to Vashon Community Care would be like making house calls—only he'd be bringing the dogs. Just a little tweak of his old life.

CHAPTER 27

"AL, I'VE GOT SOME GOOD NEWS," JAKE MOLINA SAID, "IT'S A GOOD Christmas present, only it's a day late. Thomas Claribble told the prosecutor's office he wouldn't be willing to testify against you. I think he'd been convinced by somebody," Jake said, and chuckled, "that as far as his actions went he might have to think about the Animal Cruelty Statute. He was also notified that the prosecutor's office has received a petition supporting you that had over five hundred signatures. I think that gave him the idea that it might not be a good idea to proceed. So the matter is closed."

Al quite literally breathed a sigh of relief. "Is that ever great news! Did the guy say anything about the dog?"

"He doesn't want it. It's all yours. I have to say—you sure have a lot of fans on this island."

"Thanks—thanks for letting me know, and Happy New Year!" Al hung up and went to Bert and Princess and told them the news. Now he wouldn't have to think about spending money on a lawyer and having all that hassle hanging over his head. Al wondered if they suggested to Thomas Claribble that he go to anger management. That dirtbag needed it.

BONNIE'S PLANE WAS DUE IN around seven. Depending on how many stops the shuttle had before they got to Baker's Beach, he figured she'd be home by at least nine. He couldn't wait to see her, although he realized he was also uneasy. With signing the lease on the property, adopting Ali and getting his new venture underway, and *now* with the prosecutor's office closing his case, things were going too well. So well that it made him anxious; and then it ballooned into a kind of dread. It wasn't going to work out with Bonnie. He couldn't expect to have her, too. If he was able to finally tell Bonnie how he really felt, he was sure she'd tell him she just wanted to be friends. It didn't seem possible that she would really want to be part of his life, at least in the way he wanted. But at least he knew he could count on her being kind.

To take his mind off his fears, he spent the rest of the day looking at ads on the internet for furniture. He'd rented JoAnne McKee's place furnished, and all the furniture that had been at the Burton house belonged to Eleanor. What a weird arrangement that was. Not much of a marriage, that's for sure. But he didn't want to look back. He'd need a lot of stuff for his new house because right now the only thing he had was the chair he took from his office so that Jerry Kincaid couldn't have it. He'd need a bed, a kitchen table and some chairs and living room furniture. It was a good thing there were so many sales after Christmas and in January. There was so much he had to get, he decided to make a list and then prioritize everything, but first he'd go to Granny's Attic and Treasure Island and some of the other thrift stores on the island. It would be great if he could find a lot of what he needed there.

BONNIE CALLED AL AS SOON as she got home from the airport. "Just give me a minute to change and then I'll be right over to get Princess."

"I'd be happy to bring her over. I've got her dish and dog food, I'll just bring it all."

"Oh, thanks—that'd be great."

Al wasn't sure how long to wait. The excitement he felt trumped his earlier fears and he was so eager to see her he wanted to run right over there, but he thought ten minutes might be about right. He got the dog food and the dish for Princess that

Bonnie had given him, and then put on some music. But he couldn't sit still, so he danced around the living room for a couple of songs until he thought he had probably given her enough time. Al imagined walking in on her when she was in the middle of changing her clothes and didn't think it would be such a bad idea if that happened.

When he was sure he'd waited long enough, he put Princess on her leash and then headed across the road with both dogs; he thought Bert would want to welcome Bonnie, too. He was certain Princess would have followed them and didn't really need to be on the leash, but he still didn't want to take any chances.

Bonnie opened the door as soon as she heard his knock. "Al ...." She held her arms open and he dropped Princess's leash and reached down and hugged her. Still holding her, he kicked the door shut behind him as they kissed. He never wanted to let go of her.

Bonnie opened her eyes and looked up at him. "Hello there." She laughed.

"You greeted me before Princess. I must rate." He kissed the top of her head.

"You do." Bonnie knelt down and patted Princess, who wagged her tail and put her head on Bonnie's knee. "Looks like she remembers me."

"How could she not—you're unforgettable." Then Al sang, "Unforgettable, that's what you are ... unforgettable tho' near or far—"

Bonnie chimed in, laughing, and sang with him, "That's why, darling, it's incredible. That someone so unforgettable ... Thinks that I am ... Unforgettable, too."

"I wonder if Nat King Cole would turn over in his grave?" Al laughed. "Although I think you sounded good."

"I don't know about that. We're very corny, you know—but I like corny." Bonnie kissed him on the cheek. "How 'bout a glass of wine? I'm still on East Coast time, and it's almost midnight for me, but—"

"Are you sure? Maybe you'd rather get some sleep—"

"No way." She grinned. "I'm wide awake. I think I have a bottle of Merlot." She went to the kitchen. "Are you hungry?"

"I can always eat."

"I had dinner on the plane, but I'm kind of hungry. Let me see what I have."

Al sat on the couch. "It's been really cold this week. Want me to make a fire?"

"Sure. Great. I turned the heat up when I came in, but it takes a while before it gets warm." Bonnie came out from the kitchen. "I found a big bag of popcorn. It's store bought, but it's pretty good. Think that'll do?"

"Popcorn and Merlot are the perfect pairing."

Al made the fire and got it started. "The wood is really dry, so it's catching pretty fast." Bonnie came in with wine and handed him a glass, then put the bowl of popcorn on the coffee table in front of the couch. Al closed the fire screen and sat next to her.

Bonnie sipped her wine. "I made some decisions while I was away."

Al smiled. "So did I—but you go first."

"I'm going to keep Princess. I want to be her forever home, and that part of the decision leads to where are Princess and I are going to live when Maggie comes back. Remember when I said on the phone that I wanted to come home?"

"I do. It was music to me." Al put his arm around her.

"I love this place. It's where my father is, and I'll always want to see him, whether he remembers me or not, and Maggie is family. She lives here and Al—you're here—"

Al started to kiss her, but she lay her hand against his chest. "Just hear me out—you see when I was away, I realized that sometimes you meet the right person at the wrong time. And I guess I felt like it was the wrong time for me to get attached to anyone or anything, since it hasn't been that long since my husband and then my mother died. But I found myself wanting to be with you all the time, and I realized that you're part of why this is home." She looked down for a minute, and then over at the fireplace. "It's like I'm home when I'm with you."

"I love you, Bonnie." Al said, quietly.

"Me too." Bonnie lay her head on his chest and her eyes shone. "I had such a sense of time flying when I was with my grandkids—they're growing up so fast. Time doesn't stand still between my visits. It won't stand still for me and it dawned on me that if you love someone there's no such thing as the wrong time or the right time, it just is. It just happens and I could finally let myself admit that I've probably loved you since the night you rescued Tanner from the ravine."

"I've been wanting to tell you. But I've been worried that it wasn't the same for you. Not only too soon, but—oh, I don't know—mostly that you wouldn't think I was the right person for you."

Bonnie took a sip of her wine. "I have to admit, I've been unsettled about us—because the common wisdom is never to get involved with a man who's only separated from his wife, whose divorce isn't final. But I guess you've never struck me as being particularly ambivalent about it and I decided to trust that. I hope I'm right." She looked up at him.

Al kissed her forehead. "I talked to Eleanor and we should be getting the final dissolution papers in a week or so. I'm just hoping the courts are a little faster than the King County building department, but it doesn't matter. There's no question about my *wanting* a divorce and *getting* a divorce." He pulled her closer. "Let me say it again—I love you." He was quiet a minute, then he smiled. "I also told your father I loved you, when I was there with Bert."

"Did you?'

He nodded. "But I don't think any of it computed, he was so engrossed in Susie." Al sipped his wine. "I thought a lot, too, while you were gone. And I finally figured out what I want to do with the rest of my life."

"Wow, that's pretty big."

"It is for me, although in reality it probably doesn't sound so earth shaking. But it just kind of evolved. I saw a therapist a couple of times, and he asked me what had given me the most pleasure since I'd retired. And apart from being with you, I realized that I'd loved taking Bert to see your dad. And I know we'd both had the thought of adopting Betty Bagley's dog. A while ago, when things seemed the most confused for me, I told Martha Jane I'd flunked retirement. Well, I got to thinking that dogs like Betty Bagley's flunked retirement home—they were just too big and failed the weight requirement—it was no fault of their own. So, I decided I'd legally adopt the dogs, and then I'd bring them to visit the people at the care center who had owned them. I've already leased a farmhouse near Paradise Cove, and I'll be moving the day after New Year's."

"You *are* moving fast. I'm surprised, but honestly, it's perfect—it's a wonderful plan."

"I've already adopted Ali and I told Betty at Christmas dinner. She was thrilled."

"I'll bet she was! I wish I could have been there."

"I would have loved for you to have seen her face. It was wonderful." Al reached for the popcorn and took a handful. "I'm going to apply to get non-profit status, so it can be an official program. And I can provide the veterinary care since they'll legitimately be my dogs, so there won't be any conflict with my non-compete clause."

"More wine?" Bonnie picked up the bottle from the coffee table.

"Sure, thanks."

She filled both their glasses and sat back. "I've got a name for your program."

"Really?"

"How 'bout 'Too Big to Fail?'" She smiled.

"That's it—I love it." Al set his wine down and kissed her. "I've been meaning to ask you—would you be my date for New Year's Eve?"

"Absolutely. What do you have in mind?"

"There's a great blues band playing at the Bike. I like to dance."

"So do I. Should we dress up?"

Al took a sip of his wine. "I'll wear my clean jeans."

"Okay, then I will, too." Bonnie took a handful of popcorn. "What a nice fire you made."

"Warm enough now?'

She nodded.

"Will you stay with Maggie for a while after she gets back?" Al asked.

"I know she'd let me, but I think I better start looking for a place. I've heard it can be hard to find places to rent on the island. And now that I have a dog, I might not have as many options."

Al sat forward. "Listen, Bonnie—my new place is a four bedroom farmhouse." He put his hand on her arm. "I think you and Princess should move in with me. What are we waiting for? I'm not kidding about this. I'm serious."

Bonnie took a big gulp of her wine. "You really are serious?"

"Absolutely. Dead serious. Betty Bagley told me patience wasn't a virtue when you don't have that many years left. I suppose people might think it's too fast, but I don't care. Unless your family objects, which could make it hard. You know, if they gave you a bad time about it."

"If they did have any trouble accepting it at first, I think they'd come around. They just want me to be happy. But there'd be problems, Al. There always are."

"I know, but we'd just work at figuring them out." He put his arm around her. "And if it does seem too fast, you can just stay with me while you look for a place of your own, and we can try to live under one roof later if we want to. Whatever you think is right for you."

"And you don't mean that I'd live in your house like a roommate?"

"No!" he blurted—so emphatically that it surprised both of them. "Not a roommate. Eleanor accused me of just being like a roommate and I suppose it was true. I don't want a roommate. I've been sleeping with Bert and Princess. I want to sleep with you, too."

Bonnie laughed, she tried to stop laughing because she knew he was serious, but every time she tried to stop she laughed harder.

"Okay, what's so funny?"

Bonnie finally calmed down. "Just the picture of all of us piled up. We'd have to get a king-sized bed."

"Good. They have a lot of sales on now." Al looked at her and touched her cheek. "I want to make love with you, Bonnie."

"I guess we could give it a try. I'm pretty rusty you know."

"I haven't had sex since the Bush administration. But that's another story. I just hope it's like riding a bike, you know—that you never forget how."

"I don't know about that, Al. There are a lot of drug companies making money betting on it not being so easy."

"I guess that could be an option for me, if need be."

"Don't worry, we'll have fun trying." Bonnie smiled. "How 'bout now?" She sat forward, holding his hand and pulling him toward her.

"You're serious, aren't you?"

"Sure. Why not? The worst thing that can happen is that we'll be a little creaky and it'll be a flop."

"That I'll flop, you mean." Al laughed as she pulled him up from the couch.

In the bedroom he closed the door, leaving the dogs in front of the fire. "I'm not ready for an audience."

She laughed and got in bed. "Let's take our clothes off under the covers, it won't be so cold that way."

He crawled in beside her and they held each other for a long time, afraid to move. After a while, he stroked her hair. Then her face and her throat, and slowly they helped each other shed their clothes.

"I'm glad it's dark," she whispered, as he caressed her. "I'm old and wrinkly."

"So am I," he whispered. "And you are delicious."

"Why are we whispering?" She ran her hands along his back.

"We don't want to wake the kids."

They laughed, thinking of Princess and Bert lying in front of the fire. And then they were quiet as their tenderness gave way to urgent need. And they wept with the pleasure they gave each other, and a joy so exquisite that it hurt.

IT SEEMED ANOTHER LIFETIME WHEN Al woke to hear Bert whining at the door. "I'll get him." He kissed her then he got up to let the dog in.

She propped herself up on one elbow and smiled at him. "Well, they were quiet for a while at least." She looked out the window, "You know, it's a gorgeous night. I saw the full moon as we were flying in to SeaTac. Would you like to bundle up and take the dogs to the beach?"

"You're really sure? It must be the middle of the night for you, East Coast time."

"I'd like to."

"Okay. It's a great idea."

They dressed and Al put another log on the coals, so the fire would be going when they got back. It seemed the kind of night that they'd want to last forever.

It was clear and cold and the velvet sky was bright with stars. The full moon lit the beach and made a silver path across the water. Princess and Bert trotted ahead of them and Al reached for Bonnie's hand. When they walked to Peter Point, they stopped at the driftwood log and sat for a minute. It was the place where he'd first kissed her. Al pulled her close to him and looked up at the sky. "When I see all those millions of stars twinkling up there it seems like a miracle. And when I look at you, we seem like a miracle."

"Pretty great for a couple of old farts," Bonnie said, and Al saw there were tears in her eyes.

"Pretty great," Al whispered as he held her.

They sat in silence huddled on the log, taking in the beautiful night. After a while, Bonnie put her head on his shoulder and looked up at him. "Shall we go back?" she asked. "Head home?"

Al nodded. He stood and took her hand and pulled her up. "That's what old folks do, isn't it, as they head into the last part of their lives. They walk each other home."

Al and Bonnie held hands and walked along the shore heading back to Baker's Beach. The moonlight in the winter sky lit the way as Princess and Bert walked beside them. Heading home.

J EAN DAVIES OKIMOTO is an author and play-
wright whose books and short stories have been
translated into Japanese, Italian, Chinese, German,
Korean, Danish and Hebrew. She is the recipient
of numerous awards including *Smithsonian* Notable
Book, the American Library Association Best Book
for Young Adults, the Washington Governor's Award,
the Green Earth Book Award, and the International
Reading Association Readers Choice Award. Her
picture book, *Blumpoe the Grumpoe Meets Arnold the
Cat* was adapted by Shelly Duvall for the HBO and
Showtime television series "Bedtime Stories." Jeanie,
who is also a retired psychotherapist, began writing
for adults when she and her husband Joe retired to
Vashon Island in 2004 where they (and their dogs
Bert and Willie) are visited by deer families and their
six grandchildren.

CPSIA information can be obtained
at www.ICGtesting.com
Printed in the USA
FSOW01n1148301115
14021FS

9 780989 429139